A SAVAGE INHERITANCE

HEATHER ATKINSON

Boldwood

First published in Great Britain in 2024 by Boldwood Books Ltd.

Cover Design: Judge By My Covers

Cover Photography: Deposit Photos

A CIP catalogue record for this book is available from the British Library.

Paperback ISBN 978-1-80415-823-4

Large Print ISBN 978-1-80415-824-1

Hardback ISBN 978-1-80415-822-7

Ebook ISBN 978-1-80415-825-8

Kindle ISBN 978-1-80415-826-5

Audio CD ISBN 978-1-80415-817-3

MP3 CD ISBN 978-1-80415-818-0

Digital audio download ISBN 978-1-80415-819-7

Boldwood Books Ltd
23 Bowerdean Street
London SW6 3TN
www.boldwoodbooks.com

1

Carly Savage gripped onto her sister Rose's hand as she gazed down into the gaping dark hole in the ground, watching as her father's coffin was lowered into it. Tears rolled down her face. It was almost impossible to believe that Alec Savage, who had once seemed indestructible, was gone. He'd been an enormous presence, the mainstay of all three of his daughters' lives, and without him the sisters felt cast adrift.

She looked to Rose when her younger sister's grip on her hand tightened. Sobs shook Rose's slender frame and Jane, the eldest of the sisters who was standing on Rose's other side, wrapped an arm around her shoulders. She looked over to Carly, eyes shiny with tears as Rose hung her head and wept.

On the opposite side of the grave stood their Uncle Eddie, Alec's younger brother, with his handsome sons Dean and Harry on either side of him. Eddie didn't want to show too much emotion but he was fighting a losing battle and a tear slipped from the corner of his eye. Hastily he wiped it away with a pudgy hand while the brothers stared reverently down at the grave. Eddie wanted to be strong for his nieces but his grief was too powerful.

No one had expected Alec's sudden death. He'd been thriving in the care home where he'd been staying because of early-onset Parkinson's Disease, making friends, enjoying life again when he'd fallen ill with pneumonia. His decline had been frighteningly fast and he'd passed away just two weeks later. The speed with which the illness had taken him had left them all reeling. Carly wasn't sure she'd ever recover from the shock. Her eyes connected with Dean's across the grave and she felt herself fortified a little. It was as though his strong presence fed her strength.

Flowers were tossed onto the coffin as it was lowered into the ground. Alec was being laid to rest beside his dead wife. It gave Carly some comfort that they were finally reunited but this final goodbye to her beloved father was ripping the heart right out of her.

Finally, the funeral was over. The mourners began to quietly file away but Carly was unwilling to move, not wanting to leave her dad there in that awful hole in the ground.

'I don't want to go without him,' sobbed Rose, echoing her thoughts.

'We can come and visit him any time we want,' said Jane, placing a gentle hand on her shoulder.

'It feels wrong, he belongs with us.'

Jane's heart almost broke when her little sister looked up at her with watery eyes full of pain. 'And he always will be with us, sweetheart. I promise.' She wanted to get her away before the gravediggers came to fill in the hole. No one wanted to see that. 'It's time to go to the wake. I think we could all use a big glass of wine.'

'Am I allowed one?' sniffed Rose.

'Go on then, even though you're not quite eighteen yet.'

'Come on, you,' Eddie told Rose, sliding an arm around her

shoulders. 'Let's go to the pub and have a good gab about Alec, remember him for the amazing man he was.'

Her smile was sad. 'That sounds nice.'

Eddie led Rose over to the waiting black car, the chauffeur standing by the vehicle solemnly. Harry followed them while Jennifer, Jane's girlfriend, took her hand. This left Carly and Dean bringing up the rear.

'How are you holding up?' he asked her.

'Crap,' she replied miserably. 'I can't wait for today to be over.'

'The hard part is done.'

'The burial?'

'No, the walking away.'

Carly was glad he understood that but then Dean did seem to really get her. 'It's taking me everything I have to keep walking.'

She was surprised when he took her hand. 'I'll help you.'

His hand was gentle and warm and filled her with comfort. It occurred to Carly that people might find them holding hands strange but they were the only ones left in the graveyard. The burial had been limited to close family and friends and they'd already gone, so she decided not to object.

Jane turned to them while the others got into the waiting limousines. Her eyes slipped to their hands but she didn't comment.

'Dean, you can ride with us,' she said. 'Rose is going with Uncle Eddie and Harry.'

'Thanks,' he said while Carly gave her sister a grateful smile.

In the back of the limousines were two rows of seats that faced each other. Jane and Jennifer took one side while Carly and Dean took the other. As the car set off, Dean wrapped an arm around Carly and she leaned into him as she gazed out of the window.

* * *

The wake for Alec was being held at The Horseshoe Bar. Derek, the landlord and one of Alec's oldest friends, had been at the burial and had rushed back ahead of the rest of the mourners to ensure everything was ready. Sharon, who had been left in charge during his absence, had done Alec proud. A buffet had been set up and vases containing white lilies were dotted all over the room. Behind the bar with Sharon stood a new young barman Derek had recently hired. Both wore black clothes and Sharon had even forgone her trademark gaudy lipstick.

'The first round's on the house,' Derek told Eddie when he entered with his family.

'That's really good of you, pal. Thanks,' he replied. Eddie had noted his younger son was paying Carly particular attention as they'd got out of the limo and he wanted to separate them. Not only did he not want them getting together, aware that they'd had feelings for each other for a while, but he especially didn't want his son taking advantage when Carly was so vulnerable.

'Dean, give us a hand with the drinks,' he called.

His son nodded and ensured Carly was comfortably seated with her sisters before joining his father and older brother at the bar.

The rest of the mourners were already there – staff from the care home who'd been immensely fond of Alec, along with their neighbours Mary McCulloch and Mrs Beig and some other old friends. Mourners who wanted to pay their respects but who hadn't been invited to the burial began to arrive, quietly filing in and passing on their condolences to the Savage sisters and Eddie. The mood was muted as the mourners took their food and drinks, quietly chatting together. Peanut, a good friend of the Savage family who had recently started working with them, would have been present, however he'd gone to Spain for a couple of weeks to visit old friends and he hadn't been able to get a flight back in time.

The Bitches, the girl gang Jane led, all piled in as one and headed straight over to their leader. Jane smiled, so grateful for their support. Rose's friends also arrived and similarly surrounded her. She'd recently got herself a new boyfriend, a sweet, gentle boy called Noah who she'd known most of her life. When he sat beside her and slid an arm around her, Rose burst into tears and wept on his shoulder. Her friends all leaned in with concern, taking her hands or patting her arm in support.

Jack Alexander, the only member of his family who'd been invited as he was the Savage family's new boss, walked in to see Jane being comforted by The Bitches and her girlfriend and Rose surrounded by her boyfriend and her own friends. Carly sat close to them, alone and forlorn. His cold, hard heart went out to her. His ex-girlfriend was the only person he'd ever loved and he still did passionately. Only she could make him hurt and her loneliness hurt him now. A couple of her friends approached to pass on their condolences but they didn't sit with her in solidarity as her sisters' friends did. Instead, they moved on, eager to get to the buffet before everything was gone.

Glancing around the room, Jack saw Eddie and his sons standing at the bar. Dean was also regarding Carly with concern so Jack hurried over to her before he could make a move. The two men's eyes met, their mutual hostility obvious. Dean might have worked for Jack and he did his job very well but they didn't like each other personally, their love for Carly creating a rivalry between them.

Jack smoothly slipped into the spot beside her and he glanced at Dean, enjoying his small victory.

'Thanks for coming,' said Carly.

Her skin was very pale, eyes bloodshot but she still looked beautiful.

'As if I wouldn't,' replied Jack in his thick Yorkshire accent. He'd been born in Glasgow but had moved to England with his parents when he was just a small boy, so there was no trace of his native accent. 'I didn't know your dad but he made you, so I hold him in very high regard.'

'That's so sweet,' she replied with a sad smile.

'How are you holding up?'

'Oh, you know,' she sighed. 'I feel awful now but I'm hanging onto the fact that one day it will get better. It's just so hard getting my head around the fact that he's gone. It's so hard coping without someone who's been there your entire life.' A single tear slipped down her cheek. 'He was the heart of our family and I don't know what we'll do without him.'

'I wish I could give you some advice but I can't. My dad was an evil bastard who I was glad to see the back of. No one mourned him when he died and no one has ever visited his grave. Just look at all these people,' he said, gesturing to the busy room. 'They all loved Alec. He'll never be forgotten. If you ask me, he was a bloody lucky man.'

Carly's smile was happier and she patted his hand. 'Thanks. That does make me feel a bit better.'

'Good.' Unable to help himself, he ran his fingers through the ends of her long hair. He loved her hair, it was so soft and always smelled nice. It had been two months since she'd dumped him after he'd slept with Toni McVay in order to secure his new position. He hadn't wanted to do it but it had been the only way. If he'd displeased Toni, there had been a good chance she would have killed him but not before she'd scooped his eyeballs out of his head, the fate that had befallen his predecessor. But Rod Tallan had very much deserved his punishment, especially after he'd attacked Carly twice. Jack had raised himself in Carly's estimation when he'd been there for her when Rod had attacked her but it hadn't been enough to convince her to get back with him. His new position meant he had women throwing themselves at him but he wasn't interested. Carly was the woman for him. She had an unparalleled inner strength and was as tough as nails. He'd had one dalliance since their separation but that had only been about sex and he'd been careful that the woman in question was well away from Haghill.

'Jack, don't,' she said softly when his hand moved higher into her hair, something he knew turned her on.

'Sorry,' he said, retracting his hand. 'Old habits die hard. I just came here to make sure you were okay and to show my support.'

'And it's appreciated.'

'Is there anything I can do for you?'

Carly stared back at him, tempted to ask him to take her to bed. Despite what he'd done, she missed him. She also missed his sexual talents. She hadn't been with any man since Jack and she still loved him, even though she didn't want to. What she needed right now was the warmth and physical closeness of another person, the thought of her cold lonely bed infinitely depressing, but he'd only think they were getting back together and that she couldn't allow. Finally, she'd got out of the gangland life and she was enjoying working at Death Loves Company, a bar in the city centre. Rekindling her relationship with Jack would only drag her back into that life.

'No,' she said, all these thoughts whirling through her head in a moment. 'Thanks though.'

'No problem. Do you want a drink?'

'I'll have a dry white wine.'

'Coming right up.'

Jack headed to the bar. Dean took the spot he'd vacated beside Carly and placed a glass of dry white wine on the table before her.

'How are you holding up?' he asked, unwittingly using the same words as his rival.

'I'm okay,' she replied, picking up the glass and taking a big swig.

'Jack's not bothering you, is he?'

'No. He was just making sure I was all right,' she sighed, hoping they didn't start butting heads. That was the last thing she needed.

'He shouldn't have come.'

'He's just showing us his support and he's your boss, so I wouldn't badmouth him if I were you.'

Dean muttered something uncomplimentary under his breath.

'I thought you said he was a good boss,' replied Carly.

'Put it this way, he's better than Rod but Charles Manson would have been an improvement on that arsehole.'

Jack returned to the table carrying a pint of lager for himself and a glass of wine for Carly. He frowned when he saw Dean. For his part, Dean stared back at him steadily and took a swig of lager, making it very clear he was going nowhere.

Jack took a seat on Carly's other side, the two men casting each other glares across her while she sat awkwardly between them.

'Excuse me, I need the bathroom,' she said, getting to her feet.

Carly entered the ladies' bathroom with a sigh of relief. As she didn't need to use the toilet, she turned to the mirror to reapply her lipstick. Her appearance shocked her. She'd never seen her skin so pale before, her eyes were red from crying and her hair was a mess. She was amazed any man had wanted to sit with her, never mind two of them.

As she ran a comb through her hair, the door opened and Jane entered. Before speaking, she checked that the three toilet stalls were empty.

'I saw all that with Jack and Dean,' she told her sister.

'Aye, that was awkward,' sighed Carly.

'What are you going to do? It's clear they're both in love with you. They're still out there, glaring at each other.'

'I'm going to do nothing,' she said, replacing the comb in her handbag and producing a compact of powder and a make-up brush.

'Nothing?'

'That's right. I'm no' in the right headspace to deal with their feelings. I'm just trying to get through today.'

'You're right, sod them. You concentrate on you.' Jane worried what the fallout of Jack and Dean's rivalry would be, especially as their family was now working for Jack but she didn't articulate this to Carly, not on today of all days.

'I can't be with either of them,' said Carly as she dabbed at her face with the make-up brush. 'Because it would only piss off the other one.'

'I thought you'd never get back with Jack anyway after he slept with Toni.'

'That's right, but it doesn't stop me loving him.'

'And your feelings for him don't stop you loving Dean either.'

'Aye and they'd both be furious if I started seeing someone else, which I don't want to risk as they're dangerous men. So, as long as I'm in Haghill, I can't have a relationship.'

Concern filled Jane. 'You're not thinking of leaving, are you?'

The thought had occurred to Carly but her sister did not need to hear that right now. She forced a smile and turned to Jane. 'No, course not. Haghill's my home.'

'Come and have a drink then. Derek's telling stories about Da' when he was young.'

On exiting the bathroom with Jane, Carly saw Jack and Dean still sitting where she'd left them, awaiting her return. Instead of retaking that seat, she sat on the empty stool at the bar beside Derek, who was regaling the room with stories of what he and Alec had got up to when they were children. He beamed down at Carly and wrapped an arm around her. Emotion swelled in Carly's chest. Derek was the closest she had to a father now. She rested her head on his shoulder as he continued to talk. He was quite the storyteller and she found it soothing listening to him. Carly refused to look at either Jack or Dean, although she was conscious of their eyes on her. Once their love had felt like a privilege. Now it was becoming an anchor around her neck that she was afraid would one day drown her. Perhaps leaving Haghill was the only way to escape them both?

Carly's gaze slipped to the door when it opened and Jessica Alexander strutted in wearing a very tight black dress that revealed plenty of cleavage and thigh. No one else had noticed as they were too busy listening to Derek. Carly sat bolt upright in outrage. This bitch had had an affair with her father when her mother had been dying of cancer, something Jessica was inordinately proud of. Only Carly knew about the affair in the Savage family. Jessica had revealed it to her when her sons had kidnapped and tortured her. Carly had confronted her father about it, who deeply regretted his actions and she'd promised to keep it to herself.

Carly got to her feet and hurried over to Jessica, grabbing her roughly by the arm.

'What the fuck are you doing here?' she whispered. Derek was still holding court and she didn't want to interrupt.

'I've come to pay my respects,' purred Jessica. 'As you know, Alec and I were very close.'

'Bollocks. He couldn't stand you. Get out.'

'I have a right to be here... ow,' she cried when Carly twisted her arm up her back. 'You can't do this.'

'Watch me,' Carly growled, hauling her towards the door.

This drew everyone's attention and they all turned to look.

'Jack, help me,' cried Jessica, appealing to her cousin as she was manhandled out.

'Nothing to do with me,' he replied before casually sipping his pint.

Carly shoved Jessica through the door and out into the street.

Jessica whipped round to face her. 'If you don't let me in, I'll tell everyone about my affair with your precious da',' she spat in Carly's face.

'I'll break your fucking jaw before you get the chance and you know Jack will back me up.' Carly smirked back.

The pub door clattered open behind them and Jane and Rose emerged along with Derek. When Jessica's green eyes gleamed with malice, Carly panicked, thinking she was going to blurt out her dad's dirty secret, so she punched Jessica in the face, knocking her onto her bottom. Jessica pressed a hand to her swelling cheek and regarded the sisters uncertainly as they gathered around her.

'You should leave while you still can,' Carly told her. 'Because if just one more word comes out of your mouth, the three of us will tear you apart.'

Jessica wasn't stupid and knew when she was beaten. She dragged herself to her feet and staggered slightly on her heels, hitching her handbag up her shoulder. 'You will pay for this one day, Carly. You can't go around punching people you don't like.'

'It's served me well so far. Now do one, unless you want to end up as a stain on the pavement.'

Carly held her breath, seeing the temptation in Jessica's eyes to tell Alec's daughters about her affair with him but she knew that would be stupid. All three would just launch into her and she'd more than likely end up in intensive care.

'And you're no' welcome in my pub,' Derek told Jessica. 'You've been barred for ages, so I don't know why you even bothered to turn up.'

Jessica stalked off down the street, high heels clacking loudly along the pavement, casting the sisters glares over her shoulder.

'God, I'd love to give her a good battering,' said Rose, hands curling into fists.

'You and me both,' replied Carly. 'Anyway, let's no' worry about her. We need to go back in there, for Da'.'

Rose nodded sadly and headed back into the pub, her sisters and Derek following. Carly glanced at Jack to make sure he had no objection to what she'd just done. After all, he was the big man around here now, but he just nodded.

'Right,' said Derek, retaking his seat. 'Where was I?'

Even though Jane had practically moved into her girlfriend Jennifer's flat and Rose spent most of her time at her boyfriend's or her friends' houses, the three sisters had agreed to spend the night together at the flat that had been the family home they'd shared with their father. Carly closed the door behind them and locked it with a sigh of relief. They'd left their cousins and uncle at the pub, the wake having turned into a massive piss up. They hadn't wanted to join in, preferring peace and quiet.

The three of them curled up on the couch in the kitchen to watch a film and drink more wine. Although their father had left the flat a couple of months ago to go into the care home, his old bedroom, which had originally been the living room of the flat, still lay in state holding his bed and other furniture, so the kitchen remained the centre of activity. Carly was the only one who still lived there on a permanent basis and with every passing day it felt less and less like a home.

The three of them stared at the television in silence, not really seeing the romantic comedy Rose had requested they watch, lost in their own thoughts. When the film had ended and the wine had been drunk, they all retired to their bedrooms.

Carly changed into her pyjamas but she felt restless, thoughts about her future whirling through her head, along with memories of her father.

To distract herself from her grief, she sat on her bed and brought up properties to rent around Glasgow. It was true that she couldn't have a normal relationship with a man while she was in Haghill. Jack had blown his chance with her and being with Dean would cause too much trouble. It wasn't just the fact that he was her first cousin and that Jack wouldn't like her seeing him, it was because he was in the gangland life too. Although the danger of that life had excited her, she'd hated the impact it had on others. Collecting debts from desperate people had made her feel so bad, so she'd gone back to doing the only other thing she knew how to do – bar work. She'd been made manager of Death Loves Company a month ago after Diana, the previous manager, had quit. Diana had stuck it out for a few weeks after Rod had attacked them both at the bar but had been unable to cope with being around the bad memories, so she'd left to manage another bar on the other side of the city, which was a shame because she and Carly had become good friends. Carly however had no such issues and loved her job. Although being made manager had brought with it a pay rise, she certainly wasn't earning what she'd made debt collecting but the peace of mind she now had was more important. She made enough to buy and run a nice little car and to rent a place of her own, away from Haghill. Leaving her family behind would be painful but she had no choice if she wanted any sort of a future. Her sisters wouldn't want her to leave but it was all right for them, they were happy with their respective partners. Carly just wanted the same for herself.

She looked at properties closer to her work and saw there were a couple of nice flats within her budget available to rent. Tomorrow she would make appointments to view them. It was vital that she started living for herself after putting the needs of others before her own for so long. She'd given up school to go to work and help support the family when her father had become ill, she hadn't started a relationship with Dean for fear of what everyone would say and then she'd had to keep her relationship with Jack a secret. Carly was so tired of putting herself last. Both her parents had died young, leaving behind so many unused opportunities and unfulfilled dreams. It was a stark lesson. From now on, she would live for herself.

2

Jane was up and out early the next morning to meet Jennifer for breakfast while Rose headed to Noah's, leaving Carly alone once again at the flat. Usually this would have pained her but this time she was glad because it meant she could arrange viewings for the flats she'd found online. She managed to book appointments for both properties the following day. Carly was surprised by how motivated she felt. One of the most important people in the world to her had just died and it had undoubtedly knocked her sideways but it had also filled her with determination to make the most of her life, a chance neither of her parents had got. It felt like a final gift from her father and she determined to make the most of it.

'What now?' she sighed when there was a knock at the door.

She was expecting it to be either Jack or Dean but it was neither.

'Cole,' she said with surprise.

Her ex-boyfriend stood on her doorstep looking sympathetic. His green cats' eyes were for once soft and gentle.

'I'm really sorry about Alec,' he opened. 'I would have liked to go to the wake but I didn't think I would be welcome and I didnae want to cause any trouble.'

'I appreciate that,' she replied. 'I just wish your maw had been so thoughtful.'

'You know what she's like. She doesn't like anyone telling her what to do.'

'Did you know she was going to turn up?'

'She did mention it but I told her no' to go. I thought she'd listened. Clearly, she didn't and for that I'm sorry.'

'I've got to admit that I'm surprised you're here. Our families have had nothing to do with each other since you and your brothers pointed guns at us.'

'I didn't enjoy that.'

'Ross did.'

'He loves any sort of violence but I did think a lot of Alec. I know how close you were and I can only imagine the pain you're in.'

Carly frowned. 'Why are you being nice all of a sudden?'

'Dunno.' He shrugged. 'I suppose it's just struck me what I gave up.'

Carly was put immediately on her guard when he gazed at her with wide, sad eyes. For so long he'd seemed so cold and stony; prison had changed him for the worse. Now he looked like the Cole she'd loved before he'd been sent to Barlinnie.

'The last time you spoke like this it was a set-up so your brothers could try and kidnap me,' she said.

'I know,' he sighed. 'I was stupid. There's no trick this time.'

Carly didn't believe that for a second. 'Is your family working for Jack?'

'No. Personally, I think it would be a good idea to try and build bridges with him again; he's raking in a fortune, but Ross and Dom are too proud.'

'Are you sure it's just your brothers who are too proud?'

'Aye. I made a play for the top spot and I was outmanoeuvred. I actually respect Jack a lot more for that stunt he pulled. He fooled us all.'

'Including me,' she muttered.

'I heard you dumped him because he slept with Toni McVay.'

'Thanks for reminding me.'

'I'm no' having a go. I just think he's a fucking idiot.'

'Like you wouldn't have made the same choice.'

'Actually, I'm not sure I would have.'

'Aye, right,' she replied cynically.

'What are you doing?' he said when she glanced up and down the street.

'Looking out for your brothers.'

'They're no' here. Seriously, I've no ulterior motive. I've just been doing some soul searching recently and I realised I made a big mistake. I let all the bad stuff I went through in prison turn me into something I'm not. Being made to look an idiot in front of the whole of Haghill does that to a person. Ambition and greed made me gi'e up the best thing that ever happened to me. I want you back, Carly.'

She folded her arms across her chest and regarded him sternly. 'I don't believe you. This is just part of whatever new plot you're cooking up to try and snatch power back from Jack but it won't work. Anyway, I'm nothing to do with that life any more. I just work in the bar. I'm out.'

'I mean it,' he said, eyes wide and earnest. 'I really have changed.'

'Goodbye, Cole,' she said before slamming the door shut in his face. For good measure, she locked it too.

Carly remained by the door, wondering if he'd knock again. When she didn't hear anything, she headed into Jane's room, which looked out over the front street and peered out of the window. To her relief, she saw him retreating down the road.

'Thank God,' she breathed.

She hadn't believed his words for a second. Anything good that had been inside Cole had been knocked out of him in Barlinnie Prison. Carly wondered if she should mention his visit to the rest of the family then decided against it. That would only kick off more trouble and that was the last thing they needed while they were grieving. However, she would keep an eye out, just to make sure, because Cole had proved time and again that he was very clever and extremely tricky. She wondered if Jack was going to face a challenge to his position so soon and if so, how would he handle it? Probably with lots of violence because blood ties meant nothing to the Alexander family.

* * *

That afternoon, Carly headed back to the cemetery to make sure her father's grave had been filled in properly. She was pleased to see that the job had been done very neatly. The tombstone wasn't in situ yet, it would take a few weeks for that to be made. Eddie had insisted on footing the bill for that personally and he'd gone for top of the range marble, no expense spared. Flowers were already on the grave, but Carly placed another bunch on it along with some for her mother.

'Everything's changed,' she told the graves. 'I'm determined to live my own life but I'm scared. You've always been there to guide me but now I feel lost. I know Uncle Eddie, Derek and Jane are there if I need advice but it's no' the same.'

Feeling someone watching her, she whipped round, sharp eyes scanning the graveyard but there was no one, the only movement from the yew trees surrounding the cemetery, like ancient guardians, witnesses to so much pain and grief. Despite the fact that she appeared to be the only person present, Carly grew so uncomfortable that she decided to leave.

After saying goodbye to the graves, she hurried out of the cemetery, constantly looking left and right, sighing with relief when she returned to the main road. Now she was once again surrounded by people and traffic, Carly felt a little foolish. She'd allowed her imagination to get the better of her. That was all there was to it. So why did she still feel the need to glance over her shoulder?

* * *

The prospect of going back to the lonely flat was not an appealing one, so Carly decided to head to her friend Claire's house. However, she was out, as was her other friend Sarah. Carly wasn't like her sisters, she didn't have a big friend group. She'd taken two weeks off work after her father's death, so she found herself at a loose end. Eddie, Dean and Harry were working. Jane had been given the day off but she was spending it with Jennifer while Rose was with Noah. Her family were moving forward with their own lives while Carly was being left behind.

It was tempting to go to the pub and drown her sorrows but that was a dangerous path to go down, so instead she decided to pamper herself and get her nails done at the local nail bar. After peering through the window and determining that Jessica Alexander wasn't in there, she headed inside. Carly began to unwind at the beautician's small talk.

'That's lovely, thanks.' Carly smiled when the beautician had finished painting her nails a rose pink. For once, they looked neat and even, not chipped and of unequal length as they usually were.

The till was by the window and as Carly waited to pay, she

once again felt eyes on her. Turning, she looked out but saw no one. Her attention was brought back to the beautician and after paying, Carly reluctantly stepped back out onto the street. There were a few people on the pavement, two old women eagerly gabbing away outside the newsagent's next door, but no one was paying her any attention.

Wishing she'd brought her car, Carly headed in the direction of home, constantly looking back over her shoulder as the uncomfortable feeling wouldn't go.

As she approached the door of her flat she saw her uncle's car pull up outside, which was odd as she thought he'd be out all day working.

Eddie leapt out of the driver's seat. 'Carly, doll,' he said. 'Thank God you're here.'

'Why?' she replied.

He opened the back door of the car and Harry got out first before turning to assist Dean, who held a bloodied piece of cloth to his upper right arm.

'God, what's happened?' she exclaimed rushing up to her cousin.

'Some arsehole with a knife,' said Harry, slinging his brother's good arm around his shoulders and hauling him towards the door.

'Why have you brought him here and not the hospital?'

'Because we cannae have them asking any awkward questions,' replied Eddie. 'I can suture it myself, I've done it enough times. I just need Jane's first aid kit.'

'Come in,' said Carly, hastily unlocking the front door.

Dean was able to move under his own steam but he looked pale and in pain. Harry manoeuvred him to the kitchen table and helped him slump into a chair.

Carly hastily dug the first aid kit out of the kitchen cupboard and handed it to her uncle.

'Cheers, hen,' replied Eddie. 'Harry, get his shirt off.'

Harry began unbuttoning the smart blue shirt Dean wore, which was slashed at the top of the right arm. Carly's eyes widened when she saw Dean's bare torso. His skin was covered in a fine sheen of sweat and each muscle was tense. His breathing was ragged, making his powerful chest heave savagely.

'Carly, set the kettle to boil,' Eddie told her. 'I need some sterile water. Carly,' he repeated louder when she failed to respond.

'Sorry,' she said, blushing.

She tore her eyes off Dean's body and rushed over to the kettle, filling it and switching it on. She then dug out a bowl to pour the water into. 'What happened?' she asked as she worked.

'It was a bloody ambush,' growled Harry. 'We were supposed to collect the last payment from a client. It was an old Tallan debt, one of the few remaining. Forty-five grand. The prick didn't want to pay and had half a dozen of his pals waiting for us. We hammered them but Dean got slashed in the process.'

'Thank God you lot are tough or it could have been so much worse.'

'You put the arsehole through a wall, didn't you pal?' Harry beamed down at his brother, clapping him on the shoulder. 'Sorry,' he said when Dean grunted with pain.

'Take a step back before you give him more injuries,' his dad told Harry as he began cleaning the wound with an antiseptic wipe. 'It was bleeding like a bastard at first, but luckily we managed to stop it quickly enough.'

'It looks nasty,' said Carly when the wound was revealed. It was about five inches long and a little ragged. 'Are you sure he wouldn't be better off at a hospital?'

'It's clearly a knife wound and they would have to report it,' replied Eddie.

'You said he lost a lot of blood and that can be dangerous.'

'No' that much. Trust me, I've dealt with these sorts of injuries before. The kettle's boiled, I need that water.'

With a sigh, Carly poured the water into the bowl and placed it on the kitchen table within her uncle's reach. Anxiously she watched as he prepared the suture.

'What about painkillers?' Carly asked him.

'He can have some when I've done,' replied Eddie. 'I don't want to risk raising his blood pressure and making him bleed again.'

'You cannae stitch him up without pain relief; he'll be in agony.'

'He's tough, he can take it.'

'But...'

'It's fine, Carly,' breathed Dean. 'Honestly.'

All she could do was watch as Eddie started to stitch up the wound. Dean groaned with pain and screwed up his big fists, making the muscles pop out even more. Feeling helpless, all Carly could do was watch. He looked up at her, eyes heavy with pain, jaw gritted and took her hand for comfort. Carly winced when he squeezed it hard as Eddie continued to work. She had to give her uncle his due, he completed the line of stitches neatly and swiftly. He hadn't been lying when he'd said he was experienced but it was Dean's suffering that broke her heart. Even though he was crushing her hand, she decided to suck it up and tolerate her own pain, sighing with relief when Eddie completed the last stitch and Dean's grip relaxed.

'You all right, son?' Eddie asked Dean.

'Aye,' he murmured, eyes heavy. 'Just sore. And bloody knackered.'

'You can lie down on the couch,' said Carly. 'I'll fetch you a blanket.'

'Thanks.'

As Harry and Eddie helped him to lie down, Carly rushed into her father's old bedroom, produced a clean blanket from a wardrobe and took it back to the kitchen. Dean was lying on the couch on his good side and she tucked the blanket in around him. His eyes flickered open and he managed to give her a gentle smile before they closed again.

'He looks pale and weak,' Carly told her uncle. 'What if he's lost too much blood?'

'He hasn't,' replied Eddie. 'He'll be fine. Stop worrying.'

'Stop worrying? He's been stabbed, for God's sake.'

'Aye, we know. We saw it. Now we're going back to sort out the twats who did it. We need Jane to come with us but we cannae get hold of her.'

'Jennifer was taking her out somewhere. She thought it would help to get her away from Glasgow for a few hours.'

'Fucking marvellous,' he sighed. 'You'll have to come instead.'

'Me? Oh no, I don't do all that any more.'

'We need back-up.'

'Then get Jack to go with you.'

'We cannae ask him, he's the boss. We're collecting on his behalf.'

'Then ask him to send one of his men with you.'

'No, it has to be a woman. I've got a plan. The mark's a real ladies' man and we need a woman to distract him so me and Harry can grab the money.'

'No. I'm no' in that line of work any more,' she firmly replied. 'Besides, Dean can't be left alone, not in his condition.'

'I'll get Mary from next door to sit with him,' replied Eddie. 'She used to be a nurse, so he'll be in good hands. Besides, don't you want to get some payback on the arsehole who did this to him?'

Carly really did and it showed in her eyes but she was also reluctant to get back into that world. 'I'm still trying to deal with Da's death. I'm no' in the right headspace.'

'Some action is just what's needed to help you get over it. What do you think Alec would do if some prick had hurt a member of his family?'

Her expression hardened. 'That's low, Uncle Eddie.'

'It's the truth. He'd have been raging. You've inherited that anger from him, so fucking use it and help us get some payback for Dean.'

Carly sighed and chewed her lower lip. If she was honest with herself, she was up for a good scrap and she did want to help get revenge. 'If I come, this doesn't mean I'm back in the life, okay? I'm still out. I'm only doing it this time because Dean got hurt.'

'Absolutely, sweetheart. We promise it won't lead to you getting caught up in it all again.'

'Good. Right, I'll call Mary and ask her to sit with Dean.'

'No need. I'll go up and gi'e her a knock. You need to get ready.'

'What do you mean, get ready?'

'You know, tart yourself up a wee bit. Short skirt, low top, that sort of thing.'

'Hey, that wasn't the deal,' she exclaimed.

'Sorry but it's all part of my plan. Now chop chop, we need to get back over there before he leaves. And don't forget to take your baton and pepper spray with you.'

Carly tutted before storming into her bedroom and slamming the door shut. She rummaged around in her wardrobe and produced a short black skirt along with a turquoise blouse. Then she took out her baton from the bottom of her wardrobe where it had sat for the last two months and put it in her handbag. The small canister of pepper spray beside it was slipped into the pocket of her skirt. After applying some make-up and brushing her hair, she pulled on a pair of low heels and stomped back into the kitchen.

'Will this do?' she snapped at Harry, hand on hip.

'Err, I think so,' he replied. 'Da's just gone up to Mary's.'

'Do you know about this plan of his?' She frowned.

'No' in detail.'

'This is the last thing I'm in the mood for; I'm mourning my da' here.'

'I know and I'm sorry,' he said sincerely. 'Believe me, this isnae my idea.'

Eddie returned with Mary, who immediately began fussing around Dean, who was almost asleep.

'Don't you worry, I'll take good care of him,' she assured them. 'Away you go, take all the time you need.'

'Thanks, doll, you're a lifesaver,' Eddie told her. 'Right, let's move. The sooner we get this done the sooner we can get back.'

3

Carly slunk out of the house after her uncle and cousin wondering how the hell she'd allowed herself to be roped into this. She got into the back of Eddie's car, scowling out of the window as they left Haghill behind.

'Right, this is the plan,' said her uncle. 'Blair – he's the mark by the way, Carly – lives in Cambuslang. He has quite a nice drum, actually. You're gonnae knock on his door and ask to use his phone because your car's broken down.'

'He won't fall for that,' she replied. 'Everyone has mobile phones these days.'

'Tell him your battery's died. Anyway, he won't care about your story because he'll be too busy looking at you.'

'What makes you think he'll even be interested in me?'

'Because you're a bonny lassie. And he's no' the brightest bulb in the box.'

'What if his friends are still there?'

'They're no'. They scarpered when we tore into them. He'll be all alone.'

'Or he might be expecting you to come back and he got more friends to come to his house.'

'And if he did, they'll get fucking battered too.'

Eddie's voice was choked with rage and it only just struck Carly how furious he was about what had been done to Dean. 'Does Jack know about any of this yet?'

'No. I don't want to call him until we've got the money.'

They pulled up at the kerb on a brand-new scheme that was dotted with identical white boxes with grey roofs. Eddie turned in his seat to face Carly and indicated the last house on the street.

'This is it, doll,' he told her. 'Just knock on the door, gi'e him your story and let us do the rest.'

'What if he slams the door shut in my face?'

'He won't. Undo the top two buttons of your shirt.'

She frowned. 'No.'

'If you do, I can guarantee he won't shut the door in your face.'

'Fine,' she sighed, unfastening the buttons. 'Better?'

'Aye,' replied Harry. 'Just don't breathe too hard because you'll have his eye out.'

'Fucking hilarious,' she grumbled, snatching up her handbag and getting out of the car.

She slammed the door shut as hard as she could, pleased when her uncle and cousin winced, before storming down the street. It was very quiet; no one was about and the click of her heels on the pavement seemed incredibly loud. Blair would hear her coming a mile off.

She headed up the drive to the front door while attempting to gather her thoughts. Carly closed her eyes, took a deep breath and recalled the image of Dean injured and bleeding. Then she knocked on the door. At the sound of the door being unlocked, she opened her eyes, feeling more resolute.

The door was pulled open by a rather attractive man in his

early thirties with short black hair and light blue eyes. There was a large bruise on his left cheek, no doubt from the fist of one of her cousins or her uncle. In his hands he clutched a golf club. He frowned at Carly as though she were a visitor from outer space.

'What do you want?' replied the man who she assumed to be Blair.

'Hi, I'm sorry to disturb you,' she said with the best smile she could muster. 'But my car broke down. I wondered if I could use your phone to call my breakdown company?'

Suspicion filled his eyes. 'Why don't you use your mobile phone?'

'My battery died,' she replied, putting on her best ditsy voice. 'I'm always forgetting to charge it.'

Carly tossed back her long hair and stuck out her chest, causing his eyes to widen.

'You'd better come in then,' he said, opening the door wider.

'So kind.' She smiled as she stepped inside. At least he appeared to be alone. She could see no one else and there was no sound of anyone talking or moving about. The house felt empty.

Blair closed the door behind her and indicated a room to the left. 'The phone's just in there.'

'Thanks.'

As she headed down the hall, she heard the lock on the front door being turned. Glancing back over her shoulder, she saw him watching her.

'Just in there,' he told her with a reassuring smile.

He seemed relaxed enough and Carly reasoned that he would want to keep the door locked after he'd just been attacked in his own home, but it still made her uneasy. Only the knowledge that Eddie and Harry were close encouraged her to move deeper into the house. The lounge would once have been nice with its thick cream carpet and luxurious furniture, but everything had been overturned. A large picture at one side of the room was on the floor, the glass smashed.

'What happened here?' she asked Blair as he followed her into the room.

'Someone tried robbing the place but I caught them, battered them and threw them out,' he said, throwing back his shoulders proudly.

'Oh my God, have you called the polis?'

'Naw, I don't need them. I handled the arseholes myself.'

'Are you sure you want me in here? I could destroy any evidence that might help catch them.'

'Don't you worry, sweetheart, they won't be back any time soon.'

Want to bet? Carly thought to herself. 'Where's the phone?' she asked him.

'There.'

She looked in the direction he pointed and saw the cordless phone lying on the floor beside an overturned table.

'Do you have the number?' he asked her.

'Aye, it's on my car key,' she replied before rummaging through her handbag, making a show of looking for her keys.

'Before calling them, why don't you have a glass of wine?'

'No thanks, I don't drink this early.'

'You're no' in a rush, are you?'

Carly took a couple of steps back when he approached her.

'I am in a rush,' she replied. 'I want to get home. To my husband,' she added.

He smiled. 'You're not married.'

'I am.'

'Then why aren't you wearing a ring?'

'I... lost it.'

'You're a bad liar,' he replied with an amused smile, taking another step closer.

Carly backed up again and bumped into the wall. 'Just let me make the call,' she told him, not liking the look in his eyes. Usually, she'd feel confident about taking on most people but there was something very dangerous about this man.

'Later,' he replied. 'First I want a quid pro quo.'

'A what?'

'I do something nice for you, so you do something nice for me.'

'But you haven't done anything nice for me yet.'

'I let you into my home.' He pressed his palms against the wall on either side of her head, penning her in. 'Now you have to do something nice for me.'

Blair cried out in surprise when her forehead connected with his nose. He staggered backwards, blood trickling from both nostrils. Carly pulled the baton from her handbag and advanced on him. Memories of Rod Tallan attempting to force himself on her returned and her fury spiked. Why did these creeps think they had the right to take any woman they wanted?

'Let me tell you something about me, Blair,' she hissed. 'I don't play fucking nice.'

'How do you know my name?' he exclaimed.

Carly's response was a wicked grin.

'You're one of them,' he cried, drawing back his fist.

Carly ducked and slammed the baton into his left knee. He screeched with pain and dropped to the floor.

When she heard the thud of approaching footsteps, she expected to see her cousin and uncle but instead three big men who also had bruised faces charged into the room.

'What happened?' demanded one of the men.

'The bitch headbutted me then bust my knee,' retorted Blair. 'Get her.'

Carly turned to the men, gripping the baton hard. Rather than attack, they frowned at each other.

'Why would she do that?' replied the shortest of the three. He was a sturdy-looking individual with a shaved head and large brown eyes.

'I asked to use his phone because my car broke down,' Carly told them. 'And he tried to sexually assault me.'

'What?' exclaimed the man. He looked back at Blair. 'You dirty bastard.'

'I didn't do anything,' he cried.

'You're saying this lassie's a liar?'

'Aye, I am.'

'Why the hell would she walk in here and do that to you for no reason?'

'Because she's come for the money. She's with that lot who burst in earlier.'

'What money?' Carly frowned.

'Course she's no' here for that,' the short man told Blair. 'Does she look like a debt collector?'

'I just want to call my breakdown company,' rasped Carly, eyes welling with tears. The play-acting wasn't difficult. Since her dad's death the tears had constantly been close to the surface.

'On you go, sweetheart,' the short man told her. 'We'll make sure this one leaves you alone while you make your call.'

'Thank you,' she sniffed, wiping away her tears with her fingertips.

She retrieved the phone from the floor and dialled. Thankfully Blair was too preoccupied with his injured face and knee to realise that she hadn't produced her car key from her bag for the phone number.

'Hello, yes,' she said. 'My car's broken down and I need it collecting.' She rhymed off a fake policy number and gave the address to her own answering machine at home. She hung up with a smile. 'They'll be here in an hour.'

'Good,' said the short man. 'You're welcome to wait here.'

'Thanks but I'll wait with my car,' she told him, looking warily down at Blair.

'No problem.'

Carly backed up towards the door, the three men watching her go. When she was in the hallway, she turned and ran towards the front door. She tugged at it but it refused to open. Then she realised she needed to turn the key, which was in the lock. She turned it but still it refused to open.

Carly whipped round when the three men emerged in the hallway.

'We just pressed redial,' said the short man. 'You didnae call a breakdown company. It was someone's house.'

'There must be some mistake,' she replied with a breezy smile. 'You heard me speak to them.'

'We heard you speak to someone.' The men began to advance on her. 'Blair was right, you are connected to those debt collectors, aren't you?'

'I don't know anything about any debt collectors,' she replied, gripping the baton tightly.

'Put that down,' he said, nodding at the weapon. 'Things will go a lot better for you if you do.'

'No chance. You're just as mad as your friend.'

'You can drop the pretence now. We don't want to hurt you, you're just the distraction. Tell us where your friends are and we can take it out on them instead.'

'I've no idea who you're talking about.'

'I don't know what they're paying you but it's no' worth it, so tell us what the plan is.'

'There isn't any plan,' she cried, still playing the damsel in distress. 'I just want to get my car sorted and go home.' As she spoke, Carly fumbled with the bolt on the door that in her panic she'd just realised needed unlocking. The short man rushed forward and slammed his hand against the door before she could pull it open.

'Come back in so we can discuss it,' he growled, suddenly looking angry and aggressive. He tore the baton from her hand. 'And you can gi'e me that too.'

Carly allowed him to take it. He also snatched the clutch bag from her hand and tossed it to one of his friends. 'Check it for weapons.'

'I'm going to tell the polis about you,' she told them. 'And they'll arrest you all. You're perverts just like your pal.'

He grabbed her roughly by the arm and as she was hauled back towards the lounge, she groped for the canister of pepper spray in her skirt pocket. Her hand closed around it but she kept it hidden behind her back.

Carly was flung to the lounge floor and she stared up at the three men fearfully, wondering what they were going to do. She was also wondering where the hell Harry and her uncle were. Blair was still on the floor, but he sat propped up against the side of the couch, pale and sweaty with pain.

'Why are you really here?' the short man demanded of Carly.

'I keep telling you – to call my breakdown company.'

'We already know that's a lie, so you'd better start telling the truth. We don't want to hurt you but we will if we have to.'

'I'm no' lying.'

He sighed and shook his head. 'Well, you can't say you weren't warned.'

As he drew back his foot to kick her, Carly leapt up and sprayed the pepper spray right into his eyes. He screamed in pain and stumbled backwards, tripping over the upturned coffee table and falling into one of his friends, taking him down with him. The third man stared at her in surprise before quickly recovering himself and charging at her. Carly snatched up the cordless phone that she'd used earlier and smacked him in the face with it before pepper spraying him too. Some of it struck Blair, who cried out in pain.

After snatching her baton from the short man's hand, she dashed to the door, wanting to escape the room before her eyes were also affected. As she exited the lounge, she almost ran into Harry.

'Woah,' he said, steadying her. 'You okay?'

'Where the hell were you?'

'In the office taking the money. Why, what happened?' He peered into the lounge and his eyebrows shot up when he saw the four men groaning on the floor and screeching about their eyes. 'Nice one.'

'Nice one?' she exclaimed. 'You left me to take on four of them alone.'

'We didn't mean to; we didnae know the other three were here.'

'Well you should have.'

Eddie emerged from a door further down the hall holding a sports bag. 'Let's go before they're back on their feet.'

Carly thought that was a good idea, so she decided to save the chastisement until they were safely away. They hurried out the back door, past the side of the house and down the drive, only slowing when they reached the main street.

'I can't believe you left me like that,' exclaimed Carly once they were back in the car.

'We didnae mean to, hen,' said Eddie as he drove. 'We thought Blair would be alone and we knew you could handle him.'

'You shouldn't have assumed and you were too busy getting the money to bother checking I was safe. Well, I'm never helping you again; I don't care what the circumstances are. You can sod right off,' she yelled before slumping into the back seat with a scowl. When she realised her breasts were practically bursting out of her shirt, she fastened up the top buttons.

'We let you down, sweetheart,' said Eddie gently. 'And we didnae mean to. You're right, we should have checked. Anything could have happened to you and I'll never forgive myself.'

She pouted, folding her arms across her chest.

They sank into an uncomfortable silence, which was broken when Carly realised they weren't heading back to her home.

'Where are we going?' she said.

'We need to drop the cash off with Jack,' replied Eddie.

'I don't want to see him,' she sighed.

'You don't need to. You can wait in the car while me and Harry go in.'

'Fine, just don't be long.'

Eddie parked outside a café and her cousin and uncle got out of the car, leaving Carly alone with her thoughts. She wondered why she was in such a rush to get back home. It wasn't like she had anything to do, although she was a little anxious to see how Dean was doing. Curiously she studied the café Eddie and Harry had gone into. The Cosy Café looked like a typical greasy spoon, not very inviting with its tacky bright orange front. There was certainly nothing cosy about it. This must be the place Jack was doing business from. It was a smart front because if anyone saw Eddie and Harry coming and going regularly, they'd just assume it was a favourite haunt of theirs.

Carly sighed when the café door opened and Jack stalked out

looking sexy and dangerous. She was irritated when her heart skipped a beat but she told herself it was just a lingering physical attraction. The last thing she wanted was to get back into a relationship with him. She was surprised when he pulled open the door and got into the back of the car with her.

'What are you doing?' she asked.

'Eddie told me what happened. I wanted to make sure you were okay.'

'I'm fine. Those men didnae lay a finger on me.'

'I'm very glad to hear it because I would have been majorly pissed off if you'd been hurt. For the record, I didn't want you anywhere near this. I know you're out of the life.'

'I am and this doesn't mean that I want back in.'

He held up his hands. 'I know. I just wanted to let you know that I don't condone what they did in any way.'

'Thanks, I appreciate that.'

Tenderly he cupped her right cheek with his hand. 'I wouldn't see you hurt for the world.'

'Jack, please don't,' she said softly.

He nodded, eyes flashing with hurt as he removed his hand. 'Sorry. It just constantly tears me up that I lost the best thing that ever happened to me.'

'I thought your deal with Toni was the best thing that ever happened to you?' she said bitterly.

'It turns out it's not,' he replied with a self-deprecating smile. 'Don't get me wrong, it's a great deal. I enjoy the work but it doesn't make me happy like you did, but what choice did I have? If I hadn't made my move then Cole would be running things now and no one wants that.'

Carly considered telling him about Cole's visit then decided against it because it would only cause trouble. 'You're handsome and powerful, you'll meet someone else.'

'But they won't be like you. No one's like you.'

Those dark, dangerous eyes of his briefly filled with pain, the power of which rather shocked Carly.

He smiled, dispelling all that emotion. 'I'd better get out of this car before I lose control of myself. That outfit of yours is really turning me on.'

'It wasn't my choice to wear it.'

'So I heard and I know that's not your style. It looks great on you though,' he replied with a smile and a wink. From his pocket he produced a wad of notes and held it out to her. 'For your time and trouble.'

'Thanks,' she replied, taking it from him. She'd certainly earned it and it would come in useful when she moved. 'Do you work out of this café?'

'I'm renting the flat above it, under another name of course. It's just for business.'

'I hope the café owner keeps their mouth shut.'

'They will; they've been in this game a long time. I chose them carefully.'

'I've no doubt. You certainly seem to know what you're doing.'

'That's the only good thing about prison. It teaches you how to be a better criminal.'

Carly was unable to resist a smile, despite how lousy she was feeling. Jack had always been able to make her feel better when she was down.

'Well,' he said. 'I'll let you get on with your day.' He gave her hand a gentle squeeze. 'See you around.'

He looked at her once more before getting out of the car. Carly watched him head back to the café. At the door, he paused to glance back at her before going inside.

Carly sighed heavily and sank back in her seat. Another good reason to move away from Haghill would be that she would finally escape temptation.

4

Eddie and Harry returned to the car and they continued their drive back to Haghill. Carly noted that her uncle looked angry and she guessed Jack had given him a telling off. Good.

She got out of the car without a word and stormed back into the flat, Eddie and Harry sheepishly trailing after her. Carly entered the kitchen to find Mary sitting at the kitchen table, knitting, while Dean slept on the couch.

'How has he been?' Carly quietly asked her so as not to disturb him.

'Fine,' she replied. 'Sleeping like a baby, which is good. It means the pain's not disturbing him.'

'I suppose,' Carly said uncertainly before looking back at Dean. She would have felt much better had he been treated at a hospital but it seemed no one else agreed.

'Now you're back I'll head home,' said Mary, stuffing her knitting into a canvas bag.

'No problem, doll,' replied Eddie. 'Thanks so much for your help,' he added before slipping her fifty quid.

'Any time for your family.' She smiled sweetly, patting his face before sliding the money into the pocket of her cardigan and leaving.

'You don't need to hang around if you've got things to do,' Carly told Eddie and Harry coolly. 'I'll keep an eye on Dean.' The hostile look in her eyes and the way she stood with her arms folded across her chest said they weren't welcome to stay.

'Aye, all right,' replied Eddie. 'Thanks for your help, doll.'

Carly just regarded him coldly.

The two men left in awkward silence. As soon as they'd gone, Carly checked on Dean before hurrying into her bedroom and changing back into jeans and a jumper, which helped lift her mood a little.

Dean stirred half an hour later and she hastened to his side.

'How are you feeling?' she said gently when his eyes flickered open.

'Shite,' he rasped.

'Do you want some water?' she said, hearing his throat was dry.

'Please.'

She hurried to pour him a glass as he hauled himself up to a sitting position. His torso was still bare and Carly had to fight not to look. He downed the glass of water in one.

'Do you want some more?'

'If it's not too much trouble,' he replied, his voice sounding stronger.

'Of course it's not,' she said, taking the glass from him.

She refilled it and handed it back to Dean, taking a seat on the couch beside him.

'Are you in pain?' she asked with concern.

'It aches but I can stand it.' He glanced at the clock on the wall with bleary eyes. 'I cannae have any more painkillers yet anyway.'

'Do you want something to eat?'

'No, thanks. Did Da' and Harry go back to Blair's?'

'They did,' she muttered.

He noted the anger in her eyes. 'What happened?'

Dean listened to her explain with growing fury.

'And they just left you alone in there?' he spluttered once she'd finished.

Carly nodded sombrely.

'I'll be having a fucking word with them,' he growled, shooting to his feet. His eyes widened and he swayed.

'Sit down,' she told him, taking his hand and urging him to retake his seat. 'You've lost blood; you need to take it easy.'

Dean sank back into the couch and pressed his free hand to his forehead. He retained hold of her own hand with the other. Carly considered objecting but didn't have the heart as he looked so weak.

'I cannae believe they did that,' he said when his head had cleared.

'Me neither. I was pissed off.'

'I don't blame you.'

'Jack gave me some cash as compensation though.'

'He knew about it?' he exclaimed.

'No. He was as angry as you are. Eddie and Harry dropped off the cash they'd collected with him on the way back here.'

They were both very conscious of the fact that they were still holding hands. They turned to look at each other, their eyes slipping to their joined hands before they locked gazes again. Carly thought he'd never looked more adorable with his mussed-up hair and hazy eyes.

'I want to kiss you,' he said.

'Okay,' she slowly replied, not expecting him to be so forthright. 'But I'd feel like I was taking advantage of you because you're hurt and on painkillers.'

He leaned into her, pinning her with his eyes. 'Do you think I'm weak?'

'No, course not.'

'Vulnerable?'

'I wouldn't say that but you have just gone through an ordeal and you're not thinking straight.'

'My mind's never been clearer. Or are you worried about Jack?' he added, expression hardening.

'It's nothing to do with him. I just don't want to take advantage of an injured man.'

'You won't,' he said, leaning in even closer.

Carly's eyes closed with anticipation, her heart thumping. She moaned with pleasure when Dean's lips met hers. This was so unexpected it was even more exciting. Her hand slid into his hair as he wrapped his good arm around her waist and pulled her closer. Carly allowed her hands to slide down his big shoulders to his back, loving the feel of his bare skin.

Slowly they sank back into the couch together.

'Should we be doing this?' she breathed as he kissed her neck.

'It feels right to me,' he murmured into her throat. He raised his head to look into her eyes. 'Unless you think you're too vulnerable after your da's death?'

Carly hesitated, knowing he was right but he felt so good.

'Oh no, not now,' he grunted before she could reply.

'What's wrong?' replied Carly.

'My arm's bleeding again.' He shrugged. 'It'll be fine.'

'We can't just leave it,' she said, noting the blood trickling from the corner of a stitch. 'Sit up.'

'Talk about shite timing,' he muttered.

Carly jumped up, flushed, her heart hammering, and rushed to get a sterile cloth to press to the wound.

'Sorry,' she said as he inhaled sharply with pain.

'Don't worry about it. I'm used to it.'

'Aren't you getting sick of this life? Of being hurt and put in danger?'

'I suppose but I earn good money.'

'How many times have you been hurt while working? It's twice that I know of – this injury and when the auld lady stabbed you.'

'Harry still takes the piss out of me for that one.'

'What if next time you're no' so lucky and you're stabbed in the neck or the heart?'

'I get what you're saying but there's nothing else I can do that will give me such a good income.'

'Of course there is. You're really clever; you've been taking a university course.'

'I've been getting sick of that recently.'

'Why?'

'I don't know, I suppose other things have been taking priority.'

'Don't let them. You could be anything you want to be and still make a tonne of cash without running the risk of being hurt or killed. You wanted out of the life once. What's changed?'

'The work I'm doing now pays a lot better and I enjoy the money. I know that makes me sound shallow, but it feels good after struggling for years.'

'Believe me, I understand that but I'm much happier now I'm out. Today has just reiterated that I made the right decision. I worry about you.'

'If I wasn't doing this job, could we become a couple?'

'I...' Carly trailed off, unsure how to answer.

He took her hand. 'I understand that you wouldn't want to be with me or anyone else in this life now you've got out but would it change your mind if I got out too?'

Carly didn't reply because she had no idea what to say. She'd been completely blindsided.

'That's a no then,' he mumbled.

'No, it's not. I just wasn't expecting it. To be honest, I've got a couple of appointments to view flats near my work.'

'You want to leave Haghill?'

She nodded. 'And I don't know how it would affect us.'

'I never thought you'd want to leave your sisters.'

'I don't but Jane and Rose have their own lives now and I want to get away from Jack.'

'Really?'

'Why are you frowning?'

'I always thought you'd end up getting back together.'

'No' after what he did with Toni.'

'Do you still love him?'

'That doesn't matter.'

'Aye it does. Do you still love him?'

She sighed and nodded.

'Then how can we be together?' he replied, eyes flashing.

'All the time I was with him I was still in love with you.'

'Why did you get with him if you loved me then?'

'Do we need to go into all that? Can't we put it in the past?' She couldn't have this conversation now, her head was still so messed up.

Dean's expression softened. 'You're right. That's exactly what we should do. It doesn't matter any more, but how have you forgiven me for lying to you about your da's past? That hurt you so much it stopped us from getting together.'

'Losing him has put a lot of stuff into perspective.'

'You mean you wouldn't have given Jack the time of day back then if we'd been together?'

Once again Carly hesitated. She couldn't be sure of that but

Dean's gaze demanded an answer. 'I don't know but me and Jack did happen and I can't do anything to change it.'

'You're still in love with him and I refuse to share you with anyone.' He picked up his slashed shirt and gingerly pulled it on, grimacing as he slid it over the wound.

'What are you doing?' said Carly.

'Going home.'

'You can't, you're too weak.'

'I'm fine.'

'You've lost blood, you shouldn't be alone.'

'I'll manage.'

'Don't be ridiculous.' Carly rolled her eyes as he fumbled with the buttons. 'That's right, run away. I didn't have you down as a coward, Dean.'

His head snapped up. 'I'm no' a coward.'

'Aye, ya are. You might be big and tough debt collecting but when it comes to anything emotional you run a mile.'

'I'm not running away,' he exclaimed.

'Course you are. Don't get me wrong, I understand why. You're afraid of getting hurt again and I cannae blame you but walking out is not the answer. It won't resolve anything.'

'I'm sorry but I'm no' up to having this conversation now.'

'You started it. You asked me if we could be a couple if you got out of the life.'

'And you told me you're still in love with another man. How could it possibly work?'

'Because I love you too.'

'You can't love two people at the same time.'

'I love you in different ways.'

'How?' he demanded.

'Well, I can't really put it into words. It just feels different.' She sighed, unable to explain it even to herself. 'My head's all over the place.'

His expression softened. 'You're going through a lot. I should have kept my mouth shut. It was the wrong time. I should go.'

Dean's eyes widened again and he flopped back onto the couch.

'You should really stay here,' she told him. 'You're not strong enough to be alone yet. I promise not to molest you.'

'Shame,' he replied with a wry smile.

They lapsed into that comfortable silence, the one they could only share with each other, both lost in their own thoughts.

'Perhaps now isn't the right time for us,' said Carly a few minutes later. 'I need to get Jack out of my system and get over losing my da'. You don't deserve anything less. I wouldn't like to be with someone I knew was in love with someone else.'

'Did Jack know you loved me when you were with him?'

'No. I think he had his suspicions, but I never told him. I was too afraid of what he'd do.'

'To you?'

'No, to you. It's even worse now he's the boss. After what Rod Tallan did...' Carly broke off as the memory of that creep trying to rape her returned. The man was dead now but that hadn't helped ease the trauma. Not that she ever thought Jack would do the same to her but she'd had to put up with one boss lording it over her because her family relied on his goodwill and she refused to be put in that position again.

'I understand,' Dean said sadly. 'I just hope that one day we'll get our chance.'

'I'm sure we will. I just need to get my head straight.'

Dean patted her hand. 'Then let's leave it at that.'

Carly sighed with frustration. There were her sisters enjoying happy relationships and once again she was stuck being alone because of other people. She was so sick of it. Perhaps she should forget about being with Dean and move away from Glasgow entirely? Go somewhere new, far away from both him and Jack and get out from under the yoke of Toni McVay. Maybe a fresh start was just what was needed? The thought of being so far from her family was painful and she wasn't sure she could do it. Careful thought was required and she could only think straight once she'd got over losing her father.

'Every time we're close to getting together something comes along to ruin it,' said Dean miserably.

'If we make a move too soon, then we could destroy any chance we have,' she replied.

'I know, you're right,' he sighed. 'Oh, sod it.'

Carly's eyes widened when Dean took her face between his hands and kissed her.

'What are you doing?' she exclaimed.

'What does it look like?' he replied. 'I want you, Carly.'

He kissed her again. She moaned and he pulled her onto his lap, Carly unbuttoning his shirt while his hands slipped under her jumper.

'You're confusing the hell out of me,' she said.

'We've waited long enough for this,' he murmured. 'Why wait a second longer?'

'Because one or both of us might get hurt.'

'I'm willing to take the chance if you are.'

The front door opened and a voice called, 'Just me.'

Carly couldn't work out whether her sister's timing was good or bad as she climbed off Dean's lap. He hastily pulled the blanket over his lap to hide his erection seconds before Jane entered the room.

Jane's eyes flicked suspiciously between them. 'What's going on?'

'Dean got stabbed at a collection this morning,' replied Carly.

'God, are you okay?' Jane asked him.

He nodded and gingerly pulled the shirt down his arm to show her his wound.

'Jesus. I take it you've been to hospital?'

'Uncle Eddie stitched him up,' said Carly disapprovingly. 'I said he should go and get checked out but he won't.'

'She's right,' Jane told him. 'You should go.'

'I'm fine,' he replied.

'Stubborn git,' Carly told him.

Jane noted the way they smiled at each other. 'So I take it you've been playing nurse?' she asked her sister. 'It's funny how tending to a sick man messes up your hair and turns your face bright red.'

Carly blushed deeper and ran her fingers through her long hair.

'Are you two in a relationship?' Jane demanded of them.

'No,' replied Carly. 'But we have been discussing it.'

'If Jack found out...'

'He's no' my boyfriend any more.'

'True but unfortunately he's a powerful man now capable of causing you a lot of trouble. I'm not thinking of me or the money, I'm worried about you two.'

Carly considered telling her about her plans to leave Haghill but decided against it. 'Like I said, we were only talking about it. Dean's afraid I'll hurt him again.'

'There is that too,' said Jane severely. 'I would love for you two to find the same happiness I have with Jennifer but you've got to consider the cost. Anyway, is Uncle Eddie about? I had a couple of missed calls from him.'

'He wanted you to go out on a job,' replied Carly. 'So I went instead when he couldnae get hold of you.'

Jane caught the snippiness in her sister's tone. 'What happened?' When Carly had finished explaining, she sighed and shook her head. 'That was my fault. I shouldn't have switched off the ringer on my phone.'

'Actually, it's Uncle Eddie's fault,' replied Carly. 'He's the one who left me with those men while he and Harry got the money.'

'That was completely out of order. I'm gonnae have a word with him.'

'Don't bother. I've already done it. I also said I won't help out ever again. You're best just leaving it.'

'They shouldn't even be doing any collections anyway, not with Da' just buried yesterday.'

'This one couldnae wait,' said Dean.

'Then Jack should have sent someone else.'

'Da' was afraid if he did then we'd be pushed out.'

'Bollocks. He just wanted a payday. Let me guess, it was a big collection?'

'Forty-five grand.'

'There we are then. He was thinking of his wallet, nothing more.'

'Let it go, Jane,' sighed Carly. 'I've dealt with it.'

'Fine but I'm not happy about it,' she replied, tapping her foot angrily. 'Anyway, I came back for some fresh clothes. I'm staying at Jennifer's tonight.'

'Okay,' said Carly, hiding her disappointment. Another lonely night in the flat for her.

Jane hesitated and looked to Dean. 'At least I was but I can always stay here.'

'Afraid we're gonnae start having sex the second you walk out the door?' Carly asked her with a raised eyebrow.

'To be honest, aye, I am.'

'So what if we do? It's none of your business.'

'Actually, it is because the consequences...'

'Fuck the consequences,' yelled Carly. 'It's all right for you tucked up nice and cosy in bed with your girlfriend and Rose with Noah while I'm stuck here again all alone.'

'You're right, I'm being selfish,' she said contritely. 'I should be here with you, Rose too.'

'I don't want you to put your lives on hold for me,' said Carly, shoulders slumping, once again caught between wanting to be with her sisters and not wanting to become the family pity case.

'I want to spend time with you. We'll have a girly night in. Rose can do our hair, she loves that.'

'She'd prefer to be with Noah.'

'Tough. We've just lost Da', so we need to spend more time together.' Jane looked to Dean. 'Are you spending the night here?'

'No, I'll go home. I'm feeling better.'

'I'm glad to hear it. Who wants a cuppa?' said Jane, switching on the kettle, making it clear she wasn't going to leave them on their own again.

Dean and Carly looked at each other regretfully.

The door opened again and Eddie's voice called, 'Can I come in? I want to call a truce.' He appeared in the kitchen followed by Harry, both of them looking very hangdog.

'Hey, you,' Jane barked at her uncle. 'Carly's told me what happened today and you were well out of order.'

'I didnae intend for it to go like that. I thought Blair would be alone and aye, I should have checked first, but I didnae and I have to live with the guilt of that.'

'Boo hoo,' said Jane flatly.

'I tried getting hold of you but I couldnae.' His eyes narrowed. 'Where were you by the way?'

'Out with Jennifer, as you well know. Don't try and turn this around on me. Carly's out of the game, so don't ask her again.'

'I don't intend to but you have to be available at all times. You cannae just go off grid like you did today.'

'I buried my father yesterday and I needed some time away from Haghill. Jack gave me a few days off, so I wasnae expecting to be asked to work today. He gave you three some time off too but you chose to work. That's up to you. Jack's my boss, no' you, so don't you dare have a go at me for daring to take a few hours to myself.'

'I get that but you should still have answered your phone. In our line of work being unavailable can be dangerous. What if it had been an emergency?'

'But it wasn't an emergency. You should have gone back to Jack when you failed to get the money the first time, no' told Carly to dress up like a tart and flash her bits at some creep.'

'Shut up,' yelled Carly.

They both went silent and looked at her.

'Turning on each other is just making things worse,' she continued. 'We cannae change what happened, so let it go. We're all feeling tense since the funeral but it's more important than ever that we stick together.'

'You're right, doll,' said Eddie. He looked to Jane. 'I won't involve Carly again,' he said gently. 'I promise.'

Her expression softened and she nodded. 'We have to go to the care home tomorrow afternoon to clear out Da's room. Are you coming?'

Eddie was pleased. She was extending an olive branch to him. 'Course I am. I've already told Jack none of us will be available. Get that, Harry,' he said when there was a knock at the door.

His son nodded and left the room.

Eddie looked to Dean. 'You look a bit stronger. You've got some colour in your cheeks.'

Jane raised an eyebrow but didn't comment.

'I'm feeling a wee bit better,' replied Dean.

'You ready to go home then?'

'Suppose,' he said, glancing at Carly.

Eddie caught the look and decided his son needed to leave immediately. 'I'll gi'e you a lift home, son.'

Before Dean could make a move, Harry returned to the room clutching an enormous bunch of roses.

'What are you doing with those, ya big Jessie?' Eddie demanded.

'They're no' mine,' he retorted. 'They're for Carly.'

He held the bouquet out to her and Carly took it from him with a frown. 'There's a card,' she said.

Carly placed the bouquet on the table and plucked the card from a stem.

'They're from Jack, aren't they?' said Dean.

'Aye.' She didn't add that the card said he wanted to apologise for her being dragged into that situation earlier with Blair, not wanting to reignite that old argument.

'He still wants you back,' Eddie told her.

'Tough.'

'I know he hurt you but you have to consider the circumstances. He's a powerful man now and he's loaded.'

'So what? He still betrayed me.'

'He won't do it again, he's crazy about you.'

'I'm no' getting back with him and that's all I'm saying on the matter. I'll give these flowers to Rose, she'll love them.'

'Maybe you should gi'e the matter more consideration? You'd be set up very nicely.'

'Drop it, Uncle Eddie.'

'Fine,' he said, holding up his hands. 'I just want what's best for you.'

'And that isn't Jack Alexander.'

'Fair enough. Come on, Dean. Let's get you home. Actually, scratch that. Someone needs to keep an eye on you, so you can stay with me and Harry.'

Dean sighed heavily. Unlike himself, his father and brother were messy and left their dirty socks everywhere. 'I'll be fine here on the couch.'

'You cannae stay on a couch when you're no' well. We've got a spare room, you'll have that.' His expression brooked no argument.

Everyone noticed the reluctant look that passed between Dean and Carly as he got to his feet. Eddie for his part was more determined than ever that his son and niece would not get together.

5

Carly felt a little happier the next morning. Jane and Rose had spent the night at the flat. They didn't laugh as they usually would because of the weight of their mutual grief but they did enjoy each other's company and Rose had fun styling their hair.

Eddie picked the sisters up at three o'clock that afternoon and drove them to the care home. All four were silent on the journey, sad that this was the last time they'd ever get to visit the place that had made Alec so happy in his final months.

The matron of the care home greeted them sombrely. Members of staff who had been unable to attend the funeral passed on their condolences, all of them appearing to genuinely grieve Alec. Emilio, who had been Alec's best friend in the home, had asked to see them and they headed to his room where they found him in bed.

'I'm sorry I couldn't be at the funeral,' he told them, looking genuinely stricken. 'I wanted to be there...' He broke off and swallowed. Used to Alec's condition, they patiently waited for him to continue. 'I fell and hurt my leg.'

'It's okay, we understand,' said Eddie kindly. 'Nae worries.'

'He was a good pal to me,' Emilio replied, choking up with emotion. 'One of the best.'

They spent a few more minutes with Emilio before heading into Alec's room. Alec's presence still hung heavily in the room, as though he'd just nipped out and would be back any second. Rose started to cry and Jane told her to take a walk in the gardens. Gratefully the girl left.

'I don't like this,' said Eddie. 'It feels like we've no right to touch his stuff.'

'There's no choice,' replied Carly. 'They need this room for a new patient.'

He frowned. 'They're replacing him already.'

'That's no' it at all and you know it.'

'Aye,' he sighed. 'It's just so bloody hard.'

'Let's get it over with then.'

They packed Alec's things into the boxes they'd brought. All he'd really had at the care home were clothes, toiletries, books and photographs. He hadn't been one for ornaments or trinkets, so packing up didn't take them long. By the time they'd finished, Alec's presence in the room had diminished to a mere ghostly shadow.

'It's almost like he was never here,' croaked Carly.

'Don't think like that, hen,' said Eddie, wrapping an arm around her. 'Alec was a big personality. Everyone who met him will always remember him. He's never gone.'

'That's sweet,' she replied, forcing a smile.

'Let's go to the pub, raise a glass to him.'

'Sounds good to me,' said Jane.

After loading the stuff in the car and collecting Rose from the garden, they said a final goodbye to Emilio and the staff before leaving.

'I'll miss this place,' said Eddie as he drove them down the leafy drive. 'It was nice coming here.'

The sisters didn't respond but they all felt the same way.

Leaving Alec's stuff in the back of Eddie's car, they headed into The Horseshoe Bar to find Derek serving. 'What would you like?' he asked the Savages. 'It's on the house.'

'Cheers, pal,' replied Eddie. 'I'll have a pint.'

The sisters ordered a glass of white wine each, Rose pouting when Jane changed her order to an orange juice. Derek told them to take a seat, saying he'd bring their drinks over.

The atmosphere in the pub had been rather jolly but their appearance subdued it. People came up to ask after them and Carly experienced a pang as she thought of leaving behind this community. Everyone here knew her, while moving away would mean living among strangers. Was leaving the right thing to do after all?

There was the sound of smashing glass from outside.

'What the bloody hell's that?' demanded Derek.

Jim, one of the regulars, peered out of the window to the right of the door. 'There's a bunch of men out there holding weapons.'

'What?' Derek exclaimed, rushing to join him at the window. 'Who the hell are they?'

'Nae idea,' replied Jim. 'They're certainly no' from Haghill.'

Eddie rose and joined them. 'Christ, it's Blair and six men.'

'Blair from the collection?' replied Jane.

'Aye.'

'Marvellous,' she sighed before taking out her phone.

'What are you doing?' Carly asked her.

'Calling The Bitches. It's Saturday, so most of them should be about.'

Carly smiled and nodded.

'Who's Blair?' Rose asked her sisters.

'Someone we collected a debt from yesterday,' replied Carly.

'I thought you weren't doing that any more?'

'I helped them out as a one off. It seems Blair's no' too happy about losing forty-five grand.'

'I don't blame him. That's a lot of money.'

'Then he shouldn't have borrowed off a dangerous man. It's his own fault. I'll call Harry.'

'Eddie Savage,' bellowed a voice from outside. 'I know that's your name and that you're in there.'

Fearlessly, Eddie pushed open the door and stepped outside onto the pavement. 'And how the hell do you know that? Who's been running off their big mouth?'

'That's none of your business. Now, where's that wee slag of a niece of yours?'

'Don't call her that, ya arsehole,' Eddie thundered back.

Carly stepped out of the pub, Jane and Rose on either side of her. 'Right here, dickhead,' she called to Blair, who was leaning his weight on a crutch because of his injured knee.

'Tell me right now who's been giving you information,' Eddie demanded of Blair.

'Like I'm gonnae dae that. Where's my money?'

'Where do you think? It's gone to pay off your debt.'

'I want it back.'

'Tough titty. You shouldnae have borrowed it in the first place. It wasnae your money to keep.'

'Rod Tallan's disappeared. Everyone's saying he's deid, so who the hell has my cash?'

'I repeat, it's no' your cash and it's gone to the person who took on his debts. Believe me when I say you don't want to fuck with him.'

Blair grinned. 'I'm so scared.'

'You should be. He makes your wee pals look like choirboys.'

'You know what I think?'

'I'm amazed you can think at all,' retorted Carly.

Blair pointed a digit at her. 'Put it on a leash, Eddie.'

'Who the fuck are you calling "it"?' she yelled back. 'I'll batter you again just like I did before.'

Blair's smirk dropped. 'You got lucky and wee slappers like you should always be referred to as *it.* You're just things for men like me to enjoy. You've got no use beyond that.'

'Jeezo, grab her,' exclaimed Eddie when Carly attempted to storm over to Blair. Jane grabbed her sister and had to fight to maintain a hold on her.

'I'll twist your pathetic wee baws right off,' Rose yelled at Blair.

'Hello, pretty.' He winked back at her. 'Come to me and I'll show you what a real man can do.'

'Why, do you know one?'

'Looks like you're all as mouthy as each other. Now I want to know who took my money before me and my pals get really nasty.'

Derek emerged from the pub wielding his baseball bat. 'Bring it on, big man, and we'll show you how we treat gobby shites like you in Haghill.'

Blair appeared less certain of himself when more customers emerged from the pub brandishing beer bottles and glasses.

'I take it you're the landlord?' Blair asked Derek.

'Aye I am and I want you and your gang of morons to piss aff.'

'You should stay out of this. It would be a shame if anything happened to your very nice business.'

'Like I've no' heard that threat before. You're no different to all the others who've gone after the Savages and you know what? They buried them all.'

'Aye, that's great,' said Blair in a bored tone. 'We want a name – who's got my fucking money?'

'I have,' said a voice.

Carly smiled when Jack appeared from an alleyway behind them looking dark and dangerous.

Blair and his friends whipped round at the sound of his voice.

'Who the fuck are you?' demanded Blair.

'Jack Alexander, the man who's got your forty-five grand.'

'I want it back.'

'Tough shit.'

'If you don't gi'e it back, then me and my pals will tear you apart.'

Jack's smile could only be described as amused. 'You can try.'

'Fine. Don't say I didn't warn you.'

As Blair and his friends advanced on Jack, Elijah Samson and his enormous brother Davey, two of Jack's closest associates, also emerged from the mouth of the alley. The two didn't look like brothers. It was hard to believe they were even related. Elijah, the older of the two, was thin and ferrety while Davey was huge, standing at six foot six with a big barrel chest. His sheer size caused Blair and his men to hesitate and glance at each other.

'What are you waiting for?' goaded Jack. 'I thought you were going to take your money back.'

'Too right we are,' retorted Blair.

His determination buoyed up his friends again and they began to march on the three men. Sensing movement behind them, they paused and looked back to see the Savage family approaching them, penning them in. Derek and the customers had been told to stay behind.

'You shouldn't be involved in this,' Jane whispered to Rose.

'You're no' keeping me out of it,' she stubbornly replied.

'Looks like we've got even numbers,' said Blair. 'And three of your lot are birds,' he added to Jack.

'If I were you, I wouldn't be so smug,' Jack replied. 'They're the most dangerous of us all.'

'That doesnae say much for the rest of you,' he laughed.

'One of them has already battered you once. Do you want more of the same?'

Blair grunted with rage and charged at Jack, raising his crutch as a weapon. Before he could even reach him, Davey's big hand shot out and gripped him by the throat. Blair grimaced, his legs kicking ineffectually as he fought to escape.

'Hold him,' Jack told Davey before striding up to one of Blair's friends. He dodged when the man attempted to hit him and punched him hard in the face.

The Savages and Elijah attacked too and a fight broke out in the middle of the street. Rose, with one of her trademark war cries, threw herself joyfully into the fray, ducking under one man's fist as he swung it at her and grabbing his crotch, his piercing scream filling the air as she twisted, her eyes full of malevolent glee.

Two of the men were so confident of beating the women in a fight that they barely put in any effort and only realised their error when it was too late and Carly and Jane had sent them to the ground, bleeding. Elijah took on a man twice his size, his speed giving him a huge advantage and he launched himself at his opponent, knocking him to the ground. Elijah landed on top of him and began pummelling him in the face. Jack headbutted another man, sending him to the ground before kicking him several times in the ribs, cracking a few, ensuring he stayed down.

At that moment, Harry's car sped down the road, screeching to a halt outside the pub. He and Dean leapt out.

'What are you doing here?' Eddie demanded of his younger son. 'You should be resting.'

'I'm fine,' he retorted. He pointed to the man Elijah had taken down. 'Besides, I owe that bastard some payback. He's the one who stabbed me.'

At the same time, The Bitches tore down the street, emerging from different directions.

'Are you all okay?' Jack asked the Savage family, although the question was particularly addressed to Carly.

They all nodded.

'Good.' He turned back to Davey. 'You can let him go now. He's going a funny colour.'

Davey released Blair, who fell to the ground, gasping. Jack knelt beside him and produced a knife.

At the sight of the weapon, Derek ushered his customers back inside the pub. He followed, closing the door behind him.

'You made a mistake challenging me,' said Jack. 'But your biggest mistake was attacking Carly. For that, you are going to suffer.'

He slashed Blair across both cheeks with the blade, making him yelp. He then flipped it round and proceeded to smash his teeth in with the hilt, the cracking, snapping sound making everyone wince. When he'd finished, blood was pouring from Blair's mouth. Blair spat chunks of broken teeth out onto the road. He rolled onto his front and attempted to crawl away, blood and drool dripping in strings from his lips. Jack rose and regarded him with cold, pitiless eyes. With a grunt of rage, he kicked Blair hard several times in the ribs and stomach until he collapsed back to the ground, wheezing. Carly had to admit that she was rather thrilled by this aggressive display. Jack's dark side had always been a turn-on for her.

Satisfied Blair was done, Jack turned to The Bitches. 'Ladies,' he told them. 'You may humiliate them all in your usual manner.'

The women were eagerly grinning as they rushed forward and

began to strip the fallen men, tearing off their clothes, hitting and kicking them when they protested.

'That prick's mine,' growled Dean, storming up to one particular man. Donna and Leonie, two core members of The Bitches, stood back to allow him access to the man who'd stabbed him, laughing as Dean repeatedly punched him in the face.

Jack approached Eddie and the Savage sisters. 'Well done,' he told them.

'We didnae do very much,' replied Eddie.

'Course you did.' His eyes settled on Carly. 'You handled yourselves very well.'

'I don't think you need to worry about them again,' she replied.

'Me too,' he said cheerfully. 'Well, I fancy a pint. Will you all join me?'

'Aye, all right,' said Eddie.

'Harry, I want you and Dean to make sure they leave.'

'No problem,' he replied.

Jack nodded at Elijah and Davey, indicating he wanted them to do the same and they nodded back in understanding.

Dean straightened up from punching his attacker to watch Jack place a hand in the small of Carly's back and enter the pub, the two of them happily chatting.

Jack joined the Savages at their table and Derek fetched him a pint of lager.

'Cheers,' he told the landlord. 'This is my fault,' he continued when Derek left them to it. 'I should never have sent you out on that job. This crap is the last thing you need.'

'I offered to do it,' said Eddie. 'You didnae make us.'

'I know but I still feel bad. Rose,' he told the girl. 'Once again, you were very impressive. You're a little firecracker, aren't you?'

'I have my moments.' She smiled, pleased that he'd singled

her out for praise. Once Jack Alexander had been the most mistrusted man in Haghill. Now he ran the whole scheme and everyone respected him. He was good at what he did and hadn't turned into the dictator Rod Tallan had been. Not yet, anyway.

'That's typical of the Savage sisters,' he continued. 'Faces of angels, hearts of demons.'

Jane frowned. 'I wouldnae go that far.'

'I only mean you're demons when it comes to a scrap.'

'You cannae deny that's true,' Eddie told his nieces.

'I've got a special job for you, if you want it,' continued Jack. 'It's a bit dangerous but it'll be the biggest payday you've ever had.'

'Come on, Rose,' said Carly, getting to her feet. 'Let's go and sit at another table while they talk business.'

'But...' she began.

'No buts,' Carly said sternly.

'Fine,' she sighed, rolling her eyes as she got to her feet. The two of them took another table, Carly ensuring it was at the far side of the room so they couldn't overhear.

'What do you think this job is?' Rose asked Carly as they watched Jack, Eddie and Jane talking seriously.

'I've no idea and I don't want to know.'

'Jack said it's dangerous. That worries me.'

'Me too but he wouldnae give them anything they couldn't handle.'

'Things can always go wrong. I'm so afraid something will happen to you all.' Rose smiled sadly. 'It's become an even bigger fear since we lost Da'. I couldnae stand anyone else going.'

Despondency filled Carly. How could she leave Haghill now? Her little sister's world had been torn apart and Rose wouldn't be able to stand the thought of her leaving the area, even though she wouldn't be far away. She'd been distraught when Dean had said he was moving back to Clydebank, a move he'd in the end decided against. There was no choice. She had to remain in Haghill. For years her life had been about sacrifice, putting the needs of others before her own and it seemed that part of her life still wasn't over.

Carly watched Jack as she sipped her drink. He really was gorgeous. Inside he and Dean were similar. Both were clever, stubborn, passionate and – most of all – dangerous. Jack was very charismatic; it was one reason why he made such a good leader. God, his body was stunning, but then again, so was Dean's. She sighed. Once again, she was being pulled in different directions by two different men.

'Carly.' Rose's voice cut through her thoughts.

'What?' she said, shaking herself.

'You haven't stopped staring at Jack.'

'I wasn't staring.' She blushed, tearing her gaze from him.

'Aye, ya were. You obviously miss him, so why don't you get back with him, that's if you can forgive him for what he did with Toni?'

As she spoke, the door opened and Dean entered.

'It's not as easy as that,' she replied.

Rose noted her sister's eyes slip to Dean. 'I don't know how you manage. I'd have gone crazy in your position.'

'I don't manage, that's the problem. But I can't be with Jack, especially not as he's still in the life.'

'Then what about Dean?'

'He's my cousin.'

'So?'

'Uncle Eddie's dead against it.'

'Who cares? You and Dean are adults, you can do what you like.'

'It's no' as easy as that, sweetheart. Besides, he's in the life too.'

'It's as easy as you make it. You've always made things more complicated than they need to be, Carly.'

'I'm better off on my own. It will save a lot of trouble.'

'But that's no' fair. You're so pretty, you should be out there enjoying yourself.'

'Like you and Noah?' Carly said, knowing any mention of her beloved boyfriend sent Rose off on a tangent.

'Oh God, he's so amazing,' Rose enthused. 'He's hot AF and so sweet and gentle. He writes me poetry.'

'Really? I cannae imagine him doing that.'

'Aye, he's so creative and sensitive.'

'He's a nice man, Rose. You chose well.'

'I know,' she said, starry-eyed. 'I think I love him.'

'Don't get carried away. It's easy to mistake lust and excitement for love.'

'You still love Jack, don't you?'

'Sadly, yes.'

'And you love Dean?'

Carly nodded.

'What are you going to do?'

'I've no bloody idea.'

Harry and Dean had joined Jack and the others at the table and Carly's eyes flicked between the two men her heart belonged to.

'You need to pick one,' Rose told her.

'I can't have either. Don't you see that they'd attack each other if I ever made that decision? They already hate each other as it is,' she added, noting the hard way Jack and Dean stared at each other.

'Then you need to forget about them both and move on.'

'I'm trying but it's no' that easy.'

'Besides, I don't think you do feel the same way about them both. You have stronger feelings for one of them.'

'It feels pretty equal to me.'

'Nope, you're wrong. I know which one you feel more for and that's Jack.'

Carly stared at her in surprise. She'd expected her sister to say Dean. 'What makes you say that?'

'Because you like looking at Dean but you cannae take your eyes off Jack. You still love him even after what he did with Toni, which shows how strong your feelings are for him. You've had a real relationship with him and it was great. You're no' in love with Dean, you're in lust with him. You should sleep with him and then you'll see that your feelings for him will fade.'

The thought was a tempting one but Carly decided not to tell her sister that. 'You're seventeen. What do you know about all this?'

'It's simple – I've had more boyfriends than you. There was Mason, who turned out to be a complete arsehole and Noah, but before them were Steven and Ezra.'

'Who the hell are Steven and Ezra? It's the first I'm hearing about them.'

'They were nice guys. It's not important,' she added when Carly stared at her hard. 'The point is, I've had more relationships. You've only dated Cole and Jack.'

'I cannae believe I'm being lectured in love by my wee sister.'

'You should be glad I'm here to give you advice. The only thing that's stopping you from being with Jack now is your pride, which is stupid because it's making you both unhappy.'

'He cheated on me and I cannae get past that.'

'Course you can. Besides, he only did it for you because he wanted to give you a future. I don't think he'd ever do anything like that to you again. You should give him another chance.'

'I never thought I'd hear you stick up for him after what he did.'

'I was furious with him at first but then I talked it through with Noah, he's so wise,' she said enthusiastically. 'He said he could understand Jack doing what was necessary so he could give you a future.'

'Actually, it showed he's ruthless and willing to do anything to satisfy his ambition.'

'And he's regretting it now. Anyone can see that. I reckon he's learnt from his mistake.'

'It wasnae a mistake, it was a betrayal plus he's in the life I don't want any part of.'

'You can't escape the life because our family's involved in it. You'll never be free of it, so why bother making yourself miserable? It was Uncle Eddie's fault you were dragged into it today, no' Jack's.' Before Carly could reply, Rose continued. 'Put it this way – if Jack hadn't slept with Toni, would you still be together now?'

Carly nodded.

'See, I told you. Give him another chance.'

'Has he paid you to talk to me?'

'Of course not. This is free advice and it's good advice.'

'Dean would hate it, he'd probably leave.'

'He'll have to suck it up and deal with it. This is your life, no' his. Stop letting other people control you.'

Carly turned back thoughtfully to look at Jack. He seemed to sense the attention and his black eyes stared right back at her. Desire and longing washed through her.

'I love it when I'm right,' said Rose with satisfaction.

Jack got to his feet and picked up his pint before making his way over to their table.

'I need the bathroom,' said Rose, getting to her feet.

'Wait, don't go,' said Carly.

Rose just gave her a mischievous smile before leaving them to it.

6

Jack took the chair Rose had vacated opposite Carly and placed his pint on the table. 'I wanted to make sure you were okay after that fight,' he began with concern.

'I'm fine,' she said a little belligerently. 'Like those pricks could get to me.'

'Good, I'm glad to hear it. I'm sorry you were dragged into this when you wanted to stay away.'

'As Rose has pointed out, how can I stay out of it when my whole family's involved.'

'There is that. If you are thinking of getting back in, you'll always have a job. Today proved that you're still at the top of your game.'

'Thanks, but no thanks.' Carly noted Dean glance over his shoulder at them with a scowl. She supposed she couldn't blame him for being pissed off after they'd shared a kiss earlier.

'Shame,' said Jack. 'It's a waste of your talents.'

'My talents are serving drinks.'

He leaned into her, a naughty look filling his eyes. 'You have many talents.'

She blushed and smiled back.

'My bed is so lonely without you in it,' he said.

'Don't tell me you haven't had any other women?'

'I haven't, actually.'

'Come on, Jack. I know how high your sex drive is. No way have you gone two months being celibate.' Her eyes narrowed. 'Unless you've slept with Toni again.'

'No way. It was just that once to seal the deal. Our relationship is purely professional now.'

'And there's been no one else?' she pressed.

'There has been one woman but it was just sex. She meant nothing to me.'

Carly inhaled sharply and looked down at her hands.

Jack was a little surprised by the pain in her eyes. He'd thought all the longing had been on his side alone. 'I'm sorry,' he said.

She raised her head and forced a smile. 'No need to apologise. It's not like we were together.'

'I've hurt you.'

'And not for the first time.'

'Has there been anyone else for you?'

Carly thought of the kiss she'd shared with Dean but only momentarily before she shook her head. 'No.'

He breathed a sigh of relief. 'Good.'

She frowned. 'So it's okay for you to sleep with other people but I can't?'

'I didn't mean it like that, but I won't lie – the fact that there hasn't been anyone else makes me very happy. Don't give me that sexy, angry scowl,' he said, smiling. 'If it was up to me, we would still be together. At the risk of sounding big-headed, I have women throwing themselves at me all the time but I don't want anyone else. If I had my way, you'd be my wife by now.'

Carly stared at him in amazement. 'Are you serious?'

'Deadly. You're all I want, babe. No one else will do.'

They were interrupted by Elijah approaching them. 'Jack, I need a word.'

'Not now,' he replied without taking his eyes off Carly.

'Sorry but it's important.'

Jack sighed with annoyance and got to his feet. 'Fine.' He winked at Carly. 'See you around, gorgeous.'

With that, he walked away, leaving her to stare after him in amazement.

Rose re-joined her and said eagerly, 'So, what did he want?'

'He said if he had his way, we'd be married now.'

'I knew it.' Rose grinned. 'Anna Johnson has been after him for weeks and you know how stunning she is. He just keeps knocking her back. It's really dented her confidence,' she chuckled. 'Hannah More and Olivia McGregor have tried too and he's no' interested. He just wants you.'

'So he said,' murmured Carly.

'I really think you should give him another chance.'

'If Noah cheated on you, would you give him another chance?'

'No, but Noah isn't Jack Alexander. He's much simpler. I don't mean it like that,' she added when Carly sniggered. 'I mean he doesn't have business to think about. That's all Toni was to Jack, business.'

'I don't understand why you're sticking up for him. I had thought you'd want to twist his baws off for what he did.'

'I did at first, then I saw how unhappy you are without him. He made you happier than I've ever seen you. Not even Cole gave you that look in your eyes.'

'You're just confusing me even more,' said Carly, raking a hand through her hair.

They were distracted by The Bitches entering the bar, laughing and joking.

'I want to see what they did to them,' said Rose, getting up and rushing to the door.

Carly followed and they exited the pub to see Blair's men had been stripped entirely naked, their pale bodies covered in bruises. They were crawling about the road, attempting to gather their clothes together. Their presence had forced a passing car to stop and the driver was honking the horn while aggressively revving its engine. People on the pavement were laughing and pointing at the humiliated men.

Blair was slumped on the pavement, slowly pulling on his jumper, his movements indicating he had some cracked ribs. The lower half of his face was covered in blood. He spotted Carly and Rose and scowled at them, eyes blazing with rage. Carly could tell that he was far from down and out and she wondered if he'd come after them a second time. Some people never learned.

The sisters headed back inside the pub. Carly glanced across the room and caught Jack's eye while he was still chatting with Elijah.

'Ow,' said Harry when she walked into the back of his chair.

'Sorry.' She cringed, embarrassed about being so clumsy in front of Jack. Why should she care what he thought anyway? She sighed inwardly. Maybe Rose was right. She did want him back. Great.

Carly took a seat between Rose and Harry.

'You made me spill my pint,' grumbled Harry.

'I'll buy you another,' replied Carly.

'It doesnae matter,' he sighed as though terribly put upon. 'I'm going out on a job in a minute.'

'Is this the dangerous job Jack mentioned?' she anxiously asked.

'Aye but don't you worry, doll,' Eddie told her. 'We can handle it.'

'What is it?'

'You're out, so we're no' telling you, unless you want back in?'

Carly hesitated. It was tempting to go with them to make sure they were okay but one look at Rose changed her mind. Her little sister was worried enough about her family, so she wouldn't want them all to go in case something bad happened. 'No, thanks,' she replied.

Eddie appeared disappointed but he didn't comment. 'We'd better get going then.'

'You will be careful, won't you?' said Rose, eyes wide with concern.

'Course we will, sweetheart,' said Eddie, patting her shoulder. 'Don't worry, it's no' that dangerous. We'll be back in a few hours.'

Carly and Rose remained at the table, watching them go. Dean paused to look back at Carly before he turned and followed his family out.

'What do you want to do now?' Carly asked Rose.

'I promised Noah I'd go to his.'

'I take it you'll be spending the night?'

'Aye. You don't mind, do you? I know I don't spend much time at home any more.'

'Course I don't mind,' Carly replied with a forced smile. 'You're almost an adult now and you can't always be hanging around your older sisters.' Carly herself had been chained to the family home at Rose's age thanks to their father's illness and she didn't want her to suffer the same fate.

When Rose was ready to go, Carly left with her. Jack was still there and once again his eyes followed her as she crossed the floor to the door.

'Why don't you stay and have a drink with him?' Rose asked Carly once they were outside.

'No, thanks,' she replied. 'I'll just head home.' Carly scanned the area. All of Blair's men appeared to have gone.

'We both know you'd much rather spend time with him than sit around at home on your own.'

'I'll manage.'

'So stubborn,' she sighed.

'I've no choice. I've just made the situation even more complicated.'

'What do you mean?'

'You can't tell anyone what I'm about to tell you, no' even Noah.'

'I won't, I promise.'

'I kissed Dean yesterday. Now I'm worried I've given him false hope and I'll probably end up hurting him again.'

'Well, it will only become an issue if he wants a relationship with you or if you want to get back with Jack.'

'I don't intend to do either of those things.'

'Then it should be okay.' Anxiety filled Rose's eyes. 'Do you really think the others will be all right?'

'I do. They're way too tough to let anyone get the better of them.'

'Aye, you're right,' Rose said, looking happier.

They both turned when the pub door opened and Jack exited.

'Are you off home, ladies?' he said.

'I'm going to my boyfriend's.' Rose smiled.

'You mean Noah? He's a very lucky man. I'll escort you both. We think those men have gone but they could still be hanging about.'

'That's very thoughtful but not necessary,' said Carly.

'I wouldn't be able to live with myself if anything happened to either of you.'

'That's really kind,' said Rose. 'We accept.'

Carly gave her sister a warning look but Rose just shrugged and started to walk away. Jack and Carly followed.

'We're worried about Jane and the others,' Carly told him.

'There's no need to be. I know I said it was dangerous but they're more than capable.'

'I thought you weren't going to send them out on another job just yet?'

'Something cropped up last minute.'

'Couldn't the Samsons have handled it?'

'They're on with something else. If you were working for me, I could tell you everything.'

'I'm fine being kept in the dark,' she replied although that wasn't at all true.

'I wondered if you'd have dinner with me tonight?'

Carly was annoyed by the thrill that ran through her at the prospect but she had to remain strong. 'No.'

'Why not?'

'Because we're no' a couple any more.'

'So? Friends can go out for a meal together.'

'I really don't think it's a good idea.'

'I've no ulterior motive. I just thought it would be nice after everything you've been through. You deserve to be spoilt.'

'I appreciate the thought but I'm good.'

They both scanned their surroundings as they walked, staying alert.

'I don't think we need to worry about Blair and his friends for the rest of the day,' said Carly in an attempt to change the subject. 'Especially after you smashed his teeth in.'

'Let's hope he's smart enough to take the hint.'

'I doubt it. I get the feeling he'll come back at some point.'

'I'll tell my people to keep an eye out for them. I'm concerned by the fact that you're left on your own a lot in the flat.'

'I'll be fine. I can look after myself.'

'What you need is a big, strong Yorkshireman to protect you.'

'You never give up, do you?'

'Not when it comes to you.'

Carly grinned and shook her head.

'You smiled. I call that progress.'

'I've never known such a stubborn, pig-headed man in my entire life.'

Her smile widened when he winked at her.

They dropped Rose safely off at Noah's and Carly made her sister promise to call her when she was ready to leave the next day so she wouldn't be tramping the streets alone.

'So, what now?' Jack asked Carly as they walked away from Noah's house.

'I'm going home.'

'Great, I'll come with you.'

'That might have worked once but it won't again.'

'What can I say? I'm an optimist.' He took her hand and they came to a halt in the middle of the street. 'Just tell me one thing – is there absolutely no hope of us getting back together? If you say there isn't then I'll finally accept that we're over but if there's even the slightest chance then please, be honest with me.'

Carly looked up and down the street, seeking inspiration.

He smiled. 'Thanks for your answer.'

'I didn't say anything.'

'I understand you well enough to know that means there is a chance. If there wasn't you would have told me straight. That's the best news I've had all week.'

'I'm making no promises. I'm still struggling with what you did with Toni.'

'Okay,' he said gently, releasing her hand. 'Then I won't press you any more, for now. Let's get you home.'

As they walked, they chatted about light, trifling things and Carly was glad that Jack could still make her laugh. It seemed the power he now wielded had not changed him for the worse, which made him a far better man than either Tallan brother, both of whom had previously occupied his position. However, he was only a couple of months into his reign. There was still time for the corruption to set in. What if one day he was no longer the man she loved?

Carly bid Jack goodbye at her front door and he didn't go until he'd seen her safely inside. Her left her with a smile on her face, Rose's words echoing in her head.

* * *

As it grew darker that night, Carly found herself growing increasingly uneasy. Although all the doors and windows were locked and the curtains were drawn, it felt like someone was hovering just outside the flat knowing she was alone inside. There was no reason for this feeling. She'd heard and seen nothing suspicious. It was just a sense that someone was out there, lurking.

Carly attempted to dismiss the feeling as ridiculous. It was just her imagination. She considered taking a look outside but thought that would be stupid. After all, it could be Blair and his friends out there but that wouldn't explain why she'd felt someone had been following her earlier. The only enemy she had was Rod Tallan and he was dead and buried. The thought of his vengeful spirit lurking around her home, watching with those mad, staring eyes of his was horrifying.

Carly attempted to focus her attention on the film she was watching. Usually, she'd watch a fluffy comedy or romance but instead she'd gone for an action film that Jack loved with lots of fights and car chases. This thought struck a chord deep inside her. Why had she put on this film? Was it possible she wanted to feel closer to him?

She should never have kissed Dean yesterday and she should never have given Jack hope.

'I need some wine,' she said to herself.

Carly padded over to the fridge and retrieved a bottle of white. She hesitated, thinking that she'd been drinking more than usual recently.

'I'll just have this one,' she told herself before pouring out a glass.

Replacing the bottle, she padded back to the couch with her wine and attempted to focus on the film but she was assailed by memories of when she'd watched it with Jack, smiling every time he'd cheered when the good guy had battered a bad guy and his enthusiasm for the car chases. To the world, Jack Alexander might seem dark and scary but what no one else seemed to realise was that he was fun too with a huge zest for living. He was right when he'd said that if he hadn't slept with Toni they would still be together now. Her feelings for Dean hadn't been strong enough to come between them.

Carly leapt up when there was a bang at the back door. It was aggressive and made her heart pound. Fortunately, both the rear and front doors were made of reinforced steel. It wasn't possible for anyone to break them down but this knowledge didn't make her feel much better.

After switching off the kitchen light, she crept to the window which was to the right of the door. Pulling aside the curtain, she peered out. She gasped and recoiled when a fist pounded off the glass. Her heart thudding, she raced out of the kitchen and down the hall to the front door where the baseball bat was kept propped up in the corner. Snatching it up, she rushed back into the kitchen to the sound of more pounding, first on the window and then on the door.

'Try and break that down, you bastard,' she yelled, drawing back the bat, wondering if they'd try and smash their way through the window, even though that had been triple glazed.

The banging stopped, the sudden silence somehow worse than all the noise. She raced to scoop up her mobile phone and hesitated, wondering who she should call. Her first thought was her Uncle Eddie but he'd gone on a dangerous job with the rest of the family. Distracting them could have terrible consequences. Harry, Dean and Jane were with him too. Who else could she call? Jack's name sprung to mind. No, she couldn't do that.

It was still quiet out there. Maybe whoever it was had gone? She had two options – stay in the flat and do nothing or go out there and pound into the dirt whoever was messing with her. Determination gripped Carly. She was far from some helpless female who had to call the men at the first sign of trouble.

Carly hurried into her bedroom to retrieve her baton and pepper spray. She also dug out her taser and stuck that into the back of her jeans.

'If you know what's good for you, you'll have done a runner already,' she yelled as she flung open the back door. Outside it was pitch black, although the rear garden was illuminated not only by the lights from her own flat but from the flats above too. It was enough to tell her that no one was there. Storming through the garden, she propped the bat up against an old wheelbarrow before scrambling over the wall. Dropping down on the other side, she immediately drew the taser and pepper spray, holding both out before her. The lights from the flats failed to penetrate here and the watery orange glow from the streetlights wasn't enough to illuminate the whole back street and shadows lurked everywhere. As the wind was picking up, these shadows fluttered and shifted, the branches of a large tree in the garden waving back and forth. There was the shudder of a wheelie bin threatening to topple over.

Screwing up her courage, she raced down the back street and emerged on the road that ran down the right side of her block of flats. She looked left and spied someone just turning the corner. Despite the darkness, she swore the figure hesitated and looked back at her, as though wanting her to notice them before plunging on ahead. When they rushed around the corner, she hastened to follow. Carly didn't charge blindly around the corner in case they were waiting to spring out at her. Instead, she approached cautiously, holding the taser and pepper spray out before her. She could see them up ahead, moving towards the front of her flat.

As she hurried after them, the wind picked up even more, scattering dead leaves and crisp packets across her path.

The figure once again looked back at her but Carly could make out nothing of them. They were dressed in black and wore a thick jumper with the hood pulled up. She couldn't even tell if they were male or female because the clothes were sexless and baggy. The figure crossed the road and leapt at the wall into the old cemetery directly across from her flat. They sat astride the wall for a moment and looked back at her as though daring her to follow before dropping down into the graveyard.

Carly's natural tenacity urged her to follow but common sense told her that would be a very stupid thing to do. She paused to see if they made a reappearance but when they didn't and when drops of rain started to fall, she decided to head back into the flat.

As the front door was locked, she had to go the back way. Carly hesitated at the mouth of the back street, which looked dark and threatening. She gripped her weapons tighter.

It was then she recalled that she'd charged out of the flat and left the back door unlocked.

'You fucking idiot,' she told herself before racing down the back street. She leapt at the wall and scrambled back over it, relieved to see her baseball bat was still there. Grabbing that too, she burst back into the kitchen, ready to attack any intruders but no one was there.

Quickly she checked the other rooms and was relieved to find she was alone. Carly locked the back door and rushed into Jane's room, which looked out over the front street. There was no sign of the figure she'd chased.

Carly returned to the kitchen where the credits of the film she'd been watching were rolling. What had that been about? Who was the mysterious figure?

She retook her place on the couch, keeping her weapons close and lapsed into thought, wondering what she should do about this. Of course she couldn't keep it to herself. She must tell her family when they returned. She could come up with no reason as to why anyone would target her. One thing was certain though – she definitely had an enemy.

7

'Are you ill?' was Jane's first question when Carly entered the kitchen the following morning.

'No, just tired,' she replied. 'I didnae get much sleep last night.' In truth, she'd lain awake for most of it, waiting to hear that pounding at the door again but it had never come. She'd managed to drift off a couple of times but only for about an hour or so and now she felt tired and washed out.

'Was it the wind? It did pick up a lot last night.'

'Actually, no. It was something else.'

Jane's eyes widened as she explained. 'Why didn't you call us?' she demanded once Carly had related her nocturnal adventure.

'Because you were on a job and I didn't want to distract you.'

'We were about finished by that time. You shouldn't have gone out after them alone. Anything could have happened.'

'But it didn't. If they had an end game in mind then they wanted to do it in the graveyard, no' near the flat.'

'Thank God you had the good sense not to follow them in there. Right, I'm calling Uncle Eddie. We need a family meeting.'

'Don't tell Rose. She'll only worry.'

'I won't.'

'I don't want to know the details but did everything go well last night?'

'Aye, it was fine. Nae bother.'

'Good.'

Eddie and his sons arrived at the flat half an hour later.

'How's the arm?' Carly asked Dean.

'Much better, thanks,' he replied with a tender smile.

Great. Clearly that smile meant he thought there was more between them. Why did she kiss him? Carly was surprised by how quickly her feelings for Dean seemed to be changing. She had thought her love for him was the strongest and purest of the two but it was looking like she was wrong. Christ, she was driving herself crazy.

'Hello, Carly, doll,' said a voice.

She realised her uncle was talking to her and she shook herself out of it. 'Sorry?'

'You looked away with the fairies there.'

'I'm tired. I didn't sleep very well last night.'

'Someone was banging on the back door and windows,' Jane told him.

'What?' he exclaimed. 'Who?'

'I don't know,' replied Carly. 'I chased after them and they went into the graveyard. No way was I following them in there.'

'Because you're a smart lassie. Check it out, boys,' he told his sons.

Dean and Harry nodded and hurried out of the flat.

'I don't think they'll still be there,' said Carly. 'No' unless they're simple.'

'They might have left some sort of trace. Any idea who it was?'

'No. I couldn't even tell if they were male or female. They were dressed all in black. They could fair move though. They were fast and jumped over the graveyard wall easily enough.'

'At least we can rule out all the fat bastards around here.'

'I don't understand why anyone would target me. I'm no' in the life any more.'

'That's precisely why they're targeting you. They see you as weaker now, easier to get to than the rest of us.'

'If that was the case then surely Rose would be the main target?'

'Maybe they're afraid of having their baws twisted off,' said Jane.

'You made an enemy,' Eddie told Carly. 'And now you're no' working for Toni or Jack you're fair game.'

Carly shivered and wrapped her arms around herself.

'You need to think carefully, hen – did you piss off anyone so much they'd want to get back at you now?'

'The only person I can think of is Rod Tallan and we know it cannae be him.'

'What about the Alexanders?'

Cole's unexpected visit returned to Carly but she decided not to mention it, for now. He'd only said nice things and if she mentioned it to her family they would go after him and he might not have done anything wrong. 'I don't see why they'd bother. If they were going after anyone, they'd go after Jack.'

'What about Emma Wilkinson?' said Jane. 'I wouldn't put it past her to start causing trouble again.' Emma had been the woman who'd took over running The Bitches when Jane had stepped down to look after her sick father. Jane had brutally taken the leadership back from Emma and they'd clashed a couple of times since.

'She's more likely to go for you than me,' replied Carly.

Harry and Dean returned.

'We couldn't find any trace,' said Harry. 'We spoke to a couple of wee neds who were in there vandalising gravestones but they've no' seen anything.'

'We were just wondering who could have been responsible,' said Jane. 'But we cannae come up with anyone.'

'What about Jack?' offered Dean.

'No way would he do something like that,' said Carly, narrowing her eyes at him.

'Think about it – he knew you'd be here alone. He sent us out on a job and Rose is hardly ever here any more. It's obvious he wants you back. Maybe he's trying to scare you into turning to him?'

'That's a ridiculous theory.'

'I don't think it is,' replied Eddie.

'You should be careful what you say. He pays your wages.'

'Aye but Dean's right. Jack's desperate to get you back and this could be his way of doing it.'

'He wouldn't do that to me.'

'We've seen how ruthless he is. That man will do anything to get what he wants, as we already know.'

'No' this. I know him better than any of you and he wouldn't scare me like that.'

'He might, Carly,' said Jane more gently. 'I really think you should bear it in mind, just to be on the safe side.'

'It could just have been some kid messing about.'

'Everyone around here knows no' to fuck with our family,' said Eddie. 'Anyway, no matter who it is, we need to take precautions. You cannae stay here on your own. You can come and stay with me and Harry.'

'Nae offence but your house smells and you leave dirty clothes and pots everywhere.'

'It does not smell,' he exclaimed.

'You have to admit that it does a wee bit, Da',' said Harry.

'Well, maybe but that's only because of your manky feet.'

'My feet?' he exclaimed. 'You're the stinky one, no' me.'

'She can stay with me,' said Dean.

They all turned to look at him.

'It makes sense,' he continued. 'I have a spare bedroom and I'm tidy and my flat doesnae smell.'

'No,' said Eddie.

'How no'?'

'You know why. Don't make me embarrass you by saying it out loud.'

'I've nae idea what you're talking about.'

'Course you do and I'm telling you it's no' happening. Christ, I wish Peanut was here. I know you'd be completely safe with him watching over you,' he told Carly. 'But he won't be back for a couple more days.'

'Me and Jennifer can stay here,' said Jane. 'And I can ask The Bitches to keep an eye out too.'

'There we go, the perfect solution,' said Eddie. 'When are you back at work?' he asked Carly.

'A week on Friday,' she replied, relieved that she wouldn't have to stay at Dean's. Life was complicated enough.

'Good. That makes guarding you easier.'

'I don't need a guard. Just because I'm out of the life doesnae mean I've suddenly turned helpless.'

'It's just until we find out who was responsible. Hopefully you're right and it was just some wee dick playing a practical joke. If it was, I'll tan their arse personally.'

'Are you all working today?'

'No, we've got a couple of days off now. I thought we could sort through your da's stuff, see what we want to keep.'

'Good idea,' said Jane. 'Although we should wait for Rose because I know she'll want in on that.'

'Nae bother. The boxes are at my house when everyone's ready.'

'Well,' said Harry, breaking the ensuing silence. 'If no one needs me for a while, I've got a date.'

'With Chantelle?' said Jane.

'No. We had a falling out.'

'Over what?'

'I said she couldnae sing and she smacked me around the heid with a microphone.'

'Where did she get a microphone from?'

'We were at that karaoke bar in the West End. Anyway, she dumped me and said I'd regret saying that about her when she was a famous pop singer.'

'She's a deluded idiot.'

'Aye, I realise that now. I'm taking out some nice wee bird called Genesis. She's gorgeous – legs up to her armpits, waist-length blonde hair, enormous... eyes,' he added when Jane frowned at him.

'Let's hope she doesn't want to be a singer too,' said Carly.

'She doesn't. She's a topless model. Jealous?' He smirked at his brother.

'No' really. I prefer intellectual women.'

'I've noticed men who can only pull ugly birds always say that.'

'Cheeky bastard.'

'Right, I'm off. I need to prepare. Enjoy your lonely night in.' He grinned at Dean.

'Actually, I've got a date too.'

They all regarded Dean with surprise, knowing his feelings for Carly.

'Who?' demanded Harry.

'Destiny Corrigan,' he announced with satisfaction.

'How the hell did you pull her?'

'She likes clever men, which is why I'm guessing she turned you down.'

'Who's Destiny Corrigan?' said Eddie.

'She's a lingerie model,' replied Dean.

'There's no need to look so smug.' Harry frowned. 'And I thought you only liked intellectual women?' he added scathingly.

'Destiny is an intellectual. She has a degree in clinical psychology. Does Genesis have a degree?'

Harry just folded his arms across his chest and scowled.

'Genesis, Destiny,' repeated Eddie. 'What happened to normal names like Elizabeth and Maud.'

'Maud,' sniggered Harry.

'So I'd better be off,' replied Dean. 'I need plenty of time to get ready.'

'You gonnae paint your nails and curl your hair?' sneered Harry.

Dean regarded him disdainfully before leaving without a single glance Carly's way.

'Let us know if you have any trouble again,' Eddie told Carly before he and Harry also left.

'That was weird,' Jane told her sister. 'Dean normally can't stop looking at you but today he barely glanced your way. What do you think of him dating Destiny?'

Carly shrugged. 'It's probably for the best.'

'You've changed your tune too.' Jane's forehead creased. 'Something else is going on here. Please don't tell me you're thinking of getting back with Jack?'

'I wouldn't say that.'

'Then what would you say?'

'I still love him and I've finally realised that my feelings for him are stronger than they are for Dean.'

'Something happened between you and Dean just the day before yesterday, so how have things changed so quickly?'

'I'm not sure but I know they have. I think perhaps it's Da's death. It's helped me put things into perspective. I was thinking of leaving Haghill and getting a place closer to work.'

'What?' said Jane, looking stricken. 'Why would you want to do that?'

'Because I knew I couldn't have a relationship with another man with Dean and Jack around but I changed my mind when Rose said she couldn't bear to lose anyone else. Even though I wouldn't be far away, I knew she'd be upset, so I decided to stay.'

'Thank God because I don't want you to go either.'

'Right then, I want to go out for a drive, get away for a wee bit. Do you want to come?' Carly had passed her driving test with flying colours and had bought herself a cute little black Suzuki Ignis.

'Aye, sounds good.'

Carly was pleased. She had expected Jane to say no, that she had plans with Jennifer. For once, she'd get her big sister to herself.

* * *

Carly and Jane took a trip into the city where they enjoyed a meal together and some light shopping. Carly couldn't spend like she had when she was making the big money but she could still treat herself a bit. Jane bought lunch because her sister now earned a lot less than she did.

On their return to Haghill, they were shocked to find a group brawling in the street outside the Savage family home.

'What the bloody hell's going on here?' demanded Jane as Carly brought the car to a halt further down the street, not wanting to risk any damage to her beloved Suzuki.

'It's The Bitches,' replied Carly. 'But I don't recognise who they're fighting.'

The sisters leapt out of the car and raced up to the struggling group. There were six Bitches against four men and three women.

Jane grabbed one man by the back of the shirt, dragged him backwards and hit him hard in the face. His knees buckled and she released him, letting him drop to the ground. Carly kicked one woman in the back, sending her staggering forward. Her eyes widened when the woman whipped round.

'No' you again,' she said when confronted by a woman with short blonde hair, shaved at the sides. She wore the same crop top and tight blue jeans she'd been in the last time Carly had fought her. It was Lana, girlfriend of Declan, leader of a biker gang they'd attacked on a debt collection a couple of months ago. 'What are you doing here?'

'Declan wants his money back,' retorted Lana.

'He cannae have it.'

'Rod's gone, everyone's saying he's deid and his replacement is a soft touch.'

'If he thinks that then he's in for a shock. Jack's way tougher than Rod ever was.'

'Aye, right,' she said cynically.

She swung a fist at Carly but she leapt back and Lana missed.

'Why are you doing this after I saved you from having your face slashed open?' demanded Carly.

Lana shrugged. 'That was your decision. I didnae ask you to do it.'

'You ungrateful cow,' exclaimed Carly.

'That's what you get for being a goody two shoes.'

From her pocket, Lana produced a bike chain and swung it at Carly. It was the same weapon she'd attacked her with before. The previous time they'd fought, Carly had been prepared with her own weapons but now she was unarmed. She ducked and dodged, avoiding the vicious swipe of the chain.

'Looks like your people are losing, again,' said Carly when more of the biker gang were taken down by The Bitches. Jane was at her most ferocious, kicking her opponent back into a wall before springing at him and punching him repeatedly in the face.

Lana did the sensible thing and realised the fight was over, for now. She backed away from Carly, keeping one eye on her as she called, 'Retreat.'

The fight broke apart, Lana and her cronies raced off down the street.

'Let them go,' called Jane when The Bitches looked at her questioningly. 'Is anyone injured?'

'Donna's hurt her wrist,' replied Leonie.

'Do you need to go to the hospital?' Jane asked Donna, who was cradling her right hand to herself.

'Aye, I think so. Some big bastard grabbed it and twisted it.'

'I hope you got your own back.'

'Course I did. I hit him in the baws with a crowbar.'

Jane smiled. 'Nice one.'

'I can take you, Donna,' said Carly. 'My car's just there.'

'Thanks, that would be great,' she replied.

Carly drove Donna to the hospital. As there was a long wait in A & E, Donna told Carly to go and she'd call her brother when she was ready to leave. By the time Carly returned home, it was starting to get dark but the light on in the flat heartened her. She entered to find Jane in conference with Eddie and Jack.

Her ex's black eyes met Carly's as she entered the kitchen.

'How's Donna?' Jane asked her.

'I don't know,' she replied. 'I just dropped her off. She's getting her brother to pick her up.'

'I hope she's not out of commission for long. She's one of my best fighters and that lot will probably come back.'

'Don't worry,' said Jack. 'I'll get my people to track them down and beat the shite out of them.'

'Has anyone else thought they could challenge you now they've realised Rod's no' coming back?' Carly asked him.

'I thought you didn't want to know about anything like that?' he replied.

'I don't but I should know if they're gonnae turn up on my doorstep.'

'They have. I sent your family out last night to deal with one lot of idiots and the Samsons sorted out another.'

'Just how many people are we talking about?'

'Some,' was all he was willing to reply.

Carly didn't even bother trying to force an answer, knowing it would be futile. 'Are there likely to be more?'

Jack just shrugged. 'Don't look so angry,' he said. 'You wanted to be kept out of it. It won't happen again.'

'No offence but you cannae guarantee that.'

'True. All I can do is my best.'

'Fine,' she sighed. 'I'll trust you to sort it out.'

'Thank you. We've still some business to discuss, so you're probably best leaving for this conversation, unless you want back in?'

'No thanks. I'll be in my room.'

Jack and Jane remained silent until she'd gone. Carly closed her bedroom door with a sigh and sank onto her bed. The murmur of voices in the kitchen started back up and she found herself straining to listen.

'Stop it,' she told herself.

Wanting a distraction, she picked up a magazine that sat on her bedside table and began flicking through it, paying no attention to the pages, still struggling to hear what they were saying. Carly told herself that she was only concerned in case more people came to her home to attack her, but she knew that wasn't true. A good scrap made her feel so alive. Was violence in her blood?

Carly crept to the door and pulled it open a crack.

'You can't tell her,' she heard her uncle say. 'She can't ever know.'

'I think she has a right,' replied Jack. 'Carly's smart enough to make up her own mind.'

'It would be a mistake. The lassie's reckless. She'd charge in and get hurt. We have to keep it quiet for her own sake.'

'I'm not so sure.'

'With all due respect, Jack, you're the boss but Carly's my niece. I made her da' a promise to protect her and I won't let him down.'

'Forewarned is forearmed.'

'No' yet. Not until we know more about the situation.'

'What do you think, Jane?' Jack asked her.

'I think she can handle it,' she replied.

'It's no' that I don't think she can handle it,' said Eddie. 'I just think it would be a bit much for her after everything she's been through – first that prick Rod Tallan attacking her twice, then losing her da'. The lassie deserves some peace and I want to see that she gets it.'

Carly flung open her bedroom door and stormed into the kitchen.

'What's going on?' she demanded.

'Nothing, doll,' replied Eddie innocently. 'Just a wee bit of business.'

'Don't gi'e me that, I heard every word you said. Now, what do I need to know?'

Jack turned to face her seriously. 'My cousins have been plotting to kidnap you.'

Her eyes widened. 'Why the hell would you think it would be in my best interests to keep that from me?' she demanded of her uncle.

'Because we're gonnae track them down and stop them before they can hurt you,' he replied.

'I bet it was Cole's idea,' she said, eyes narrowing. Now she knew the real reason for his so-called sympathy. He'd been on a scouting mission.

'Actually, no,' replied Jack. 'Dominic and Ross have come up with it between them. Cole's the one who told me about it. He said they're out of order and he wants to stop them.'

'Do you trust him?'

'God, no. I'm well aware this could be another plot on his part but I have to take the threat seriously. I'd be letting you down if I didn't.'

'I appreciate that,' she said more gently. 'When did he tell you?'

'This morning. Ross and Dominic have left Haghill. I've got people looking for them. They're both pretty thick, so it's only a matter of time before I find them. They're nothing without Cole and Jessica.'

'I bet that bitch is in on it too. She hates me.'

'She swore to me she isn't but I don't trust her either.'

'Cole hasn't gone into hiding then?'

'No, he's still in Haghill but I'm watching him closely. I'm afraid my feelings for you have put you in danger. They know that hurting you is the best way to get at me and for that I'm sorry.'

'It's no' your fault but this is something you will always have to put up with. Whoever you love will be in danger. That's the price you pay.'

Sadness filled his eyes and he nodded.

'You should leave Haghill until we've found them,' Eddie told Carly.

'No way. I will not let that pair chase me out of my home. Besides, it's only Ross and Dominic. I could handle them on my own.'

'But we don't know if anyone's helping them,' said Jack. 'There are people who don't like me running things.'

'Whoever took over from Rod would have had the same problem,' said Eddie. 'It's nothing personal.'

Jack nodded. 'I know. At least I can rely on your family.'

'Course you can. What we need to discuss is how we're going to protect you, Carly.'

'I can protect myself,' she replied.

'We know that but we don't know how Ross and Dominic are gonnae come at you or who they're working with. We have to take precautions. First of all, I think it would be a mistake for you to stay here. You're too vulnerable. What if what happened last night was down to them? If it was, they could have easily snatched you because not only did you run out after them alone, but you left the back door open for anyone to wander in.'

'I had plenty of weapons.'

'What if they'd snuck up on you from behind? Or you'd been overwhelmed by numbers? You're one hard lassie but anyone can be taken down. Thinking you're invincible is a mistake.'

Carly nodded. 'You're right. Sorry.' She looked to Jack. 'I take it you know about what happened last night?'

'I do,' he replied.

'Do you think it was Ross and Dominic?'

'I wouldn't like to say either way but I do think you should stay elsewhere.'

'Preferably away from Haghill,' added Eddie.

'Jane and Jennifer said they'd stay here with me,' replied Carly.

'Nae offence to either of them but that won't be enough.'

'Then Harry can stay too.'

'You need to go somewhere Ross and Dominic can't find you.'

'We don't even know if Cole's telling the truth. By leaving, I could be playing right into their hands.'

'That's an excellent point,' said Jane. 'At least in Haghill everyone knows you. If you go somewhere with strangers, who's to look out for you?'

'True,' said Eddie.

'I'm staying,' said Carly. 'Dominic and Ross sodding Alexander are no' driving me away and if this is a plot of Cole's, then I will make him regret it.'

The corner of Jack's mouth lifted into a smile. 'That's what I like to hear but if you do stay, we need to take precautions and that is only sensible.'

'Jane, Jennifer and Harry can stay here,' she said again. 'And no one's getting through either door unless we want them to.'

'And if someone does bang on the back door again, you do not run out after them and leave the door open,' said Jack severely.

'I've learnt my lesson. I won't do it again.'

'Good. Well, I'll leave all the security arrangements with you and your family, you're all more than capable. In the meantime, I'll track down my idiot cousins.'

'What will you do when you find them?'

'Give them a world of pain for daring to think of hurting you.'

His gaze connected with Carly's for a few seconds before he got to his feet. 'Right, I need to get back on the hunt.'

Carly smiled inwardly at the darkness that filled his eyes. She really did pity Dominic and Ross, who were hopelessly outclassed.

'Call me if you need me, anytime,' Jack told Carly.

'I will.'

He gave her hand a gentle squeeze before leaving.

Eddie didn't speak until Jack had closed the front door behind him. 'I cannae help remember what Dean said about Jack trying to scare you into turning to him. If he is, then he's come up with the perfect way.'

'Wrong because he knows I'd never be scared of Ross and Dominic,' said Carly. 'He'd have to use someone far scarier than those idiots.'

'It's hard to argue with that,' replied Jane.

'Just bear in mind Jack could be behind this, for whatever reason,' pressed Eddie. 'I hope to Christ he's no' but we cannae take the chance.'

'It's just sensible, Carly,' said Jane reasonably.

'Okay, fair enough,' said her sister, even though the prospect caused her intense pain. 'I'll bear it in mind.'

'He's clever and willing to do anything to get what he wants,' said Eddie. 'He's already got his lucrative deal with Toni. There's only one more thing he wants and that's you, doll. You don't usually see Jack's type in this sort of work. Aye, he's smart and likes strategizing but most people are involved in this life for the money, plain and simple and their greed usually gets the better of them. Toni McVay has only lasted so long because she doesnae let greed get the better of her.'

'Being totally terrifying also helps,' said Jane wryly.

'Aye, it does but her brains are in charge, no' her lust for money. Jack's cut from the same cloth. He likes the creature comforts, just as we all do but he's no' into all the posh cars, big houses and flashing the cash about. All that stuff gets people caught. He just enjoys playing the game. You're the one thing he wants, doll, and he always gets what he wants.'

8

Carly was annoyed. She'd gone from feeling lonely to being followed around everywhere. Jane, Jennifer and Harry wouldn't even let her go to the corner shop alone.

'You've got to give me some space,' she exclaimed when they insisted on marching her between them on their way to the pub that evening. 'Harry, you nearly stood on my foot again. Next time I will punch you right in the face. I bet your new girlfriend won't fancy you with a big red swollen nose.'

Harry held up his hands while taking a couple of steps to the left.

'We're just trying to do our best for you,' Jane told Carly.

'Sorry,' she sighed. 'But I don't like having babysitters. You know what we should do – track down Ross and Dominic ourselves.'

'You're best leaving that to Jack and his people. They've got better resources.'

'But we know the area better than they do.'

'I think it's a good idea,' said Jennifer. 'And it'll be fun.'

'Let's do it,' said Carly eagerly.

'Look at you,' smiled Jane. 'You cannae wait to get stuck back in.'

'Well, Jennifer's right. It will be fun.'

'I'm up for it,' said Harry.

'Jack won't appreciate us interfering,' said Jane.

'He won't mind if we tell him it was Carly's idea.'

'I'm not sure...'

'Wouldn't you like to find Ross and Dominic and batter their heids in?' Carly asked her sister.

Mischief sparkled in Jane's eyes. 'I'd love it but where should we start?'

'Their bitch of a mother will know.'

'Jack will have already spoken to her.'

'Aye but he won't hit her until she gives up her sons like we will.'

'Now that does sound like fun.' Jennifer smiled, eyes gleaming. 'I've always hated that cow. She went to school with my maw and they never got on. She looked down on my maw because my grandda' was a sewage worker. She always gives me and every member of my family a snooty look when she sees us, like she's so fucking special. I cannae wait to bring her down a peg or two.'

'Then what are we waiting for?' said Carly. 'She'll be at the nail bar right now. That's where she is most afternoons.'

'Just don't get carried away,' said Jane as they turned up a different street, heading away from the pub. 'Remember she's our boss's cousin.'

'He cannae stand her,' said Carly.

'Maybe so but she's still a member of his family and not retaliating when someone hurts her will make him look bad. Just bear that in mind.'

'I will,' said Carly as she confidently strode down the street, looking forward to getting some payback on that bitch.

* * *

Jessica exited the nail bar and took a moment to admire her nails in the sunlight. They'd been painted a sparkly pink in time for her date that night.

'Pretty,' said a voice.

'Thanks,' she replied.

Jessica looked to her left and frowned when she saw Carly Savage leaning against the wall, arms folded across her chest.

'What do you want?'

Carly straightened up and approached her. Jessica stood her ground but she regarded the younger woman warily, aware of the violence she was capable of.

'I want to know where Ross and Dominic are.'

'Oh, I see. You've had Cole and Jack. Now you want to move onto the next one. You won't be satisfied until you've shagged every man in my family.'

'From what I've heard, you won't be satisfied until you've shagged every man in Glasgow,' retorted Carly. 'Don't you think you're a bit old for putting it about so much?'

Jessica's eyes flashed. The thing she hated most was being reminded of her age. 'You wee bitch,' she said, drawing back her hand to slap her.

Carly caught her wrist and squeezed, enjoying Jessica's wince of pain.

'Jack won't stand for you treating me like this,' she objected.

'We both know that Jack likes me a lot more than he likes you.' Carly smirked. 'Now tell me where your sons are.'

'I've no idea. They're adults, they don't have to check in with their mummy any more.'

'They're no' capable of taking a dump on their own. They'll still be in touch with their precious maw.'

'And I'm telling you they're not. Now, if you'll excuse me, I've got an appointment at the hairdressers.' Jessica attempted to tug her wrist free but Carly refused to let go.

'Is there a problem, Jess?' rumbled a deep voice.

Carly turned to see a shaven-headed man standing behind her. He was quite handsome and he was huge, shoulder muscles bulging through his smart suit.

'Help me, Armstrong, she's hurting me,' whined Jessica, putting on her best Little-Girl-Lost voice.

Carly rolled her eyes. Jessica was certainly too old to pull that one.

'Right, Missy,' said Armstrong. 'If you know what's good for you, you'll let her go right now.'

Armstrong's eyes widened when he was yanked backwards and slammed to the ground by Harry. Jennifer and Jane assisted Harry to pin him there when he attempted to rise.

When Carly looked back at Jessica, she was enormously gratified by the fear in her eyes.

'I repeat,' said Carly. 'Where are Ross and Dominic?'

'I don't know,' she replied, this time much less full of herself. 'Honestly. They just told me they were moving out of Haghill, that they'd got jobs.'

'What sort of jobs?'

'As mechanics.'

'Why didn't you just tell me that in the first place?'

'Because I don't want you and your family harassing them.' Jessica winced again when Carly squeezed her wrist harder.

'You don't care about that. You don't care about anyone but yourself. It's why your sons all turned out to be cold, vicious bastards. If you don't tell me where they are, then I'll do to your nose what Jane did to Emma Wilkinson's and I know you don't have the cash to fix that damage.'

The threat of physical deformity was Jessica's Achilles' heel. 'Okay, they're in Bishopbriggs. That's all I know.' She gasped with relief when Carly released her wrist.

'There,' said Carly. 'That wasn't so hard, was it?'

Jessica glowered at her as she shook out her wrist.

'If you've lied to me, I will come back and splatter your nose right across your face.'

'Just go,' said Jessica, narrowing her green cat's eyes at her.

Carly gave her an infuriating smile before turning to her friends. 'We're going to Bishopbriggs.'

Before Armstrong was released, Harry punched him hard in the stomach, ensuring he stayed down.

Jessica didn't rush to her beau's side as he groaned in pain on the pavement, arms wrapped around his torso. Instead, she glared at Carly Savage's retreating back, swearing she would figure out a way to get the cow back.

* * *

Bishopbriggs was four miles from Glasgow city centre.

'My uncle lives here,' said Jennifer. 'I could ask him if he's seen Ross and Dominic.'

'Will he know them?' asked Carly.

'That pair of pricks have a habit of making themselves known.'

'True.'

Jennifer's uncle lived in a nice bungalow on Kelvin Drive and was a jovial, cherry-cheeked man in his early sixties with a pot belly. He was short, only standing at five foot four with curly white hair. He put Carly in mind of a gnome. The only thing ruining this image were his hands, which were enormous, almost abnormally large and hanging down by his sides, the knuckles thick and knotty.

'Jen.' He beamed, clearly delighted to see his niece. 'And you've brought friends too. Come away in and I'll put the kettle on.'

'Lovely.' Jennifer smiled as they all stepped inside.

The interior was as whimsical as its owner with its cutesy little ornaments, flowery curtains and the chihuahua asleep on the rug.

'Aren't you going to introduce me then?' he asked his niece.

'Uncle Finlay, this is my girlfriend, Jane,' she said, taking her lover's hand.

Jane regarded Finlay warily, wondering how he would react to that news. To her surprise though, the little man hugged her, the top of his head just reaching her shoulder.

'How lovely to meet you at last,' he told Jane as he released her. 'Jennifer's told me lots about you. I'm so pleased she's finally met someone who makes her so happy.'

Jane beamed at him gratefully. 'Thank you. She makes me really happy too.'

'That is wonderful to hear.'

'This is Jane's younger sister, Carly,' said Jennifer.

'Good looks obviously run in your family.' Finlay smiled, taking Carly's hand in his own enormous paw and giving her a little bow. 'Actually, I have another niece who's single...'

Jennifer cringed. 'Carly's no' gay,' she told him.

'Oh. In that case, I have a nephew...'

'And this is Harry,' Jennifer hastened to say. 'He's Jane and Carly's cousin.'

'A fine, strong-looking boy,' he said, patting Harry heartily on the shoulder.

'Boy?' Harry frowned.

'Sit down and I'll make the tea.'

Carly, Jane and Jennifer sat on the couch while Harry took the wooden chair in the corner. Finlay vanished into the kitchen and returned a few minutes later carrying a tray laden with cups on saucers, sugar, milk, a plate of biscuits and an enormous teapot. He placed it on the coffee table and beamed at them all.

'I'll be mother,' he said, making Harry grin.

After the tea and biscuits were doled out, Finlay took a seat in the armchair and regarded them all with a benevolent smile. 'So, what's the reason for this visit then?'

'Can't I drop in on my favourite uncle?' said Jennifer.

'Aye, any time, but I sense a tension in the air.'

'You're right, as always.' She smiled. 'Uncle Finlay is the shrewdest man I know,' she told the room. She turned back to her uncle. 'We're looking for two people who've apparently moved here from Haghill, if our information's to be trusted.'

'They're no' a pair of brothers, are they?'

'God, yes. Ross and Dominic Alexander.'

'Oh. This pair are called Rob and Damien Alton.'

'That must be them,' said Carly. 'They havenae even the imagination to use names starting with different letters.'

'Can you describe them?' Jennifer asked her uncle.

The descriptions Finlay rhymed off perfectly matched Ross and Dominic Alexander.

'That's them,' replied his niece. 'Where can we find them?'

'They're working as mechanics at a local garage.'

'Bloody hell,' said Carly. 'Jessica was telling the truth. That's a shock.'

'They're pretty crap at the job. Everyone's been complaining about their work. It's only a matter of time before they're booted oot.'

'Have they been up to anything dodgy?' said Jane.

'Probably, knowing that pair but I cannae say for sure.'

'We need to check out this garage,' said Harry.

'Great,' said Finlay, eagerly leaping to his feet. 'I'll come with you.'

'I'm no' sure that's wise,' replied Harry with a patronising smile. 'It could get rough.'

The change in Finlay was shocking. His jovial grin fell, his eyes narrowed and his entire demeanour changed from a happy gnome to a malevolent goblin.

'What the fuck did you say to me, boy?' he growled, voice several octaves deeper than it had previously been. His enormous hands snapped open and closed, making a disturbing slapping sound, the thick joints popping out.

Harry looked to his cousins in astonishment. Carly and Jane stared back at him with equal surprise.

'Don't take it personally, Uncle Finlay,' said Jennifer, leaping to her feet. 'He doesnae know what he's saying.' Her tone was gentle and placating, completely unlike her usual way of talking.

'He thinks I'm just a fucking fanny,' roared Finlay, pointing one enormous digit at Harry. 'He thinks I'm some weak lassie who cannae fight but he's so fucking wrong.' Spittle flew from his lips and he ended this statement by gnashing his teeth.

Jennifer gently placed her hand on his shoulder, as though she were attempting to placate a wild animal. 'That's because he doesnae know what you can do. Why don't we go and show him?'

Finlay stared hard at Harry, his eyes bulging. He took a deep breath and his body relaxed, those huge hands going limp. The happy, harmless smile returned.

'I think that's a wonderful idea,' he said. 'I'll grab my shoes and coat.'

With that, he hurried out of the room.

'What the actual fuck?' Harry whispered to Jennifer, not wanting to incur Finlay's wrath again.

'I'll explain later,' she whispered back.

The five of them left the house, Finlay leading the way, talking excitedly.

'It's been a while since I've done anything like this. It's just like old times.'

Jennifer shook her head when Jane looked at her questioningly. 'Is it far?' she asked her uncle.

'It's a wee bit of a walk. We're probably best driving there, especially as it looks like rain.'

They all piled into Harry's car. He was a little uncomfortable when Finlay sat up front with him to give directions but the wee man was all bonhomie. No sign of his earlier aggression.

The garage where the Alexanders were allegedly working was located in a damp, manky backstreet. The rusting iron gates stood open, revealing an interior of chaos and despair. Numerous cars stood about in varying stages of dismemberment, some missing doors and wing mirrors, others with their bonnets propped open, the innards spilling out or missing entirely.

'Now remember,' said Jane before they got out of the car. 'We don't know for certain that it is Ross and Dominic in there, so let's ascertain what's going on before we do anything drastic. I'm particularly addressing you there, Harry.'

'Me?' He frowned, pointing at himself.

'Aye, you. And Carly.'

'What have I done?' demanded her sister. She sighed and nodded when Jane arched an eyebrow. 'Aye, all right.'

They all climbed out of the car and strode through the gates into the compound. There was a mechanic in dirty blue overalls working on a car, but his face was obscured by the bonnet.

'Hello,' called Jane.

The man peered around the side of the car but he wasn't either Alexander brother. 'What ya wantin'?' he called back.

'Charming customer service,' Jane told her friends with a

smile. She looked back at the mechanic. 'We're after Rob and Damien Alton. Are they here?'

'They were,' he replied, straightening up and wiping his hands on a rag that was so filthy it put more dirt onto his hands than it got off. 'Until they got sacked for stealing parts from the cars, and I mean the good motors people brought us to fix, no' the shite ones,' he added, gesturing to the wrecks that surrounded them.

'People actually bring their cars to you to fix?' Jane replied, surprised.

'Aye. Don't be fooled by the state of the place. My boss is a bloody genius. He can fix anything and he taught me,' he added with a lot more pride than any of them would have credited him with. 'Another reason Rob and Damo were sacked was because they were pretty shite mechanics.'

'Do you know where we can find them?'

'Probably in one of the local boozers. That's where they usually spend their time.'

'Do you know where they're staying?'

'Havenae a scoobie. They kept that to themselves.'

'All right. Thanks for your time.'

'Nae bother,' he replied before disappearing under the bonnet again.

Jane turned to the others. 'What do you think?'

'I reckon he's telling the truth,' said Carly.

'Aye, me too,' replied Harry.

Jennifer and Finlay nodded in agreement.

'Is this garage really a good one?' Jennifer asked her uncle once they were back in the car.

'They have a brilliant reputation,' he replied.

'Seriously?'

'I've used them. No' for a while because I havenae had a car for a few years but they always did a good job. They usually leave a bit of grease on your steering wheel but you can trust them to fix your motor.'

'Where's the nearest pub?'

'There are a few around here. What sort of place do these Alexander fannies like?'

'Bear pits usually.'

'They're all quite nice around here. There's nowhere I'd class as a bear pit.'

'Then we'll just have to drive around them all.'

The first they tried was a swanky bar and restaurant but there was no sign of their quarry there. Their second port of call was a pub with friendly staff and customers alike. They stopped to have a drink, Harry a little put out because he was stuck with orange juice as he was driving. Their subtle enquiries revealed no one had seen Rob or Damien Alton. Finlay knew a couple of the regulars who told him they'd not seen either man, so they moved on.

The third pub they tried was a beautiful old building with a beer garden.

'This also looks too nice for the Alexander brothers,' said Carly.

'They have live music on here regularly,' Finlay told her. 'Are they into that?'

'God no. Ross especially hates anything even remotely like culture.'

'That doesn't bode well for our search,' replied Jane. 'But we still need to check it out.'

They headed inside. The pub was warm and welcoming, some of the tables occupied by people enjoying a meal.

'It smells lovely in here,' said Harry. 'Why don't we stop and have something to eat? I'm starving.'

'You're always starving,' replied Carly. 'But the smell's making me hungry too.'

'Fine, we'll grab a bite to eat,' said Jane. 'We might be able to find something out from the staff.'

They took a table and were approached by a pale, sad-looking waitress.

'Are you okay?' Jane asked her when she stood before them, looking limp.

'Fine,' she sniffed. 'Just... just...'

With that, she burst into tears and ran off.

'No' again,' said the curvy, middle-aged woman behind the bar. She approached their table. 'I'm so sorry about that,' she told them. 'She's having boyfriend trouble. I was understanding at first but she's really trying my patience now. I don't see why she should get so upset over some nae-user. Anyway, that's no' your problem.' She broke into a big smile. 'Finlay, it's been a while.'

He leapt to his feet and took her hand. 'The fair Shirley. I don't know why I've stayed away for so long. You're the most beautiful woman in Bishopbriggs.'

'Oh, you,' she giggled. 'Such a charmer.'

'I merely tell the truth,' he gallantly replied before kissing her hand.

Shirley giggled again and blushed.

'What's all this then?' said a voice.

They turned to see a large, sturdy man who looked pretty pissed off. 'Have you got hold of my wife again Finlay? You cannae leave her alone.'

'I'm only being polite,' Finlay replied, smile falling as he released her hand. 'Have you got a problem with that, Mark?'

The big man suddenly looked very wary and shuffled uncomfortably. 'Naw, course not. I know you're just being friendly.'

The smile returned to Finlay's face. 'That's all right then. You can go. Shirley's more than capable of giving us what we need.'

Finlay's tone and gaze were suggestive. Shirley glanced at her husband, abashed, while Mark appeared both angry and afraid. Mark glared at Finlay once more before turning on his heel and stalking back to the bar.

Finlay retook his seat with the air of a triumphant conqueror.

'Well,' said Shirley with a forced smile. 'What can I get you all?'

They gave her their orders and she scurried back to the bar looking sheepish.

'Have you been up to your old tricks with the local women?' Jennifer demanded of her uncle.

He smiled and shrugged. 'It's no' my fault they find me irresistible.'

'Really?' said Harry.

Finlay rounded on him, the mayhem returning to his eyes. 'Why do you sound so fucking sceptical?'

'I don't,' he hastily replied, noting his hands were doing that weird snapping thing again. The last thing he wanted was to be hit by those knobbly bastards. 'I just... I...'

'Don't start on him, Uncle Finlay,' said Jennifer. 'You promised Maw you'd rein yourself in. That's why you had to leave Rutherglen.'

'I'm no' like that any more. I'm older and wiser.'

'And still horny by the sounds of it.'

'Some things never change,' he said, smiling.

'That Mark seemed scared of you,' Carly told Finlay. 'Are you a terror on the quiet?'

Her naughty smile broadened his grin. 'I was known as the Terror of Clydeside in my younger days and I still have my moments.'

'Really?' repeated Harry.

Finlay scowled at him. 'You're a baw hair away from a severe doin', ya wee fanny.'

'Uncle Finlay, please,' hissed Jennifer. 'Remember your promise.'

He sighed and nodded, the tension leaving his body. 'I do remember. What?' he added when she continued to stare at him. 'I didnae touch him,' he added, gesturing to Harry. 'Although the prick deserves a beating.'

'Hey, you – ow,' said Harry when Jane kicked him under the table, her look urging him to keep his big mouth shut.

'I bet you've some great stories to tell,' said Carly in an attempt to diffuse the situation.

Finlay smiled at her enthusiasm. 'Aye, I dae. I should write a book, it would be a best seller. It would be full of fights and shagging.'

'Sounds like my kind of book.'

'Because you're a wee terror too, aren't you?' he told her playfully. 'I knew your da'.'

The mention of her father caused Carly's grin to drop and pain to fill her eyes.

'Sorry,' he replied. 'I didnae mean to upset you.'

'You didn't. It's just still so raw.'

'Aye, I get that but you should be proud. Alec Savage was one hell of a man.'

'He certainly was,' she said with a sad smile.

'How did you know him?' Jane asked Finlay.

'Through his brother, Eddie. He was pals with a mutual friend of mine, a skinny prick called Murray who was murdered, stabbed through the heart. The polis never did catch who did it. Shame.'

Carly's blood froze in her veins. She looked to Harry, who stared back at her similarly startled. They were the only two at the table who knew Alec had been the one to kill Murray.

'That's terrible,' replied Carly. To her astonishment, her voice sounded relaxed and sympathetic.

'Aye. If I ever get my hands on who did it then...'

Finlay held out those huge, ugly hands of his and curled the fingers as he imitated throttling the culprit.

'You were good pals with Murray?' Harry asked him.

'Aye. We grew up together. He was like a brother to me. Unfortunately, he took a bad path, began dealing drugs. I reckon he was killed over a drug deal. I warned him often enough that he was in with a bad crowd but he wouldnae listen.' Finlay shook his head. 'Such a waste. He had a good heid on his shoulders but he let the drugs get the better of him.'

'I don't remember Da' mentioning a murder,' said Jane. 'Do you, Carly?'

Her sister just shook her head.

'It's no' the sort of thing a father would tell his daughters,' said Finlay. 'It's a sad story that happens the world over, it's nothing new. It's just awful when it happens to someone you know.'

The young waitress who'd run out earlier in tears returned carrying their drinks.

'Are you okay?' Jane asked her kindly.

'Fine,' she sniffed. 'I just hate men. I might become a nun.'

'Don't tar us all with the same brush, doll.' Finlay winked at her. 'Some of us are gentlemen.'

Harry was astonished when the girl blushed and giggled just as Shirley had done, even though Finlay was old enough to be her grandfather.

'Oh, I know you are.' She smiled at him. 'But you're the exception, no' the rule.'

'Tell me who he is and I'll make him pay.'

'You won't know him, he's no' lived here long. He's called Rob Alton.'

'You've been seeing Rob Alton?' Jane demanded of her.

'Aye, why?' the girl replied, a little nonplussed by the aggression in Jane's tone.

'He's cheated on other women we know.'

'I'm not surprised,' she rasped. 'He's been cheating on me with Hannah who works in the kebab shop. You should see her, she's so ugly with her big buck teeth and her fat arse. He has no class.'

'You've got that right. Do you know where he's staying? We'd like to have a catch-up with him.'

'I do actually,' the waitress said, malice filling her eyes as she hoped these people would get revenge for her. 'He's renting a ground-floor flat on Emerson Road. Forty-three A.'

'Thanks so much.'

The waitress wandered off looking much happier.

'Brilliant,' said Harry. 'And we didnae have to threaten anyone to get what we wanted.'

'I'm disappointed,' said Finlay. 'It's been a while since I've had a good rammy.'

'Don't worry,' Jennifer told him. 'You might still get one yet.'

9

After enjoying a very hearty lunch at the pub, they all got back into Harry's car and drove to Emerson Road. They located the house – a grey pebble-dashed semi opposite a three-storey block of flats in a cul-de-sac. Harry turned the car around in the turning circle at the end and parked two houses down from their target's home.

'Ross's BMW is parked outside,' said Jane with satisfaction. 'He didn't even have the good sense to change motors.'

'So what do we do?' said Finlay with an enthusiasm reminiscent of a puppy out for its first walk. 'Charge in and beat the shite out of them?'

'Like it,' said Harry, earning himself his first smile from Finlay.

'We need information from them first, so don't get carried away,' said Jane. 'Let me do the talking.'

'Okay, doll, we'll follow your lead,' said Finlay.

They got out of the car and headed down the street, casually strolling up the driveway. There was no front door. Instead, there were two doors at the side of the house, one for each flat. Jane rang the bell for forty-three A.

'Carly, Jennifer, cover the back,' said Jane.

The two women nodded and disappeared around the corner. There was the sound of approaching footsteps and the door was pulled open by Dominic Alexander.

'Got you, ya bastard,' said Jane.

'Shit,' he cried before turning and racing back into the flat.

The three of them rushed inside, Jane leading the way. They saw Dominic run into the kitchen and they followed, bursting in just in time to see him yank open the back door. Carly's fist met his face and he staggered backwards. Harry wrapped an arm around his waist and slammed him down onto the kitchen table. When Dominic opened his mouth, either to cry for help or give a warning, Finlay clamped a hand down over his face, his hand so huge only Dominic's eyes were visible over the top of it.

'We've got him,' Harry told Jane as he and Finlay kept Dominic pinned down.

'Let's check the rest of the flat,' Jane told Carly and Jennifer.

The three women rushed through the flat together but it was clear no one else was home.

'Where's Ross?' Jane demanded of Dominic when they returned to the kitchen.

Finlay removed his hand so he could speak.

'He's no' here,' cried Dominic. 'He's gone away to... to... Perth. Aye, Perth. He's staying with a pal.'

'You're a shite liar,' chuckled Finlay.

'We know he's close because his car's parked outside,' Jane told Dominic.

'He didnae take his car. He went on the train.'

'Bollocks. Why would Ross bother going to Perth? And if it is all innocent, then why are you hiding out in Bishopbriggs?'

'We're no' hiding out. We got offered jobs here as mechanics.'

'Shite mechanics. You got the sack.'

'That wasnae our fault,' he whined. 'They accused us of nicking when we didnae do anything.'

'Course you did, it's in your natures. You wouldnae have been able to help yourselves. We know you two are plotting to kidnap Carly.'

'We're no',' he exclaimed.

'Don't bother to deny it.'

'Why the hell would we want Carly? Nae offence,' he added when the woman herself scowled.

'You tell us,' retorted Jane.

'I don't know anything about it, I swear.'

'The problem is, Dominic, that your word means absolutely nothing. We cannae trust anything that comes out of your mouth, especially since the last time you pretended to work with us when all the time you and your brothers were working against us.'

'I don't get why you'd think we'd want to kidnap Carly. I mean, what would it achieve?' he cried, eyes wide.

'You know how much Jack cares about her and you want to use her to blackmail your cousin into giving up his position.'

'That wouldnae work because of Toni McVay. She's the one who says who runs things, no' us.'

'Toni McVay?' breathed Finlay, looking a little shocked. He turned to his niece. 'Just what the hell are you involved in?'

'I'll tell you later,' she replied.

'Toni allowed Jack to take over from Rod Tallan,' Jane told Dominic. 'So you probably thought she'd do the same thing again with you and Ross, only she thinks you're a pair of doughnuts.'

'We're no' trying to take over. We just want to get on with our lives.'

'Liar. Harry, Carly, go and keep a look out for Ross while we get what we want out of this fucking cabbage.'

Harry and Carly left the flat and walked down the path to the street but there was no sign of Ross.

'What did you think about what Finlay said about Murray?' Carly asked her cousin.

'We cannae be sure he was talking about the same person.'

'It's likely though, isn't it?'

'Maybe but it's best to forget about it. It's no' like Finlay can go after Uncle Alec for it.'

'You're right. It just gave me a shock.'

'Aye, me too. I take it Jane and Rose still don't know?'

'No they don't and I want to keep it that way. I made a promise to Da'.'

Harry nodded. 'I understand.'

They both continued to scan the street.

'What if Dominic's telling the truth?' said Carly. 'Cole could have been lying for his own purposes.'

'It wouldn't surprise me. He's a shifty bastard.'

'I just can't see what his play is. Jack's far too strong for Cole and his numpty brothers to challenge and Cole's smart enough to realise that.'

'Ambition and greed can make people do stupid things.'

'Perhaps.'

'Maybe Cole's working for Jack and he's agreed to help his cousin scare you into getting back with him? We both know Cole would be more than happy to drop his brothers in it for a position in Jack's crew.'

Carly had to admit that last part was true but she still shook her head. 'Jack wouldn't do that to me.'

'I disagree.'

'You've no' seen the Jack Alexander I know. He wouldn't do it,' she said firmly.

'I hope you're right. Really,' he added when she regarded him sceptically. 'He's a pretty good boss, actually. Much better than Rod bloody Tallan. I just want everything to settle down so we can concentrate on making some serious money. I'm sick of all this conspiracy shite.'

'Me too.' Carly hesitated before saying, 'So is it serious with Dean and the lingerie model?'

'I was wondering when you'd get round to asking me that,' he said.

'I'm just curious. I've decided you're right and we can't be together.'

'Seriously?' he said, surprised.

Carly nodded. 'It's complicated because we're cousins and because I still love Jack.'

'Do you want Jack back?'

'I don't know. I'm all mixed up inside.'

'That's probably the grief. Don't make a decision either way until you're over it.'

Harry grinned and nudged her playfully with his shoulder. 'Anyway, if you had any sort of taste, you'd fancy me over Dean.'

Carly chuckled. 'Modest as ever, Harry.'

He winked at her. 'That's me.'

A door in the block of flats across the road opened and Ross Alexander charged out accompanied by four males in their early twenties.

'Heads up,' said Carly.

She and Harry got to their feet and moved to greet them, the two groups meeting in the middle of the street.

'What the fuck are you doing here?' demanded Ross, strutting along with his chest puffed out, full of bravado.

'Just having a quiet word with your brother,' replied Carly stonily.

'You'll fucking leave him alone,' he snarled as the five men converged on them.

'We've a few questions for you too, like why do you want to kidnap Carly?' said Harry.

'Kidnap her?' Ross retorted with a curl of the lip. 'Why the hell would I want Big Mouth? She drives me up the fucking wall.'

'Who are you calling Big Mouth?' snapped Carly.

'You, ya gobby bitch.'

A smirk creased her lips. 'It's nice to see you back on your feet after my wee sister almost pulled your baws off.' She looked to Ross's friends. 'Did you know that he got bested by a seventeen-year-old girl? Twice?'

When one of Ross's friends chuckled, Ross turned his death stare on him and he went silent.

'See what I mean? A big mouth,' he exclaimed, pointing at Carly. 'And a liar too.'

'Your hospital medical records say differently. It was weeks before you could walk upright again.'

When the same man who'd chuckled earlier burst out laughing, Ross punched him in the face and he collapsed to the ground.

'Anyone else find it funny?' he bellowed at the men.

They all shook their heads.

Ross glared at them before turning his attention back to Carly and Harry. 'You made a mistake coming here. You're no' on your turf now and Jack has no say here. We're gonnae batter your heids in.'

'I'd like to see you try,' growled Harry.

'You're gonnae see right now.'

As Carly reached for the stun gun concealed in her jacket pocket, Finlay exited the Alexander flat and ambled down the path towards them, looking more gnome-like than ever. Carly expected derision from Ross and his friends, for them to jeer and make fun of his appearance, but on the contrary, they suddenly appeared wary, the machismo draining right out of them.

'I didnae know you were here, Finlay,' said Ross.

'Aye, well I am,' he snapped back. 'I hope you weren't about to attack my pals?'

'Us? Naw, course not,' Ross replied in a placating tone. 'We're good friends, aren't we Carly?'

'No,' she replied. 'We hate each other's guts.'

Ross narrowed his eyes at her before turning to look back at Finlay. 'We were just having a wee chat; we're from the same neighbourhood.'

'Aye, I know. Jennifer's my niece.'

'You mean Jennifer as in Jane's girlfriend?'

Finlay nodded hard, glowering at the men.

'Oh,' said Ross, looking increasingly nervous.

Harry and Carly glanced at each other, amused. Ross was a hard, violent man who loved a good scrap but now he looked positively scared, as did his friends, who were all slowly backing away. Carly was finding Finlay increasingly intriguing. What had he done to frighten men such as these?

Ross's eyes nervously flicked to Finlay's hands when they began that disturbing snapping motion again.

'Don't you fannies dare take another step,' Finlay snarled at the men.

Obediently they all came to a halt.

'Now you lot are gonnae tell these two what they want to know,' he continued, gesturing to Carly and Harry. 'And if you don't, so help you God.'

Ross looked to the Savages, took a deep breath, as though screwing up all his pride and dignity into a little ball and said, 'What do you want to know?' His voice was hoarse with suppressed rage and humiliation. Carly's and Harry's smirks did not help and his green eyes flashed.

'We've already told you,' said Carly. 'Or have you forgotten already, ya thick bastard?'

Ross grunted and when it looked like he was going to lunge at them, Finlay cleared his throat, causing him to immediately go still.

'As I've already said,' he replied through gritted teeth. 'I've nae idea what you're talking about.'

'That's no' what we've heard,' said Harry.

'Then whoever told you was just stirring trouble. Me and Dom have started a new life here; we've got a good crew around us.'

'For what?' said Carly. 'Nicking sweeties off weans? Mugging old ladies of their pension?'

'No,' he barked.

'Then what?'

'That's none of your business.'

'Tell her,' growled Finlay.

'With all due respect,' Ross told him deferentially. 'That's no' fair. You know the score. I cannae dae that.'

'You bloody well will, unless you want to wake up one night with my hands around your neck?'

The prospect made Ross swallow hard, his hand unconsciously going to his throat. 'We're lending money to those who cannae borrow from a bank.'

'And breaking their kneecaps when they can't pay the extortionate interest?' retorted Carly.

Finlay glowered at Ross. 'You dirty bastards.'

'It's no' extortionate,' he retorted. 'It's quite reasonable actually.'

'You're lying,' said Harry. 'You cannae count the fingers on both hands. You're dealing drugs, aren't you?'

'Maybe,' Ross replied. 'And that's all I'm saying on the matter. It's my business, no' yours.'

'It is mine though,' said Finlay. 'I live here. This is a decent neighbourhood and I'm no' letting you spoil it.'

Ross nodded and looked back at Carly. 'Whatever's going on is nothing to do with us. Your info's wrong. We just want to get on with our lives.'

They all turned to look when Jane and Jennifer exited the flat.

'What have you done to my brother?' demanded Ross.

'Nothing much,' replied Jane casually. 'He's fine. Well, he will be in a few days,' she added with a wicked smile. 'We didn't do him any permanent injury.'

Ross was about to yell back at them, until he recalled that Jennifer was Finlay's niece.

'I don't think they're anything to do with it,' Jane told Carly and Harry. 'Dominic would have told us after what we did to him.'

'What did you do to him?' said one of Ross's friends with more curiosity than anger.

It was Jennifer's turn to smile wickedly. 'Let's just say it involved a nine-volt battery and his willy.'

The men all winced.

'I wouldn't go in there for a while,' she continued. 'It smells like fried pubes.'

One man was unable to repress a snigger, which he hastily pretended was a cough when Ross glared at him.

'You'd no right to torture my brother,' Ross exclaimed.

'Oh aye,' said Jane, stepping forward. 'Just like you had no right to torture Carly, you sick bastard.'

'Did he do that to this lovely lassie?' demanded Finlay.

'He did,' replied Jane while glaring stonily at Ross.

'Ya vicious prick,' roared Finlay, spittle flying from his lips. 'You don't treat a woman like that.'

It appeared he was about to advance on Ross when they were interrupted by a car driving towards them. They were all standing in the middle of the road and made no effort to move.

The battered-looking Ford Mondeo pulled up at the kerb and Jack got out of the driver's seat while Cole jumped out of the passenger seat.

Jane glanced at her sister and noted the way her face lit up at Jack's appearance. His eyes met Carly's and he smiled back at her.

'You tracked them down before we did,' said Jack as he and Cole strolled up to them casually. 'Nice work.'

'Thanks,' replied Carly. She wondered if he'd be pissed off that they'd come here when they'd been told not to but he didn't seem at all angry.

'I want a fucking word with you,' said Jack, pointing a digit at Ross.

'I've already told this lot me and Dom don't want to kidnap Carly,' replied his cousin. 'You might like her, but she annoys the living fuck out of me.'

'Get inside,' said Jack in a tone that brooked no argument. 'The rest of you, fuck off,' he told Ross's friends. 'Let's go inside,' said Jack, noting people peering at them through their windows. 'We're making an exhibition of ourselves.'

Ross was urged towards his flat by a shove in the back from Jack, the Savages, Jennifer and her uncle trailing after them.

They all entered the small kitchen to find Dominic curled up in a ball on his side, his jeans around his ankles, arse bare.

'Urgh,' said Jack. 'Pull up your kecks, for Christ's sake.'

'I cannae move,' he groaned. 'They electrocuted my bits.'

'Who did?'

'Jane and her girlfriend.'

When Jack turned to face her, Jane tilted her chin defiantly.

'Good work,' he told her.

'Thanks,' she replied, surprised.

'Go and sort yourself out,' Jack told Dominic impatiently. 'We've things to discuss. Cole, Harry, give him a hand. It'll be quicker.'

The two men dragged Dominic off the table and yanked his jeans and underwear back up but not before everyone had got a glimpse of his shrivelled, injured member.

'Argh, my bits,' cried Dominic.

'Don't be a baby,' Jennifer told him. 'It'll be fine in a few days.'

'You sound like you've done it before,' Jack told her.

'I have,' she said, smiling. 'It's a very effective way of making someone talk.'

'I'll bet. We'll talk in the living room. I can't stand the stink in here.'

They all headed into the poky lounge where there was a pair of two-seater black leather couches and not much room for anything else. The enormous television had been wall-mounted.

Jennifer and Jane took one couch together while Finlay took another. Carly was about to take the final seat when Ross got there first. Jack grabbed him by the back of his jacket and hauled him to his feet.

'Let the lady sit,' Jack told him before gesturing with his free hand for Carly to take a seat beside Finlay.

'Thank you,' she replied magnanimously, unable to resist giving Ross another smirk. She saw anger spark in his eyes and he shifted from foot to foot with the pressure of containing it.

Carly just grinned and shook her head.

Jack stood at the head of the room, Cole on one side, Harry on the other. Ross elected to lean against the wall, arms folded across his chest, radiating hostility. Dominic had been dumped in a corner where he slumped, quivering with pain.

'Right,' said Jack, turning to Ross. 'We were told that you were planning to kidnap Carly and use her against me. Is that fucking true?'

'For the tenth time, no,' Ross yelled back. 'I'm sick of being asked the same question over and over. She's a nagging fishwife. I don't know what you see in her.'

Jack pointed a digit at him. 'Watch your fucking tongue.'

'Who told you I wanted to kidnap her anyway?'

'Cole did.'

Ross rounded on his younger brother. 'What do you want to be stirring the shite for? Why cannae you just leave us alone to get on with our lives?'

'I'm no' stirring the shite,' he replied, face expressionless. 'I was told that was your plan.'

'By who?'

'A pal of yours, Billy Wilde.'

'That fud? I havenae seen him for weeks. I don't even know where he'd get that idea from.'

'He said you told him.'

'I didn't tell him anything,' Ross cried, rapidly losing his patience. 'Has everyone lost their bloody minds? Like I said before, me and Dom came here to start new lives. We cannae get a foothold in Haghill any more.'

'So, you thought you'd try and pollute this place instead with your mankiness?' Finlay glowered.

Jack frowned when he saw how warily Ross regarded Finlay, which made him study the older man with interest. 'What's your name?' he asked Finlay politely, recognising Ross was afraid of him for a good reason.

'Finlay Campbell,' he replied. 'And who the fuck are you?'

'Be careful what you say,' Cole told him.

'No, it's okay,' said Jack. 'It's a fair question. I'm Jack Alexander.'

'I take it that's supposed to mean something? Because it doesnae.'

'Uncle Finlay,' said Jennifer, warning in her voice. 'Jack runs Haghill now and he has a powerful boss. You should show him some respect.'

Finlay shrugged. 'He's a Sassenach.'

'Actually, he's Glasgow born and bred. His family moved to Yorkshire when he was a wean and he's moved back now.'

'I suppose that's okay,' he said a little indignantly. 'I just don't like the English.'

'I wish you wouldn't say things like that,' said Jennifer, exasperated. 'You sound racist.'

'I'm no' racist. I just think they're arseholes,' he sniffed, folding his arms across his chest.

Jennifer cast Jack an apologetic look; he just smiled.

'It seems someone's trying to stir trouble in our family,' Cole told Jack. 'I believe Ross.'

'How fucking big of you,' said Ross sarcastically. 'Why did you no' just come to me in the first place? Why did you run to Jack telling tales? Is it because your own big plan failed and now you hope to get some scraps from his table? I bet Billy didnae tell you anything. You just made it up so Jack would think you were on his side, ya crawling wee shite.'

Jack turned to Cole with a suspicious look.

'That's not it at all,' said Cole calmly. 'I care about Carly too and I didnae want to see her get hurt. I thought I was doing the right thing.'

'Don't talk about your feelings,' said Ross. 'We all know you don't have any.'

Carly regarded Cole curiously, wondering if his brother was right.

'I think someone's been messing us about,' said Jack. 'Or

they're just trying to stir the shit between our two families. I think it's safe to say you're in no danger, Carly. Does everyone agree?'

'I do after talking to Dominic,' replied Jane.

'Me too,' said Jennifer.

'Harry?' Jack asked him.

'I think she's safe,' he replied. 'And even if someone did try anything, she'd just batter them into next week.'

Jack winked at Carly. 'I can't argue with that.'

She smiled back at him.

'In that case, we should head back to Haghill. We have things to discuss.'

'You're leaving already?' said a disappointed Finlay. 'But we've no' even seen any action yet, unless you count that fucking Jessie having his bits shocked,' he added, pointing at Dominic, who was too sore and exhausted to care about insults.

'You've had enough fights to last a lifetime,' Jennifer told him. 'You're supposed to be retired.'

'Aye, well, I'm getting bored.'

'What about the promise you made my maw?'

He sighed. 'I know, I know.'

'Good,' she said, giving him a hard look.

'Well,' said Jack. 'We've probably attracted enough attention to ourselves for one day. I'll meet you at Carly's flat,' he told the Savages. 'I want a word with this pair in private,' he added, gesturing from Ross to Dominic.

Cole remained behind with his family while the Savages and Finlay left.

'What did you make of that?' Harry asked the others once they were back in his car.

'I'm not sure,' said Jane thoughtfully. 'It was all a bit weird. Maybe Jack will have more to tell us. There could be stuff he didn't want to say in front of Ross and Dominic.'

'I agree it was strange,' said Carly. 'But I really don't think Jack's behind it.'

'Nae offence,' replied Harry. 'But you wouldn't. We all know you're still sweet on him.'

'Well, I cannae help that,' she sighed. 'I wish I could, believe me.'

10

After dropping off a disappointed Finlay, who was still grousing that he hadn't seen any violence, they returned to the Savage sisters' flat. Fortunately, Rose was out. Jack and Cole turned up twenty minutes later and they all gathered around the kitchen table to talk.

'Ross and Dominic aren't involved in any plot against you, Carly,' opened Jack. 'I'm 100 per cent certain about that.'

'What about the business they're setting up in Bishopbriggs?' Harry asked him.

'I've known about that for a couple of weeks and it's way too small fry to worry me.'

'I take it you've already spoken to Billy Wilde?'

'I've tried but he's left the area. His mum told me he's flown to Greece for a few weeks.'

'That proves it then,' said Harry. 'He's been stirring up trouble.'

'Possibly but I would like to make sure, so we can be certain that Carly's safe.'

'How will you do that?'

Before Jack could reply, the front door opened and Eddie and Dean entered.

'Just us,' called the former. 'Oh,' he added when they entered the kitchen. 'We didnae know a meeting had been arranged.'

'It was a spur of the moment decision,' replied Jack. 'Take a seat.'

'There isn't one left,' said Dean, adopting the cold attitude he usually used with Jack.

'You can take the couch,' Jane told them. 'We can move our chairs.'

The two men took a seat on the couch and Jane and Jennifer turned their chairs side-on, so they would be included.

'Now, we've ascertained that Ross and Dominic are not plotting to kidnap Carly,' said Jack.

'We've only your word for that,' retorted Dean.

'You have our word too,' said Jane. 'We tracked down Ross and Dominic to a flat in Bishopbriggs.'

'With Jack?' said Eddie.

'No, we did it off our own backs.'

Eddie shot to his feet, expression thunderous. 'You were all told to leave it alone. Why can you no' do as you're fucking told?'

'We weren't gonnae sit on our arses when Carly could be in trouble,' replied Harry. 'It's no' our style.'

'No, your style is rushing in before you've engaged your bloody brains.'

'It's all right,' said Jack. 'I admire their tenacity and they did a good job. They found Ross and Dominic before I did.'

'Still,' said Eddie, simmering down a little. 'They should learn to obey orders,' he added before sitting back down.

'I agree,' said Dean. 'It was dangerous. Anything could have happened. Did you take Carly with you?'

Harry nodded.

'Well that was stupid. Why would you do such a thing when you thought there was a possibility they wanted to abduct her? It would have been like leading a lamb to the slaughter.'

'Don't call me a lamb,' Carly told him. 'And I'm fed up with everyone insinuating that I'm helpless.'

'No one thinks that,' Jack told her.

'Since I got out of the business, I've been treated like I'm made of glass and I'm tired of it.'

'Sorry,' said Jane. 'We'll try not to do it again.'

Carly gave her uncle a hard look and he nodded in agreement.

'What's the deal with your Uncle Finlay?' Jack asked Jennifer in an attempt to break the awkward silence. 'He's an interesting character with the biggest hands I've ever seen.'

'That's a very polite way of putting it,' she smiled wryly.

'Finlay?' said Eddie. 'Your uncle's no' Finlay Campbell, is he?'

Jennifer nodded.

'Well, I didnae know that. He's one crazy bastard.'

'I can't deny that,' she replied. 'Although he has calmed down a lot in the last few years, ever since he retired.'

'Wait, that was him being calm?' said Harry, eyebrows shooting up his forehead.

'Aye,' replied Jennifer.

'Bloody hell.'

'He said he was a friend of Da's,' Carly told her uncle.

'Did he mention me?'

'Briefly.'

'Cheeky sod,' he muttered. 'Although, he always did like Alec more than me. Alec was the only person who was never feared of him.'

'Why were people afraid of him?' said Harry. 'Apart from the weird thing he does with his hands and his Manson lamps stare.'

'He was the main enforcer for a dealer called Scrappy Wilson,' replied Jennifer.

He frowned. 'Scrappy Wilson?'

'Aye. He became pretty influential around the whole of Glasgow back in the nineties. Uncle Finlay punished whoever Scrappy told him to. He was known for suffocating them with his bare hands or strangling them to death. His hands are freakishly strong. He even throttled the favourite horse of some posh boy who got into Scrappy for a lot of money and thought he could get out of paying it back. That incident made him famous in the area.'

'So that's why everyone seemed so scared of him,' said Carly.

'No' just because of that. He's done lots of other bad things. In 2007 he got arrested for malicious wounding. He caused a lot of havoc in prison. He served ten years and when he was released my maw begged him to turn over a new leaf. Uncle Finlay promised, he said he never wanted to go back to prison and my maw's the one person he listens to. He moved to Bishopbriggs to start over and he's kept his promise, sort of. Although he's no' strangling people on behalf of drug dealers any more, he has got up to mischief.'

'Like shagging the landlord's wife?' Harry smiled.

'He's a real ladies' man.'

'I should ask him for some tips.'

'Don't bother. He'd just tell you to sod off. He doesn't take any shite off anyone. He usually reacts violently to insults and unfortunately he gets a lot of them thanks to his appearance. People think he's a pushover. When they realise he's not, it's usually too late.'

'So you don't think he'd like to come out of retirement?' Jack asked Jennifer.

'No. Those days are behind him.'

'Shame. I would have paid him well. A horse strangler would be enough to shit up anyone.'

'So,' said Carly. 'Can I go about freely again, without a babysitter?'

'I reckon so,' replied Jack. 'Ross and Dominic are no threat and Billy Wilde's gone to Greece. I don't think it was a serious threat, just some shit-stirring.'

'Good,' said Carly. 'Being watched every second has been getting on my nerves.'

'We were only trying to do our best for you,' said Jane, looking a little hurt.

'You're right, I'm sorry,' said Carly, immediately contrite. 'You know me and my big mouth.'

'Ross does.' Harry grinned. 'He couldnae stop going on about it.'

'Well, that's one less thing to worry about,' said Eddie. 'So we can all go back to normal.'

'Have you forgotten about whoever was banging on the back door the other night?' Dean asked him.

'Oh, aye.'

'It would be wise for you not to be alone here at night, Carly,' Jack told her.

'I know and I won't be.'

'Jennifer and I will be here,' said Jane.

'Then that's settled. In the meantime, I'll continue working on finding whoever was banging on the door. Now, if you don't mind, we have other business to discuss,' said Jack. 'Sorry, ladies.'

'Nae worries,' replied Jennifer, getting to her feet. 'Come on, Carly, I'll buy you a roll at the café.'

The two women left the flat together and headed down the street.

'Don't you get pissed off with being cut out of all the action?' Jennifer asked Carly.

'I didn't at first but I have lately. No' because I want to get back into the business but because I miss the excitement and the plotting,' she slowly replied.

'And the fighting?'

'I don't miss that.'

'Course you do.'

'Well, maybe a little bit, but not enough to get dragged back into it all.'

Jennifer frowned when Carly stopped and looked back over her shoulder. 'What's wrong?'

'It feels like someone's following us.'

Jennifer whipped round. 'I cannae see anyone.'

'Me neither but I know someone's there. Let's check it out.'

'Wait,' called Jennifer. 'Oh hell,' she added when Carly broke into a run. Left with no choice, Jennifer sprinted after her. They reached the end of the street, which was a four-way junction and they looked up and down each road but they saw no one.

'Don't you think it's weird that the area's totally deserted?' said Carly. 'There's normally someone about.'

'It's just a coincidence,' replied Jennifer, stifling a shiver. She was a strong, tough woman who wasn't easily spooked but she was getting a bad feeling. Whether that was because there was genuine danger or Carly had infectious paranoia, she wasn't sure. 'Let's go to the café,' she continued, glancing up at the sky. 'It looks like it's gonnae start pissing down.'

It started to rain before they'd reached the café, so they ran with their heads down, continually glancing over their shoulders.

They entered the warm, cosy café that sat on the main road to the smell of coffee, shaking the raindrops from their hair.

'I'm glad you two are here,' the owner of the café told them, a small, greying man with an elaborate moustache. 'I've had some trouble with a pack of wee bastards. Wayne Mitchell's youngest is leading them. They run in, snatch the Tunnocks Teacakes off the counter and run out again. When I stopped putting food out on the counter, they started pelting my window with stones. They even cracked one. The evil wee sods need a good sorting out.'

'We'll speak to them,' replied Jennifer.

'Good because if they don't stop then I'll end up roasting them in my oven. Bloody hooligans,' he huffed, cheeks turning red with anger. 'I blame the parents, they don't gi'e a shite.'

'Nae worries, Norrie. We'll sort it.'

'That's good to hear. Whatever you want is on the house, to say thanks.'

'Cheers,' said Jennifer.

Carly and Jennifer took a seat at a table, the latter ordering her roll and a cup of tea while Carly just ordered a coffee.

'Did you feel someone was following us?' Carly asked her.

'I did but I'm gonnae be honest – I'm no' sure it was my imagination.'

'I'm no' sure myself but it's not the first time I've felt it. I first noticed it when I went to visit my da's grave the day after the funeral and I've felt it on and off ever since.'

'Have you told your family?'

Carly shook her head.

'Why not?'

'Because, like you, I was worried I was imagining it. I can't trust my own feelings right now.'

'I get that but you should still have warned them, especially after someone was banging on your back door. That wasn't your imagination.'

'But if I tell the family, I'll be given another babysitter.'

'So? Your safety is the most important thing.'

'I suppose I didn't want to worry them either, no' until I was sure.'

'Let's see if we notice it again on our way back.'

'Okay.' Carly smiled, glad they'd settled on a plan and that Jennifer wasn't classing her as a nutcase just yet.

On the walk back from the café, Jennifer and Carly remained on high alert but that feeling of being followed didn't return.

'That definitely felt different to earlier,' said Jennifer as they approached the Savage home.

'Aye, I didn't feel anything there. Maybe I'm losing my mind?'

'I don't think so. Your family has enemies and you've got to remember that you're the only person Jack Alexander cares about. If someone got hold of Jessica or one of her sons and threatened to hurt them, Jack would just say go ahead and not think about it again. In fact, he'd do that if they got hold of anyone, except you. You're the only person he'd ever put himself out for.'

'You think?'

'Definitely.' Jennifer couldn't help but smile at Carly's smile. 'Why don't you just get back with him and have done with it?'

'It's too complicated.'

'No, it's not. You're both happiest when you're together. It doesn't get any simpler than that.'

'But he's in the life,' she said a little lamely.

'You're a Savage, you'll never be out of it, no matter how hard you try.'

'I thought Jane was a straight talker but you're like a bullet between the eyes.'

Jennifer laughed. 'It's one reason why me and Jane get on so well. It's impossible to insult each other.'

Carly loved the joy that lit up her eyes at the mention of Jane's name. Their love was pure and genuine and Carly would like to share something similar with a partner of her own.

'Why don't you go on a date with Jack instead, see if the old magic's still there?' said Jennifer. 'You cannae decide that when you're always surrounded by your family.'

'That's a great idea. He did ask me out for dinner.'

'Go for it. Just make it clear you're not an item, you're just seeing how the land lies.'

'Thanks, I will. You're very wise, Jennifer.'

'Sometimes. At other times, I'm a bloody idiot.'

The two women looked at each other and laughed.

They returned to the flat to find everyone was still present. Carly was pleased that Jack was still there. She'd already decided to test out Jennifer's idea. All she needed to do now was talk to him alone.

'I'd better get on,' Jack said, rising to his feet. 'Things to do.'

Carly didn't want to say anything to him in front of everyone, so all she could do was watch him leave.

'Go after him,' Jennifer whispered in her ear.

'I can't. It would be too obvious,' she whispered back.

'What are you two up to?' Eddie asked them, eyes narrowed with suspicion.

'Nothing,' they both said sweetly.

'Hmmm,' he said, regarding them doubtfully.

'So what are you all up to now?' said Carly, hoping they'd all leave so she could go after Jack. 'Do you have any jobs on?'

'No,' replied Eddie. 'We've got the rest of the day off. We thought we'd go to the pub if you want to come?'

'I don't know, I feel like I've been drinking quite a bit lately. I think I'll stay here and read a book.'

'Really?'

'Aye. I like to read,' she snapped when he still appeared dubious.

'Okay. Well, you can join us there if you change your mind. Remember, keep all the doors locked and if someone starts banging on them, don't go running outside after them. Call us instead.'

'I will.'

'Maybe I should leave Harry behind to sit with you?'

'For God's sake, I'm no' a wean. I'll be fine.'

'And we won't be far if something does happen,' said Jennifer.

'Well, I suppose it would be okay. Just be careful, won't you, doll?' Eddie told Carly.

'I will.'

'Good. Let's go then.'

'I'll catch you up,' Dean told the rest of the family. 'I need a word with Carly.'

'No problem, son,' said Eddie.

Normally her uncle would have objected to them being alone together and when he didn't she knew he and Dean had already spoken and arranged this between them.

The family departed and Carly watched them go regretfully.

'I just wanted to say,' began Dean. 'That my da's right, nothing can happen between us.'

'Oh,' she said, a little surprised by this turn of events.

'I should never have kissed you the other day especially after what you've just been through,' he said sympathetically. Gently he took her hand. 'It would cause too much trouble in the family when what we all need is stability after losing Alec.'

'You're right,' she said. 'It's just a shame that we'll never get to explore what's really between us. It's a risk we can't take.' Carly smiled, a little relieved about this. 'Do you really like your lingerie model?'

'I do. She's an intelligent woman and is only using the modelling to earn some extra money. She's studying to be a psychiatrist. Destiny wants to help people heal.'

'She sounds a remarkable woman.'

'She really is. I'm sorry, Carly.'

'Don't be. I'm just happy that you're happy and you're absolutely right when you said we can't risk dividing the family. Since Da's death, we need each other more than ever.'

He nodded and smiled. 'Friends?'

She smiled back. 'Always.'

Dean leaned in to kiss her but turned his head at the last moment and kissed her cheek instead.

'I'd better go,' he said. 'I'm meeting Destiny for drinks and I need to get changed first.'

'Have a nice time,' she replied, her smile feeling increasingly strained.

'Thanks. Are you sure you'll be okay here alone?'

'Course I will. Don't worry about me. Go and enjoy yourself, you deserve it.'

He gave her hand a gentle squeeze before getting up and leaving. Carly turned to watch him go but, for the first time, he didn't look back at her.

When he'd closed the door behind him, Carly slumped back in her seat, surprised by this turn of events but thinking it could only be for the best.

11

Carly decided to stay in for the rest of the day, feeling a little down, meaning she wasn't in the mood for talking to Jack. She was assailed by memories of her father, some happy and warming, others sad and despondent and she wanted to be alone to work her way through the emotion.

Rose briefly popped back for a change of clothes. She'd been invited to the wedding reception of a relative of Noah's at a posh hotel. After changing and applying her make-up, she departed again with her boyfriend. Jane called Carly to say they were going on from the pub for a meal at the local Chinese restaurant and asked if she wanted to join them but Carly turned down the invitation, her grief too raw.

As she couldn't be bothered cooking, she made herself a bowl of cereal and sat down in front of the television to watch some crappy soap opera. The rain had started up again and the strong breeze whipped it against the glass. Thanks to the thick black clouds, it was going dark prematurely which increased the feeling of isolation and Carly started to wish that she had gone out with the family after all.

She jumped when there was a bang at the back door.

'No' again,' she gasped, her heart pounding with shock. It was a good job her cereal bowl was almost empty otherwise she might have catapulted the contents all over herself.

After placing the bowl on the table, she got to her feet and hesitated, wondering what she should do. Already she knew it wasn't a visitor. If it was, they would have knocked on the front door and not so aggressively. She'd promised her family to call them if anything happened but she didn't want to jump to conclusions. For all she knew, it could be something innocent. First, she had to ascertain that it really was the intruder.

After retrieving her taser, pepper spray and baton from her bedroom, she turned off the lights and television and approached the kitchen window. Slowly she pulled aside the curtain and recoiled when she was confronted by a shadowy figure standing just on the other side of the glass instead of at the door as she'd expected.

Carly let the curtain drop and took several steps back, weapons ready as she expected the assailant to try and come in through the window. She held her breath, waiting for something to happen but the silence went on and on, stretching her taut nerves right along with it. For once, she didn't know what to do. Should she look again or call her family?

There was a bang at the front door, making her jump again. Anger surged through Carly. So they were playing that game again, were they? Well, this time she'd teach the sod a lesson.

She charged down the hallway towards the front door, taser at the ready.

'Take this you bastard,' she yelled as she flung open the front door.

'Jesus,' cried Jack.

He managed to throw himself aside as she pressed the trigger.

The barbs just missed him and went flying down the path that led up to the front door. They hit his car parked at the kerb and dropped to the ground.

'Oh, sorry,' said Carly.

'Are you just tasing everyone who comes to the door now?' he exclaimed.

'No, sorry. I thought it was the intruder. They were banging at the back door again.'

'What? I'll take a look.'

He charged into the flat and through to the kitchen, Carly following after closing and locking the front door. He tugged at the back door but it was locked.

'I'll open it,' said Carly, snatching up the key off the counter and unlocking the door.

Jack tore it open. 'Stay here and lock it behind me,' he said before dashing outside into the wind and rain.

Carly obeyed and rushed to the window, yanking back the curtain to peer out but she could see nothing.

As she wondered whether she should follow in case he needed help, Jack knocked at the front door and she let him in. He was soaking wet and shaking the rain from his short black hair.

'I couldn't see anyone,' he said, closing the front door and locking it behind him before following her through to the kitchen.

'God, this is driving me mad,' she sighed, placing the baton, pepper spray and taser on the dining table. 'Why does no one else see this creep?'

'He makes sure of it. Making you out to be crazy is a good way to isolate you.'

'I am not crazy.'

'I know that, even if you did just try to tase me.'

'Sorry, I shouldn't have done that. It's lucky you're fast. Oh,

God, I could have really hurt someone. What if it had been old Mrs Beig? I might have given her a heart attack.'

'Well it wasn't,' he said, gently taking her by the shoulders. 'Everything's okay. Are you hurt?'

'No, he didn't get near me.'

'That's a relief. It must have been terrifying for you.'

'You must be joking. It takes more than some prick playing pranks to scare me.'

He smiled at her fierce expression. 'Of course. What am I saying? Have you called your family?'

'No. I was about to when you turned up.'

'Well, you don't need to now. It seems safe. Did you get a better idea this time of who it was?'

'Unfortunately, no. I'm still clueless.'

'I'll find them and make them pay, I swear.'

'You won't need to because I'll do it myself.'

He smiled when she tilted back her head. 'I've absolutely no doubt. You don't know how to fail, Carly.'

'I wouldnae go that far. I'm a massive failure at relationships.'

'From what I remember, ours was pretty wonderful.'

They smiled at each other.

'Well,' said Jack, breaking the moment. 'I was going out for something to eat. I just wanted to stop by to see if you wouldn't change your mind about coming with me?'

'Actually, I think I will.'

'Really?' he beamed.

'Unless you were just being polite?'

'Course not. I'd love to have dinner with you.'

'Great. I'll go and get changed.'

Carly hurried into her bedroom, trying to dampen her own enthusiasm. It was just a meal, as friends. It didn't mean she was going to reconcile with him. She didn't know if she could overcome what he'd done in the past or even if she wanted to overcome it all.

She selected her outfit very carefully – black trousers and a pretty lilac top. Presentable but there was certainly nothing about it that would give him hope of anything sexual to follow. After applying a little make-up and brushing her hair, she returned to the kitchen.

'You look lovely,' he said. 'I mean, you always look lovely but you look especially lovely tonight.' He sighed and shook his head. 'Stop saying lovely, you wanker,' he told himself.

'I appreciate the compliment. So, where do you want to go?'

'I know a lovely five-star restaurant in the West End... Have I said something wrong?' he added when she shuddered.

'Posh restaurants remind me of Rod Tallan.' Jack's predecessor had attempted to rape her in the back room of an exclusive restaurant. Fortunately, Carly had managed to fight him off but the trauma still remained.

'Oh God, of course. Sorry, I should have thought.'

'It's okay but I really would prefer somewhere not posh.'

'Well, I do know a nice quiet little Italian bistro. It's family run and cosy.'

'Sounds perfect,' she said, smiling.

Jack drove them to the restaurant in the city centre in his old Ford Mondeo. He could have afforded a brand-new motor but he still had to look as though he was living within the means his parole officer thought he had.

As there was no parking outside the restaurant, he found a space a couple of streets away and Carly couldn't help but be pleased when he held an umbrella over her the entire walk there.

'It seems you've become a gentleman.'

'Don't tell anyone. It'll damage my reputation.'

They enjoyed a nice, intimate dinner together. The restaurant was warm and homely with friendly staff who appeared to genuinely enjoy their work. The food was delicious and they drank luscious Italian coffee instead of alcohol as Jack was driving and Carly didn't want to drink alone. Carly was pleased that he didn't want to discuss their relationship or the possibility of getting back together. They just talked and laughed.

When they'd finished their meal, Jack said he'd drive her home. After he'd paid, they left the restaurant together and began the walk back to the car. Jack offered Carly his arm and she took it.

'I really enjoyed that,' she said. 'Such nice people and their food is the best.'

'It certainly is,' replied Jack. 'I only discovered it a month ago and I've eaten there loads since. I'll have to be careful or I'll start piling on the pounds.'

'Naw, you look fitter than ever.'

'So you've been looking?' he asked with a twinkle in his eye.

Carly was glad it was dark because she blushed.

Suddenly as they rounded the corner onto a quieter street, two men jumped out at them, both holding knives.

'Gi'e us your fucking money,' growled the taller of the two. Their faces were obscured as their hoods were pulled up.

Jack frowned. 'You what?'

'Are you fucking deif? I said gi'e us your money.'

'Piss off. No,' he cried when the taller man pointed his knife at Carly.

'If you don't gi'e us what we want, we'll cut her.'

'I don't think so,' retorted Carly.

She punched the man in the wrist, causing him to cry out and drop the weapon, while simultaneously kicking him in the stomach. As he folded, she brought her knee up into his face, knocking him sideways. Jack jumped back when the second man swiped at him with his own knife in panic. The man staggered backwards when Jack's fist met his face. Carly had kicked her own opponent to the ground and punched him three times in the face before nudging his knife down the drain with the toe of her shoe. Jack did the same with his opponent's blade.

'What's going on out there?' called a voice from one of the upper tenement windows to their left. 'Eric, call the polis.'

Jack took Carly's hand. 'Let's get out of here.'

She nodded and they raced down the street together. Carly understood why he wanted to run. A man in his position could not afford to get caught up in a police investigation, even though they were the victims. Toni McVay would not appreciate that.

Jack and Carly hopped into the car, adrenaline pounding through them both. They stared at each other, breathing hard from the excitement and exertion before they locked in an embrace, frantically kissing. Jack's hand slid into her hair, sending tingles shooting down her spine, making her moan.

'Way-hey,' called a voice.

They looked out of the window to see three neds eagerly staring at them.

'Bastards,' muttered Jack, furious about the interruption.

'Never mind us, carry on,' called one of the neds while his friends made lewd gestures.

'We'd better get out of here,' said Carly, sinking back into her seat and pulling on her seatbelt. 'Just in case someone did call the polis.'

'Aye, you're right,' replied Jack, glaring at the neds, wondering if he could get away with running them over.

Jack drove them out of the city, being careful to stick to the speed limits, despite his eagerness to get away.

'Well, that was different,' laughed Carly once they'd left the city centre safely behind.

'I bet they weren't expecting to have the shit beaten out of them,' he said, grinning.

'The pricks deserved it. Hopefully it'll make them think twice about trying to mug people.'

'I doubt it. They're probably too thick to get the hint. You looked like you enjoyed yourself.'

'I could try denying that I enjoy a good fight but I know you wouldnae believe me.'

'You're right, I wouldn't.' His grin widened. 'I enjoyed it too.'

Their smiles faltered when they returned to Haghill and reality set in.

'I'll drop you off at home,' said Jack more sombrely, disappointed that their evening together was ending.

'Okay,' she sighed, the prospect of returning to the cold, lonely flat depressing. She wanted to spend more time with him. Best of all, when she'd kissed him earlier, she hadn't thought about him and Toni McVay together at all. She wanted to test if that had been because it had been in the heat of the moment or not. 'Actually, can I come back to yours for a drink? I'm having a nice time.'

'Absolutely you can,' he beamed. This was going better than he could ever have hoped.

'I want to make it clear that I'm no' coming back for sex, even though we kissed earlier. Just for a drink and to talk, that's all.'

'I understand.'

'I'm trusting you to continue to behave like a gentleman.'

'I'll do my best, that's all I can say.'

'I suppose that'll have to do.'

Jack parked outside his flat, got out of the car and rushed to open Carly's door for her while bowing low.

'All right, there's no need to take the piss,' she told him, although she was smiling as she said it.

They headed up to his flat and Jack went into the kitchen to pour them a glass of wine each. Carly sat on the couch in the living room and looked around with a smile as it struck her how much she'd missed the place. On the surface, the small flat was nothing special. It was a typical bachelor pad with its sagging couch, pile of CDs heaped in the corner, flat-screen television and the mess you'd expect from a man living alone but she'd enjoyed plenty of nice times here. When they'd had to hide their relationship from their families, this flat had been their sanctuary from the world, the one place where they could be a real couple and totally relax together.

'Here you go,' he said, handing her a glass of white wine. He placed the half empty bottle on the coffee table and took a seat on the couch beside her, cradling his own glass.

'Thanks,' she replied before taking a sip. 'My favourite.'

'I've always kept a bottle in, hoping one day you'd come back.'

'Remember, we're just friends.'

'I know,' he said, determined not to say or do anything that might drive her away. He realised this was his one chance to get her back. Carly Savage was not the sort of woman to give second chances, so he recognised that this must mean she still felt something for him.

'What would your family say if they knew you were here?' he asked her.

'I'm no' sure. They all respect you as a boss, they say you're really good at it.'

'They do?' he said, pleasantly surprised.

'Aye. You're a natural. I don't think they'd object. They've all been fighting your corner recently, especially Rose and Jennifer. They think I'm letting my pride get in the way of being happy.'

'And would being with me make you happy?'

'I don't know. Anyway, let's not talk about that now.'

Jack was disappointed but he nodded. Putting any pressure on her at all would be a big mistake but he knew if Carly didn't take him back then he'd be a bachelor for the rest of his life. No other woman could compare to her. Once again, she'd just proved that when she'd battered that idiot mugger.

'So, what do you want to talk about?' he said. 'Or would you like to watch a film? I downloaded a new action film. It's got lots of car chases in it, although none of them are as scary as your driving.'

'Cheeky sod,' she laughed. 'Go on, let's give it a go.'

Jack put on the film and they sank back into the couch together to watch, although he found it hard to concentrate on the film. He kept glancing sideways at her, unable to take his eyes off her. It was difficult to believe she was here. He wondered if he could get away with sliding his arm along the back of the couch and then around her shoulders, or if that would lead to a punch in the balls. Perhaps he should take her hand? God, he'd never felt less sure of himself in his life. Being the big man around here meant nothing when he was with Carly. She had the habit of stripping away all the trappings of power and influence and only leaving the bare bones of a man. That was probably why Rod Tallan had felt the need to possess and control her. He couldn't stand being left exposed and seen for what he really was.

The sound of her mobile phone ringing was so startling it almost made him physically jump.

'It's Jane,' she said before answering. 'Don't worry, I'm safe. I'm at Jack's,' she told her sister. Carly coloured slightly and glanced his way. 'I'm no' sure,' she slowly replied. 'Maybe.'

Jack was straining to listen to what Jane was saying while at the same time attempting to look like he was concentrating on the film. Unfortunately, although he could hear Jane's voice, he couldn't make out the words.

'Either way, I'm fine. Aye, see you later,' said Carly before hanging up. 'The family got worried when they returned to the flat and I wasn't there.'

'Do you have to go home?'

'No, course not. They know I'm safe here.'

'Why didn't you tell them about the intruder?'

'Because they'd insist on piling round to discuss it and I don't want that.'

Jack was pleased. That meant she wanted to be alone with him. 'Do you want a refill?' he asked when she finished her glass of wine.

She smiled. 'Aye, how no'?'

As he refilled her glass, his hand shook with tension and desire.

She frowned. 'Are you okay?'

'Yeah, why?'

'I've never seen your hand shake before.'

'Just nervous, I suppose.'

'Why are you nervous?'

'Because you're here.'

'Why would that make your hand shake?'

'I'm terrified of saying or doing something that will make you yell at me and run out of here.'

'You make me sound like some sort of ogre.'

'No, I don't mean that at all. I'm worried about me messing up, not you. The last thing I want is for you to leave after I've missed you for what seems like forever but is only two months. I want to keep you here and never let you go... Oh Christ,' he sighed when her eyes widened. 'Now I sound like some sort of psycho. I don't mean I want to keep you prisoner, I just...'

Carly's heart went out to him when his eyes flickered as he hunted around for the right words. Jack was a stallion in the sack but he'd never got the hang of romance.

'I love you, okay,' he continued. 'And I know I can never love another woman like I love you because there is no one else like you. Everything I've achieved has felt so bloody pointless without you.' He exhaled slowly with relief that he'd finally found the right words.

'I love you too, really I do,' she said gently, realising how much it was taking him to bear his heart. 'But I'm still not convinced we have a future together.'

'Let's not think about the future. Let's just think about this moment, the here and now and if that goes okay then we can think about the next moment and then the next one and then the next.'

'Actually, that does sound nice.'

'And in this moment, all I want to do is kiss you and hold you after driving myself crazy longing for it for weeks. I'm not talking about sex, not unless you're comfortable with that. I just want to be close to you again.'

Carly put her glass down on the coffee table. 'Okay.'

'Really?'

'Aye but we're taking it slowly.'

'I understand,' he said, also placing his glass on the table.

Jack slid his arm around her and she leaned into him, resting her head on his chest. They both stared at the television screen, a violent fight playing out, but neither of them saw it. Carly's eyes grew heavy with pleasure as Jack slid his fingers through her hair. She could hear his heart pounding in his chest. For his part, Jack could only think about her warmth pressed against him, the silkiness of her hair. Contentment filled him. Finally, he felt true peace.

When Carly looked up at him, their gazes locked, the film entirely forgotten. Slowly Jack lowered his head and gently brushed her lips with his own. When the kiss ended, Carly's eyes rolled open, her cheeks filling with colour.

Jack was startled when she kissed him hard, locking her arms around his neck and straddling him.

'I thought you wanted to take things slowly,' he murmured into her mouth, sliding his hands up her back.

'I didn't want to,' she replied between kisses. 'I just thought it would be sensible, but I want you so much.'

He was delighted when she tore open his shirt, revealing the grinning devil tattoo on his chest. Carly's look was fierce as she ran her fingers across that tattoo. Jack exhaled shakily as her hand moved lower, caressing his stomach before sliding down to his crotch. She smiled, pleased with how hard he was.

Jack's shirt was yanked down his shoulders, pinning his arms to his sides. Carly's smile was sultry and wicked and it excited him unbearably.

'Do whatever you want to me,' he told her, his voice hoarse with desire. In that moment, he was her willing slave. No one else could have ever made him feel like that.

She pulled his shirt down lower and used it to tie his hands together behind his back.

'This is new,' he said.

After kissing a trail down his neck and chest, Carly got to her feet.

Jack's smile dropped. For one horrible moment, he thought she was going to walk out and leave him, that she didn't really want him and it was all some horrible joke. He was both relieved and excited when she pulled her top off over her head. Her shoes and trousers followed suit, her movements enticingly slow, until she was standing before him in just her underwear. He eagerly watched as her bra was slowly removed and cast to the floor. Only her panties remained.

'How much do you want me?' she said, standing before him proudly, a hand on her hip, chin tilted.

'More than anything I've ever wanted in my life,' he rasped, heart feeling like it was beating out of his chest.

She took a step closer and he leaned forward in an attempt to kiss that smooth, flat belly, which was level with his face but she stepped back again out of reach.

Carly smiled at his grunt of frustration. 'So I see.'

She moved closer and this time allowed him to kiss her belly. Her head fell back and she ran her fingers through his hair when he pressed his lips against her panties. As he attempted to pull them down with his teeth, she stepped out of reach again.

'I'll do that,' she told him before sliding the panties down her legs with excruciating slowness, loving the wildness in his eyes and the way he shifted with impatience.

Carly let the panties slide down her ankles and she elegantly kicked them off. She straddled Jack again and gave him a deep kiss as she unfastened his jeans and pulled down his underwear. He groaned loudly as she slowly bore down on him, their foreheads pressed together.

Carly wanted to continue moving slowly and sensuously but he felt too good and all too soon she was throwing back her head and moving faster, the pleasure quickly building inside her, crying out loud as he kissed her breasts, his hands still tightly bound behind him. She moved like a fury, taking him inside her again and again, her cries filling the air. Sex between them had always been passionate, even a little aggressive, but he'd never seen her give herself over so entirely to the act before and completely lose herself in the moment. Even Jack with his limited understanding of women realised that she was reclaiming him from Toni. This was something they needed to move through if they were to have any sort of future together. The pleasure was intense, more than it had ever been before and he fought with everything he had to contain it until she was ready.

With an almost primal cry, Carly flung back her head, her hair arcing through the air, hands pressing down on his thighs and finally Jack could give in to the intensity of the pleasure.

Carly collapsed forward onto him, breathing hard. She wanted to feel his arms around her and frowned when it didn't happen. Then she recalled that they were still trapped in his shirt. She sat up to free his hands before settling back into his chest.

'Bloody hell, that was incredible,' he panted, holding onto her tightly.

'It certainly was,' she replied with a satisfied smile.

He kissed her hair. 'You're amazing.'

'You're not so bad yourself.'

'Come back to me, babe,' he whispered in her ear before kissing it.

'Tempting but I'm still not sure.' Actually, she was 90 per cent sure she wanted him back, but she'd enjoyed teasing him so much she wanted to do it a little more.

'So stubborn,' he grunted.

'I cannae help it. It's who I am and what about taking it one moment at a time?'

'Well, I reckon we've just shared one incredible moment together, so it's time to move onto the next one and that's me and you getting back together. We both know this is where we belong.'

Carly's smile broadened but he couldn't see her reaction because her face was pressing against his chest. Jack took her silence to mean something different.

'Don't you agree?' he said.

'Maybe, maybe not.'

'I'm still inside you and you're giving me an answer like that?'

'Perhaps.'

Another grunt. 'I think you're still enjoying teasing me.'

'Guilty as charged,' she replied before sitting up so she could look into his eyes. 'All right, let's give it another go.'

'Yes,' he exclaimed. 'Thank you. You won't regret it, I promise.'

'But you've only got this chance. Blow it again and we're over for good. A couple of months ago I never thought I'd ever be saying this; you hurt me so badly but something inside you has changed. You've grown up a lot and I think that gives us a much better chance.'

He cupped her face in both hands. 'I won't let you down again, I swear. Without you, nothing mattered and it was fucking horrible.'

'You'd better not, because if you cheat on me again, I will kill you.'

'I love how you live up to your name, my little savage.' He smiled. 'I don't care who they are. Nothing and no one will make me bugger this up again, I promise,' he said softly, before kissing her. 'You're far too precious to me. I love you so much.'

'I love you too.'

They shared a deep kiss and smiled at each other.

'You've forgotten one thing,' he said.

'What?'

That dangerous look that always made her tingle filled his eyes.

'My hands are now free.'

She squealed with surprise when he flipped her onto her back in one deft movement, her thighs wrapping around his waist. Carly's cries of pleasure filled the air again as he made passionate love to her.

12

Carly woke up in Jack's bed with his warm body pressed against her own. She lay still with her eyes shut, trying to work out how she felt about the situation. It had occurred to her last night that she'd agreed too quickly to them getting back together and in the cold light of day she may regret her decision but she didn't experience anything like that. It just felt nice.

Opening her eyes, she saw he was lying on his side facing her, one arm around her waist. Love swelled inside her. Jack had been right. This was where she was meant to be. Already she knew she would have no regrets.

Part of her wanted to wake him so they could pick up where they'd left off last night, but the other part wanted to watch him sleep. Jack looked so peaceful, not an emotion he experienced often. Instead, she nestled into him and wrapped both arms around him.

'Morning, beautiful,' he murmured, eyes rolling open.

'Sorry, I didn't mean to disturb you.'

'Don't you worry about it. I don't want to waste time sleeping when you're lying here next to me, naked.' He went from sleepy to completely alert in an instant, rolling on top of her and kissing her.

'Do you have any plans today?' he asked her.

'You mean other than hanging around the flat, bored? Nope.'

'Good because I'm taking you out for the day.'

'What about your businesses?'

'David and Elijah can manage between them. I haven't had a day off since I started, so I'm due one.'

'I don't want to get in the way of your work.'

'You could never do that. I said you come first above everything and I meant it. I think it would be a good idea if we spent some time together outside Glasgow. How do you fancy a trip to Edinburgh?'

'I love Edinburgh,' she exclaimed.

'We can set off this morning, spend the whole day and stay the night at a nice hotel, all on me of course.'

'Sounds brilliant, especially if you're paying for everything,' she laughed.

'I want to spoil you rotten.'

'You need to be careful about how you splash the cash until your parole's over.'

'Toni's got that covered. She's put me on the books of one of her legitimate businesses, which is under the name of one of her legit puppets. My parole officer was really pleased I landed a job paying eleven hundred a month working in the warehouse of a timber merchants who are known for employing ex-cons. Are you okay?' he added when her forehead creased.

'I suppose it was the mention of Toni.'

'I won't mention her again,' he hastily said.

'No, it's okay. I actually quite like Toni and she didn't know we were an item.' Carly didn't add that Jack hadn't told her they were but then again, neither had she.

'She likes you too. She's got a lot of respect for your family.'

'And she's really never tried anything on again?'

'Nope. She just did it to seal the deal. She doesn't get involved with people she works with, so you can rest assured it won't happen again. I won't let it either.'

'God, I hope you mean that.'

He stroked her face with his fingertips. 'You're my girl, no one else.'

'I'd better be or you'll find yourself separated from your genitals.'

'It's weird how I actually enjoy being threatened by you.'

'Even though I mean it.'

'Especially because you mean it,' he said before kissing her.

Jack drove Carly back to her flat so she could pack a bag for their trip. Carly prayed the whole family wasn't gathered in the kitchen and it was a relief to find just her sisters and Jennifer.

'Oh aye.' Jennifer smiled, eyes flicking between Carly and Jack. 'What's all this then?'

'Are you back together?' said Rose eagerly.

'We are,' smiled Carly.

'Finally. I thought you'd never get round to it.'

'What do you all think?' said Carly, regarding Jane a little warily.

'Are you happy?' asked her older sister.

Carly took Jack's hand. 'Very.'

'Then that's all that matters.' Jane turned her stony glare on Jack. 'But if you hurt her again then it won't matter that you're my boss. You will suffer.'

'So Carly's already told me and I won't let her down,' he replied. 'This time, it's for keeps.'

'You'd better be telling the truth,' said Rose equally as coldly as her sister. 'I've always liked you but if you cheat on Carly again, I will twist your baws even harder than I twisted Ross's. I'll make sure you can never walk upright ever again.'

He nodded seriously. 'Understood and I won't hurt her again. You can count on it.'

'I hope so,' said Rose severely. 'For the sake of your baws.' She frowned at Jennifer when she sniggered.

'I don't think my tackle has ever been threatened so much,' said Jack. 'Not even in prison.'

'Jack's taking me to Edinburgh,' said Carly. 'We'll be spending the night there. I just need to change and pack a bag and we'll be off. Jane, can I borrow that light blue jacket of yours? It's too warm for my coat.'

'Course you can.'

'Where is it?'

Jane sensed her sister wanted to talk to her alone. 'At the back of my wardrobe. I'll dig it out for you.'

'Thanks.'

Carly followed Jane into her bedroom and shut the door behind them.

'I take it this is about more than my jacket?' said Jane.

'It is,' replied Carly, lowering her voice to a whisper, not wanting Rose to overhear and be worried. 'The intruder came to the flat again last night and began banging on the back door.'

'The bastard,' hissed Jane.

'Jack came to the front door at the same time. I nearly hit him with my taser because when he knocked, I thought it was the intruder. He took a look but he must have scared them off because he couldn't see anyone.'

'Jack turned up at the same time as the intruder?'

Carly nodded.

'Have you considered that they might be one and the same person?'

'No way. It wasn't him.'

'How can you be so sure?'

'It was chucking it down at the time. Jack would have been soaked if he'd been lurking in the back garden all that time but he was only slightly damp after walking from his car to the front door. Besides, the intruder was dressed in a thick black jumper and black trousers. Jack was wearing his leather jacket and jeans.'

'He could have come around to the front, pulled off the jumper and trousers, thrown them into the boot of his car and pulled on his leather jacket.'

'If that was true he would have been left in his boxer shorts,' said Carly snippily, folding her arms across her chest. 'It wasn't him.'

'He could have paid someone to do it.'

'I know it in my heart. Don't raise your eyebrow at me,' she snapped.

'This isn't what you want to hear, I get that, but you have to bear it in mind and I would be letting you down if I didn't point it out to you. You'd do the same if our positions were reversed,' she added when Carly continued to regard her indignantly.

'Fine. Noted,' she said coldly.

Jane sighed and shook her head before opening her wardrobe and delving inside. 'I hope you know what you're doing?'

'I do, thank you very much. I just wanted to tell you so you can make sure Rose isn't left alone here at night, in case the prick comes back.'

'Don't worry, I'll make sure she's safe. Here it is,' Jane added, plucking the coat from the back of the wardrobe and holding it out to her.

* * *

After waving off Jack and Carly on their trip and Rose had left with her best friend, Tamara, Jane called her uncle and cousins and told them they needed a meeting. The three men gathered around the kitchen table in the flat with Jane and Jennifer.

'Has something else happened?' said Eddie.

'Aye, it has,' replied Jane. 'The intruder came back last night when Carly was alone.'

'What?' he exclaimed. 'Why didnae she call us?'

Jane told them everything, watching Dean particularly closely as she explained about Carly and Jack's reconciliation. There was no tightening of his jaw, nothing to indicate that the news angered him and she'd got pretty good at reading his moods. He just listened with concern.

'I knew that would happen,' said Harry. 'They've been pining for each other ever since they broke up.'

'What I'm wondering,' said Jane. 'Is whether Jack turning up just at that moment was more than a coincidence.'

'You mean he was the intruder?'

'Or he got someone to do it so he could charge in like her knight in shining armour.'

'Carly doesn't need a knight in shining armour,' replied Dean. 'If one did charge through the door, she'd stick the heid on him.'

Harry snorted with laughter.

'None of us can argue with that,' said Eddie. 'And Jack must know that. Scaring Carly wouldnae work. She's too stubborn.'

'Anyway,' said Jane. 'If that was his plan then it worked because they're currently loved up in Edinburgh. Carly won't even consider the possibility that he's behind it but I think we'd be failing her if we didn't take the opportunity to find out what we can while they're away.'

'Okay, that's fair,' said Eddie. 'But Jack can't find out what we're up to.'

'How do we go about it?' said Harry. 'Because if we start asking questions, there's a hundred gobby bastards around here who'll run to him telling tales hoping for a pay-out.'

'We take a leaf out of the polis's book,' said Dean.

Harry looked disgusted. 'I'm gonnae pretend you didn't say that.'

'There are a few people on this street with security cameras and doorbell cameras. We'll say some wee ned was throwing stones at the window and we want to gi'e them a telling. Hopefully we'll find the intruder on that footage.'

'That's a good idea,' said Jane. 'It's certainly a start anyway. Hopefully we can at least rule out Jack, then we'll know Carly's totally safe with him.'

* * *

Carly hadn't felt this good in a long time. She was wrapped in a complimentary fluffy white bathrobe, reclining on a huge four-poster bed in the suite of one of the most luxurious hotels in the city, sipping fancy French white wine. Beside her was Jack in his matching bathrobe, his free arm wrapped around her shoulders while he enjoyed an expensive brandy. It felt wrong to be this happy when she'd only laid her father to rest a few days ago but he was the one who'd told her to seize the day, so she thought he would approve.

'This is the life, isn't it, babe?' Jack smiled. 'You should only have the best and finally I can give it to you.'

'I'm with you for you, no' for what I can get out of you. I was happy when you were just living off benefits.'

'Which makes you unique. I kept getting hit on by gold-digging tarts who couldn't care less about me.' He shuddered. 'They were horrible. You're more woman than the lot of them put together.'

She smiled. 'There were that many of them, were there?'

'There were a few but don't worry, I didn't touch any of them. I do have standards.' He ran his fingers through her hair. 'High standards, actually. Right, get dressed because we're going out for dinner.'

'Into the Old Town?'

'If you like.' He smiled, pleased with her enthusiasm.

'I love the Old Town with all its gothic architecture.'

'And you never know, we might find a quiet wee wynd we can sneak down together.'

'You've a one-track mind. I don't want to eat anywhere fancy though. Just somewhere relaxed.'

Her nervous expression made him a little sad. Rod bloody Tallan had certainly done a number on her. 'You know I'd never do to you what he did.'

'I do. I've just been put off posh restaurants for life. Besides, I don't like places like that. I cannae relax in them.'

'Okay, we'll find a nice, casual place to eat and have a few drinks.'

'Sounds good. I don't get to Edinburgh often, so I want to make the most of it.'

'We can come here as often as you like now.'

'You shouldn't make promises like that. I know you're a very busy man.'

'True but David and Elijah can be trusted to run things when I want to take time off.'

'They're such opposites. How do they get on working together?'

'Pretty well, actually. David's more thoughtful, not as quick to anger, while Elijah knows when it's necessary to get heavy. Both are very intelligent and can be relied on not to fuck things up in my absence.'

'Do they get along? I would have thought having two lieutenants might make things complicated.'

'I didn't think you wanted to know about all that?' he smiled.

'I cannae help being curious.'

'There's always a spot for you if you ever change your mind, although now that we're seeing each other again, I admit I would be worried if you were doing something dangerous.'

'Don't worry, I'm happy working at Death Loves Company.'

'That's probably for the best. It is a lot safer. Don't scowl at me, Carly. I love you and I don't want you putting yourself in any danger. I know more than anyone that you can handle yourself.'

'Fair enough.' Carly unfastened the tie on his dressing gown and spread it open, exposing that gorgeous body and all the tattoos, a Spartan warrior on his left arm and a Viking berserker on the right. 'But let's play some more before we go out.'

'I hope Carly and Jack are getting along okay,' said Jane anxiously. She and Jennifer were heading to a neighbour's house on the next street as they had a CCTV camera that looked out over the alley that ran behind the block of flats where the Savage sisters lived. 'What if it doesn't work out and she's stuck there alone?'

'Edinburgh's only an hour from here. She can easily make her way back.'

'But she's left her car here and the buses and trains don't run all night.'

'She's smart and tough, she'll be fine. Anyway, I don't think they will fall out. They looked really loved-up earlier.'

'I know but I'm worried. I'd feel much better if we could confirm that Jack isn't behind this intruder business.'

'Hopefully we can do that now.'

'I'm so worried she's just made the biggest mistake of her life.'

'Or she's just made the best decision.'

'I didn't think you were so up on Jack Alexander,' frowned Jane.

'I'm not but I am up on Carly being happy.'

'Perhaps you're right. Anyway, here we are.'

The owners of the house were a pleasant couple in their late fifties called Alan and Rachel Cunningham. They'd known the Savage family for many years and were on good terms with them, so they happily invited Jennifer and Jane in.

'This is going to sound like a weird request,' opened Jane. 'But we know you have a CCTV camera out back and we wondered if we could take a look at the footage from last night?'

The Cunninghams knew what sort of business the Savages were involved in, so they didn't ask any questions. Jane didn't even have to roll out the story about the neds throwing stones. Instead, Rachel brought up the footage on her laptop, placed it on the kitchen table and she and her husband quietly left them to it.

Jane and Jennifer sat down together at the table to watch. On the screen they saw a figure clad in black head down the back street and scramble over the wall leading into the garden behind the Savages' flat. There was the vague sound of a few bangs and the figure scrambled back over a few minutes later before vanishing off screen, heading in the direction they'd come.

'Well that told us nothing,' said Jennifer. 'I cannae even tell if they're male or female.'

'Let's look at the first night they attacked the flat,' replied Jane.

An identical figure did the same – scrambled over the back wall into the garden and emerged a few minutes later. The only difference this time was that the figure was quickly followed by a furious Carly who tore down the back street after them.

'Jeezo, look at her go.' Jennifer grinned. 'The lassie's got a huge set of baws on her. There's no' many people who would have done that.'

'It was reckless. Anything could have happened. She had no idea who she was dealing with.'

'Aye but it was really brave. Carly was always going to end up with someone like Jack. Do you think a lassie who can tear outside after an intruder like that could ever settle with someone dull and ordinary?'

'No, I suppose not, although I had hoped she would when she went legitimate.'

'That won't last either.'

'You're right. I think the only person who doesn't realise it yet is Carly. Being with Jack will drag her back into the life, she must know that.'

13

Jane and Jennifer managed to track the intruder through various neighbours' CCTV footage as they headed away from the Savage flat.

'I'm pretty sure now that it's a man,' said Jane as they looked at their fourth piece of footage.

'Aye, they don't move like a woman but it's so hard to tell how big they are,' replied Jennifer. 'They're not enormous but they're no' wee, so that doesn't help much.'

The figure vanished off screen with such swiftness they were both startled.

'Where the hell did he go?' said Jennifer.

'Let's rewind it.'

'There, look. He ducks down the alley that runs between a block of flats and the Stewart brothers' garage.'

Jane's eyes narrowed. 'The same garage where Ross and Dominic used to work.'

'But we were certain that Dominic was telling the truth.'

'The worm could just be a good liar. The intruder must have

taken the short cut down the alley. I bet he comes out the other side.'

They knocked on the door of a house that faced the opposite end of the alley and which had a doorbell camera. The footage told them the intruder never emerged from that alleyway.

'They must have gone into the garage,' said Jane. 'There's no door into the flats on that side of the building.'

'Why don't we go and check it out?'

'Aye, okay. I'll call Uncle Eddie and get him to meet us there.'

She phoned her uncle, who told them not to go near the place alone and to meet him outside the pub instead. It wasn't far from the garage and they could walk there together.

Eddie was already waiting for the two women with his sons and the five of them hurried through the darkened streets to the garage. He told Harry and Jane to wait at the mouth of the alley to keep a lookout while he went to investigate with Jennifer and Dean.

'Look,' said Jennifer excitedly. 'There's a wee door at the side of the garage. Why have I never noticed it before?'

'The door looks brand new,' said Eddie. 'I reckon this entrance has only recently been installed.'

'Jane can break in. She's done it before.'

'No. I noticed they've got a new alarm on the building, probably because Jane broke in before. We cannae risk involving the polis in this.'

'It's possible the intruder lives in the flats next door and is nothing to do with the garage,' said Dean. 'We cannae just make assumptions. That could be dangerous for Carly.'

'Aye, you're right, son. Let's discuss it with Jane and Harry.'

They exited the alley to find Harry was alone.

'Where's Jane?' demanded Eddie.

'A pal of hers came out of the flats, so she's gone in to talk to her,' he replied.

'She shouldnae have left you on your own.'

'Why? I'm no' simple. I can be left alone,' he sniffed.

'I mean because anyone could have snuck up on you.'

'We've seen no one, apart from Jane's pal. How did you get on down there?'

'We found a side door into the garage that wasnae there before.'

'Intriguing. Are we breaking it down?'

'No we are not and we need to find Jane. That's more important.'

They headed inside the block of flats.

'Which flat is she in?' Eddie asked Harry.

'Number six on the first floor.'

They hurried up the stairs and Eddie banged on the door. When no one answered, he knocked again.

'I don't like this,' he said when there was still no response. He tried turning the handle but the door was locked. 'Are you sure you've got the right number?' he asked Harry.

'Aye, that's what she told me.'

'Who does she know in here?' Eddie asked Jennifer.

'I don't know,' she replied, looking worried.

'Let's break down the door,' said Harry.

'Good idea, go ahead.'

He put his foot to the door. There was a crack and it swung open.

'Jane,' cried Jennifer, rushing in first.

'No, hen,' exclaimed Eddie but she was too fast and he was unable to stop her.

'Jane,' repeated Jennifer as the three men followed her inside. She peered into the first doorway, which was a small kitchen. No one was there. She continued rushing through the poky, cluttered flat but found no one. It felt like the occupant had just left, as though they'd missed them by just a minute.

'I'll try calling her,' said Jennifer, taking out her phone and dialling Jane's number. 'She's not answering. Where is she?' she cried, on the verge of panic. She pointed a digit at Harry. 'You should have stayed with her. Why did you let her go off alone?'

'This isnae my fault,' he retorted. 'I told her to wait until you lot came back but she refused and I didnae want to go as I was keeping lookout. I'm only one man, for Christ's sake. I can't split myself in two.'

'This isnae your fault, son,' said Eddie. 'You're right, Jane should have waited for us to come back. You cannae blame him for this, Jen.'

'I know,' she rasped, tears filling her eyes. 'I'm sorry, Harry. I'm just so worried about her.'

'It's okay,' he replied, patting her shoulder. 'Me too.'

'Let's check the rest of the flats,' said Dean.

'But we stick together,' said Eddie as they rushed back out into the hallway. 'I'm no' losing anyone else.'

They knocked on the doors of the other two flats on that level. When they were opened by the occupants, they charged inside calling Jane's name but no one had seen her.

'Jane,' yelled Jennifer as they rushed up to the second floor, Eddie puffing and panting his way up behind them.

'I'm here,' they heard her call back.

They emerged on the first floor to find Jane exiting one of the flats. Jennifer flung her arms around her.

'Thank God,' she breathed. 'We've been so worried.'

'You should have told me you were coming up here,' said Harry. 'We've been running around like arseholes, barging into people's flats looking for you.'

'Sorry, Emily said it would only take a minute.'

'Emily?'

Jane nodded at the elderly woman who emerged from the flat behind her. The woman's skin was very pale and transparent, the blue eyes that looked back at them bright and twinkly.

'She's a good friend of Mary McCulloch's,' continued Jane. 'Her bedroom window overlooks the Stewarts' garage and she's seen some very interesting things. Emily's friend Jemima lives in this flat. It's directly above her own and Jemima's seen some interesting things too.'

'Have you, doll?' said Eddie, addressing Emily directly.

'Aye, I have,' she replied, in a thin, croaky voice. 'Do you want to see?'

'I'd love to.'

As they entered the flat, Jennifer took Jane's hand. 'Don't ever scare me like that again,' she told her.

'Sorry, I didn't think it would take that long. Emily had quite a lot to tell.' Jane kissed her. 'I'll make it up to you later.'

The two women followed the others into the flat where a second elderly woman waited. She was a lot more robust looking than Emily with stout calves encased in thick tights, her feet stuffed into furry slippers.

'Looks like we've got the entire clan.' She smiled, hands on her square hips. Her voice was deep and loud. She gave the impression of the headmistress of a girls' school. 'Come away through and I'll explain.'

They all gathered in the cramped bedroom to peer out of the window into the garage below.

'During the day, it's just the normal activities you'd expect to see in any garage,' announced Jemima, sounding like she was giving a lecture to her pupils. 'But at night, things take a very different turn. There are shadowy figures coming and going at all hours. I can hear whenever they come because that side door into the garage squeaks. I struggle sleeping because of my bad hip and I'll sit in the dark, watching them going about their dirty business. They've no idea I've been spying on them,' she said proudly.

'Has that door always been there?' said Eddie.

'No. It was only installed about a month ago.'

'What have these shadowy figures been doing?'

'Sometimes they pile into the office. I assume they're having a meeting and they'll leave the light on. Other times they drop off packages before leaving straight away.'

'Packages?'

'Aye. Don't ask me what's in them because I don't know.'

'Have you ever recognised any of these people?'

'No. My eyes aren't what they used to be. I can't say exactly what they're up to. All I know is that it's something nasty and I'll tell you something else – they all know the code to the alarm system. Nothing happens until around midnight. Auld Mr McWhirter lives in the flat above this. The poor soul is really bad with his knees. The council should get him into a ground-floor flat, it's scandalous. Anyway, he's seen a lot of strange stuff going on in the garage too.'

'Can he identify the shadowy people who turn up?' said Eddie.

'He recognised one of them.'

They all waited expectantly when she went silent, looking very pleased with herself.

'Who was it, doll?' pressed Eddie.

'A woman. Jessica Alexander.'

* * *

'I knew that bitch must be involved,' seethed Jane as they stormed out of the block of flats after bidding goodbye to Jemima and Emily.

Before leaving, Eddie had called out an all-night locksmith to repair the broken lock on Emily's front door and given her a wad of cash to cover the bill.

'I bet Jessica's the mastermind of whatever's going on,' continued Jane. 'The scheming cow would never be content with being cut off from all the money her sons were earning.'

'Let's go and make her tell us what's going on,' said Jennifer determinedly.

'Just calm down,' Eddie told them. 'Let's no' rush in. We need to think about how we're gonnae tackle her first.'

'What's to think about?' said Jane. 'It's no' like she can stand up to us.'

'But she is Jack's cousin. We have to tell him what we've found out first.'

'Da's right,' said Dean. 'Only Carly could get away with making her talk and she's no' here.'

'But they won't be back from Edinburgh until tomorrow,' said Jane. 'Anything could happen in that time. For all we know, Jessica's planning a coup to take over from Jack. I bet Cole's in on it too. He's only pretending to be on Jack's side.'

'Maybe or it could be something else altogether.'

'Doubtful. We tracked the intruder to that garage.'

'It's still no' enough proof to go after Jack's own cousin,' said Eddie. 'But there's nothing to stop us approaching the Stewart brothers. They aren't related to Jack and they're certainly no' friends of his.'

Jane smiled. 'That is a very good idea.'

'Anyone know where we can find them?'

'They're probably in The Wheatsheaf,' replied Jennifer, referring to The Horseshoe Bar's nearest rival, which was frequented by the Alexander family.

'We don't want to risk tackling them there and word getting back to the Alexanders,' said Eddie.

'I know where Freddy Stewart lives but his wife and weans will be there.'

'We don't want to speak to him in front of them either.'

'Belinda won't let him smoke in the house, so he has to go outside when he wants a ciggie, which he does a lot.'

Eddie smiled. 'Perfect.'

14

'Freddy.' His wife's shrill voice echoed after him as he hurried to the front door. 'The cludgie's blocked again.'

'It'll have to wait, I'm going for a smoke,' he snapped back.

'But wee Johnnie wants to go.'

'Wee Johnnie will have to tie a knot in it,' he snarled before storming outside and slamming the front door shut behind him. *Wee* Johnnie was an appropriate name for his second youngest son who had a bladder the size of a teabag. It was his fault the toilet kept getting blocked because he always stuffed half a bloody bog roll down it each time he went.

'The bastard's costing me a fortune in plungers and toilet roll,' Freddy muttered to himself as he lit a cigarette. He drew in a lungful of smoke and tilted his head back as he exhaled, feeling his nerves start to unwind again. With four children, his small three bed home always felt cramped and chaotic. These brief but frequent forays outside with his cigarettes gave him a much-needed break from it all. Belinda was always nagging him to quit, saying she was worried about his health but if he was dead at least he would get some bloody peace.

Freddy gazed up at the night sky. Only the moon and Sirius were visible because of the light pollution. One of his dreams was to visit a place where the night sky was full of stars, where the reality wasn't masked by the pollution of the human race.

His thoughts were interrupted by footsteps. He turned to see Jane Savage heading towards him looking pissed off, accompanied by her girlfriend, Jennifer, who looked equally menacing.

More footsteps caused him to turn the other way and he saw Eddie Savage and his two sons approaching. If he hadn't suffered with arthritis in his back, Freddy would have considered making a run for it but knew they'd easily catch him and he'd lose all dignity. All he could do was hope to talk his way out of whatever trouble he was in.

'Evening.' Freddy smiled, hoping they weren't here for him and were just passing through. To his chagrin, they formed a semi-circle before him.

'Something wrong?' he said, attempting to sound friendly and relaxed but his voice trembled slightly with nerves.

'Aye there is,' said Eddie. 'Mainly with your garage.'

'What's wrong with my garage? We've no' had any of your motors through, so I don't know what you've got to complain about.'

'I'd rather let a rabid monkey with a chainsaw have a go at my car than any member of your family and I'm no' talking about that side of the business. I want to know what's going on there at night?'

'Night?' said Freddy, feigning innocence. 'Nothing. It's closed at night.'

'No' according to what we've heard. People have been coming and going, getting up to all sorts of shady shit. As you're one of the owners of the garage, you must know what they're doing.'

'Well, I don't. I'm always here at night. If something is going on at the garage, then it's nothing to do with me.'

'If that's true then how come the intruders know the code to your fancy new alarm system.'

Freddy's eyes widened with panic. 'I...'

'You're coming with us right now and you're taking us into the garage.'

'Wait, no, I...'

'Freddy, come and unblock the cludgie, for Christ's sake, you lazy, useless arsehole,' screeched Belinda from inside the house. 'Johnnie's gonnae piss himself.'

'Grab him, boys,' Eddie told his sons.

Harry and Dean took one of Freddy's arms each and propelled him down the street. Eddie, Jane and Jennifer followed.

'Don't be so rough,' exclaimed Freddy as they turned the corner. 'You're hurting my back.'

'Stop struggling and it'll stop hurting,' growled Dean.

Freddy forced his body to relax and some of the pain eased. 'I'm gonnae be sore in the morning. I hope you're happy with yourselves?'

'We're fucking delighted,' said Harry, rolling his eyes.

Eddie glanced at his watch. 'It's no' far off midnight. I wonder if anyone's gonnae be at your garage?'

'Of course they're no',' retorted Freddy. 'You're all aff your heids.'

'You'd better hope for your sake that you're right.'

It was only a few minutes' walk to the garage and they arrived to find it was quiet, the gate and side door still closed and locked.

'Told you so,' said Freddy smugly.

'Why did you have that side door installed?' Eddie demanded of him.

'Side door?' he said innocently.

'Aye? Why would you need that? It's just another way for someone to break in, unless you wanted an entrance that wasn't visible from the main street.'

'Dunno.'

'Dean.'

Freddy yelped with pain when Dean twisted his arm, forcing him forward.

'My back,' cried Freddy. 'My fucking back.'

'We don't gi'e a shite about your bloody back,' said Eddie. 'And the pain will only stop when you start telling us the truth.'

'Malcolm's arranged it all, no' me,' he cried.

'Your brother?'

'Aye.'

'Why would he do that?'

'I don't know, I swear to God.'

'People have been seen carrying packages in and out. Who are they and what's in those packages?'

'I'll talk, I'll talk, just please let me stand up straight. I cannae take the pain.'

Dean looked questioningly at his father, who nodded, so he released him. Freddy slowly straightened up, a hand to his lower back.

'I don't know what's in them,' he sighed, exhausted, scared and in pain. 'All I know is that it's been set up by Jack Alexander.'

'Jack?' Eddie frowned. 'Bollocks.'

'That's what his cousin Jessica told me. She's working for him.'

'Doing what?'

'I don't know and neither does my brother. They're just paying for the use of our premises.'

'Who pays you?'

'Jessica. She told us the money was from Jack.'

'How much?'

'A grand a week. Jack's the one who arranged for the door to be built in, no' us.'

'Why?'

'Nae idea. Me and my brother don't use it, we only use the main gate. We just let them use our garage at night and we're never here when they are.'

'Have you ever seen Jack at your garage personally?' Jane asked Freddy.

'Well, no, but Jessica's often mentioned his name. I just assumed it was some sort of sideline he was running that he didnae want Toni McVay to find out about. Jessica said we'd all lose our eyeballs if we breathed a word. Oh God, I told and now I'm gonnae be blinded and my eyeballs carried around in a glasses case,' he wailed.

'If you don't keep the bloody noise down,' Eddie told him. 'I'll scoop out your eyeballs myself.'

This threat caused Freddy to go abruptly silent.

'I thought Jack would be too smart to go behind Toni's back,' said Jennifer.

'Aye, he is,' replied Eddie. 'I reckon Jessica's behind this, no' him.'

'We can't know that for sure,' replied Dean. 'Especially after the last stunt he pulled.'

'I think it's important that we don't assume anything either way,' said Harry. 'We really don't know what's going on.'

'A very wise thing to say, son,' said Eddie. 'We make no assumptions,' he told the others. 'We don't know what those packages contain or what's going on.' He looked to Freddy. 'You can bugger off now and don't breathe a word of this to anyone, no' even your brother.'

'Like I'd dae that,' he replied. 'I don't want to be in the Alexander family's bad books.'

'Well you're already in ours, so just watch yourself, okay? One wrong move and we'll ensure that every part of your body hurts for the rest of your miserable life.'

'I understand,' he said before frantically hobbling away.

Eddie glanced at the time on his phone. 'It's nearly the Witching Hour. We'd better get back up to Emily's flat.'

They hurried back into the block of flats. Emily opened the door to them and escorted them into her bedroom.

'It shouldn't be long,' said the old woman, switching off the light, plunging them into blackness. 'Although they don't come every night, so I hope you're no' wasting your time.'

'What if they do?' Dean asked his father.

'We just observe and take it from there.'

'Here they come,' said Emily excitedly.

Two dark figures flitted down the street together. They walked so casually Eddie assumed they weren't the people they were waiting for and were going to pass them by. However, they turned down the small alley beside the flats and walked straight to the side door into the garage.

'Can anyone tell who they are?' Eddie asked the room.

They all shook their heads.

'We could open the window a crack,' suggested Emily. 'We might be able to hear something that'll give us a clue.'

Eddie beamed down at her. 'You're enjoying this, aren't you, hen?'

'Aye I am. I love spy films – James Bond, Jason Bourne, the more violent the better. I don't like all the old black and white films my friends enjoy. I want action.'

Eddie was so surprised to hear this from such a frail, elderly lady that he just stared at her in surprise.

Dean opened the window a crack and they all strained to listen.

'Is one of them wearing high heels?' said Jennifer. 'I can hear a click clack.'

'You're right,' said Jane. 'I bet it's Jessica Alexander.'

One of the figures unlocked the side door and they stepped inside. While the one they suspected was Jessica closed the door, from their elevated position they could see the other sprint into the Portakabin that acted as an office and a few beeps followed.

'They're putting in the code to disable the alarm,' said Emily.

'You don't need to watch any films,' Eddie told her. 'You're a great spy yourself.'

'Thank you,' she twinkled back at him. 'You're no' so bad yourself.'

He did a double take when she gave him a distinctly flirtatious look. Eddie took a few steps to the right, placing Dean between Emily and himself.

'Shall we go down there?' Jane asked her uncle.

'No. We cannae risk it. Let's just watch.'

The second figure joined the first in the office.

'I wonder if they're waiting for someone else to turn up?' said Jennifer.

'At least we know they're no' waiting for Jack seeing as he's in Edinburgh with Carly,' replied Eddie.

Dean pointed to the office. 'I could sneak down there and listen in.'

'It'll be risky. What if they see you?'

'I'll make sure they don't.'

'I don't like it. It's too dangerous.'

'I'll be fine, I promise, Da'.'

'I'll go with you.' He frowned. 'Why are you pulling a face?'

'Nae offence but you're no' exactly stealthy. They'll hear you coming a mile off. Jennifer can come instead. She moves like a ninja.'

'Aye, all right but it looks like they're waiting for someone else to turn up, so wait until they've arrived.'

Dean nodded in understanding.

Five minutes later, another two shadowy figures appeared and entered the office.

'Right, that's your cue,' Eddie told Dean and Jennifer. 'And for Christ's sake, be careful. Jane, Harry, you go too but stay outside the garage in case they need help, then follow whoever comes out first.'

Anxiously he watched them go, praying they'd be all right.

'Aww, bless,' said Emily, placing a hand on his arm. 'I can see how worried you are.'

'I'm constantly terrified of sending them into a situation they cannae handle,' he replied.

'Don't be. They're all very tough. I'm sure they'll be able to deal with anything that comes their way.' Emily's hand slid up his shoulder and her fingers brushed his neck. When Eddie regarded her with surprise, she winked and nodded at the bed. 'Why don't you let me take your mind off it?'

'Err, thanks but... I have a girlfriend.' It was a lie but he was willing to say he was a eunuch if it made her back off.

'I won't tell,' she said with another wink.

When her hand slid down to his bottom, Eddie actually considered hurling himself out of the window.

'I need to concentrate on what's going on outside,' he said, moving away from her again.

'You'll give in to me one day,' she said. 'I may be an old woman now but in my younger days I was a right wee raver. Every man in Haghill wanted me.'

'Aye, I'll bet,' he mumbled, keeping watch at the window. He spied Dean and Jennifer sneaking into the garage, Harry and Jane crouched down by the wall outside it. Hopefully they'd find something that could tell them just what the hell was going on.

He sighed when a thin, frail arm slid around his waist.

'I do like a chunky monkey,' Emily twinkled at him. 'A woman needs something to hang onto.'

Eddie frowned. 'Chunky monkey?'

* * *

Dean waved at Jennifer to hide behind a car and keep watch while he approached the Portakabin. Keeping low, he quickly made his way across to the office and crouched down below the level of one of the windows to listen. One voice was definitely Jessica's. The other three were male and it was hard to discern who they belonged to. Someone who had lived in Haghill their entire life might have known. Still, he could hear exactly what they were discussing. He didn't dare look in through the window in case he was spotted.

'You dirty bastards,' he whispered to himself as he listened.

The meeting didn't last long. Within five minutes, it broke up and they all got to their feet. Dean turned and scurried back the way he'd come but he wasn't quick enough to reach the gate and he was forced to duck behind a Honda Civic as the office door opened, light pouring out onto the ground.

'Urgh,' said Jessica's imperious voice. 'This place is filthy. I always end up with grease on my boots.'

Dean peered around the car and saw Jennifer still crouched behind the Mercedes SUV he'd left her behind. When she looked at him questioningly, he indicated for her to remain where she was.

Two of the men said their goodnights and left the garage by the side door, leaving Jessica with the fourth man.

'I don't know why you hired Mason,' continued Jessica. 'He's a cretin.'

Dean attempted to see who she was speaking to but he couldn't without giving away his position. Frustratingly the only person he could see was Jessica.

'He has his good points,' replied the voice.

'I've never seen any, apart from that pretty face of his but he's as useful as a chocolate teapot.'

'I didnae want him, I wanted his brother. Unfortunately, they came as a package deal.'

'Emma and Karen would have been better.'

'I disagree. Karen's too quick to anger and Emma's lost her bottle since the Savages attacked her in her own home.'

Dean craned his neck a little further and finally saw the owner of that second voice.

There was a crash from the rear of the compound and Jessica and her companion went charging off in that direction to discover the source of the noise. Dean looked back at Jennifer and frantically waved, indicating for her to move while the going was good.

The two of them raced out of the garage. Harry and Jane weren't there, so they assumed they'd followed the two who'd already left.

'What was that crash?' Dean asked Jennifer as they ran back into the flats.

'I threw a wrench at a car window.'

'Genius,' he replied, making her smile.

Dean knocked before opening the door into Emily's flat so as not to startle the old lady. He frowned when he saw his father backed up against the wall, Emily attempting to put her arms around his neck.

'What's going on here?' he said.

Emily turned to him with a smile. 'Your father's very shy, isn't he?'

'Not normally,' he replied.

Eddie stepped out from behind Emily and hastened to his son's side. 'What did you find out?'

'Quite a lot actually,' he replied, looking suspiciously from his father to Emily and back again.

'Looks like they're leaving,' said Emily.

They gathered at the window to watch Jessica and the man exit the compound, the latter pausing to lock the side door behind them before they continued on down the street.

'That's our cue to leave too,' said Eddie, anxious to escape Emily and her octopus arms. 'We need to contact Jane and Harry, see what they've found out.' He turned to the old lady. 'Thanks so much for the use of your flat, doll. It's been very educational.'

'I intended it to be even more educational for you, sweetheart,' she replied with another lascivious wink. 'Come back and see me any time. I can show you things that would make your hair curl.'

'Let's go,' Eddie told Jennifer and Dean while backing up to the door. 'Quickly.'

They left the flat and hurried down the stairs.

'She really fancies you,' Jennifer told Eddie.

'It's no' her fault, it's my animal magnetism,' he called back over his shoulder. As he was leading the way he failed to see Dean and Jennifer's amused smiles.

Once they were outside, Eddie looked up and down the street.

'Let's go this way,' he said, indicating left, which was the opposite direction to which Jessica and her accomplice had gone. 'We don't want to risk bumping into them. Did you find out anything?'

'I did,' replied Dean. 'I snuck up to the office while Jennifer kept watch. Those packages contain weapons.'

'Really? I was expecting you to say drugs.'

'That's what I assumed it would be too. They're bloody armourers now.'

'Oh, Christ, that's all we need,' said Jennifer.

'What sort of weapons?' said Eddie. 'Please don't tell me guns?'

'I cannae say for sure but there was mention of Berettas.'

'Jack must be involved. He was the one who hooked up Cole and his brothers with guns before and they were Berettas.'

'But he took the firing pins out of them,' replied Jennifer. 'He knows those idiots shouldn't be allowed anywhere near guns, so why would he do this?'

'Like I said, I cannae be 100 per cent certain,' replied Dean. 'They used the word *weapon* more than anything else. They could be dealing in anything.'

'Maybe they managed to get hold of Jack's contact behind his back?' said Eddie.

'We have to face the fact that Jack could well be involved in this,' said Dean. 'I know he's a good boss but we'd be stupid if we didnae consider the possibility, especially as Elijah Samson was there.'

'What?' Eddie and Jennifer said in unison.

'Aye,' sighed Dean, looking troubled. 'One of the other two men looked familiar but I cannae mind who he was. I didnae recognise the fourth at all.'

'So none of Jessica's sons were there?' said Jennifer.

'Nope.'

'Then it's looking like they're not involved.'

'We cannae rule that out for certain yet,' said Eddie. 'Right, we need to meet back up with Harry and Jane, see what they found out. Perhaps they could gi'e us some of the answers we're missing.'

15

'You two first,' Eddie told Jane and Harry when they'd convened back at Eddie's house.

'One of the men we followed was Mason who seduced and tricked Rose,' said Jane, eyes flashing with anger. 'We tracked them to The Wheatsheaf. Naturally we couldn't go inside, so we waited for them to come out. They were only in there ten minutes. We think the second man was Mason's brother or a relative at least because there was a strong resemblance between them.'

'He's his brother,' said Dean. 'I overheard Jessica telling the others that Mason was useless and Elijah Samson said he only employed him because he really wanted his brother.'

Jane and Harry blinked at him. 'Elijah?' said the latter.

'Aye. I crept right up to the office and listened in. They're dealing in weapons.'

'Oh, great. That's just what this country needs – a bunch of inbred fannies giving every numpty in the city guns.'

'I didn't hear exactly what types of weapons but there was mention of Berettas.'

'Marvellous,' he sighed. 'Where the hell are they getting guns from?'

'Either Jack's involved and is using his own contact,' said Eddie. 'Or Elijah's running the whole show.'

'Which indicates Jack's involved,' said Jane.

'Or Elijah's set it up behind his back.'

'The question is what do we do about it?' said Jennifer. 'Do we approach Jack?'

'No,' said Eddie. 'No' until we've a better idea of what's going on. We need to keep digging, see what else we can find out because we've only just scratched the surface. This is a conspiracy and we cannae trust anyone but each other.'

'And Carly,' said Jane.

'Of course but we need to keep this from her. She's seeing Jack and if he is involved then we have to look out for her. If he isn't and we tell her before we've got all the facts, we could ruin their relationship. We tell no one else yet, okay?'

The other four nodded, looking solemn, faces tight with worry.

* * *

Carly was smiling as Jack drove them back to Haghill. They'd had such a lovely time in Edinburgh and she felt closer to him than ever.

'It feels wrong being this happy when my da's just died,' said Carly, the guilt settling in her heart again as they turned onto her street.

'I'm not a parent but I do know that your dad would have wanted you to be happy,' replied Jack. 'He wouldn't want you moping about.'

'That's true. All he ever wanted was for me and my sisters to be happy.'

'And you really are?'

'Absolutely,' she said, resting her hand on his thigh. 'I've had an amazing time.'

'Me too. I wish we could have stayed longer but I've got a meeting this afternoon.'

'It's okay, I understand. Maybe one day soon we can go away for a few days?'

'Sounds good. Where would you like to go?'

'I'm not bothered. It's just important that we're together.'

He parked the car outside her flat and turned to face her. 'In that case, shall I surprise you?'

She smiled. 'Yes please.'

He leaned into her. 'Now that I can do.'

They kissed passionately, unwilling to relinquish each other yet.

'I'll walk you to the door,' he said when the kiss eventually ended.

'You don't have to.'

'I'm taking no chances with this intruder about.'

They got out of the car together, holding hands as they walked up to the front door.

'Do you want to stay at mine tonight?' he asked her.

'You're not sick of me yet then?'

'That could never happen. I love you far too much.'

As they kissed again, the front door was pulled open by Harry. 'Oh, it's yourselves,' he said. 'I take it you had a good time in Edinburgh?'

'It was wonderful,' enthused Carly.

'Good.'

'Didn't you have a collection this morning?' Jack asked Harry.

'Aye and we've done it.'

'Any problems?'

'Naw, it went smoothly and we got the full amount.'

'Nice one.' Jack looked back at Carly. 'See you later, babe. I'll pick you up at seven, if that works for you?'

'It does. See you then.'

They shared another quick kiss, conscious of Harry still standing there. As Jack headed back to his car, Carly stepped into the flat and closed the door behind her.

'What?' she said when Harry grinned at her knowingly.

'You look a lot better.'

'I feel better. It's amazing the difference a change of scenery can make.'

'I don't think the scenery's responsible.'

'It is, but only a wee bit,' she said, smiling. 'What's going on, a family meeting?'

'Naw. We're just hanging out. We were about to make a cuppa, if you want one?'

'Please. I'll just dump my bag in my bedroom.'

Carly opened her bedroom door, chucked the bag inside and headed into the kitchen to find the family gathered there, including Rose.

'Wow, it looks like the operation to separate you from Noah was successful,' she told her younger sister.

Everyone was heartened by the sparkle in Carly's eyes. Even Dean smiled.

'Ha ha,' retorted Rose. 'I bet you and Jack end up the same way.'

'Perhaps,' Carly said, unable to repress a smile.

'How was Edinburgh?' said Jane as she prepared the mugs for the tea.

'Lovely,' she replied, sinking into a chair at the table. 'We stayed at a gorgeous hotel and found a fantastic little restaurant in the Old Town. I wish we could have stayed longer.'

'And you got on well?'

'Very. It was what we needed to clear the air and start our relationship up again on a stronger footing.' As she spoke, she glanced at Dean, wondering if he would be disapproving but he didn't appear at all angry or pissed off.

'That's good to hear,' said Eddie. 'So you're a definite item again?'

'We are. How have things been here? Have I missed anything?'

'No' really, just the usual stuff.'

'Right, I've got to get to college,' said Rose, picking up her backpack from beside the couch and slinging it over her shoulder.

'Do you want a lift?' Harry asked her.

'No thanks, it's not far and Noah's meeting me at the end of the street. We're walking together. He's so romantic,' she enthused before leaving.

Harry smiled. 'I wish all the women I knew were so easily pleased.'

'Just so you all know,' said Carly. 'I'm stopping at Jack's tonight, so we need to make sure Rose isnae left here alone.'

'I'll sort that out, don't worry about it,' Jane told her. 'Now then, we need to discuss this intruder.'

Carly's happy smile faltered. 'Do we have to?'

'Aye. The problem won't go away just because you had a nice time in Edinburgh. I think we should set a trap for them.'

'What sort of trap?'

'We want to arrange it so he actually comes into the house and we can all take him down.'

'Okay but we never know when he's gonnae turn up, so how do we manage it?'

'We'll just have to try the same thing each night until he does turn up.'

'Try what exactly?'

'We need to make it clear to the intruder that you're alone and vulnerable.'

'How do we do that?'

'Have you parading before the windows, probably in something skimpy and enticing.'

'I am not prancing about like that for hours.'

'We thought we'd go into the pub tonight and make it clear the rest of us are going on somewhere else, like a nightclub. You say loud enough for everyone to hear that you're no' in the mood and that you're going home. The intruder will know you're alone and strike.'

'What if the intruder's no' in the pub?'

'Then we'll think of something else.'

'No, sorry. It's way too vague. Anyway, Jack's picking me up at seven and I'm spending the night at his. He knows about the intruder, so he might be able to come up with something.'

'Okay but we'll try it tomorrow night if Jack doesn't have any better ideas.'

'Fine by me. Right, I'm going to call Briony. She's the one I left in charge of Death Loves Company. I want to make sure there haven't been any problems in my absence.'

The others didn't speak until she'd headed into her bedroom to make the call.

'Are you sure we shouldn't tell her what we've found out?' said Jane anxiously.

'Aye,' replied Eddie.

'If Jack is involved then she could get caught up in it too and if he's not that means people he thinks are allies are plotting against him. Either way, it puts her in danger. At least if she knows then she can be prepared.'

Eddie considered this statement. 'What do the rest of you think?' he said.

'I agree with Jane,' replied Jennifer. 'Her personal safety has got to be our priority over her new relationship.'

'But if she's put on her guard it might alert Jack to the fact that she knows something and that in itself could be dangerous,' said Dean.

'Actually, that's a good point,' replied Jennifer.

'I don't think we should tell her just yet,' said Harry. 'We don't have a definite picture. All we've got is spotting a few people walking about in the dark and Dean catching part of a conversation. If we tell her and we're wrong, we could cause her a lot of problems. Let's wait until we know for certain.'

'She finally looks genuinely happy again,' said Dean softly. 'Let's no' spoil that for her.'

'Aye, okay,' said Eddie. 'We'll find out what's going on properly first, then we'll tell the lassie.'

* * *

Carly lay curled up in Jack's arms on the couch in his flat that evening, wondering how she'd thought she could live without him. Things had changed so quickly and if she was honest with herself, her head was still spinning. Life was good at delivering relentless body blows and just when you thought you couldn't take another hit, it turned around and gave you something wonderful.

'Do you want a glass of wine?' Jack asked her.

'No, thanks. I could go a brew though.'

'Coming right up.'

He kissed her, got to his feet and headed into the kitchen. Carly settled into the warm spot he'd left on the couch, eyes growing heavy with contentment as she stared at the television, listening to the sound of Jack moving about in the kitchen, whistling happily to himself.

Carly sat bolt upright when there was a loud thud at the front door, which shook in its frame, so hard was the blow.

'Babe, are you okay?' said Jack, rushing back into the room.

'Someone's at the door,' she replied.

There was another enormous bang and Jack whipped round to face the door. He peered through the spyhole.

'There are four men out there,' he whispered to Carly.

'Who are they?' she whispered back.

'I don't recognise them.'

'What do we do?'

Before he could reply, one of the men yelled through the door, 'We know you're in there, Jack. Open up or we'll break it down.'

'Who the fuck are you?' he called back.

'We'll tell you when you let us in.'

'Piss off, you're not coming in.'

Carly held up her phone. 'Shall I call my family?' she whispered.

Jack nodded and she immediately began dialling.

'What do you want?' Jack called through the door, hoping to stall them.

'To talk.'

'About what?'

'I'm no' shouting it through the door.'

'Then you're not getting in.'

'You may as well open up because if you don't, we'll just break the fucking thing down.'

'Go for it, prick,' retorted Jack.

The man continued to spit more threats at him through the door but Jack didn't respond. He rushed to the cupboard in the hallway leading to the bedrooms and produced two baseball bats before hurrying back into the living room and handing one to Carly.

'I've called Uncle Eddie,' she whispered. 'They're on their way.'

'Nice one but that lot will break down the door before they get here. I can see four men but there may be more.'

'We can take them,' she said, making him smile. 'I've got an idea.'

Dumping the bat on the couch, Carly rushed into the kitchen and returned holding a can of bug spray, as well as a bottle of cooking oil. She handed the spray to Jack and tipped the oil onto the wooden floor before the door.

'Clever,' he said.

'This is your territory. They've nae idea what they're walking into. We have to take advantage of that.'

Jack wrapped an arm around her waist and yanked her close. 'You see, this is why I love you.'

They kissed hard before releasing each other when the banging on the door started up again with renewed violence. The intruders had done talking. This time they were knocking it down.

Jack indicated for Carly to stand behind the door so she wouldn't be seen when it was kicked in and she was careful to place herself so she wouldn't be hit by it. Jack held the bat in one hand and the can of bug spray in the other, watching the door start to crack. With one last bang, it was slammed open and the burly, bearded man he'd seen through the spyhole charged in. The man shrieked when he got a face full of bug spray. Unable to see, he slipped in the cooking oil and crashed to the floor. The second man ran in and ducked, avoiding the cloud of spray but he got a baseball bat in the stomach from Jack. His trainers slipped in the oil with a squeak and he hit the floor hard, landing beside his friend.

It was only then Jack saw there were in fact seven men altogether, not the four he'd initially thought. A third man leapt over his friends, avoiding Jack and the cooking oil but he'd failed to realise Carly was there, who slammed her bat into his back. With a pained cry, he was sent toppling forward over the couch. Determined not to give him time to get up, Carly pursued him, hitting him in the ribs and crotch with the bat, ensuring he stayed down. Three were down but there were four still to deal with and these men were sensible enough to have their own weapons ready.

Jack staggered backwards as he avoided a swipe with a crowbar but his attacker slipped in the oil and down he went. While Jack began to tussle with another intruder, Carly made swift work of the man who'd just fallen with her bat, going for his ribs and knees. She also delivered more hits to the two men who'd already fallen in the doorway but that still left three to deal with.

While two of the remaining men went for Jack, one of them turned to Carly. He brandished a small hatchet, which she had to admit she found a little scary.

'Put the bat down and I won't use this on you,' he told her, indicating the hatchet.

'Go fuck yourself,' she retorted while keeping one eye on Jack. He'd knocked one of the two men out with the bat but he was still fighting the second and she was appalled to see that one of them had a knife.

'No,' she cried when his right forearm got slashed, the sight of his blood terrifying.

The man with the hatchet took advantage of this distraction to grab her by the hair, yank back her head and press the blade to her throat.

'Drop the bat or I'll cut her fucking head off,' he yelled.

16

The man's threat caused the fighting men to go instantly still.

'No, let her go,' bellowed Jack.

'Drop the fucking bat.'

'Don't do it, babe,' said Carly.

Jack immediately threw down the bat, his eyes wide with fear for his girlfriend. 'There, I've done what you want. Just let her go. You want me, not her.'

'True but now we know we can use her to control you.'

'Why, what do you want?' Jack exclaimed with frustration. 'Just fucking tell me.'

'You're stepping on our toes, you twat. You're selling weapons and that's our business.'

'Weapons?' Jack frowned. 'No, I'm not. I've got enough on my plate without getting into all that too.'

'Aye, ya are. Don't lie to me. We've tracked the sales back to Haghill and everyone knows you're the big man around here.'

'I am but I swear, I wouldn't touch weapons. I'm not an armourer.'

'Our information says different. Now you and your little girlfriend here are coming with us.'

'Where?'

'Somewhere we can talk in private. The walls in these flats are paper thin and we don't want to be overheard. If you behave yourself then she won't be harmed, no' much anyway. I cannae say the same for you but you can at least keep her alive.'

Carly knew the man was lying. She'd seen their faces. She and Jack would both be dead before sunrise if they went with these men. His grip on her had relaxed slightly and the blade of the hatchet wasn't pressed right against her throat any more, giving her a little breathing space. He was standing side on to her, his left hand in her hair, the hatchet in his right, so he could strike with one downward blow of the weapon. She had to act now, while his attention was diverted.

'Okay, I'll do anything you want,' cried Jack. 'Just please let her go.'

As the man replied, Carly grabbed his hand holding the hatchet and dragged it forward while simultaneously pulling herself to the left. His hand moved with her and the hatchet slammed into the inside of his left forearm. He screamed with shock and pain and Carly tore herself free of his grip, feeling a few strands of hair come away in his hand. Before he could recover, she punched him hard in the face before yanking the hatchet free from his arm and rounding on the men. They all gaped at her in amazement while their friend continued to wail and bleed.

Jack snatched up the bat he'd dropped and smashed the man closest to him in the face with it. He then grabbed one man by the front of the jacket and slammed him painfully against the wall, banging him off it a few times for good measure to stun him before letting him drop.

Jack stepped over the injured men and knelt before the one who'd held the hatchet to Carly's throat. 'You're staying here and answering some questions,' he growled in the man's face. 'And you're gonna pay for threatening my girlfriend.'

The man glared back at him, hand clamped to his injured arm, blood trickling through his fingers.

Jack straightened up. 'The rest of you can fuck off.'

'Yeah,' chimed in Carly. 'Before I go to town on you with this bastard,' she added, waving the hatchet around in the air.

They whipped round to face the door at the sound of footsteps charging up the stairs to Jack's flat. Carly sighed when her uncle and cousins appeared.

The three men came to a halt in the doorway to gape at the carnage inside.

'What the bloody hell happened here?' exclaimed Eddie.

'These pricks were just leaving,' said Jack. 'Except this one,' he added, gesturing to the bleeding man. 'He's got some explaining to do. Make sure they all leave. And watch the cooking oil on the floor.'

'Nae problem,' said Eddie. 'Right, you bunch of pricks, you've got two choices – walk down the stairs nice and quietly or me and my boys will throw you down them and have a bet on whose neck snaps.'

The men left obediently, although it took some longer than others because of their injuries. When a couple of the men were too slow for Eddie's liking, he nodded at his sons, who dragged them out the door and kicked them down the stairs. They then followed them out to make sure they left.

While this was going on, Jack stared down at the bleeding man with rage in his dark eyes, fantasising about how he was going to punish him for what he'd done to Carly.

'We should stop the bleeding,' said Carly, who was still holding the hatchet. 'He cannae talk if he bleeds to death.'

'You're right,' replied Jack. He turned to her and took her face in his hands. 'Are you okay?'

'I'm fine. You're injured though.'

'It's just a scratch. Look, it's already stopped bleeding. Besides, I wasn't the one who had an axe held to their throat.'

She shrugged. 'I've faced scarier people than him.'

Jack thought that was such a sad statement. He kissed her before pulling her into his arms, so relieved she was okay.

They relinquished each other when Eddie and the others returned.

'I'll get something to stop him bleeding,' said Carly. She handed the hatchet to Jack before heading into the bathroom.

'Just so you know,' Jack told his prisoner. 'I'm going to cut bits off you with your own weapon for what you did to her.'

'What did he do to her?' demanded Eddie.

'He held this to her throat,' replied Jack, holding up the axe.

'You piece of shit,' growled Harry before kicking the man in the face. His head snapped back, blood bursting from his nose.

'Steady on, son,' said Eddie, pulling him backwards. 'He cannae talk if he's all messed up.'

'She got her own back on him,' said Jack proudly. 'She made him hit himself in his own arm with the axe.'

'That's our Carly,' said Eddie proudly.

They went silent when she returned to the room carrying bandages. Kneeling beside the man, she put pressure on his wound, making him wince. When the bleeding had stopped, she wrapped a thick bandage around his arm. Now the danger was over, she could appraise him better. He was in his early thirties, the same age as Jack but he was nowhere near as attractive with his low forehead, thick monobrow and jutting jaw. His thin dark brown hair was messy and it looked like he hadn't shaved in a few days. He regarded her with small, mean eyes that were light brown in colour and were sharp with intelligence and hate. Beads of sweat had formed on his face from the pain in his arm.

'There,' she said once she was satisfied with her work. Delving into his jacket pocket, she produced the man's wallet and tossed it to Jack, who caught it in one hand.

'Maybe you should leave for the questioning, doll?' said Eddie.

'No way,' replied Carly. 'It was my neck he held an axe to and I want to know why.'

'And you've a right to know,' replied Jack. He produced a driver's licence from the man's wallet. 'Nick Kramer. Thirty-two years old. Lives in Bearsden. What the fuck is all this shite about me selling weapons, Nick?'

As Jack's gaze was on the prisoner, he failed to notice the look that passed between Eddie and his sons, but Carly was quick to catch it, although she didn't comment.

'That's what I've heard,' retorted Nick.

'From who?'

'From everyone.'

'Who's everyone?'

Nick shrugged. 'Dunno.'

He jumped when Jack slammed the hatchet into the wall beside his head.

'Don't fucking dick me about,' he bellowed. 'If you don't give me something useful then there's no need to keep you alive, is there?'

Nick appeared unmoved but Carly guessed he took Jack's warning to heart because he continued to talk. 'There's a couple of people I know who've bought guns and they say you're running the show.'

'Then they're fucking lying. I don't deal in guns.'

'That's what they told me.'

'So you decided to come here mob-handed instead of approaching me, did you, genius? You broke into my home, you threatened my girlfriend.' Jack yanked the hatchet out of the wall and raised it above his head. 'Did you seriously think that was a good idea?'

'Listen,' said Nick, looking increasingly nervous. 'I'm just going off what I've been told. I was only trying to protect my business. Surely you understand that?' He cringed when the blade met the wall just to the right of his head.

'I don't understand you lot bursting in here waving weapons around,' yelled Jack. He tore the axe out of the wall and slammed it into the wall to the left of Nick's head, each blow getting closer to its target. 'I'm not unreasonable and I would have respected you a lot more if you'd approached me and talked it out man to man but you couldn't do that. You had to take the coward's route.'

When the hatchet was once again slammed into the wall to the right of Nick's head, the blade caught the top of his ear, hacking off a small chunk. Nick cried out with pain and clamped a hand to the injury.

'I'll keep going until you're nothing but a pile of bits on the floor unless you give me better information,' snarled Jack.

'Trevor Wilson,' exclaimed Nick. 'That's one of the people who gave me your name. He's bought off me for years but he came to me taking the piss saying someone was undercutting me and he was going to them from now on.'

'Where does Trevor live?'

'Bearsden. We've known each other for years. The other was Garth Thomson. He's from Coatbridge. He's bought off me for a couple of years. He gave me the heads up that someone was stealing my business.'

'I'm not, for Christ's sake. Someone's been using my name.'

'Err, Jack,' said Eddie. 'Can I have a word?'

Jack stared down at Nick, who regarded him warily, eyes flicking to the hatchet in his hand. 'Okay,' he eventually replied. 'Watch him,' he told Dean and Harry as he followed Eddie into the kitchen. 'What's this about?' he said impatiently.

'I think Jessica and Elijah are running the weapons and using your name to do it.'

Jack blinked at him. 'You fucking what?'

Eddie related their previous night's adventure.

'You should have come to me immediately with this,' exploded Jack.

'We didnae know what was going on,' replied Eddie. 'We wanted to confirm it first and for all we knew we'd stumbled on a sideline of yours.'

'Sideline. As if I'd be stupid enough to get involved in guns.'

Eddie didn't think it would go down well if he mentioned the guns Jack got for himself as well as his cousins previously. 'It's all on me. I didnae want to approach you until I knew for sure what was going on. The rest of the family was just obeying my orders.'

'Who knows about this exactly?'

'Just me, my boys, Jane and Jennifer. We've kept Carly out of it.'

The news that Carly didn't know came as a huge relief to Jack. He didn't like the thought of her keeping something like this from him. 'Well thanks to your order Carly could have been killed.'

Eddie's eyes remained fixed on the weapon in Jack's hand, wondering if it was his turn to have the top of his ear cut off.

'I didnae think something like this would happen. I fucked up and I'm sorry but I really thought gathering more information was the right way to go rather than approaching you with some half-baked story.'

'All right, I can understand that but if you weren't Carly's uncle, I wouldn't let this drop so easily,' Jack thundered. 'I won't let anyone put her in danger, not even her own family. Do you understand?'

'Aye, I know and I don't blame you. I feel fucking awful.'

'Good, you should. And you said Elijah was there?'

Eddie nodded. 'Dean saw him with Jessica. Mason and his brother were there too.'

'And Dean's certain it was Elijah?'

'Aye.'

'Weird. I can't imagine him doing something like that. We get on so well.'

'In this business, personal feelings mean nothing.'

'I want you to find out everything you can. Make it your priority. We need to know if we're going to have more arseholes like Nick and his friends coming into Haghill. In the meantime, I need to find somewhere else to live. Thank God Carly's tough. If she wasn't then God knows what would have happened.'

Eddie saw the fear in Jack's eyes as he spoke and realised his feelings for Carly were genuine. 'Aye she is. That lassie can handle anything that's thrown her way.'

'She could have been hurt because of me.'

'No, not because of you, because of whoever's using your name.'

'We need to shut this down asap. First though, we have to deal with Nick.'

Eddie was relieved that Jack no longer seemed to be angry with him. 'How do you want to handle it?'

'I've got somewhere we can take him but I don't want Carly left alone. Is Jane at home?'

'No, she's at Jennifer's. You can stay with Carly. Me and the boys will deal with Nick.'

'Okay, we'll do it that way. I'll call Toni first, I want to make sure this Nick doesn't work for her.'

'Will you give her the full story?'

'Course. Bad things happen to people who hide stuff from Toni McVay.'

Eddie waited while Jack called Toni.

'Nick's nothing to do with her,' said Jack when he'd hung up. 'She thinks he's an arsehole, so she said we can do whatever we want with him.'

'Toni must have worked out from what you told her that you're seeing Carly?'

'She did and she didn't mention it but she was pissed off that Carly was put in danger. She likes her. Toni is also furious that someone's running weapons through Haghill and she wants that put to bed asap. Give Nick a proper pasting, I'm talking intensive care but don't go all the way. I want him to tell people what he's learned and we might need him to give us more information in the future. Break a couple of joints too, ensure he stays out of our hair for a while.'

'Will do. Just to clarify, this involves your family members...'

'Do whatever's necessary. It doesn't matter that they're blood.'

'Understood.'

'Right, I need to arrange somewhere else to stay and to get Carly out of here. I don't want to take her back to her flat, it's not safe. There's a spare flat above the café where I have my office. No one's staying there and the owner gave me the key, he said I could use it anytime. We can both stay there until this is wrapped up.'

'Good idea. How are you gonnae deal with Elijah?'

'Carefully. He is not someone I want as an enemy, but I really think something else is going on. Elijah, even though he loves violence, hates guns. Plus just owning one can send you to prison for years and he's not fucking stupid. I think you're right and we don't have the full picture yet. Once you've dealt with Nick, you and your boys get a few hours' rest then get straight on this. You don't do anything else, okay? This is your priority. Jane and Jennifer too. They're smart and they've lived here their entire lives. Their inside knowledge could be vital.'

'Carly might want in on this after what happened tonight.'

'If she does then she has that right.'

'After what just happened, you need to keep her out of it.'

'Do you think I can force Carly to do anything? I wouldn't even try. She knows her own mind and if she wants back in that's her decision.'

Eddie's eyes narrowed. 'You want her back in, don't you? You must realise it would be much easier for you to maintain your relationship with her if she was part of your world.'

'The decision is her own. I wouldn't dream of dictating to her because that's not the sort of man I am.'

With one last glower at Eddie, Jack stormed back into the living room. Nick jumped, eyes widening when he marched up to him still holding the hatchet and glared at him with such hate Nick expected to be hacked to pieces at any moment.

'Get him the fuck out of my sight,' growled Jack. 'Eddie knows what to do.'

Between them, Dean and Harry hauled Nick to his feet and dragged him towards the door.

'Let me know the moment you find out anything,' Jack told Eddie as he left with his sons.

'I will,' he replied. 'See you later, doll,' he told Carly before they all left.

Jack let the hatchet drop to the floor as Carly flew into his arms.

'We were lucky tonight,' she told him.

Jack cupped her face in his hands and leaned back slightly to look into her eyes. 'You'll always be in danger while you're with me. Are you sure I'm worth the risk?'

'Absolutely,' she replied without even pausing to consider her answer.

'I want you to think about it very carefully. You wanted out of the life but we've only just got back together and look what's happened already. Our lives will always be affected like this.'

'I already know that and it's no' enough to put me off. I was so unhappy without you and now I'm happy again. Besides, you know how much I love a good scrap.'

He smiled and wrapped his arms around her waist. 'You were magnificent. Thank God you can handle yourself.'

'I can, so you don't need to worry.'

Jack kissed her but inwardly he was afraid that he could get the only person he had ever loved killed. Until now, he'd never understood the old saying *if you love something let it go.*

'Right,' he said, swallowing down the emotion he felt rising in his chest. 'First, I need to get the front door sorted before I'm robbed blind, then we need to spend the night somewhere else.'

'My flat?'

'I was thinking the flat above the café. I've got the keys and it's clean and cosy.'

'Sounds good.'

He felt all that turbulent emotion rise inside him again as the desire to protect Carly fought with his need to be with her. Was letting Carly go the right thing to do for her? It certainly wouldn't be for him.

* * *

Eddie hardly got any sleep that night. He'd lain awake staring at the ceiling, trying to figure out how he would find out what Jessica and Elijah were up to. The first thing he needed to do was gather information, so he decided to go and speak to his old friend, Daphne.

The next morning, he and his sons headed over to the strip club she still owned and ran. They arrived early, before the club opened and apart from Daphne herself, only the cleaners were present.

Daphne bustled up to him wearing her usual tight top and black trousers, bosom threatening to burst out of her pink blouse.

'Eddie,' she said, bright red lips curving into a smile. 'Lovely to see you again, sweetheart.' She eyed Harry and Dean appreciatively. 'And what have you brought me this time?' She circled the two men like a hungry shark, assessing them with a practised eye. 'Perfect timing because I've got a show tomorrow night that this pair of Adonises would be perfect in. It's called Snow White and the Seven Dicks and I'm not satisfied with two of the dicks, they're far too wee and puny.' She smiled when Harry laughed. 'At least they've got more of a sense of humour than those two wee madams you brought me.' She noted Dean's hard, unamused look and her smile fell. 'Well, one of them does anyway.'

'Why did you bring madams here?' Harry asked his dad. 'Is it a brothel?'

'No' those sort of madams, ya fanny,' retorted Eddie. 'She means Carly and Jane. We came to speak to Daphne the last time there was trouble in Haghill. And they're no' here to be part of your show,' Eddie told Daphne. 'These are my sons.'

'Really? You sired two such impressive specimens as these?' she said, continuing to examine them closely, prodding at their backs and running her hands over their biceps with the practised study of a farmer at the cattle market.

'Aye,' frowned Eddie. 'Why shouldn't I?'

'No reason. I take it their maw was the good-looking one?'

'You cheeky cow.'

Daphne smiled. 'You know I'm only playing. I'm assuming you're here for some information?'

'Aye, no' to be insulted.'

'I'd no idea you were so sensitive,' she said. 'Come on through to the office so we can talk in private. The cleaners are nosy bitches.'

Daphne led the three men into her office at the back of the club.

'Why do you no' get a real office?' Eddie asked her. 'It's like a bloody broom cupboard.' There was even less space with Dean and Harry's bulk.

'If you want to be rude you can do it outside on the pavement and you'll no' get the information you want,' Daphne yelled back at him.

'All right, no need to get your knickers in a twist.' Eddie produced a roll of notes from his jacket pocket and placed it on the desk.

'Consider my knickers untwisted,' she said before picking up the money and stuffing it into her bra. She caught Harry looking and gave him a wink. 'Now, Eddie, what do you want to know?'

'About guns.'

Her smile dropped. 'I don't have anything to do with those things. Do you think I'm fucking mad?'

'I'm no' after one. I want to know if you've heard if anyone else has started dealing in them?'

'Why do you want to know?'

Eddie could sense she was being cagey, which wasn't like Daphne. They had a good working relationship and she knew she could trust him.

'Because someone has started dealing in them and it's causing us some trouble.'

'Like what? Has someone shot at you?'

'No. Let's just say other people with interests in that business are blaming someone for being an armourer when they really have nothing to do with it.'

'I see. You want to share that person's name with me?'

'No. Sorry, doll.'

'It's okay. You don't need to tell me. I know you work for Jack Alexander who took over from Rod Tallan, who was a major arsehole by the way. Everyone was glad when that prick vanished. So someone's dealing guns and saying Jack's really running the show?'

'I'm saying nothing.'

'It's a good job I can read you like a book. Actually, I have heard something. We have a regular client who's obsessed with one of my girls, Chastity. He comes four nights a week just to see her and he's been boasting to her about how much money he's making selling guns.' Daphne gathered her information through the strippers who worked in her club. Both she and her girls made a lot of cash by either selling the information to interested parties or blackmailing their clients.

'Who is he?' said Eddie.

'He says his name's Charlie but I've already confirmed that's an alias. He's very tight-lipped about himself, so it was a surprise to Chastity when he started bragging about selling fifty grand's worth of handguns. He was really splashing the cash, buying lots of champagne. He even bought a diamond necklace for Chastity. He said he'd finally made it big and could provide for her. The poor sod's working up to asking her to leave this business and marry him, I just know it. The berk doesnae realise all my girls get asked the same thing several times a year but they always turn the men down because they make a tonne of cash here and they don't have to tie themselves down to some fat, ugly bastard for life.'

'Has this Charlie given any names?'

'Naw but he did mention a pub once – The Wheatsheaf. He didnae say where it was but I do know there is a pub with the same name in Haghill.'

'What did he say about The Wheatsheaf?'

'You know the rules, sweetheart.'

Eddie sighed and produced another roll of money, which also disappeared inside her bra.

'He said that's where he does business. He was really trying to big himself up. I don't know why he thought mentioning some manky old pub would do that but he really is obsessed with her. I reckon he'd do anything for Chastity.'

'What does this Charlie look like?'

'He's no' as bad as most of the gleekit bastards we get through here but he's nothing special either. I'd say he's about forty-five. Average height, thinning brown hair and brown eyes.'

'That could be a million people,' said Harry.

'Exactly, son,' replied Eddie. He looked back at Daphne. 'When is this Charlie due back in?'

'Tonight. He promised to bring Chastity a bracelet to match her necklace. He usually gets here at about eight.'

'Then we need to be here too,' Eddie told his sons.

'Exciting,' said Daphne. 'It'll be like a sting operation. He always goes into one of the private rooms. No funny business though,' she said haughtily. 'I don't run a knocking shop. The customers can just get a private lap dance and there's waitress service too. I always have a member of my security team on guard duty outside the rooms when a girl is inside with a client.'

'And being in a private room makes the clients more comfortable about spilling their guts to the girls,' said Dean.

Daphne smiled at him. 'I'm glad to see that you're more than just a pretty face.'

'Right, we'll come back tonight,' said Eddie. 'And remember Daph, no' a word to anyone.'

'Don't lecture me, I know the score,' she told him bad-temperedly. 'Now bugger off, I'm busy.'

'I love that silver tongue of yours, doll.'

Daphne smiled reluctantly. 'You're still a charmer, Eddie. Have your boys inherited that talent of yours?'

'I have,' said Harry. He jerked a thumb in his brother's direction. 'He hasn't. He's way too quiet and intense.'

Daphne regarded Dean with interest. 'Still waters run deep, don't they, sweetheart? I wonder what's going on in your deepest, darkest depths?'

'No' much,' said Dean flatly.

'Now I know that's not true. Right, away you go, Savage men. I need to get on with my paperwork.'

Eddie and his sons left the club and returned to his car.

'That Daphne's an interesting woman,' said Harry.

'You fancy her, don't you?' said Dean.

'I wouldnae say fancy but I bet she knows a thing or two.'

'Don't even think about it,' said Eddie. 'She'd scare the living shite out of you.'

'What do we do now?' Dean asked his father.

'Whatever our next move is must be subtle. The usual tactics won't work.'

'What about our prison contacts?'

'I doubt they'll know anything. Contacts can only tell us so much. We need to find out the scale of their operation. Surveillance might be our best option.'

'You mean we need to return to Emily's flat?'

Eddie didn't like the thought of being molested again. 'No. We need to pick a target and monitor them carefully. Jessica and Elijah are the brains of the outfit. No way do I want to follow Elijah because he'll realise pretty quickly and we cannae risk him being alerted before Jack's ready to make his move. Jessica's smart too and might realise so we go for the stupid one and that's Mason.'

17

Carly felt Jack shifting restlessly in the bed beside her. She opened her eyes to find him staring up at the ceiling, lost in thought. They were safely ensconced in the flat above the café.

'Can't sleep?' she said.

'No, I've hardly closed my eyes all night,' he replied. 'My mind's too busy trying to figure out what's going on.'

'Have you considered confiding in David? He's no' stupid enough to get involved with guns.'

'I have but I don't want to take the risk in case greed's got the better of him and he is involved.'

'I don't think he would be. David has a sense of honour that's quite rare. I doubt he would plot against you, it's no' his style.'

'I'll consider it but for now I don't want to tell anyone else. You and your family are the only people I trust.'

Carly smiled and slid her arm across his waist.

'I've also been lying awake wishing I'd never pulled off that coup to take over from Rod,' continued Jack. 'Life was simpler when I was just an employee. My stupid ambition put you in danger last night.' He turned onto his side to face her. 'Seeing that blade pressed to your throat made me realise you're the single most important thing to me, more so than my work. I'm going to figure out a way to get out of working for Toni to make sure you're never put in danger again.'

Carly's eyes filled with tenderness. 'I really appreciate that but you're still reeling from the shock of the attack. We both are. You'll change your mind when everything's calmed down.'

'No, I won't and the only way we can really be free of the life is to move away from Glasgow. I'm thinking somewhere quiet and rural with no gangs battering the shite out of each other all the time.' He placed a hand on her belly. 'Somewhere with good schools.'

'Are you serious?'

'I am. I want to marry you and have kids.'

'But...'

'Oh God, I've brought that up way too soon, haven't I? I hope I haven't scared you off. Unless you don't want an ex-con as the father of your children? I couldn't blame you for that. Actually, I don't even know if you do want kids because I've never asked, I've just assumed...'

'You're babbling and that is not like you.'

'I've had what I've heard is called a dark night of the soul. That attack made me re-evaluate my entire life. I wish I hadn't interfered with Cole's takeover but I was left with no choice. He was dropping your family right in it by using your name. At first, my intention was to try and protect you but then I realised I could turn it to my own advantage and I was happy to do so. Now look what my ambition's done – it nearly got us both killed. If you weren't so bloody hard it would have done. We were only saved thanks to your skills, not mine.'

'That's no' true. It was a joint effort.'

'No, you saved us. It made me realise that these attacks will continue as long as I'm in this job. How many attacks has Toni McVay had to fend off in her time?'

'And she's survived.'

'But one day she might not and if that happens we're all dead too. We will spend our lives in danger and so will any of our children. Christ, I'm still making assumptions. Carly, do you want kids? Do you want kids with someone who was in prison for attempted murder?'

'If you mean do I want weans with you then aye, I do.'

He smiled at her. 'I used to think my dream was the big house, the cars and money, but now I realise it's you and four kids.'

'Four?' she exclaimed.

His eyes twinkled. 'Is that too many for you?'

'Definitely. I was thinking two.'

'Okay, two then. A nice house further up north with a bit of land, some chickens, a goat...'

'A goat? Is this Jack Alexander lying next to me or did the body snatchers come along in the middle of the night and swap you?'

He laughed. 'No, it's me, babe. Last night made me realise what's important and that's us. My only worry is that I won't be able to get a job with my criminal record, so I've been thinking I'll become self-employed. I'll do a course, train in something new and set up my own business. Then it won't matter about my record. I did a course in web design in prison, I was pretty good at it too. I reckon I could make a go of it. In fact, I can start building the business up now so it's ready to go when we do make our move.'

'You really think you'd be satisfied with that life? No excitement, no danger. Just working from home raising chickens and goats?'

'And you and our kids. Definitely. What's wrong?' he added

when he realised she didn't share his enthusiasm. 'Don't you like my idea?'

'I bloody love it. My worry is that once the shock of last night has worn off, you'll change your mind and decide to stay as you are. I'm scared of getting my hopes up.'

'This isn't some whim. I really mean it but we'd have to leave Glasgow. Could you leave your family behind?'

'To be honest, I was already seriously thinking of moving away from Haghill. I even booked appointments to view a couple of flats. Then I realised Rose wouldn't be able to cope with me leaving so soon after Da's death, so I changed my mind. The truth is, I could happily leave Glasgow. I know it's the only way I can truly avoid the business my family is in because as long as I'm here I'll always get dragged into it simply because my last name is Savage.'

'What about Rose?'

'She's got Noah and her friends, she spends most of her time with them anyway. I'd just need to give her a few months to get over losing Da' and then I think she would be fine. She's practically an adult now anyway. I've spent so long living for other people and now it's time to live for me. Just as long as we go somewhere I can still visit my family, I'll be happy.'

'I was thinking Perthshire. It's beautiful around there and it's still close.'

'I don't really know that area, apart from Crieff. My parents used to take us to MacRosty Park for days out.'

'We can explore that area, look at available properties.'

'What sort of property could we get up there though? I don't earn that much and you're not supposed to be earning a lot either.'

'We'll figure something out. We can do anything when we're together, babe.'

His enthusiasm was infectious and she smiled. 'You're right. We'll manage it, but what about Toni? What if she won't let you go?'

'I've been thinking about that too. What I need to do is find someone to replace me and make her think that they'd be better at the job.'

'David?'

'That's exactly who I had in mind, which is why I'm praying he's not involved in this gun business.'

'He won't be, I'm willing to bet on it. Maybe you should take him into your confidence?'

'I want to get a bit more information before doing that. Hopefully your family will be able to find something out.'

* * *

'This is a waste of time,' sighed Harry.

'Shut up and keep watch,' Eddie told him.

'We've been watching for three hours and the walloper's still in his wanking chariot. What if he doesnae get up until teatime? That's another four hours of sitting about doing nothing. It's driving me mad.'

'You're driving me mad. Stop whining like a big Jessie.'

'I'm no' built for sitting about,' said Harry sulkily.

Even Dean was beginning to lose patience with his brother. 'Well piss off then and leave it to me and Da'. But you can guarantee the moment you're gone something will happen.'

'Aye, I know, which is the only reason why I'm still here.'

'Look, he's coming out,' said Eddie when Mason emerged from his ground-floor flat. 'Happy now?'

'Ecstatic,' Harry replied flatly.

Mason was a handsome twenty-one-year-old man with dark

hair and eyes. His charm had ensnared Rose into a trap so the Alexander brothers could use her to control her family but Rose had turned the tables on her captors and escaped. The Savage family had punished Mason by beating him up, slashing his face with a knife and almost drowning him in a kitchen sink. He still sported a scar on each side of his face from the knife Jane had used on him but the scars didn't appear to have slowed him down with the ladies because he was accompanied by a woman wearing too much make-up and a dress two sizes too small.

'She could be a relative,' said Dean, putting into words what they were all wondering.

The two of them got into Mason's BMW that was parked on the street and began to frantically kiss.

'Let's hope she's not,' said Harry.

The two eventually relinquished each other and Mason started the engine and drove off. Eddie allowed them to get to the top of the street before following.

'The roads are pretty quiet,' said Dean. 'What if they notice us?'

'We'll play that by ear,' replied his father.

Mason dropped the woman off at a flat just a couple of streets from the Savage sisters' home.

'We'll mention her to the sisters,' said Eddie. 'They might know who she is.'

Mason continued to drive on and they followed. Sure enough, he parked outside The Wheatsheaf and went inside.

'I get the feeling that place is the centre of operations, which means Lonny the landlord is involved,' said Eddie as he drove on and turned the corner. He parked at the kerb and switched off the engine.

'What are you doing?' Harry asked him.

'Wondering what to do next.'

'Let's stop fannying about and just go in there.'

'We cannae. It's Alexander territory.'

'So? Ross and Dominic are no' here any more and we're working on Jack's behalf. That just leaves Cole and who gi'es a solitary shite about that prick?'

'If we suddenly turn up then they'll know that we know.'

'Then we need to come up with another excuse for going in there.'

'We could say we need to speak to Cole urgently,' suggested Dean.

'What could we possibly have to discuss with him?' said Eddie.

'Carly. That'll make him come running.'

'I doubt it,' said Harry. 'They're ancient history.'

'I'm willing to bet that he still has feelings for her.'

'That ice-hearted arsehole doesnae have feelings for anyone,' said Eddie.

Dean shrugged. 'It was just a thought.'

'Let's go for it,' said Harry.

'You really think it could work?' replied Eddie.

'I don't know. Maybe.'

'And what if he doesnae come running?'

'We don't need Cole to come running. For all we know he's no' in on this gunrunning operation anyway. We just need to take a look at what's going on in that pub and test their reaction to us.'

The three of them got out of the car. As they rounded the corner, they saw another person heading into the pub.

'Is that Hairy Bill?' said Harry.

'Who?' replied Eddie.

'You know, the guy who worked for Rod. He was the Plague Doctor at Death Loves Company. He works for Jack now.'

'You're right, it is him,' said Dean.

'Does this mean he's turned against Jack too?'

'Don't jump to conclusions,' said Eddie. 'He could just be going in for a drink.'

Once Hairy Bill had gone inside, the three of them walked down the street and pushed at the door into the pub.

'It's locked,' said Eddie.

'That's a bad way to do business,' said Harry.

'Because they're no' in there for the usual pub business. Something else is going on. Let's go around the back.'

They headed around the corner to the back street. The pub had a backyard that was hidden by stone walls and a sturdy wooden gate.

'Boost me over,' said Harry.

'Just hold your horses there, son,' said Eddie. 'They might see you.'

'Naw, they won't. They'll all be in the main bar.'

'You don't know that for sure.'

'The only way to confirm it is for one of us to go over that wall. If I get seen, I can always jump back over.'

'I don't like it.'

'We've nae choice.'

'I'll go with him,' said Dean.

'Aye, all right but you're on your own lads because there's no way I can drag my arse over that wall.'

Eddie watched Harry go over first followed by Dean. He continually looked up and down the street, watching for anyone approaching. A breeze moaned mournfully up the alley, scattering litter along with it, making him feel even more alone.

'You silly old sod,' he told himself.

Sensing movement, he looked up and saw Harry peering down at him from the over the wall.

'Jesus,' breathed Eddie, pressing a hand to his chest. 'Do you have to stare down at me like Chad?'

'Who?'

'Never mind. What's going on?'

'The back door's open and Dean's listening. He can hear the landlord, Lonny, talking.'

'What's he saying?'

'I don't know, Dean's still listening but the point is the back door's open, so we can sneak in if we want.'

'Naw. Just listen and don't let them see you.'

Harry nodded and dropped down out of sight.

Eddie waited for another anxious ten minutes before his sons scrambled back over the wall.

Dean didn't speak until the three of them were safely back in Eddie's car and they'd left The Wheatsheaf behind.

'I heard five different voices,' began Dean. 'One was the Lonny the landlord, another Mason. One I think was Hairy Bill but I didnae recognise the other two. Jessica definitely wasnae there because they were all male voices.'

'Cole?' replied Eddie.

'Nope and not his brothers either.'

'What were they discussing?'

'Ditching the garage as a meeting place. They've realised someone was there last night.'

'Do they know it was us?'

'Our names were mentioned but they don't know for sure. They think the Stewart brothers have sold them out. I reckon the Stewarts could be in some hot water.'

'Let's keep an eye on their homes and see what happens. Did they mention Jack at all?'

'They did mention telling the boss but they didn't say a name.'

'Bugger,' he sighed. 'But at least that tells us someone else is running the show.'

Fortunately, the Stewart brothers lived close to each other.

While Dean watched the home of the older brother, Malcolm, Eddie and Harry kept an eye on Freddy's. Sure enough, half an hour later, a car screeched to a halt outside Freddy's home and Hairy Bill climbed out along with Mason and his brother. They strode manfully up to the front door and Bill pounded his meaty fist on it. The door was opened by a woman Eddie and Harry took to be Freddy's wife, her face falling at the sight of three aggressive males on her doorstep. Eddie wound down his window so he could hear what was being said.

'Where's Freddy?' Bill demanded of the wife.

'At work,' she replied. 'Why, what's going on?'

'We want a word with him.'

'Then you'll have to go to the garage because he's no' here.'

'We don't believe you,' growled Bill. 'And we're coming in.'

'The hell you are. I've just got the baby to sleep. You'll wake him and are you fucking deif? Freddy's no' here.'

When he attempted to enter the house, the wife kneed him in the balls before slamming the door shut in his face.

Bill, who had dropped to his knees, slapped Mason's hands away when he attempted to help him up.

'Maybe we should go to the garage,' said Mason. 'I really don't think he's here.'

'Aye,' gasped Bill. 'Gi'e me a minute.'

'We should get Freddy's wife on our side,' said Harry. 'She's tougher than those puddings.'

'Let's get a head start on them and go over to the garage,' said Eddie.

'Aye, okay. I think it'll take Bill a while to stand up straight anyway.'

Before they set off, Eddie called Dean, who said it was all quiet at the older Stewart brother's house, so his father told him to get his arse over to the garage pronto.

Eddie parked his car on the next street and he and Harry hurried over to the garage, the main gate standing open. They passed it on the other side of the street and peered inside to see both Stewart brothers busy working on cars, along with a third, younger mechanic. Dean arrived a minute later and the three of them ducked behind a parked car to watch the front of the garage.

It took Bill and his two friends twenty minutes to make the short walk from Freddy's house. Bill limped along, looking pale and unwell. Before entering the garage, he stopped and leaned against a wall, taking in a few deep breaths.

'Should we leave this till later?' Mason's brother asked him.

'Naw, we're doing it now. It cannae wait,' he snapped back.

'Then you should wait out here. You look like you're gonnae fall over.'

'I'm fine,' he growled irritably.

Mason's brother scowled with irritation and he looked like he wanted to punch Bill right in the face. The brother looked just like Mason but he was taller, stronger, sturdier and Eddie thought he would be capable of causing a lot of carnage if he so chose. In comparison, Mason himself looked limp and weak.

'Well I'm going in,' grunted the brother. 'You can wait here.'

'No, Alfie, wait,' said Bill, limping along behind the brothers as they strode determinedly into the garage.

'Hey, you,' Alfie told the young mechanic. 'Piss aff, we need a word with your bosses.'

The Stewart brothers regarded their visitors warily.

'It's okay, Rory,' Freddy told him. 'You can take your break early.'

'Aye, all right,' he said before dumping his tools, wiping his hands on a cloth and hastily leaving the compound.

Once the young mechanic had gone, Eddie and his sons

rushed across the road and pressed themselves back against the wall so they could hear better.

'We want to know who the fuck you've been mouthing off to,' opened Alfie.

'What do you mean?' replied Freddy, looking a little nervous.

'I mean someone came here last night and we think you told them about the operation.'

'We fucking didn't,' growled Malcolm. 'Someone probably decided to have a poke around. It's no' like the garage is hidden.'

The eyes of Bill and the two brothers fixated on Freddy, whose cheeks had turned scarlet.

Alfie frowned. 'You're keeping something from us.'

'I'm not,' said Freddy. 'I've nae idea what you're talking about.'

Alfie took an aggressive stride towards Freddy, making him flinch. 'Jack Alexander knows about it, doesn't he?'

The incorrect name made Freddy relax, the colour vanishing from his cheeks. 'Course he doesn't.'

'So it's no' him?' said Alfie.

'Naw, I've never even spoken to him.'

Alfie's gaze was sharp and clever and Freddy became increasingly uncomfortable as those penetrating eyes bore right into him.

'Someone else then,' said Alfie. 'Someone affiliated with him.' His lips spread into a slow smile. 'The Savages.'

All the blood instantly drained from Freddy's face, telling Alfie everything he needed to know.

'What did you tell them?' demanded Alfie.

'Nothing,' he exclaimed. 'They just... they wanted to know about the side door.'

'Jesus,' sighed Malcolm.

Alfie grabbed Freddy by the throat and threw him back onto the bonnet of a car.

'Argh, my fucking back,' shrieked Freddy.

'When did they approach you?' growled Alfie, gripping him by the throat.

'Last night,' he replied hoarsely.

'What do they know about it?'

'Nothing, apart from it was put there by Jack.'

'That's really all you told them?'

'Aye because I don't know anything else. Please, my back.'

Alfie stared at him thoughtfully before releasing him and straightening up with a smile.

'Well that's all right then.'

'How is it all right?' said Mason.

'Because the Savages will think Jack's up to something behind their backs and it'll cause trouble between them. Separating Jack from that family will take away a lot of his support. Nice one Freddy, you did good.'

'I did?' Freddy said with wonder.

'Aye.' Alfie produced a knife from inside his jacket with lightning speed and pressed it to his throat. 'But if you open your fucking mouth again, I'll cut out your tongue and gi'e it to my dog as a treat. Got it?'

'A-aye, Alfie,' he stammered. 'I've got it. It won't happen again.'

Alfie studied him hard before releasing him and replacing the knife in his jacket. 'Good. By the way, we're shifting locations, so we'll no longer be paying you.' He looked to his friends. 'Let's go.'

Eddie, Dean and Harry rushed to place themselves behind a large white transit van parked a little further down the street. They peered around it to watch Alfie, Mason and Bill walk away.

'Well, it's clear who's the most dangerous one out of that lot,' said Eddie when the three men had turned the corner at the top of the street. 'I don't know much about this Alfie but I think I need to find out asap. Do you know anything about him, boys?'

His sons shook their heads.

'I'll speak to my contacts but that is one dangerous sod. We also need to find out if Cole's involved in this as he made out he's now on Jack's side. If he is in on it, I can see a big clash of personalities occurring between him and Alfie. Both are strong leaders.'

'Maybe that's why Cole's teamed up with Jack?' offered Dean. 'He's probably realised Alfie's a big threat.'

'Aye, probably, son.'

'How do we confirm if Cole's involved?' said Harry.

'I'm no' sure yet.'

'Lonny's a weak coward, we'd easily be able to get him to talk.'

'But he'd alert the others.'

'They already know we're onto them, so who cares?'

Eddie looked to Dean. 'What do you think?'

'Let's see what we can find out at the strip club tonight. We might get information that turns out to be vital to us.'

'Good idea. All right, we've got a plan.'

18

Carly took a shower in the flat above the café, enjoying the warm spray that soothed her muscles, which ached after the previous night's fight. Jack had already left for work. What work that was she had no idea, she hadn't asked.

She dressed and headed into the lounge, her damp hair streaming down her back. Jack had told her to stay in the flat until he got back, wanting to confirm that there was no immediate danger to her. She wondered if he really meant what he'd said about moving away. How would a man like him cope with living the quiet life? She wanted to believe him but she couldn't help but feel it was just a fantasy brought on by the shock of the attack.

Carly tensed when there was a knock at the door. Jack hadn't mentioned anyone would be visiting.

'Jack, are you in there?' called a voice.

Carly rushed to her handbag and produced the taser, which she'd collected from her flat along with her baton and pepper spray last night before coming here.

'Who is it?' she called.

'Elijah,' he replied. 'I need to talk to Jack urgently.'

'He's no' here.'

'Where is he?'

'I don't know, he said he had to go out on business.'

There was a hesitation before he said, 'You can open the door. I don't bite.'

Carly wasn't so sure about that. 'Jack's no' here,' she repeated.

'Okay. I'll gi'e him a call, see if I can get hold of him.'

She strained to listen but could hear nothing. When a minute had passed, she peered through the spyhole again and was shocked to see Elijah was still standing there, smirking.

'Why don't you open the door so we can talk?' he said.

Carly didn't reply. Instead, she stood ready with the taser. When she looked again, he'd gone.

'Thank God,' she breathed. Taking out her phone, she called Jack.

'Hi, babe,' he said cheerfully.

'Elijah was just here looking for you,' she replied. 'He said it was urgent.'

'You didn't let him in, did you?'

'No. I told him you weren't here and that I didnae know where you were. He wanted me to open the door, but I refused. He stood out in the hallway for a couple of minutes looking creepy, but I think he's gone now.'

'You did the right thing. Do you need me to come back?'

'No, I'm okay. I've got my trusty taser.'

'Good. Don't open the door to anyone, apart from me or your family. I'm on with finding another flat no one knows about.'

'Okay.'

The call ended and Carly wandered over to the window to look down onto the busy main street, which teemed with cars and pedestrians. Elijah stood on the pavement leaning against a car, chatting with – to her surprise – Cole. Elijah spotted her looking and he nudged Cole, who turned to look up at her. Both men just stared at her while she stared back.

'Freaks,' she muttered, taking a step back.

When she looked out of the window again a few minutes later, both men had gone but this didn't make her feel any better as she didn't know if they were in the café below or possibly even on the stairs. She wondered if she should call her family. The last thing she wanted was to sound like she needed a babysitter but she did think they needed to know that Cole and Elijah were hanging around together.

'Uncle Eddie,' she said when he answered her call. 'I'm sorry to disturb you when you're busy. I just thought you should know that Cole and Elijah were talking together outside the café. They looked like they were up to something. No, I'm fine. Jack will be back soon. Okay, bye.'

Carly hung up and stared at her phone. It was strange how since she'd got out of the life she was being treated like the weak one who needed looking after, even after what she'd done to those intruders just the previous night. She supposed her uncle was only looking out for her by asking if she needed one of them to sit with her, but it still dented her pride.

Rather than switch on the television, Carly returned to the window to watch the world go by. There was a dog-grooming salon directly opposite and she found it entertaining watching the pampered pooches being taken in and out. One little white dog came out looking hilariously floofy and the dog's expression said he didn't approve of his new look.

Just down from the café was the park in which the Alexander brothers and their friends had chased her and Dean in the dark. Carly could see the trees from the window and the memory gave her chills. In her mind it felt like she was in the same situation, stumbling about in the dark, unable to see her true enemy. Had

Elijah really turned against Jack? Whose side was Cole on? Was Jack serious about them leaving together? It was enough to make her head spin.

* * *

Eddie related what Carly had told him to his sons.

'It's definite then,' said Harry. 'Cole is in on it.'

'Not necessarily,' replied Dean. 'This is still not enough to confirm it for sure.'

'I agree,' said Eddie. They'd just pulled up outside the house he shared with Harry and had been about to get out of the car when his phone rang. 'It's Jane,' he said. 'All right, doll?' he added, putting the phone to his ear. 'We're on our way.' He hung up and tossed his phone into Harry's lap.

'Christ, watch where you're throwing that,' exclaimed his son when it hit him in the crotch.

'Jennifer got a call from her Uncle Finlay. Something's going on in Bishopbriggs.'

* * *

After collecting Jennifer and Jane, Eddie drove the five of them into Bishopbriggs. Finlay was waiting for them at the top of the street where Ross and Dominic lived, eyes alight with excitement.

'I thought I'd keep an eye on these wallopers for you,' he said once he'd been introduced to Eddie. 'I've got a pal who lives on this street and he called me to say three men arrived an hour ago. They stood lurking outside for a bit, watching the flat of that pair of Alexander pricks. Then they burst in, there was some yelling and shouting and now it's all gone quiet.'

'What did these men look like?' Eddie asked him.

'One was a fat hairy bastard with a limp. The other two were younger, one really mean-looking, the other the drippy wet lettuce type. So, are we gonnae charge in there?' he said eagerly.

'This could be our chance to find out what's really going on,' said Harry. 'We could burst in and confront them all.'

'You've seen the size of that flat, it's toaty,' replied Eddie. 'What do you think's gonnae happen with eleven of us piled in there? It'll be bloody chaos and we know Alfie carries a knife. Christ knows what other weapons they have.'

'Then what do we do? Just hang about here like pricks?'

'Did the three men arrive in a car or on foot?' Eddie asked Finlay.

'In a car,' he replied, pointing down the street. 'The blue Audi.'

'That'll be a bastard to break into. Boys, let its tyres down and don't let anyone see you.'

Harry and Dean nodded and raced off down the street.

'We need to find out what's going on in that flat,' said Eddie.

'We can do that,' said Jane, gesturing from herself to Jennifer.

'Aye, all right but be careful.'

'What should we do?' Finlay asked Eddie as the two women jogged away.

'We keep watch.'

'I don't want to hang around here like a big Jessie, I want some action.'

'We need to be on hand to act, we've nae idea what's gonnae happen now.'

They both whipped round to face the house when there was a loud bang.

'Jen,' cried Finlay before breaking into a run.

Eddie followed, both men puffing and panting. Mason and Alfie were fleeing from Ross and Dominic's flat, Bill limping along behind them as quickly as he could. In one hand, Alfie held a gun.

Eddie managed to grab the back of Finlay's coat and shove him into a neighbour's garden before leaping in after him. The next thing he knew, Finlay's huge hands were around his neck, squeezing the life out of him.

'What the fuck are you doing?' growled Finlay. 'You're trying to stop me from saving Jen. What have you got against her?'

Eddie was desperate to explain that he had nothing against her and was only trying to stop them both from getting shot but the words were choked in his throat. Tears of pain filled Eddie's eyes, tongue protruding from his mouth as the darkness began to close in. Then Finlay was being pulled off him and he could breathe again.

'Da', are you okay?'

Eddie just lay there, staring stupidly up at his sons, who were fighting to keep a hold of Finlay.

'Da'?' repeated Harry more urgently.

Eddie coughed and slowly sat up, grimacing at the pain in his neck. 'I'll be okay,' he rasped.

'Let me at him,' growled Finlay, struggling to tear himself free of the brothers' grip. 'I'm gonnae kill him.'

'Uncle Finlay,' exclaimed Jennifer, rushing up to them. 'Did you just try to strangle someone *again*?'

All the aggression left Finlay's body in an instant. 'No,' he said nonchalantly.

'Aye, he did,' said Harry. 'We had to pull him off Da'.'

Finlay turned sheepishly when Jennifer glared at him.

'Please don't tell your maw,' he said to his niece.

'I might have to,' she retorted. 'Anyway, that'll have to wait. You need to come into the flat.'

'Did they shoot Ross and Dominic?' said Dean.

'Ross was winged but he's okay. Jane's sorting out his wound. They're ready to talk.'

'Wait,' said Eddie as Dean helped him to his feet. 'Where did those three wallopers go?'

'They drove off in their car,' replied his son. 'We let the tyres down on the wrong Audi.' Dean nodded at Finlay. 'He told us the blue Audi when it was the black one.'

'I cannae help it if I'm colour blind,' Finlay snapped back. 'Get the fuck off me,' he told the brothers. 'Or are you trying to feel me up?'

'We'll let go if you promise no' to strangle our da' again.'

'Aye, I promise. Now get off,' he snapped, shrugging himself free of their grip.

'You need to come now,' said Jennifer.

They followed her down the street and into Ross and Dominic's flat. Jane was in the kitchen with the brothers, bathing the wound on Ross's right upper arm.

'What happened here?' said Harry.

'I'll tell you what fucking happened,' thundered Ross. 'I was shot. It was that twat, Alfie. The prick shouldnae be in charge of a hairdryer, never mind a gun. I'm gonnae rip his fucking heid off and—'

'Did you know they're dealing weapons?' interrupted Eddie, his voice still weak and raspy after being throttled.

'Oh, Jesus, is that what they've been up to?'

'Are you seriously telling us you didn't know?'

'We knew something was going on and that it wasn't good. It's why we got out of Haghill. We thought Jack was behind it and that he might come for us.'

'Is he behind it?'

'We're still no' sure. Alfie pointed a gun at me and kept asking me over and over if I'd grassed them up to your family. When I said what was I supposed to have grassed them up about, he shot me in the arm and said the next time it would be my heid. Then

Dom did the first useful thing he's done in his life. The kettle had just boiled and he flung the lot at them. They panicked and ran. I think the bang of the gun scared them too. They weren't expecting it to be so loud, the fucking pussies. You have to stop them, they're aff their fucking heids.'

'Oh, *we* have to stop them, do we?' said Harry. 'What about you? Aren't you gonnae help?'

'They don't want to because their maw's involved,' said Dean.

'Our maw is not involved,' snapped Ross. He winced and looked at Jane. 'Careful, that bloody hurt. I have just been shot, you know.'

'Stop being a big baby,' she told him. 'You were grazed, that's all. Your washing machine got the worst of it.'

Ross turned in his seat to look at said appliance and saw a hole in the machine to the right of the door. 'Bastards,' he grunted. 'We're gonnae have to replace that.'

'Your maw is involved,' said Eddie before coughing.

'Here,' said Dominic, handing him a glass of water.

'Cheers,' he replied, accepting it from him and gingerly taking a few sips, wincing at the pain in his neck when he swallowed.

Jennifer glared at her uncle, who hung his head.

'We know Jessica's involved in this,' continued Eddie. 'Which is why those three thought you were in the know too.'

'But we're not,' exclaimed Dominic. 'We moved from Haghill to get away from all this shite and it's followed us here,' he added, looking miserable.

'Do you seriously expect us to believe that you're innocent after everything you've done to our family?' said Dean.

'This time we really are innocent. Well, me and Ross are anyway. After Jack stabbed us in the back, we knew we had to get out because it was just a matter of time before he came for us. He knows we'll always be a threat. When we heard something weird was going on in Haghill, we realised it was time to leave.'

'When did you hear that something weird was going on?' said Dean.

'Long before you lot did,' smirked Ross.

'It was about a month ago,' said Dominic, who was the more reasonable of the two brothers. 'Maw started coming home with money again but she was more subtle with it, no' splashing the cash like she used to. She told us she was involved in something but she wouldnae say what it was, said we'd run our mouths off and ruin it. Then we got word that someone in Haghill was dealing in guns. That's heavy shit, too heavy for us.'

Harry scowled. 'Even though you threatened us with guns only a couple of months ago?'

'Oh, they did, did they?' barked Finlay, hands starting to snap open and closed again.

'Take it easy, Uncle Finlay,' said Jennifer, patting his shoulder.

He simmered down but continued to glare at the Alexander brothers.

'We confronted Maw about it,' continued Dominic. 'She admitted she knew about it but swore she wasn't involved and that she wasn't getting her money from it. We didnae know if Jack and Cole were involved. Cole had started sucking up to Jack, trying to get back in his good books. He'd already turned against me and Ross and we worried the pair of them would ensure we could never be a threat again, so we left. We couldnae even trust our own maw not to turn on us either,' he said sadly.

'Do you think Jack's involved?' Jane asked him.

'I wouldnae put it past him.'

Jane lapsed into thought as she considered the implications for her sister.

'Hey, I'm bleeding here,' snapped Ross.

Jane's face creased with anger. 'After everything you've done to my family, you're lucky I'm no' pouring salt all over the wound, you whingeing bastard. You kidnapped and tortured my sister and now you're demanding that I patch you back up. Well, fuck you, Ross. For all I care, you can get an infection and die. Getting shot was just karma for all the bad stuff you've done. I wish Alfie had hit you between the eyes instead,' she yelled, throwing down the cloth she was using to clean the wound and getting to her feet.

Ross glowered at her, picked up the cloth and began dabbing at his injury.

'You're right, Jane,' said Dominic. 'This is a punishment. You cannae get away with all the stuff we've done over the years. Now look at us – forced out of our home, hiding here from our own family.'

'Serves you bloody right,' Harry told him.

Dominic just nodded.

'You're ones to talk,' said Ross, who looked both defiant and malevolent. 'Just look at all the things your family's done over the years. You're just as bad as us and if karma's come for us then it's coming for you too.'

The Savages looked at each other, knowing they had no come-back to that.

'Do you know for sure if Jack is involved in this gun operation?' Eddie asked the Alexander brothers.

'We've no proof of anything,' replied Ross. 'But he was the one who supplied us with guns before, so what does that tell you?'

'Do you know where Alfie and the others were going?'

'Naw. As if they'd share that with us.'

'Our families worked together before and we did it pretty well. We could do it again to stop this gun ring.'

'Piss off. I've already been shot once and I'm no' risking it again. We're getting out of Glasgow until the whole thing's died down.'

'We are?' said Dominic, unable to repress a smile of relief.

'Aye. We don't need this shite and if we stick around, we'll probably get killed. Moving to Bishopbriggs wasnae far enough.'

'So you're gonnae run away like your da' did?' sneered Harry.

'Aye because it's the sensible thing to do.'

'What if your maw needs help? She's in way over her head,' said Eddie.

Ross's smile was cruel and unpleasant. 'Believe me, that bitch can take care of herself. If there was a nuclear war, she'd be the only survivor. She'll have something up her sleeve to protect herself.'

'What about Cole?' said Eddie. 'He's your wee brother.'

'That prick made it quite clear he wants nothing to do with us any more, so fuck him. From now on, it's just me and Dom.'

Eddie wondered what sort of life Dominic would lead being constantly bullied by his older brother's stronger, more aggressive personality, but that wasn't his problem. He had his own family to worry about.

'Is Cole really on Jack's side now or is he plotting against him?' he asked Ross.

'Christ knows. The only person that sly git shares his plans with is Maw, or at least that's how it used to be. I doubt he even does that any more. One thing I do know about my brother is that he has big ambitions and he won't be satisfied for long taking orders from someone else.'

'Anything else we should know?'

'Naw. We've been kept in the dark as much as you.'

'Let's go,' said Eddie. 'We're wasting our time here. They've both lost their bottle.'

Ross shrugged. 'We don't gi'e a shite what you think about us.

At the end of the day, we'll be far from here living the good life while you lot are in intensive care or deid.'

Eddie just glowered at him before turning and leaving.

As they all filed out, Finlay turned back to Ross, whose malicious smirk fell at the angry look in his eyes. Before he could react or even move, Finlay's fist met his face and knocked him flat on his back, the chair tipping with him.

'That's for torturing lassies, ya cowardly prick,' bellowed Finlay.

Ross didn't hear him. He just stared up at the ceiling, dazed.

Dominic jumped when Finlay rounded on him.

'Let's go, Uncle Finlay,' said Jennifer, urging him towards the door.

'They deserve to be punished for what they've done,' he thundered.

'Aye and they will be. They're a pair of losers who'll never amount to anything. Let that be their punishment.'

Dominic retreated into the doorway leading deeper into the flat, preparing to run if the little man decided to attack.

'Maybe you're right,' said Finlay before departing with his niece, leaving Dominic to breathe a sigh of relief.

19

Carly was immensely relieved to see Jack when he walked into the flat two hours after Elijah had knocked on the door.

'All right, babe,' he said, pulling her into his arms when she ran to him.

'I'm glad you're back safe, I've been so worried,' she replied. 'How did you get on?'

'Good news. I've found somewhere else for us to stay. I want to move you there right now.'

They both turned to look at the door when there was a knock on it.

'Get ready, babe,' he told Carly.

She nodded and produced her taser as Jack peered through the spyhole.

'It's David,' he told her.

'You should let him in.'

'You think we can trust him?'

'Aye, I'm sure we can.'

'Well, okay but be on your guard.'

'I will,' she replied, replacing the taser in the back of her jeans.

Jack opened the door a crack. 'Are you alone?' he asked David.

'Aye, why?'

'Come on in.'

David watched with confusion as Jack peered suspiciously down the stairs before closing the door and locking it. 'What the hell's going on now?' he demanded.

'What makes you think anything's going on?' replied Jack.

'You're being furtive and things feel weird again.'

'Nothing's going on.'

'Have you forgotten that I've been through two wars already? Everyone's being shifty like they were when Neil and Rod attacked each other and then again when Rod lost the plot and went on the rampage. I really don't want to go through all that again, so I insist on being told what's going on.'

Jack glanced at Carly again, who nodded.

'Sit down, David,' he said.

He obeyed and regarded them with confusion as they sat together on the couch opposite him.

'I take it you two are back together?' opened David.

'We are,' replied Jack. 'But that's not the issue. What do you know about guns?'

Jack purposefully kept this statement vague, wanting to test David's reaction to the word *guns*.

'Not much,' he replied. 'I'm more of a knuckleduster type of man myself. Guns can also land you a hefty prison sentence. Why?'

'Because someone in Haghill has started dealing in them and they're using my name to do it.'

'Oh, Christ, that's all we need,' he sighed. 'Which fucking prick is responsible?'

'We're still trying to confirm that, but we do know that Mason and his brother are involved, the same Mason who seduced and tricked Carly's younger sister, Rose. Bill's in on it too.'

'I don't know Mason but I know Bill and I said he shouldn't be trusted, didn't I?'

Jack sighed and nodded. 'You did.'

'I kept saying we should kick him out but you wouldnae listen.'

'I can't argue with that.'

Carly was surprised Jack was allowing David to speak to him like that, which went to show how much he respected his lieutenant's opinion. She didn't think Elijah would have got away with it. David had a way of making you feel like a naughty child being told off by the headmaster.

'There's a possibility Elijah's also in on it,' continued Jack. 'What do you think of that?'

'Well, he has been acting shifty lately,' replied David. 'Sneaking off to make furtive phone calls and no' being where he said he's gonnae be. He could have a bit on the side. That was my first thought because I don't think he'd betray you.'

'He came to the door earlier wanting to speak to Jack urgently,' said Carly. 'And he was being creepy and weird.'

'That's just Elijah.'

'He was standing outside the café talking to Cole Alexander and they were both staring up at the flat. It was really strange.'

'Cole's just as creepy and weird as he is.'

'He didn't used to be. Before he was sent to prison, he was sweet and kind.'

'Prison does that to a lot of people.'

'Why are you so sure Elijah wouldn't betray me?' Jack asked him.

'Because his family's doing better than they ever have before and that's thanks to you.'

'That's not enough of a reason.'

'I know but he just seems really loyal to you. He was ready for cutting Dillon Crockett's throat when he bad-mouthed you. I managed to stop him but Elijah still put him in intensive care. Naw, I don't believe he's a traitor.'

'Still, I would like proof one way or the other.'

'That's fair. So, what's the plan for dealing with this?'

'At the moment we're still gathering information. We don't know who's involved exactly. My priority is keeping Carly safe.'

'You don't need to keep that lassie safe, she's perfectly capable of doing it all on her own.'

Carly beamed back at David. After feeling like the weak one, it was good to hear that.

'She doesn't want to get dragged back into our world,' replied Jack.

'With all due respect, if you've reconciled then she's already back in. Maybe you should just do what you do best, Carly, and that's no' managing a bar.'

'No, I'm definitely out,' she replied, thinking of the future she and Jack were planning together. That was the important thing.

'Shame because your skills are being wasted.'

'We're heading over to the new place now,' said Jack. 'Do you think you could confirm whether Elijah's involved in dealing weapons?'

'I can try. How quiet are we keeping this?'

'As quiet as possible. They're already aware the Savage family are onto them, which tells them I know about it too, so they won't hang about.'

'You need to keep a low profile. You're the biggest danger to them, Jack, meaning they might try and take you out before you can hit them. Don't tell anyone where you're staying, no' even me and take the back door out of here, just in case. That's a busy road out there but these pricks must be reckless to be dealing in guns in the first place, so they might try anything, no matter how stupid. Does Toni know about this?'

'I'm keeping her informed.'

David nodded. 'I appreciate you confiding in me.'

'Thank Carly for that. She said I could trust you with this.'

'I won't let either of you down.'

'I know you won't,' replied Carly.

David got to his feet. 'Right, I'll let you get on and I'll do some discreet digging. I'll concentrate on finding the buyers. They'll lead us back to the vendors.'

'Good idea.'

David left and Jack lapsed into thoughtful silence.

'You're sure he's not involved?' he eventually asked Carly.

'Aye, it's no' his style. He won't let you down just as he's never let me down.'

'He's got a soft spot for you.'

'Only because we were thrown together during the war between Neil and Rod but it showed me what type of man he is and he's definitely loyal. Neither has he ever wanted to be in charge.'

'He's the smart one,' sighed Jack. 'I feel like I've aged ten years in the last two months.'

Carly smiled and ran her fingers through his hair. 'If it helps, you don't look to have aged at all.'

He grinned and kissed her, pressing her back into the couch.

'No,' said Jack, releasing her and sitting up. 'We need to move to the new location first. I can't relax here. Let's pack up and go.'

Carly recognised the sense of this, and she packed her overnight bag while Jack gathered his things together. Ten minutes later they headed down the stairs, which led them to the café. Instead of exiting that way, they left via the back door, emerging in a paved yard and out onto the back street. They paused to look left and right but no one was about.

'Where's your car?' said Carly.

'I left it on Marwick Street.'

They stuck to the back streets, watching for anyone following them.

Jack drove them to their new digs, taking a convoluted route until he steered them down a small turning opposite the Glasgow Kelvin College Campus. Carly frowned as the road curved to the right to reveal several static caravans. Two were obviously occupied as there was patio furniture and garden ornaments outside them and furniture visible through the windows. It looked like a tiny community tucked away from the main thoroughfare. The road turned into a dead end, the turning circle lined with caravans, which was where Jack parked the car.

'Why are we here?' she said.

'This is where we're going to be staying until the danger's passed.'

She frowned. 'In a caravan?'

'Don't you like caravans?'

'I've nothing against them. I just assumed we'd be staying in another flat.'

'Then you assumed wrong. Come on, let's take a look. I've been told it's a nice caravan.'

'Okay,' she slowly replied before getting out of the car.

She followed him to a particularly nice-looking caravan with latticed windows and decking outside. He produced a key and unlocked the front door, which looked like the front door of a house complete with letterbox and not one of the flimsy doors typically found on caravans.

Carly smiled as they stepped inside. 'This is lovely.'

The interior was plush and spacious with a comfortable couch and two armchairs. There was a large flat-screen television mounted on the wall and an expensive mahogany dining table. The open-plan kitchen contained top-of-the-range appliances.

'Surprised?' said Jack knowingly.

'Actually, I am.'

'You like it?'

'I do. I think we'll be very comfortable here. I've lived in Haghill my entire life and had no idea this was even here.'

'Only two of the other caravans are occupied and they're at the other end of the compound. The others are empty, so we won't be disturbed.'

'Sounds good.' She smiled, sliding her arms around his neck.

'Don't tell anyone about this place yet, not even your family. If someone is intending to use you against me then the more people who know your location the bigger the chance there is of you being found. I suspect that was the intention of the intruder at your flat.'

'You think he wanted to kidnap me?'

Jack nodded. 'That's why he tried to lure you into the graveyard.'

Carly shivered. 'My family will want to know where I am and I don't like keeping something like that from them.'

'It's only for a little while. Hopefully David and I can get this wrapped up soon. I just want you to stay safe.'

'Okay, I won't tell anyone.'

He kissed her. 'Thank you. Right, I've got to go out again, but I'll be back soon and I'll bring some supplies. In the meantime, make yourself comfy. There are books and games in the cupboard,' he said, gesturing to the cabinet under the television. 'Call me if you need me.'

With that he left and Carly began to explore her new temporary home. There were three bedrooms, two were small and both contained single beds but the master was quite a decent size complete with a dressing table and en suite.

Carly returned to the lounge to call Jane and ask her how the family was getting on in their hunt. Jane said they were making progress but didn't give her any details. Once again, Carly was being kept out of the loop but she only had herself to blame. She hoped this didn't go on for much longer as she had to go back to work in just over a week. Thank goodness she'd taken all the time she was owed and booked a solid two weeks off otherwise she would have been a sitting duck at the bar.

Carly didn't tell Jane about the flittin, deciding her sister knowing her location could put them all in danger. She felt bad about concealing information but it was for the best. It also saddened her that the mere knowledge of her whereabouts could put her family's lives in danger. It seemed she was kidding herself that she could leave the gangland life behind. Once you were in, you could never escape.

* * *

Daphne's strip club was a startling contrast to how it had been when Eddie, Dean and Harry had visited earlier in the day. A huge doorman was on duty now, sporting sunglasses even though it was getting dark. Clearly, he'd been briefed about their arrival because he nodded for them to go straight in.

They entered the main club to find the majority of the tables were occupied. Alannah Myles's 'Black Velvet' thrummed through the speakers as a woman stripped on stage to the whoops and cat calls of the audience. The lighting was muted, only the stage illuminated. Waitresses in tight dresses stalked from the bar to the tables and back again carrying trays of drinks. More doormen were inside looking serious and professional, keeping a lookout for any punter getting too heavy with the women. Those who weren't dancing were mingling with the customers, sitting with them and quaffing the most expensive drinks the club had to offer.

Daphne was waiting to greet them at the door wearing her usual black trousers and a tight blouse, hair piled on top of her head. She escorted them to a table at the side of the room from which they could watch everyone discreetly.

'Has Charlie arrived yet?' Eddie asked her as they took their seats.

'No,' she replied, removing the *reserved* sign from their table. 'But Chastity's over there, the black-haired lassie in the pink latex dress.'

Harry's eyes widened at the sight of the raven-haired beauty chatting up a fat businessman. 'I can see why Charlie's smitten with her.'

'He'll be in to see her soon, have no worries.'

Daphne asked the men what they wanted to drink and she pouted when they ordered a pint of lager each.

'Still a cheapskate, Eddie. You should be drinking champagne.'

'No' everyone who comes in here drinks champagne.'

'I'm going out of my way to help you. I turned down real customers so you could have this table. The least you can do is buy more than three pints.'

'We'll take a bottle of champagne,' said Dean impatiently. 'I'll pay.'

'Now that is a gentleman,' she told Eddie while nodding at his son. 'You could learn a lot from him.'

With that, she stalked off and relayed their order to one of the bar staff.

'You shouldnae have done that,' Eddie told Dean. 'She would

have added a load of expensive drinks to our order anyway. She'll still do it even though you've asked for champagne.'

'It's fine. I just want to concentrate on the job so we can get out of here.'

Harry smiled. 'Are you uncomfortable?'

'Aye, a bit.'

'Why? It's just lassies taking their clothes off, or have you never seen a naked woman before?'

'Course I have. I've just never had to pay for the privilege while I'm guessing you have?'

'Don't start, you two,' said Eddie. 'We're here to work. Now concentrate, try to spot any familiar faces.'

Harry had trouble keeping his eyes off the girls. Fortunately, his father and brother were on the ball and Eddie spotted someone they knew being led to a table on the opposite side of the room by Daphne.

'Hey,' he said to his sons. 'That's Lonny.'

They all turned to look at the landlord of The Wheatsheaf as he happily settled himself at the table, eyes widening when Chastity strode over to him. She took the seat beside his and the two began chatting like old friends.

'He must be deep in this gunrunning ring and no' just letting them hold their meetings in his pub,' said Eddie.

'It's looking that way,' replied Dean. 'Unless he's just using what he overhears at those meetings to impress Chastity.'

'Bugger, I bet that's what the wee worm's doing. He hasnae got the balls to be involved in something like that.'

'That still means he has all the information though.'

'Good point, son. Let's stick with the plan. Harry, get your mind off that lassie taking her clothes off and onto the job.'

'Sorry,' Harry said, tearing his eyes off the stage. 'But it's hard to concentrate in here.'

'Maybe you should leave it to me and Dean?'

'No, I'm good,' he replied. 'I can do this.'

'It looks like she's taking him into the back room,' said Dean.

They watched Chastity rise, take Lonny's hand and lead him away from the table and through a side door. As they moved, Chastity glanced over at their table and winked.

'We're on,' said Eddie. 'Dean, go and listen. I don't trust Harry no' to get distracted.'

His younger son nodded and left the table.

'Keep an eye out,' Eddie told Harry. 'There might be more people here that we know.'

The woman dancing to 'Black Velvet' finished her routine and left the stage. Their drinks were brought over by a tall blonde with enormous fake breasts. Eddie grinned when Harry's eyes almost fell out of his head as she leaned over to place the bottle of champagne on the table.

'What's your name, beautiful?' he asked her.

'Roxy.' She smiled back at him.

'Pretty, like you.'

'For God's sake,' muttered Eddie, rolling his eyes. 'Do you think she doesnae hear that every night in this place?'

'Shut up, Da',' Harry hissed at him.

'Your da's right, I do hear that every night,' said Roxy. She reached out to stroke Harry's face. 'But none of them are as handsome as you. Ask for me if you'd like a private dance.' She winked at him before walking away, Harry's eyes glued to her backside.

'Wow, she's gorgeous,' enthused Harry.

'You mean plastic,' said Eddie. 'Nature didnae create that, some surgeon with a scalpel did. Gi'e me natural every time.'

'He's no' a surgeon, he's an artist.'

Dean returned to the table twenty minutes later looking pissed off.

'What's wrong with your face?' Eddie asked him.

'Lonny's full of shite. He's making himself out to be Marlon Brando back there. Anyone who didnae know him would think he ran the whole of Glasgow rather than a shitey back street pub.'

'So it's all bollocks?'

'Perhaps. Lonny didn't mention Cole, so I don't think he's involved but he did say that he's running the whole operation with his partner, some sheep-shagging ex-con from Yorkshire.'

'Jack,' said Harry, narrowing his eyes.

'We cannae trust a word Lonny says; he's just bragging to impress a stripper,' replied Eddie.

'But there was some truth to what he was saying,' said Dean. 'He also mentioned the Stewarts' garage.'

'I'm done with this shite,' grunted Eddie. 'Let's grab the wee fanny and make him talk.'

'You cannae dae that here,' said Dean.

'Then we'll wait for him to leave and grab him outside.'

'Christ knows when he'll leave, he's obsessed with that stripper.'

'We'll wait as long as it takes.'

'Fine by me,' said Harry, smiling when a woman dressed as a nurse appeared on the stage and began stripping to Bon Jovi's 'Bad Medicine'. Then Harry frowned and slowly got to his feet, squinting at the woman. 'No, it cannae be.'

'What's wrong?' said Eddie.

'That stripper – it's Genesis.'

'Your girlfriend?' said Dean.

'Aye.' He was gaping at the stage but this time there was no pleasure in his eyes. Instead, anger filled them as he noted all the men ogling her. 'Hey,' he yelled. 'Stop looking at my girlfriend.'

The music was so loud that no one beyond the tables closest to his own heard.

'Get off there right now,' Harry exclaimed, storming towards the stage.

'Should we stop him?' Dean asked his father.

'We could try but it would cause a big scene. We're best leaving him to it.'

Dean anxiously watched his brother jump onto the stage. Genesis realised he was there, her eyes widening. She stopped dancing to talk to him, while the customers started booing.

'Great,' sighed Eddie when the doormen rushed up to the stage.

'We really should do something,' said Dean.

'They're going now,' said Eddie when Genesis took Harry's hand and hastily led him off the stage. 'It's okay.'

'It's not okay, the doormen are following them.'

'More fool them then.'

'I'll make sure he's okay,' said Dean before getting up and rushing towards the stage.

Daphne stormed up to Eddie, expression hard. 'Your son's messed up Genesis's routine. Her naughty nurse is one of our most popular shows.'

'Sorry about that, doll, but she's his girlfriend and he didnae know she was a stripper. He thought she was a topless model.'

'What's the difference? Either way, she's getting her tits out.'

'She told him she was working for a classy magazine, he didnae realise—'

Daphne pursed her lips when he went abruptly silent. 'You mean he didnae realise she was really working at a shitey old strip club.'

'That's no' what I was gonnae say.'

'Aye it was. Well, you can take your sons and get out of my crappy business if it's no' good enough for you.'

'Take it easy, Daph. That's no' what I meant at all. This is a great place.'

She trembled with indignation, causing her bosom to wobble.

'Why don't you sit down and have a drink with me?' said Eddie, indicating the bottle of champagne. 'You work too hard, you need to relax a wee bit.'

'Well,' she said, thawing to his charm slightly. 'I suppose one wouldn't hurt.' Daphne stopped one of the waitresses as she passed by. 'Go and tell the doormen to leave Genesis and her boyfriend alone and tell Amethyst that she's going on now.'

'Yes, Ms Daphne,' the girl said obediently before tottering off.

Daphne sat beside Eddie and he filled a glass for her. So far, neither himself nor his boys had touched the champagne, wanting to stay clear-headed but he reasoned that calming down this formidable woman was reason enough for a drink.

20

Dean and Harry returned to the table to find Eddie and Daphne laughing together, half the bottle of champagne gone.

Harry frowned. 'This looks very cosy.'

'There you are.' Eddie grinned. 'Sit down, boys, have a glass of champagne. It's bloody lovely stuff.'

'We're supposed to be working, no' getting pished.'

'Take the pole out of your arse, son. Here you go,' Eddie said, pouring a glass of champagne and holding it out to him.

Harry snatched it from his hand and slammed himself down into a chair. 'I dumped Genesis.'

'Never mind,' said Daphne. 'You're a good-looking man, you'll soon find someone else.'

'I know but I liked her. She's a proper dynamo in the sack.'

'Is that the only reason you liked her?'

'No. She smelled good too.'

'I think you'll get over it.' Daphne wrapped an arm around his shoulders. 'You need the comfort and understanding of an older woman.' She frowned when she saw her two doormen limping back to their posts. 'What happened to them?'

'They got in Harry's way,' replied Dean, also taking a seat.

They all looked to Daphne wondering if she'd be annoyed but on the contrary, she spluttered with laughter.

'I should sack them and give you two their jobs,' she told the brothers.

'Harry couldn't work here, he'd be far too distracted,' replied Dean.

'Hey, you made a joke,' she said, smiling. 'I knew you could do it. You shouldn't be so serious all the time.'

Dean just stared back at her, unamused.

'Charlie's coming back with Chastity,' said Eddie, not wanting to use Lonny's real name in front of Daphne.

'He lasted longer than I thought this time,' chuckled Daphne.

'What do you mean?'

'I mean that he cannae contain his excitement when she strips for him.'

'I thought you didn't allow anything like that in your club?'

'I don't but there's nothing I can do about men getting carried away and coming in their pants.'

Harry choked on his champagne. Dean slapped him hard on the back.

'I'm fine,' protested Harry. 'No need to be so rough. We should spread the rumour around Haghill that he comes in his pants while watching strippers,' he added mischievously, nodding in Lonny's direction.

'We need to use this to our advantage,' said Eddie. 'Do you think we could have a wee word with Chastity?' he asked Daphne. 'Obviously we'll pay her for her time.'

'One of you can in the back room,' she replied. 'She charges 500 pounds.'

'For one strip?' he exclaimed.

'You can always not talk to her,' she said frostily.

'I'll do it,' said Harry. 'It would be money well spent. She's gorgeous.'

'You got over your broken heart pretty quickly,' Eddie snapped at him.

'Like Daphne said, there's plenty more fish in the sea,' he replied cheerfully.

'No. You'll get overwhelmed by her nakedness and no' ask the right questions. I'll do it,' he said with a martyred sigh.

'Shall I nip home and pick you up a spare pair of pants?'

'If you weren't my son, I'd knock you out of your fucking chair for that remark.'

'I'll let Chastity know she's got another client.' Daphne smiled, getting to her feet and bustling across the room to her.

'It was only a joke,' said Harry when his father glared at him.

'Well, it was no' funny. I'm a real man, unlike him,' he retorted, nodding in the direction of Lonny, who was lolling back in his chair, looking spent but happy.

Daphne returned and told Eddie that Chastity was waiting for him in the private room before moving to greet a new customer.

'Sure you don't want me to sacrifice myself instead?' Harry asked his father.

'No, thanks. I can handle it,' Eddie replied, getting to his feet and running a hand through his thinning hair before striding off.

'So, how's it going with you and Destiny?' Harry asked his brother while they waited for their father to return.

'Aye, good,' he replied, looking more cheerful at the mention of his new girlfriend. 'She's fascinated by Voltaire; we had a really good discussion about his work.'

'Oh, aye. Voltaire. He plays for Juventus, doesn't he?' Harry grinned.

'Very funny. He was a French writer and philosopher. How

many women do you know read Voltaire?' It was Dean's turn to smile. 'What am I saying? None of your girlfriends can read.'

'Actually, they can,' sniffed Harry.

'I'm talking about books without pictures.'

'You can be really up yourself sometimes, Dean. Anyway, I'm just surprised you've given up on Carly for a Voltaire-reading lingerie model.'

'It had to be done. I still love her, but it would have been too complicated. Da' was right, everyone would have called us freaks because we're cousins. It would have caused trouble in the family and that's the last thing I want after losing Uncle Alec.'

Harry didn't like to mention that he and Jane had been coming round to the idea of them being a couple. 'You're right, it's for the best, although I bet Carly's a wildcat in the sack.'

Dean glowered. 'Don't talk about her like that.'

'You know I mean no disrespect, it's just who I am. Are you really okay about her being with Jack?'

'I'd be a hypocrite not to be when I'm seeing Destiny.'

'It must hurt though.'

'Aye, it does but I'll deal with it. He makes her happy and that's what's important.'

'You're a bigger man than I am.'

'So all the ladies say.' Dean smiled.

'Cheeky bastard.' Harry grinned back.

They watched Amethyst perform her routine on stage, which involved a snake and a feather duster. They kept one eye on Lonny, who gazed at the stage, transfixed while steadily drinking champagne.

As Amethyst's routine finished, Eddie returned to the table.

'You just missed one hell of a show, Da',' said Harry. 'I'd nae idea anyone could bend like that and I've dated three women who were double jointed.'

'I bet it was nothing compared to the show I've just seen,' he replied. 'That Chastity is one hell of a woman, no wonder Lonny's obsessed. And no, I don't need to change my undies,' he snapped at Harry when he smiled. 'She told me some useful stuff. Lonny has been loaded lately. He could only afford one strip a month but now he's paying for them every week, as well as the best champagne.'

'Aye, he's coined up,' said Harry in a bored tone. 'We already know that.'

'What we didn't know was that he came here last week with another man. Daphne was off sick, so she didnae see him. That man perfectly fits Alfie's description, although he called himself Alan. They were both flashing the cash and enjoying themselves with the girls. Alfie particularly liked Genesis.'

Harry's expression turned thunderous. 'What?'

'He told her some really interesting things when he was pished. Chastity's gonnae have a word and get her to talk to us.'

'Well I won't be here for that,' he muttered, folding his arms across his chest.

'Maybe you should gi'e her a break?' said Dean. 'She's only trying to make some money.'

'By stripping for men.'

'You were happy enough when you thought she was a topless model. What's the difference between men looking at her here and through the pages of a magazine?'

'The magazine's at a distance. The men aren't anywhere near her.'

'No touching is allowed.'

'So? How would you feel if it was Destiny? Ha,' he added when Dean didn't reply. 'You wouldnae be happy either.'

'All I'm saying is you should gi'e her a chance to explain. You wouldn't let her say two words backstage, you just ranted at her and stormed off like a wean.'

'I'd had a shock,' he barked.

'Shut your geggies,' said Eddie. 'Here comes the lassie.'

A sheepish Genesis approached the table, her huge blue eyes fixed on Harry. 'I believe you want to talk to me,' she mumbled.

'Aye,' replied Eddie. 'Sit down, doll,' he added, patting the chair between himself and Harry.

Genesis looked hopefully at Harry, who sniffed and tilted his head away from her. She swallowed hard and her eyes turned shiny with tears. She'd changed out of her naughty nurse outfit and wore a tiny black skirt and black bikini top that struggled to contain her large silicone breasts.

'Did Daphne tell you who we wanted to discuss?' Eddie asked Genesis, drawing her attention back to himself.

'She did,' she replied, wiping away a single tear when it escaped from the corner of her eye and rolled down her cheek.

'Good. What can you tell us about them, doll?'

'Well, they called themselves Charlie and Alan. They had a lot of money and they were very generous with it.'

'Stripped for them, did you?' said Harry without deigning to look at her.

'No,' she retorted. 'They just wanted to talk.'

Harry snorted in response.

'I'm not good enough to talk to either now, am I?' she told him. 'I'm just some bimbo who should shut up and look pretty. That's all you want, isn't it Harry?'

'No but I don't want someone who strips off for a living either. Ow,' he exclaimed when Dean kicked him under the table.

'Ignore him,' Dean told Genesis. 'He's a dick.'

'Hey you,' he huffed.

'Shut it, Harry,' Eddie told him. After giving his older son a warning look, he turned back to Genesis. 'What else did they do?' he said gently.

'They both got pretty drunk. Alan especially cannae take champagne. It goes straight to his heid. I got the impression he'd usually be pretty tight-lipped but he was gabbing away, they both were, bragging about how much money they make.'

'Did they say how they made it?'

'No' exactly but I got the impression it was illegal. They also mentioned a garage but to be honest, I lost what they were saying because they were so pished. They didnae make much sense. They wanted to surround themselves with girls though. At one point there were six of us sat with them.'

'Three each,' said Harry bitterly. 'That worked out well.'

'If you cannae contribute anything useful then you can bugger off,' Eddie told him.

'Fine,' he huffed, getting to his feet. 'I'll wait outside. Hey,' he exclaimed when Dean grabbed his arm and yanked him back down into his seat.

'He was looking around then,' Dean told him. 'I didnae want him to see you.'

'Nice save,' replied Eddie, glancing over at Lonny, who was stretching and yawning. 'Sit there and don't say a word,' he told Harry. 'Now, doll,' he continued, turning back to Genesis. 'What else can you tell us?'

'No' much really. Oh, I did see Alan texting someone. I read the message over his shoulder,' she mumbled, looking a little embarrassed.

This wasn't a surprise because they all knew Daphne's girls gathered blackmail material for their boss.

'We're no' judging,' said Eddie kindly. 'What did it say?'

'It was to someone called Jack. Alan was telling him that he was taking the next delivery at ten o'clock the following night. He seemed a bit scared of this Jack if you ask me. He was trying to placate him when he replied he should have done that delivery that night instead. Jack said he'd cut his stomach open too if he didn't stop being such a lazy bastard. It gave me a shock reading that because there was so much hate in it and it sounded such a horrible thing to say to someone. Alan's hand actually started shaking and he replied that he'd get right on it. I've never seen anyone sober up so quickly in my life. The two of them left. Charlie didn't want to go and Alan practically dragged him out by the arm. I hope I've helped?' she added when the three men glanced at each other.

'Aye, you've been great, doll,' said Eddie. He produced some cash from his pocket and held it out to her. 'For your time.'

'No need. I did it for Harry,' she replied, glancing sideways at him.

'That's good of you,' mumbled her ex.

'I do hope you'll let me explain properly why I work here,' she said. 'You might understand then.'

'He'll call you,' Dean answered for his brother.

'I can speak for myself,' Harry barked back at him.

'Go on then, tell Genesis you'll call her and arrange to discuss it properly.'

'Don't look at me,' said Eddie when Harry turned to him for assistance. 'Your brother's right, you should gi'e her the chance to explain.'

'Fine,' he sighed as though put upon. 'I'll call you,' he told Genesis, only deigning to give her a sideways glance.

'Thank you, I appreciate that.' She got to her feet and planted a kiss on his cheek before walking away.

'That's a nice lassie,' said Eddie.

'I agree,' replied Dean. 'There's something really sweet about her and I think you like her more than you've let on, it's why you got so angry about her stripping.'

'I'm no' discussing it any more,' grunted Harry. 'I agreed to talk to her, so can we drop it now. But at least she confirmed that Jack's been lying to us and he really is in on it.'

'Wrong,' said Eddie. 'Alan, or rather Alfie, was texting someone called Jack. We don't know that it was him. It could have been someone using his name.'

'But the stomach cutting thing...'

'Anyone could have written that. It's still no' enough proof.'

'So this has been a total waste of time.'

'No' completely,' said Dean. 'At least we found out that your girlfriend's a stripper.'

'You're really asking for a smack in the mouth.'

Dean just smiled in response before turning to his father. 'What do we do now because the way I see it, we're no closer to solving the mystery?'

'Right, we're doing it my way,' said Harry, watching a drunken Lonny attempt to pull on his jacket. 'We're grabbing that fanny once he's outside and we'll make him tell us what's going on because I'm sick of this spy shite.'

'Aye, all right,' said Eddie.

After leaving money on the table to cover the drinks, the three of them casually got to their feet and followed Lonny out the door. They passed the doormen, who glowered at Harry.

'Don't worry, boys,' he told them. 'The bruises will fade in a few days.'

They exited the club and saw Lonny winding his way down the street, staggering from side to side. He attempted to flag down a passing taxi but the vehicle refused to stop. After giving the car the finger, he continued on his way.

'Grab him now and take him down that back street,' Eddie urged his sons.

Harry and Dean rushed up behind Lonny, grabbed one arm each and ushered him down a side street. Lonny was so shocked that he didn't even protest until he was halfway down the alley.

'Wh... what's going on?' he babbled.

He was shoved up against a wall and under the glare of a streetlight he was finally able to see his abductors. 'Oh, thank God,' he breathed. 'It's just you.' The fright he'd got had scared him sober.

'No' the response we were expecting,' said Harry.

'Who did you think we were?' Dean asked him.

'Nobody,' Lonny said innocently.

'Aye ya did. Who?'

Dean punched him hard in the stomach and he dropped to his knees and emptied his guts all over the dirty cobbles. The brothers leapt backwards, narrowly avoiding having their shoes splattered with sick.

'You're gonnae start talking,' Eddie told Lonny. 'And if you don't, my boys will beat the shite out of you and leave you in this stinking alley for the dogs to piss on.' They all turned to look when a young couple who'd clearly just left one of the surrounding nightclubs staggered down the alley together, frantically kissing. They stopped when they saw the three aggressive men glaring at them and the fourth on the ground, groaning in pain.

'Fuck off,' spat Harry.

The couple jumped and sprinted out of the alley together.

The three men turned back to Lonny.

'Now you're gonnae tell us if Jack Alexander is or isn't in on your gunrunning operation,' said Eddie.

Lonny stared up at them. 'Then you do know?' he panted, still trying to recover his breath.

'Course we know. We just want you to confirm who exactly is involved. Is Jack in charge?'

'Aye. Do you really think anything happens in Haghill without his knowledge?'

Eddie glanced at his sons, who looked equally troubled.

'He says he knows nothing about it,' added Eddie.

'Well he would, wouldn't he? All he cares about is money and getting Carly back and she wouldn't want to be with a man who's dealing in guns. He's a greedy bastard and he'll do whatever's necessary to get what he wants.'

'Did he set the whole gun ring up?'

'Aye. It's making big money too. It's no' just guns but blades too, illegal ones you cannae buy.'

'If that's true then why would he send us to find out who's behind the ring? He must have known one of you would talk.'

'Because he wants Carly all to himself without any interfering family. He can be charming when he wants to be but the man's a grade-A psycho. He keeps saying how he cut that druggie's stomach open in self-defence but you can guarantee it was on purpose. He's a sadistic twat. He was probably hoping you'd run into Alfie and he'd shoot you. That guy's a psycho too and he loves guns. He's been itching to shoot a real person and no' just targets.'

'He's already shot Ross Alexander.'

'That fanny barely classes as human and I heard he only winged him. Shame Alfie didnae put a bullet right through his skull. It would have served him right. He was always playing the big man in my pub, demanding free drinks.'

'Never mind all that. We want to know about Jack.'

'I've told you everything I know. Jack just wants money and your niece. I bet by now he's taken her away somewhere none of you know about and told her no' to tell you where she is to protect you and her.'

'He was the one who pretended to be an intruder to scare her?'

'I don't know about that but it sounds like something he'd do.'

'What about Cole? Is he in on it too?'

'You must be joking. Jack knows how clever Cole is and he's afraid of him taking everything from him. He's luring Cole into a false sense of security to make him think he's forgiven him but only so it'll make it easier to take him out. He hates Cole because he was Carly's first love, it drives him mad. He's so jealous.' Lonny's eyes flicked to Dean. 'You're in danger too, he knows there was something between you and her. Everyone says that's weird because you're cousins but personally, I find it hot.'

Dean kicked him in the ribs, sending him sprawling face down onto the cobbles.

'Easy, son,' said Eddie. 'Where's Jack now?' he asked Lonny.

It took him a moment to reply. Slowly he dragged himself up to a sitting position, an arm wrapped around his aching ribs and stomach. 'If you keep hitting me,' he wheezed. 'I'm no' gonnae be able to talk at all.'

'Just get on with it,' said Eddie impatiently.

'I don't know, he doesnae share his every move with me.'

'Do you meet with him personally?'

'Naw. I'm too lowly for the likes of Jack Alexander. All the information I get comes from Alfie.'

'So you've never heard any of this directly from Jack's own lips?'

'Naw but why would Alfie make it up?'

'That's a good question. When's the next delivery?'

'Tomorrow night. Ten o'clock.'

'Who's the buyer?'

'I don't know, I'm never told that. I just let them stash some of the stock in my cellar. They pay me very well for the risk. I only know when the deliveries are being made because Alfie and Mason arrange to collect the items from my pub.'

'Why have they been using the Stewarts' garage?'

'For their meetings. They don't want to risk being overheard.'

'So you don't know who the customer is?'

'Naw, they don't tell me that either. I only know times and dates. You won't tell them I grassed, will you? Alfie will fucking kill me.'

'Your secret's safe with us but if you've fed us a load of old bollocks...'

'I havenae, it's all true,' Lonny exclaimed.

'We want the names of everyone else involved, then you can be on your way.'

'No problem. Well, there's Alfie's brother, Mason, Jessica Alexander, Bill who works for Jack and two blokes from The Drum,' he said, referring to Drumchapel, a district north-west of the city. 'They're pals of Alfie's. He wanted to bring in a couple of faces not known around here.'

'And Jack approved of that?'

'It was his idea. He wanted strangers in case your family clocked on to what was going on.'

'So you've never spoken to Jack face to face about this operation? You only have Alfie's word that he is involved?'

'Aye but why would he lie?'

'I can think of many reasons.'

'Do you seriously think something like this could go on under Jack Alexander's nose without him realising?'

'He's no' infallible.'

'Trust me, he knows. You sound really bloody naïve. I expected more from a Savage.'

'Are you wanting another punch in the gut?' snarled Eddie.

'No,' squeaked Lonny, returning to his usual cowardly self. 'And don't forget, Jack's the one who got his cousins the guns. Do you think Alfie and Jessica could get hold of weaponry like that? No way, they don't have the contacts.'

'It sounds like they're the ones in charge.'

'They are, after Jack. He has overall control but he talks only to them directly. He's smart, he doesnae want to get his hands dirty. He's given himself plausible deniability and he's letting the others take all the risk.'

'What about Elijah Samson? Is he involved?'

'Not that I know of but I wouldnae be surprised if he's cottoned on to the operation and wants it for himself. He's a tricky one is Elijah and a real predator. He might be working behind the scenes against Jack, although I've never had any direct contact with him myself. I've told you everything I know. Can I go now?'

'Aye, piss aff. I'm sick of looking at you but if you warn anyone that you've spoken to us...'

'Jesus, like I'm gonnae dae that. They'd kill me.'

'You let them collect the guns as usual from your pub tomorrow. If you don't interfere then you might just get through this alive.'

'Aye, I've got it.'

Lonny got to his feet and pressed his hand against the wall when he swayed. He took a few deep breaths before tilting back his head and exiting the alley with enormous dignity, the effect ruined when he tripped up at the mouth of the alley and vanished around the corner.

'What do you make of that, boys?' said Eddie.

'It's looking more and more like Jack's behind everything,' replied Harry.

'Aye but can we take that fud's word for it? Like he said, he's no' spoken to him directly. This could still be someone using Jack's name like Cole used ours during his attempt to take over from Rod. I won't believe it until we've got proof that he's directly involved.'

'Should we warn Carly?'

'Aye, I think so. Let's call her. We cannae risk paying a visit in case Jack's there.'

Eddie took out his phone to call his niece but she didn't pick up.

'That should have woken her,' he said. 'She always keeps her phone close, even at night. I don't like it.'

'There could be plenty of reasons why she's no' picked up,' said Dean. 'Maybe her battery died or she's accidentally turned the ringer off.'

'I'll try calling Jack.' Eddie wasn't sure whether to be nervous or relieved when Jack answered.

'I hope you've got some good news for me, Eddie,' he said.

'We've managed to confirm some of the people involved.'

'Who?'

'Your cousin Jessica, Mason and his brother Alfie, Lonny who owns The Wheatsheaf, although he is only on the periphery, Hairy Bill who works for you and two unknowns from The Drum.'

'I can't say I'm surprised by any of those names.'

'We shouldn't discuss this any more on the phone. Shall we come to the flat?'

'We're not there any more. I've moved Carly to a safe location.'

'Where? We'll come to you.'

'I'm not telling you that. I'm trying to keep her safe. The more people who know where she is, the more danger she's in.'

Fear for his niece spiked inside Eddie. 'Can I have a wee word with her?'

'No problem.'

There was the sound of the phone being passed over and Carly's sleepy voice came on the line. 'Hi, Uncle Eddie.'

'All right, Carly, doll?'

'Aye, I'm fine. Are you?'

'We're all good, thanks. Where are you?'

'I cannae tell you that.'

'You know you can trust me.'

'I know I can but people are after me and you knowing my location will put you all in danger. I'm no' risking that.'

'Don't you worry about us, we can take care of ourselves but you're all alone.'

'I'm with Jack.'

'Am I on speakerphone?'

'No.'

'The information we've been given indicates he's the one we're looking for.'

'I don't believe it,' she replied, lowering her voice.

'No one we've spoken to so far has had direct contact with him about it. It's all through a second party but you have to bear in mind that this could all be down to him.'

'It isn't,' she retorted, her voice becoming tight with anger.

'I know you love him, sweetheart, but you have to stay on your guard, okay? It's the smart thing to do. I promised your da' I'd keep you safe and this is me fulfilling that promise. I've only got your best interests at heart.'

'I understand,' she said more gently. 'But I know that you're barking up the wrong tree.'

'Is he still with you?'

'No, he's gone into the bathroom, so he obviously has no problem with us talking in private. What does that tell you?'

Eddie thought it told him nothing. For all they knew, Jack could have bugged the room and was listening in. 'Just please remember that we've no' proved his innocence. Jack could be behind this gun ring and he could also have been the intruder at the flat. Stay on your guard, doll. It's only what your da' would tell you to do.'

'That's a cheap shot, Uncle Eddie.'

'No, it's wise advice. Please tell me where you are.'

There was a pause and he thought she was going to tell him. 'He's coming back,' she whispered. 'I'm in a caravan. Got to go,' she added before hanging up.

Eddie frowned at his phone when the dial tone sounded. 'Bugger,' he sighed.

'What did she say?' replied Harry.

'She's adamant it's nothing to do with Jack.'

'She has got it bad.'

'Definitely. She won't hear a word against him, which is crazy because this is Jack Alexander we're talking about.'

'Did she tell you where she is?' said Dean, looking anxious.

'She only said she's in a caravan.'

'Then she could be anywhere,' he exclaimed. 'There are loads of caravan sites in Scotland. What if he's taken her out of Glasgow? We'll never find her.'

'The lassie's smart. We have to rely on her to take care of herself.'

'I'd feel much better if we at least knew where she was. The fact that he's keeping her location a secret speaks volumes.'

'Aye it does,' said Harry. 'Like Lonny said, Jack wants her all to himself without any interfering family and finally he's got her. Christ only knows what he'll do now.'

21

'Has Eddie hung up?' Jack asked Carly as he climbed back into bed.

'Aye,' she replied, handing him back his phone. 'He's really worried about me.'

'Because he's a good uncle.'

Jack wrapped an arm around her and Carly nestled into his chest, feeling a little unsettled after that conversation. 'He is. I feel bad for not telling him where I am. He'll think I don't trust him.'

'It's for the best. You're in danger. Your family tracked the intruder at your flat back to the Stewarts' garage, which is the centre of operations of this gun ring. Or at least it was. If they're smart, then they will have switched locations by now. The two things are connected and I am not risking you getting shot. These people are probably willing to torture your family to get your location out of them.'

The thought horrified Carly but she kept her uncle's words in mind. God, she hoped Jack wasn't at the bottom of all this. It had been painful enough when Cole and Dean had hurt her, but her heart would be well and truly shattered if Jack had betrayed her.

'Eddie gave me some names. Let me do a little digging first. Just give me another day.'

'Okay but it's so painful being separated from them.'

He ran his fingers through her hair. 'I envy you. I've never been close to any member of my family. They're all crooks or paedos. You're the only person I've ever connected with and it means so much that you came back to me.' He rolled on top of her and kissed her. 'Never leave me again.'

'I won't, I swear. Anyway what about all this trouble?' she said, deciding to do a little probing. 'What are the names Uncle Eddie gave you?'

'He didn't tell you?'

'No. He's still trying to keep me out of it.'

'Well so far he thinks it's Mason and his brother Alfie, Jessica, Bill and Lonny.'

'Lonny? But he's such a wee wuss.'

'He's on the periphery apparently.'

'Well, they're no' very scary. I feel a wee bit better actually. You'll easily crush them.'

'Don't underestimate Alfie. He's bloody dangerous. It's one reason why I want you kept well away from this.'

'And while you're protecting me, who's protecting you?'

'I can handle it. I got used to watching my own back in prison.'

'I'm glad that you decided to trust David. I'm sure you can rely on him but what about Elijah? I don't trust him.'

'I'll get to the bottom of it. For now, we need to get some rest, although...'

Carly moaned when he kissed her neck. As he moved lower, her gaze slipped to his mobile phone sitting on the bedside cabinet. If only she could look at it... No, she would not do that. Snooping through her partner's phone would be the start of a slippery slope for their relationship. She had to have faith in the man she loved because if she didn't, who would?

* * *

Eddie and his sons headed over to Jennifer's flat where Jane was staying, wanting to avoid the family flat in light of everything that was going on. Rose had been told to spend her time between Noah's and Tamara's homes until the trouble was over.

'Wow, look at this place,' said Harry. 'I'd no idea you were so into plushies, Jen.'

The living room of Jennifer's flat was full of cuddly toys. They were piled up on the couches, perched on shelves and heaped up in the corner.

'I've collected them for years,' she replied. 'Some of them are pretty valuable.'

'Do you cuddle them?'

Jennifer smiled at the twinkle in his eye. 'Sometimes.'

'Never mind the cuddly toys,' said Eddie. 'We've more important matters to discuss.'

'What have you found out?' Jane asked him.

Eddie explained everything that had happened that evening.

'Jesus, we have to find Carly,' exclaimed Jane.

'That's just what I've been saying,' replied Dean.

'She had the chance to tell me where she was and she didnae take it,' said Eddie grimly. 'Jack's really done a number on her.'

'She obviously trusts him,' said Jennifer. 'Maybe she has good reason?'

'Or he's got her all to himself like he wanted and he's going to ensure it stays that way,' said Jane.

'Is he that type of man?'

'That's just it, we don't know what type of man he is. He only came to Haghill a few months ago.'

'We've no direct proof that he is involved,' said Eddie. 'All we have is a stripper reading a text message over someone's shoulder and Lonny saying someone told him Jack was running the show. That's no' enough to directly accuse a man like that, especially as Lonny's a lying wee rat.'

'And there's Toni McVay to consider in all this,' said Jane. 'What would she do if she got wind that Jack was gunrunning without her permission?'

'Whatever it was would involve some eyeball scooping,' said Jennifer.

'Our priority has to be getting Carly away from him,' replied Jane. 'Whether Jack is involved or not, she's going to get caught in the crossfire.'

'Did you find anything out?' Eddie asked her. He'd tasked Jane and Jennifer with following Jessica Alexander.

'Nope. All she did was potter from the nail bar to the café where she gabbed with her cronies. It was a total waste of time.'

'The next drop is going to be tomorrow night at ten o'clock starting at The Wheatsheaf. Let's get some rest, so we're fresh for that.'

'But what about Carly?' demanded Jane.

'Try calling her in the morning and talking some sense into her because she won't listen to me. Hopefully she'll tell you where she's staying.'

* * *

Jack left the caravan at eight o'clock the next morning. Carly watched him leave from the window, wishing he could stay. Even though some of the other caravans were owned, it appeared no one was currently in residence and no vehicles drove down the road. She was all alone here. The main road was just at the top of the cul-de-sac but she couldn't see it from the caravan, making it feel like it was miles away.

She switched on the television, wanting some background noise. When her phone rang, she rushed to answer it.

'Hi, Jane,' she said, pleased to hear her sister's voice.

'Carly,' she replied, sounding relieved. 'Are you okay?'

'Aye, I'm fine.'

'Where are you?'

'I can't tell you that.'

'Come on, it's me,' said Jane, gently coaxing. 'We don't have any secrets from each other.'

'It's to protect you.'

'I appreciate that but what if something happens to Jack and no one else knows where you are?'

'I don't want to put you in danger.'

'You won't. We have each other's backs.'

'I'll think about it.'

'Don't you trust me?'

'Course I do but I'm so afraid of something happening to you.'

'It won't. If you like, I'll keep it to myself. I won't tell anyone else.'

'No' even Uncle Eddie and Jennifer?'

'No' even them, I promise.'

'Well, okay. I'm in a caravan on Plant Street.'

'I think I know where that is. So you're close, that's a relief. You just told Uncle Eddie you were in a caravan and we've been driving ourselves mad trying to work out where that could be.'

'Sorry but I couldn't say anything else at the time.'

'Because of Jack?'

'He thought it was for the best and I know what you're going to say so don't say it. Jack isn't the one running this gun ring. Someone's using his name.'

'That's possible, I'll admit.'

'Keep what I'm about to say to yourself but he said he wants out. He wants me and him to leave Glasgow together and start a new life.'

'Seriously?'

Carly heard the doubt in her sister's voice. 'Aye and I believed him,' she said defensively.

'He's only been running things for two months and he wants out already?'

'It's not what he'd thought it would be and he knows that I'll always be in danger as long as he's the boss. He said he's realised that I'm the most important thing to him, more so than the job.'

'Toni would never let him out.'

'Admittedly, that is a big obstacle but if anyone can find a way it's Jack.'

'Jennifer said you can come and stay at her place with me. That would be safer than the caravan.'

'I'm fine where I am. I know you think Jack's guilty but I don't, meaning someone's setting him up and they will use me to get to him. I won't do anything to put him in danger.'

'Oh, Carly,' Jane said gently. 'I knew you loved him but I'd no idea it went this deep. Just please remember that Jack plotted his takeover without telling you about it. The same thing could be happening now.'

'It's not. Trust me.'

'I do but I still wish you'd come to Jennifer's.'

'I'm fine here and you know where I am now.'

'And I'm relieved about that. If you change location, promise you'll let me know, no matter what Jack says.'

'I promise and you'll keep me updated?'

'Course. I love you, Carly.'

'Love you too.'

Carly hung up, glad her voice hadn't cracked with the emotion she was feeling. This whole situation had been scary to begin with as it involved guns but it was starting to feel even more dangerous. In the past she'd always been surrounded by her family, known she had them to back her up, so being here alone in this strange place was making her feel sad and uneasy. It was tempting to go to Jennifer's but all Jack's enemies had to do was get hold of her and he'd do whatever they wanted. She could tolerate the isolation for him. Besides, it would only be for a little while, she hoped.

* * *

Jane hung up from her call with Carly and sighed with frustration.

'She won't come,' she said.

Jennifer wrapped an arm around her waist. 'Because she's stubborn, like you.'

'She's afraid of putting Jack in danger. At least I know where she is now.'

'Where?'

'Sorry, I promised not to tell anyone, no' even you or Uncle Eddie.'

'I understand. The best thing we can do is get to the bottom of all this as quickly as possible, then things can go back to normal.'

'Uncle Eddie says we've to be at the next drop tonight.'

'And we will be but surely there's something else we can do in the meantime?'

'I wish I could think of something but I can't. No one's going to talk and tell us what's going on, the stakes are too high. We've no choice but to wait until the drop tonight and we can only hope that Lonny's kept his mouth shut or we won't get that either.'

'He's such a coward he wouldn't dare tell his wee pals that he talked.'

Jane dragged an agitated hand through her hair, eyes full of worry.

'Why don't we take a break for a few hours?' said Jennifer, taking her hands in her own.

'I can't relax. Carly's in danger and I have to help her.'

'You can't help her if you burn yourself out with worry and don't forget – the more we go running around asking questions the more likely we are to scare off Alfie and the others from making that drop tonight. So far that's the only chance we have to get to the bottom of this.'

* * *

Rose scowled as she watched Mason blatantly walking down the street as though he wasn't a lying, cheating wee prick.

'Bastard,' she hissed to herself.

'What's he doing?' said Tamara.

'Get back,' whispered Rose.

The two girls ducked behind the corner, crouching behind a couple of wheelie bins as Mason and his brother Alfie strode down the street that ran across the top of the one they were on.

When the brothers had passed, the two girls came out of their hiding place and watched them turn right at the bottom of the road.

'Let's go,' said Rose.

'Why are we following them?' asked Tamara as they hurried down the street together.

'My family's in trouble and that pair are something to do with it.'

'How do you know?'

'I overheard Jane on the phone to Uncle Eddie. They're trying to keep me out of everything as usual by telling me to stay at yours and Noah's.'

'Maybe there's a good reason for that. I mean, the last time your family was in trouble you were kidnapped.'

'And I escaped all on my own.'

'I know but this could be really dangerous. Mason's an arsehole but I've heard his brother's really violent.'

'He can be taken down with some baw twisting just like any other man.'

'What if you can't get close enough to twist his baws? I really wish you'd think this through more.'

'I've thought about it enough. Now be quiet and wait here.'

Rose cautiously peered around the corner and saw the brothers talking to a man she didn't know outside the bookies. She was too far away to hear what they were saying.

'I need to get closer.'

'Don't you dare,' said Tamara. 'If you do, I'll tell your sisters.'

Rose narrowed her eyes. 'You wouldn't.'

'I would. It was so scary when you went missing last time and I'm no' going to allow it to happen again. If you want, we can keep following them but you keep your distance.'

Rose thought this was actually pretty sensible advice from her friend, who was usually up for an adventure. It struck Rose just how much her own abduction had affected Tamara. 'Okay.'

'You promise?'

'I do.'

Tamara breathed a sigh of relief. 'Thank you.'

It appeared that Mason and Alfie were just having a friendly chat with the bookie before continuing on their way.

'I bet they're going to Jessica Alexander's house,' said Rose.

Sure enough, the girls watched the two brothers enter the matriarch's home.

'We need to find out what they're discussing,' added Rose.

'How?' demanded Tamara. 'We'll only do that by going inside and you promised we wouldn't get that close,' she pressed, knowing Rose Savage took her promises very seriously.

'We won't. There might be an open window we can listen through.'

When Rose rushed towards Jessica's home, Tamara was sorely tempted to call Jane but didn't want to risk her friendship with her best friend, so she decided to leave that until she really had to.

They headed around to the back of the house and found the rear gate was standing open slightly.

Rose ducked down and peered through the gap. When she saw no one, she snuck through, only needing to nudge the gate open very slightly.

'I cannae believe we're doing this,' whispered Tamara.

'Shh,' Rose hissed at her over her shoulder. She pointed at the kitchen window which also stood open to allow in some fresh air as the day was close and muggy.

When they heard voices from inside, the two girls pressed themselves back against the wall beneath the window.

'Do you want a coffee, boys?' they heard Jessica say.

'No thanks,' replied a cold voice. 'We cannae stay.'

'Shame. I do enjoy visits from handsome young men.'

This comment made Rose pull a face.

'Is everything ready for tonight?' said the hard voice.

'Aye, don't worry. It's all in hand.'

'The Savages know something's going on. They might interfere.'

'If they do, you can shoot them.'

Jessica spoke so casually it froze Rose's blood in her veins. She glanced at Tamara, who had turned pale.

'That's only a last resort,' said the hard voice. 'The last thing we need is for the polis to get involved. What we want is a distraction, something to ensure they're too busy to bother us.'

'Such as?'

'We were hoping your clever brain would come up with something.'

'We could always snatch the youngest, Rose. I would like some payback on that wee bitch for what she did to Ross.'

Rose's lips curled into a wicked smile at the memory.

'The situation is too important for you to use it to settle old scores. Besides, that didnae go very well for your sons the last time. The girl got hold of a shotgun and blasted her way out.'

'We'd take better precautions.'

'No, it has to be something different. We need to cause some chaos on the scheme so they're too busy mopping that up to bother us.'

'Actually, I know just the people. They'll be very keen to help,' replied Jessica.

'Good. Make sure they're here by nine o'clock, then we can ensure the Savages are kept well out of our way.'

'You can rely on me.'

'Great. See you later.'

'Sure you can't stay?' purred Jessica.

'We've a lot to do,' said the man Rose assumed was Alfie, his voice growing colder with each word.

'Okay, I'll see you out,' replied Jessica.

There was the sound of their footsteps leaving the room,

heading towards the front of the house. Rose nudged Tamara and the two girls slipped out of the gate and rushed down the back street. They saw Mason and Alfie pass by and they ducked back until they'd gone.

'Should we keep following them?' said Tamara. Her heart was still hammering with nerves as she'd been terrified they'd be caught but she was also enjoying the flood of adrenaline.

'No,' replied Rose. 'We need to tell the family.'

22

Jane and Jennifer were dragged out of bed by a frantic knock at the door. Both women were relieved when they opened it to Rose and Tamara.

'You won't believe what's happened,' began Rose excitedly.

They listened to her explain with growing incredulity.

'What the hell did you think you were doing?' exploded Jane when she'd finished. 'They could have caught you.'

'But they didn't,' Rose retorted.

'They might have done. Have you any idea how dangerous Alfie is? He could have done anything to you.'

'Or you could say well done and thank me for getting you some pretty important information,' Rose snapped back at her sister.

'This isn't a game, for God's sake. This is real life and it's brutal and dangerous. Don't you understand that?'

'Course I do. I was kidnapped by two men with shotguns but did I let them stop me? No. I got hold of one of their guns and used it to escape. When are you going to realise that I'm no' a helpless wean and that I'm just as tough as you and Carly?'

'The lassie has a point,' said Jennifer.

'At least someone has some faith in me,' sniffed Rose.

'Fine,' exclaimed Jane. 'Well done, Rose. You're tougher than Rambo.'

Rose screwed up her face. 'Who?'

'It doesn't matter. I know you're tough, sweetheart. The point is that these men are tough too and they wouldn't think twice about hurting you and Jessica would be willing to do anything to you to get what she wants.'

'That stupid bitch,' said Rose dismissively. 'I could easily take her.'

'Give me strength,' grunted Jane, raking both hands through her hair.

'I wonder what form this distraction will take?' said Jennifer.

'Christ knows. It might be something we've no choice but to deal with. I'll call Uncle Eddie, get him round here.'

Eddie and his sons arrived twenty minutes later and all three gave Rose a hard look when Jane had got them up to speed.

'I regret nothing,' she told them defiantly.

'Aye, that's bloody obvious,' said Eddie. 'It's no' your fault, chaos is in your blood. I expect Jane's already told you off, so I won't waste my breath. Besides, you did good.'

'At last, some appreciation of my work,' she huffed, narrowing her eyes at Jane, who scowled back at her.

'At least we know we can ignore whatever distraction they're gonnae set up,' continued Eddie.

'What if they set fire to our homes or kidnap one of us?' said Jane. 'They might give us no choice but to deal with it.'

'Then it's a good job you lead a girl gang full of tough, hardened women who can handle practically anything.'

Jane smiled. 'You're right, it is.'

Eddie looked to Rose and Tamara. 'You two have done brilliantly but you can leave the rest to us.'

'No way,' said Rose, folding her arms across her chest while Tamara frantically shook her head. 'I'm almost eighteen and I am not being kept out of this. If it wasn't for me, you wouldn't even know there was a distraction being planned.'

'And I helped,' said Tamara defiantly.

'You're too young.'

'Carly and Jane were up to all sorts when they were our age,' said Rose.

'That doesn't mean we want the same for you,' said Jane.

'When are you gonnae let me decide what I want?' she exclaimed. 'It's my life, no' yours.'

'Let her help,' said Harry. 'She's always been really useful before, it's no' like she needs babysitting.'

'Thank you, Harry.' Rose beamed, flinging her arms around him.

'You're welcome,' he said, patting her on the back. He looked a little nonplussed when she remained hanging from his neck like a limpet.

'Send her out with The Bitches,' said Dean. 'She can handle it.'

Rose released Harry to hug him instead.

'I feel like I'm fighting a losing battle here,' sighed Jane.

Rose turned to face her, tilting her chin and planting a hand on her hip. 'Aye, ya are. I'm a Savage and I can do this. Why are you laughing?' she demanded.

'Sorry,' said Jane, holding up her hands. 'Fine but you stick by my side the whole time. Got it?'

'Got it,' Rose and Tamara said in unison.

'No' you,' Jane told Tamara.

'Aww, why not?' she whined.

'Because Rose can fight. You can't.'

'I've never been given the chance. I might be really good at it.'

'No. I'm sorry but it's far too dangerous. You can go home now.'

'That's no' fair,' said Rose. 'Tamara helped me today.'

'And we're very grateful but I refuse to put her in danger.'

Rose decided not to push it.

'But you can let us know if you hear or see anything weird,' Jane told Tamara.

'So I'll be a lookout?' she replied eagerly.

'Aye, if you like.'

'Great,' she said, placated.

'It doesnae need all of us to do the other thing,' said Eddie, not wanting to go into details in front of Rose and Tamara. 'Me and the boys will handle that.'

'What thing?' said Rose.

'Never you mind.'

She pouted again but didn't comment as she'd been given more than she'd thought she'd get. Most of all, she wanted to get hold of Mason and give him the ball twisting of a lifetime. She'd never got her own back on him for setting her up and she determined that soon she would have her revenge.

* * *

Jack arrived back at the caravan three hours later with more supplies.

'I got that strawberry conditioner you wanted,' he said, unpacking the carrier bag onto the dining table. 'It shows how much I love you buying this bright pink bottle. I felt like a proper dick wheeling it around in a trolley.'

'I appreciate your sacrifice,' she said, smiling. Anxiety filled her eyes. 'Have you found out anything else?'

'I met with Elijah and we just talked business. There was nothing out of the ordinary.'

'What did he want to discuss urgently with you?'

'It was something and nothing.'

'Then he was using it as an excuse to find out why I was in the flat above the café?'

'Probably. He is a nosy sod.'

'But he seemed so creepy.'

'That's just Elijah.'

'You don't think he's involved then?'

'My gut says he isn't but I've not managed to come up with any evidence either way. I got hold of the bloke who told Nick Kramer I was in charge of the gunrunning ring but he said he'd just heard my name bandied about in the pub and so had other people.'

'What happened to Nick?'

'Your uncle and cousins put him in hospital. He should be there for several weeks with two broken kneecaps and a broken elbow and wrist.'

'So someone's running around giving out your name on purpose to throw the scent off themselves.'

'Exactly and when I get hold of them, I'll fucking kill them.' The darkness fled from his eyes when he smiled. 'Anyway, you don't need to know about all that.'

'But I do. I'm deep in this too, Jack. You should know, Jane called while you were out and I told her where I was.'

Jack's eyes flickered. 'That was a dangerous thing to do.'

'I made her promise no' to tell anyone, no' even Uncle Eddie or Jennifer.'

'Can she be relied on to keep her mouth shut?'

'Aye she can and don't talk about my sister like that. She was the one who held everything together when our da' got ill. If it wasn't for her, Christ knows what would have become of us all, so show her some fucking respect.'

'I'm sorry, babe, I didn't mean it to sound like that,' he said, taking her in his arms. 'Of course I respect Jane. Anyone who can control The Bitches is to be admired, as is someone who can inspire such love and loyalty in you. I'm just so bloody tense; this situation is getting to me. Someone's plotting against me and I don't have the full picture yet. I'd never admit this to anyone else but it's scary.'

Her expression softened. 'I understand. Has Toni been able to find out anything?'

'Nope. Whatever's going on is being hidden from her too, which has pissed her off big time. She doesn't want idiots dealing guns in her city because the police automatically think she's behind anything criminal. But she's still leaving it to me to sort out.'

'She's testing you.'

'Yep and if I fail it's very possible she'll kill me, that's if whoever's behind this plot doesn't do it first.'

Carly wanted to tell him not to say things like that but it would be stupid because that was the truth. He was in so much danger and she hated it. 'What can I do to help?'

'Just keep yourself safe. Don't give me that angry look, it gets me really hot.' He smiled when she scowled. 'And I'm not patronising you if that's what you're thinking. Knowing you're safe means I can concentrate on sorting this out. Now, I've got an hour free,' he said, pulling her closer. 'How about we take a shower together?'

'Have you seen the size of the shower? It's toaty.'

'I'm game if you are.'

She laughed and he kissed her. Carly kissed him back passionately, praying he was telling her the truth and he wasn't the one behind this gun ring because if he was then the man she loved would become her enemy.

* * *

'Can you see anything?' whispered Harry.

'You're looking at the exact same thing I am,' Eddie whispered back. 'Why would I be able to see something you can't? What do you think I have, bionic eyes?'

'All right, chill. I only asked.'

'As soon as I see something, you'll see it too.'

They were stationed around the back of The Wheatsheaf while Dean kept watch from the front. Dean had messaged them five minutes ago to say that Alfie, Mason and Bill had just gone in the front door. If they were collecting the guns from the pub then Eddie was willing to bet that they'd leave by the back door.

'What's taking them so long?' sighed Eddie.

'Maybe they're having a pint first?'

'They'd be bloody stupid to drink before going out on an errand like that.'

'From what I've seen of them they're no' too intelligent. The scheme seems quiet. No sound of any chaos.'

'There's time yet,' said Eddie sagely. 'There's time.'

* * *

Jane and Jennifer waited with Rose in the graveyard across the street from the Savage sisters' flat. They'd switched the lights on inside, so it looked like someone was home. They figured that if someone was going to cause trouble, then they'd most likely start here. Jane had also stationed a couple of The Bitches outside Eddie and Harry's house and Dean's flat. The rest of the women were spread out across the estate, ready to let the others know should there be any trouble.

'God, this is tense,' said Jane quietly. 'It's like the calm before the storm.'

'Maybe Jessica couldn't get anyone to do her bidding in time?' said Rose.

'I doubt it. That bitch is an expert at causing trouble.'

'The attack could be something more insidious than a full-on assault,' said Jennifer.

'That's very possible,' replied Jane. 'Which is why we need to stay alert. God knows who she called in.'

'It's probably Ross and Dominic,' said Rose. 'In which case, we'll easily take them.'

'Let's hope.' Jane's phone vibrated in her jacket pocket and she tugged it free. 'Hello? Right, okay. No, keep watch. It could be innocent. If they try going inside, then grab them. Keep me informed,' she said before hanging up. 'That was Donna. There's someone wandering around outside Uncle Eddie's house.'

'Who?' said Rose.

'They cannae see, it's too dark and they're all in black.'

'Maybe the same will happen here,' said Rose, scanning the area. As always, she was eager for some action but standing in the graveyard at night made her nervous. Normally she didn't think twice about the place, she'd got that used to living across the street from it. She glanced over her shoulder at the yawning blackness, the vague outlines of the gravestones visible in the streetlights. Every zombie film she'd ever seen replayed through her head and she moved a little closer to her older sister.

Jane's phone rang again only this time it was Leonie, another of her most trusted women.

'Holy shit,' she said as she listened to Leonie talk. 'Aye. I'll send some of the other girls over. Don't do anything until they arrive, you'll be outnumbered.'

'What's going on?' said Jennifer when she ended the call.

'Five people are attacking the pub,' she replied, already dialling. 'Tricia, take Carla and Alice and head over to The Horseshoe Bar. It's being targeted.'

'Should we get over there too?' said Rose.

'No. I doubt that's all the trouble Jessica Alexander has cooked up. She'll be trying to divide our forces. Rather than one big attack, I reckon she'll have set up several smaller ones.'

'Did Leonie recognise the people attacking the pub?'

'No but Derek was already laying into them with his baseball bat and Brenda was throwing pint glasses at them, so I reckon they'll soon be driven off. They're obviously targeting locations in the scheme connected to our family, so someone will turn up here, I know it.'

The three women looked down the darkened street, wondering if someone was already watching them.

'They're coming out,' said Harry excitedly.

'Aye, I can see,' retorted Eddie. 'Keep down. I'll call Dean and tell him to get his arse over here.'

The two of them slid down further into the seats of the car Eddie had rented for this occasion, not wanting his own car to be spotted. They watched Alfie exit the back of the pub carrying a black sports bag, followed by Mason and Bill. The three of them got into Mason's BMW and drove off.

Dean emerged from the shadows, ran over to the car and leapt into the back seat. They set off just as the BMW turned the corner at the bottom of the street.

They followed the car out of Haghill and into nearby Cranhill where it pulled up outside some flats beside Cranhill Park. Eddie parked further down and they watched the three men enter a block of flats carrying the bag.

'I don't know anyone who lives here,' said Eddie. 'Do you, boys?'

Dean and Harry shook their heads.

'Want me to check it out?' said Dean.

'No. We've nae idea who lives there or how many people are inside. For now, we wait and watch.'

* * *

'I'm getting cold,' said Rose, stuffing her hands into her jacket pocket.

'You can always go to Noah's or Tamara's if you want,' replied Jane.

'No, I'm good,' she replied while doing her best not to look into the depths of the graveyard.

Jane scrambled for her phone when it vibrated again. 'Aye? That's great,' she breathed with relief. 'Who are they? Nope, never heard of them. Strip them, kick them off the scheme then get over here as quickly as you can. I think something's about to go down.'

'Was that Leonie?' Jennifer asked her.

'Aye, they've sorted out the fannies who attacked the pub. They were just some arseholes from Parkhead. They didn't put up much of a fight.'

'That's a relief. Maybe Jennifer just hired amateurs after all?'

'Do you hear that?' said Rose. 'It's an engine.'

The three women strained to listen and heard a distinctive rumble.

'Oh shite,' sighed Jane. 'That's a motorbike, more than one.'

'Is it time to put the plan into action?' said Rose excitedly.

'It is, although we hadn't planned for motorbikes when we should have done after what happened recently.'

'The plan will work on them too,' said Jennifer. 'Probably even better than it would on cars.'

'Let's hope.'

The three of them snatched up the small fireworks that lay on the ground at their feet and produced a lighter each from their coat pockets.

'No' yet,' said Jane, eyes on the approaching motorbikes.

Under the streetlights they could see there were six bikes altogether rolling down the road.

'It's probably Declan and his gang who we collected a debt from,' said Jane. 'The same ones who turned up here the other day. I bet Jessica sent them here that time too. She recruited them, putting all the blame on our family for what happened at their clubhouse.'

'That sounds like something the sly bitch would do,' replied Jennifer.

'Let's give them the traditional warm Haghill welcome,' said Jane.

Rose grinned. 'All right.'

They lit the fireworks and stood back as they rocketed across the road and struck the bikes. There were shrieks and yells from the riders and passengers alike who threw themselves off the vehicles and ran for cover as more fireworks came their way.

While they were still reeling from the multiple blasts, Jane, Jennifer and Rose picked up the homemade smoke bombs they'd prepared that day made from potassium nitrate and sugar, lit them and hurled those too at the disorientated bikers.

'Ready?' Jane asked Rose and Jennifer.

They both nodded.

'Then let's go. Rose, don't leave my side.'

The three of them raced out of the graveyard together, the two Savage sisters carrying a baseball bat each while Jennifer wielded her preferred golf club. They began laying into the bikers with the weapons while they were still reeling from the fireworks and smoke, being careful to target their ribs and knees, ensuring they stayed down while not doing them any permanent or fatal injury.

Rose released her traditional war cry, which sounded terrifying when combined with the smoke. To Declan, leader of the bikers, she appeared to emerge from the fog like a demon queen, her eyes wild, a blood-curling shriek flying from her lips as she slammed the bat into his ribs, causing a couple to crack before she vanished again. Breathing hard and in pain, Declan frantically looked around for her, clutching tightly onto the bike chain he held in one hand, eyes darting left and right, afraid she'd emerge from the smoke again to attack him.

Another wild cry echoed behind him but before he could turn something hard connected with his back and he was knocked forwards to the ground, jolting his injured ribs and making him scream with pain. The demon queen planted one foot on his back, unleashed another hellish cry, long hair streaming out behind her before he was kicked in the face, stunning him and she vanished once more.

Seeing he was down and out, Rose scouted around for fresh prey. She was just in time to spot a woman with short blonde hair shaved at the sides charging at her. The woman swung a bike chain at her. Rose used the bat to prevent the chain from making contact with her chest but it knocked the weapon from her hand.

'I'll kill you for what you did to my boyfriend, you little bitch,' screamed Lana.

Rose assumed she was referring to the useless cabbage she'd just taken down. She pulled a taser from her pocket and fired. The probes hit Lana in the stomach and she shrieked and jiggled before collapsing. Rose turned and jammed the weapon into the stomach of the man running up to her from behind, using the electrodes on the end to good effect.

The smoke was starting to clear and she saw Jane and Jennifer fighting back to back, surrounded by five large bikers.

'Rose, where are you?' yelled Jane as she continued to fight.

Rose was touched. Her sister was in the middle of a tough battle yet she was still concerned for her safety.

'Right here,' she called back, snatching up her bat, racing up to one man and applying the taser to his arm. She was a little surprised when he didn't drop like the other two had done, so she swung the bat at the back of his knees and he fell, enabling Jane to kick him in the face.

Jane and Jennifer drew their own tasers and fired, taking down two more men. Rose rammed the tip of her bat into another man's crotch and the final man looked startled to realise all his comrades had fallen. Looking panicked, he turned and fled.

The three women let him go and regarded the carnage, unable to believe what they'd just done.

'That was amazing,' exclaimed Rose, waving the bat excitedly in the air.

Jane produced a handful of cable ties from her pocket. 'Let's make sure they can't cause us any more trouble.'

Hastily the three of them began binding the bikers' wrists together with the cable ties, Rose grinning when she pulled the tie tight on one man's wrists and he groaned with pain.

Before they could finish, there was the sound of more engines and they saw two cars approaching.

'Oh, hell, who's this?' exclaimed Jennifer.

'It could be someone who's on our side,' said Rose hopefully.

Jane drew back the baseball bat. 'I doubt it.'

23

The cars rolled to a halt just behind the bikes. Rather than form a neat line at the kerb, they parked side by side in the middle of the road, blocking it entirely. From each car climbed four men.

'Oh, hell, it's Blair,' said Jane.

'We can take them,' replied Rose.

'Don't be ridiculous. We're out of fireworks and smoke bombs. We need to get out of here.'

'I agree,' said Jennifer.

As they turned to run down the street, they saw another car approaching. The three women watched as it too came to a halt in the street. Rather than four men, only one climbed out, an enormous figure wearing a huge hat. In one hand they carried something and Jane at first feared it was a weapon, until they walked under a streetlight.

'Peanut,' she exclaimed with delight.

'I'm back,' he said, grinning. 'What do you think of the sombrero? I also got a straw donkey. Isn't he lovely? I call him Juan.'

'Could you be any more cliched?' said Jennifer. 'I'm surprised you're no' wearing a matador's costume.'

'Cheeky,' he said. 'Well, I'm really relaxed after my holibobs and...' He trailed off when he saw all the bikers lying on the ground and the gang of aggressive-looking men. 'What the fuck's going on here?' he exclaimed.

'It's a long story,' said Jane. 'But we've just twatted this lot,' she added, pointing to the bikers on the ground. Her hand swung to Blair and his men. 'And they're here to hurt us too.'

'Like hell they are,' he growled. 'Stay here, Juan,' he told his straw donkey as he placed it carefully in a neighbour's garden. He picked up a chain dropped by one of the bikers and began swinging it menacingly. 'Where's Eddie and the boys?'

'They're on with something else,' Jane told him as the four of them faced the approaching group of men. Blair was limping badly, his mouth swollen and bruised and he hung back behind the others, clearly only here to see those he felt had wronged him get their just desserts rather than inflict any actual punishment himself.

'I've got a smoke bomb left,' said Rose, pulling it from her pocket.

'Throw it,' said Jane.

Rose lit it and hurled the bomb, which landed between the two groups.

'Split,' said Jane.

Peanut and Jennifer stepped to the left while she and Rose stepped to the right. When the men burst through the cloud of smoke between them, they attacked them from the sides. Not expecting the attack to come from this angle, the men were caught on the hop and when Leonie and another two women charged into the fray a few seconds later, they were left disorientated and confused.

Five minutes later, The Bitches were tearing off the men's clothes while slapping and punching them, the air filled with their cackles. Peanut looked on, his deep roll of laughter joining the women's.

Declan came round at this point and watched the scene with mounting horror as it appeared this entire bloody scheme was filled with demon queens.

'You're next,' Rose told him gleefully.

Declan cried out when she began tearing down his jeans.

'Rose,' exclaimed Jane. 'Stop that.'

'But I thought...'

'Leave it to The Bitches.' She pointed the bat she held at Blair, who was rapidly limping back to the cars. 'Sic him.'

With a cruel smile, Rose charged and Blair's eyes widened when he saw the banshee running at him, looking fierce and feral. He flung open the door and leapt into the driver's seat. When he tried to pull it closed, a baseball bat was shoved in the crack and it refused to shut. The door was flung open with a force that belied the slender frame of the girl. Rose reached inside, her hand clamped down on his crotch and violently twisted.

Jane smiled maliciously as she enjoyed Blair's screams of pain. It served him right for what he'd tried to do to Carly. Hopefully his limp would now be permanent.

'What about her?' Leonie asked Jane while pointing to Lana, who'd come round from being tased and was regarding the scene with astonishment, hands cable-tied behind her back.

'Leave her. I've got some questions for her.'

Lana stared up at Jane defiantly as she loomed over her, the baseball bat resting on one shoulder.

'What else has Jessica Alexander got planned?'

'Who?' said Lana with feigned innocence. She swallowed hard when Jane produced a knife from her belt.

'My sister's no' here to stop your face from being slashed now,' said Jane coldly. 'Personally, I don't gi'e a shite about you. I'll happily cut you to ribbons if it gets me what I want.'

'Look, I don't have all the details,' said Lana more reasonably. 'I was just told that we were to come here and distract you and your sisters.'

'Jessica's arranged more attacks, no' just this one. What else is she going to do?'

'I don't know. Wait,' she cried when Jane straddled her and drew back the knife, ready to cut. 'I did hear someone mention a fire.'

'Where?'

'Your uncle's house.'

'Fuck,' Jane said, scrambling to her feet. Before she could call Donna, her phone rang and Donna's name flashed up on the screen.

'I've heard there's going to be a fire... oh, thank Christ. Aye but stay alert. There's more to come, I know it.' Jane hung up and looked down at Lana. 'Your friend's attack on my uncle's house was stopped before it could even begin. What else have you lot got planned?'

'Nothing, I swear,' she cried. 'That was it for us but I did hear something about a Trevor Wilson. I don't know who Trevor is but he's from Bearsden. Apparently he's disappeared and his friend's really pissed off. Jessica said your family killed him.'

'But we didn't,' she exclaimed.

'That's what Trevor's pals think and they are dangerous fuckers. They're into guns.'

'How are they gonnae come at us?'

'They're going to your cousin Dean's flat to kill him.'

Jane breathed a sigh of relief. Thank God Dean wasn't there. 'How many of them are there?'

'I don't know exactly, about two or three.'

'Why Dean?'

'They were told he was the one who killed Trevor.'

'That's bollocks. Someone's setting Dean up.' Jane hesitated as she wondered if that person could be Jack. Dean was his closest rival for Carly's affections. Was he afraid of a reconciliation between them and using this as a cover to get him out of the way?

Jane called Dean. She couldn't risk him going home and walking into a trap.

'Dean,' she said with relief when he answered. 'Whatever you do, don't go home. Jessica's sent some friends of someone called Trevor Wilson to your flat and these are serious people with guns. They're going to kill you because, for some reason, they think you killed Trevor. Who is he by the way? Right, I see,' she said when he explained that it was the man who'd told Nick Kramer that Jack was selling guns. 'No, I know you didn't kill him,' she added when he protested his innocence. 'But someone's told them you have. We can deal with them.' She sighed when her uncle came on the phone and told her not to go anywhere near the flat. 'But we can't just leave them there. If Dean doesn't return then they might decide to hunt him down and they could come to our flat or your house. Peanut's back, I'll speak to him.'

Before her uncle could protest further, Jane hung up and dashed up to Peanut, who was watching The Bitches gleefully.

'These are some cracking women you've got, Jane,' he said.

'Aye, I know. Listen, I need your help.'

His expression grew incredulous as she explained.

'Can't I go away for a wee holiday without you lot landing yourselves in the shite?' he exclaimed when she'd finished.

Rose joined them and pointed to the car she'd left Blair in. 'What about him? He's just curled up in there, crying.'

'Forget him, he's nothing,' replied Jane. 'We've a much more serious situation to deal with. Men are waiting at Dean's flat to kill him.'

'Oh my God, we have to warn him,' she cried.

'Don't worry, I've already done it. The question is, what do we do about it?'

'You're doing nothing about it,' Peanut told the sisters. 'I won't let you anywhere near them.'

'We should grab Jessica Alexander,' said Rose. 'She's arranged all this and she doesn't know that we know about her involvement. We need to take advantage of that.'

'You're right,' said Peanut. 'If anyone can give us the full details of this assault, it's her.'

Jane nodded. 'You, me and Jennifer will handle that,' she told him. 'The Bitches can ensure this lot leave the scheme. I don't want anyone going near Dean's house.'

'What about me?' said Rose.

'You've done your bit, you can go to Noah's.'

'No way, I'm coming with you.'

'Out of the question. Armed men are in Haghill and I don't want you anywhere near them.'

'Fuck that, Jane,' Rose yelled rebelliously.

'Don't ever speak to me like that again,' her sister snarled back but Rose was unmoved.

'I'm sticking with you. I've proved that I'm more than up to the job. Besides, the safest place on this scheme is beside you and Peanut.'

Jane sighed and shook her head. 'We don't have time for an argument. You can come. Leonie,' she called. 'Make sure they leave,' she said, waving a hand at their vanquished foes. 'We're going for Jessica. Jen, you're with us. Let's go get the bitch.'

* * *

'We cannae just do nothing,' said Harry in frustration. 'The answer to everything is going on in that flat right now and we're sat here like lemons.'

'You're right,' said Dean. 'We have to do something.'

'But they've got guns,' said Eddie. 'And I'm no' risking you two getting shot.'

'Let me do a bit of reconnaissance then,' said Dean.

'No. It's too dangerous.'

'I won't let them see me.'

'You cannae go on your own,' said Harry. 'Anything could happen.'

'I'll be fine.'

'No,' said Eddie firmly. 'We'll wait till they've gone, then we'll go up there and find out who that flat belongs to. At least that will even up the odds a bit.'

Ten minutes later, Mason, Alfie and Bill exited the block of flats.

'Alfie's no' carrying the bag any more,' said Harry. 'Meaning this must be the drop-off place.'

The three men got back in the BMW and left.

'Let's go,' said Eddie.

They climbed out of the car and cautiously approached the building. The door had been left open, so they slipped inside.

'Second floor,' said Eddie.

His sons jogged on ahead while he hauled himself up the stairs after them, swearing to himself once again that he must start eating healthier and exercising more. His beer belly was becoming a real hindrance.

'Judging from what we saw through the windows, I'm guessing it's this flat,' said Harry, pointing to the door of flat ten.

Eddie nodded. 'Let's no gi'e them time to react.'

Harry kicked the door in. They raced inside, pumped up full

of aggression and prepared for action only to find a beautiful redhead reclined on her side on the couch wearing only a skimpy negligee that revealed long, slim legs and plenty of cleavage.

'I was told you were handsome but I wasn't expecting such lookers,' she purred.

The men stared at her in amazement.

'Who the hell are you?' exclaimed Eddie.

'My name is Desiree. That's French for much desired.' She winked.

'I'll bet you are, sweetheart,' said Harry, eyes eagerly drinking her in.

'Why don't you come and sit beside me. The whole night's been booked for you.'

'For me?' he replied, pointing to himself.

'For all three of you.'

'By who?' said Eddie.

'The men who just left. They dropped off a bag of tricks they thought you'd enjoy.'

Dean snatched up the black sports bag they'd seen Alfie carrying and unzipped it to reveal a pile of sex toys. On top was a note that simply read: *Ha ha.*

'Lonny grassed to them, the fucking worm,' snarled Dean, throwing the bag across the room. 'They were onto us all the time.'

'And now we've lost them and they've gone off on their real delivery,' groaned Eddie.

'I'm gonnae cut Lonny's baws off and shove them down his throat.'

'Let's go. We might still be able to catch up with them.' Eddie grunted with annoyance when Harry remained where he was, smiling at Desiree. He grabbed his son by the back of the jacket and dragged him towards the door.

'See you later, Desiree,' Harry called over his shoulder.

'Come back any time, handsome,' she called back.

They raced back to the car, leapt in and drove around Cranhill, hoping to spot the BMW but there was no sign of it.

'This is one major fuck up,' said Eddie. 'I'd better let Jack know. He's going to be really pissed off.'

'He might already know,' said Dean tightly. 'He could have even planned all this.'

'Christ, I hope not.'

* * *

The Wheatsheaf was busy. They were having a quiz night and all the customers were silent, listening to Lonny reading out the questions when Jane, Rose, Peanut and Jennifer stormed in. They'd been to Jessica's house but found no one at home. The next-door neighbour, who loathed Jessica, had been quick to tell them that she was at the pub.

'What is the capital of Croatia?' said Lonny as they entered.

'Zagreb,' replied Peanut.

Everyone turned to look, the atmosphere immediately turning hostile when they saw it was two members of the Savage family and their associates.

'Get out,' said Lonny.

Everyone heard the panic in his tone.

They ignored him and proceeded deeper into the pub, scanning the faces of the customers. Sure enough, there was Jessica sitting between Emma Wilkinson and Karen.

'I thought we told you to stay out of Haghill,' said Jane, pointing at Emma with the baseball bat.

'Fuck off,' Emma retorted. 'I go where I want. I don't obey you, bitch.'

Jane slammed the bat down on the table she was standing beside, knocking over the pint glasses of the men sitting there. When they leapt to their feet in outrage, Rose aimed her stun gun at the crotch of one man while Peanut grabbed the other by the front of his shirt and threw him against the bar.

'I'll deal with you later,' Jane told Emma. She turned her attention to Jessica. 'It's you we want.'

'Me?' said Jessica innocently and without a flicker of fear. 'What have I done?'

'You know full well but your plan's failed. Blair and Declan and their gangs have already been seen off the scheme.'

'I don't know who you're talking about.'

'Aye ya do but we want to know who else is going to try and hit us.'

'Really, I know nothing about it,' Jessica said so casually Jane ground her teeth together in anger. Jessica picked up her glass and took a sip of wine. 'Now I suggest you leave before you get torn apart. Everyone here is loyal to my family.'

'You mean Jack?'

'No. They're loyal to me.'

'Now why would they be? You're just a desperate old hag chasing after anything in trousers.'

'Look at that jacket she's wearing,' sneered Rose. 'It actually has shoulder pads. What is this, the 1980s?'

'You mouthy wee coo,' snapped Jessica.

'Come and say that to my face without those dogs sitting beside you.'

Karen leapt to her feet, smashed her pint glass on the table and pointed at Rose with the jaggy end. 'I'll fucking say it to your face.'

'Any time.' Rose grinned, pressing the button on the taser, making it crackle.

'This is fuck all to do with the rest of you,' Jane told the room. 'We just want Jessica. If you feel she's worth the trouble then fine, you can take us on but I promise you this – you will be leaving here with broken bones, if you're lucky.'

The majority of the customers were just here for an evening out and didn't want to get involved in gang warfare. Just half a dozen men present who were always up for a scrap decided to take Jane up on her offer. They got to their feet and began to surround the newcomers.

'You two get Jessica,' Peanut told the sisters. 'Me and Jen will handle this lot.'

Jessica merely smiled when Emma and Karen leapt up to tackle the sisters. She reclined back in her seat to watch the fight, confident in the abilities of everyone around her to protect her.

When the men charged at Peanut and Jennifer, Peanut picked up one man and used him as a battering ram to knock down the others.

'Hey, you only left one for me,' protested Jennifer before punching the single man remaining on his feet while the others groaned on the floor around them.

'Oh, sorry, doll,' said Peanut, placing the man he held back on his feet, where he swayed on the spot, dazed. 'There you go.'

Jennifer headbutted the man and he dropped. They turned their attention to Jane and Rose. Jane had thrown Emma back into one of the booths and was repeatedly punching her in the face, smiling when she felt Emma's nose break. Emma screamed in pain and despair, only recently having had her nose fixed after the last time Jane had broken it.

'That'll cost you another five grand to put right,' said Jane with satisfaction as she got to her feet, leaving her sobbing in the booth. 'You've gone soft,' she added with disgust. Emma had once been a force to be reckoned with but her bottle had gone since she'd lost leadership of The Bitches.

Karen was putting up more of a fight. She swiped at Rose with the broken glass, her rage only fuelled by the smirk on Rose's face; she was far too fast for Karen. Rose knocked the glass from her hand with the baseball bat, making her yelp with pain before hitting her in the shoulder with the stun gun. Karen collapsed back into the booth.

Jessica's expression turned from smug to panic in seconds. She scrambled to her feet and when she attempted to leave the table, Jane slammed the bat into the wall beside her head.

'Going somewhere?' she said.

Jessica tried to leave the other way but Rose did the same with her bat and Jessica found herself penned in.

'Come with us nice and quietly and you won't get hurt,' Jane told her. 'Well, not much anyway, but if you fuck with us then we'll ensure any man who looks at you from now on will see only an ugly, scarred mess. You got it?' she hissed.

Jessica nodded. 'I... I do.'

'Good.'

Jane's hand went into Jessica's hair and she dragged her out from behind the table, upending it.

'Don't be fucking stupid,' Peanut told one man when he decided to be chivalrous and intervene.

The man held up his hands and retook his seat.

Everyone turned to the door when it burst open.

24

'Uncle Eddie?' Rose frowned when he rushed in with his sons.

He didn't hear her, too set on pursuing his quarry. His gaze settled on Lonny. 'Ya grassing wee prick,' he bellowed. 'Get him, boys.'

Lonny squeaked with fear and attempted to rush towards the back door but Harry and Dean were too quick. They grabbed him and hauled him backwards between them, kicking and screaming.

Eddie finally noticed his nieces. 'What are you doing here?'

'We came for this bitch,' replied Jane, indicating Jessica.

'Peanut,' he said, face lighting up. 'Am I glad to see you, pal.'

'This is some big mess, Eddie,' he said as the two men shook hands.

'Aye, I know. More's happened too. I'll get you up to speed very soon. First, let's get these arseholes outside.'

Lonny was dragged out of his own pub by Dean and Harry, protesting all the way. Jessica left in a more dignified manner, escorted out between Jane and Rose, her expression cold and defiant, all the colour drained from her face.

'Right, you,' said Jane, shoving her up against the wall the moment they were outside and producing the knife from her belt. 'We know you sent Trevor Wilson's pals to Dean's flat to kill him. Now you're gonnae tell us how many of them there are and what sort of weapons they're carrying or I'll cut up your fucking face and laugh while I do it.'

'It wasn't me,' Jessica shrieked, eyes locked on the tip of the blade, all smugness and poise gone. 'Jack told them Dean killed Trevor.'

'But I didn't,' retorted Dean. 'We went with Jack to speak to him but that's it. Trevor was alive when we left him.'

'Someone went back and slit his throat.'

'It wasn't us.'

'But... it must have been.'

Jane frowned. Jessica appeared to be genuinely confused. 'Why are you so sure?'

'It's what Jack told me and he should know.'

'Christ, he really is behind all this, isn't he?'

'Well of course he is. Who else could wind us all up like this?'

Jane turned to her uncle. 'Did you follow Alfie to the drop?'

'Aye and it was a set-up. It was some prostitute's flat and there wasnae a gun in the bag Alfie was carrying. They knew we were there and we lost them.'

'Jack knew the plan?'

Eddie nodded grimly.

'Oh, hell.' Jane turned back to face Jessica. 'Why is Jack plotting against our family?'

'Why do you think? He wants Carly all to himself with no one to interfere.'

'Which is why he sent those men to my flat to kill me?' said Dean.

'He can't stand it that you and Carly have a history.'

'What about Cole?' said Jane. 'He has history with her too.'

She shrugged casually, seemingly unconcerned about the fate of her youngest son. 'I've no idea but if Jack is jealous of Dean then he's probably jealous of him too.'

'What other surprises have you set up for us on the scheme?'

'Aren't a gang of bikers and Blair and his people enough for you?' Jessica was starting to relax a little now that she wasn't being horribly beaten and her belligerence was returning with it.

'Where have Alfie and Mason gone?'

'How should I know? They don't tell me everything.'

Jessica gasped when Jane slashed the front of her jacket with the knife.

'The next time it'll be your fucking face,' snarled Jane.

'Look,' Jessica said, voice shaky. 'They're doing the next gun drop but I don't know where. I only know how much money is involved.'

'That's typical of you. And how much is involved?'

'Four grand.'

'And you think it's worth the risk for that? That's no' even a grand a piece split between you all.'

'That's just one drop. We've been pulling in forty grand a week so far.'

'So Jack's definitely behind this then?' said Harry.

'Aye,' replied Jessica.

'Have you spoken to him directly about it?' said Eddie. 'And I mean face to face, no' just over the phone.'

'No, of course not. He's not stupid. He's distancing himself from it all to give himself plausible deniability should the polis get wind.'

'Again no one's spoken to him directly about it,' said Eddie. 'I don't like it.'

'It's a smart move,' replied Jane.

'Aye but it's no' enough proof. I think something more's going on.'

'She's protecting someone,' said Rose, nodding at Jessica.

'The only person she protects is herself,' said Jane, scowling at Jessica. 'She doesn't care about anyone else, no' even her own sons.'

'How long have you been involved in this weapons dealing ring?' Eddie asked Jessica.

'About two months,' replied Jessica proudly.

'And are you seriously telling me that you've never discussed it with Jack directly?'

'No. Everything's done by burner phones, which we change every couple of days. Text message only so we can't be recorded saying anything. As I said, plausible deniability.'

'What about David and Elijah?'

'David,' she chuckled. 'Knows nothing. I do believe Elijah's started to clock on though.'

'So Elijah isn't involved?'

She shook her head.

'That's something at least,' sighed Eddie. 'I really don't want to fight the Samson family.'

'Rose, Jennifer, watch her,' Eddie told them before nodding the rest of them over so they could discuss it in private.

'I've still nae idea what's going on,' said Peanut.

'Basically, Carly's back with Jack and then we found out someone's gunrunning in his name,' replied Eddie. 'But we're no' sure if Jack's really behind it. He denies it.'

'Right,' Peanut replied slowly. 'I get the feeling a lot's been missed out there but I'll pick it up as I go along.'

'What about the armed men in my flat?' said Dean.

'We'll deal with that later. One thing at a time. We have to work out if Jack's involved.'

'Cole might know,' said Jane. 'He's been hanging around him a lot lately.'

'Good idea. Get his location out of the old witch, hen.'

Jane nodded and returned to Jessica. 'Where's Cole?'

'How should I know? He's an adult, he goes where he likes.'

Jane pressed the tip of the knife into her left cheek, making Jessica shriek.

'I'm not lying,' she cried as she felt the blood run down her cheek. 'I swear to God. He keeps as much as he can to himself.'

'I'm going to fuck up your face, Jessica and let's face it – you've had it coming for a long time.'

'No, please,' she screamed.

Jane hesitated and looked to Rose, not wanting to do something like that in front of her little sister.

'Go on,' urged Rose. 'You're right, she does deserve it. She was the one who messed up Cole, breaking Carly's heart.'

Instead, Jane pocketed the knife and punched Jessica hard in the stomach, sending her to the ground.

'I really don't think she knows where Cole is,' she told the others. 'If she did, she would have said.'

'You're right,' said Eddie.

'We need to get to Carly.'

'Why? She's safe. She's the only person we know Jack doesn't want to hurt. She's best staying where she is, well out of it. Finding Cole is our priority,' said Eddie. 'But who will know where the wee bastard is?'

'Alfie and Mason,' said Dean. 'And we don't know where they are either.'

'Maybe Jack knows?' offered Harry. 'Or is that too mad an idea?'

'Actually, no,' said Eddie. 'I'll gi'e him a bell.'

They all listened as he made the call.

'Hi Jack. Aye, we think we've mopped up the worst of it. Listen, do you know where Cole is? Right, okay. We think he could be. We'll check it out. Cheers.' He hung up and said, 'As far as he knows, Cole's at home but he doesnae have his address. Does anyone know where he lives?'

They all turned to Jessica.

'Fifty-four Brora Street, Riddrie,' she said in a resigned tone. 'The ground-floor flat.'

'You stay here,' said Eddie. 'Make sure that coo doesnae warn him,' he added, nodding at Jessica. 'Me and the boys will go and fetch him.'

'I'll come too,' said Peanut.

'Aye, okay, but Jane, keep The Bitches close.'

The men jumped into Eddie's car, which set off at a pelt. Brora Street was only a five-minute drive and they screeched to a halt outside number 54. The men leapt out of the car and tore up to the front door. Eddie put his shoulder to it without bothering to knock and they rushed inside.

'No one's here,' exclaimed Eddie. 'If Jessica was lying, I'll kill the bitch myself.'

'I don't think she was,' said Dean. 'I mean, someone clearly lives here, they're just no' here right now.'

'Maybe if we could prove Cole lives here it would be a start.'

'There's no photos,' said Peanut. 'But then he doesnae seem like the sentimental type.'

'The twat isn't,' said Eddie, who was getting seriously pissed off with the entire situation.

'There's a jacket hanging on the back of the door,' said Harry. 'I've seen Cole wearing that.'

'It's no' enough confirmation. Tear the bloody place apart, I don't care, just find some proof.'

Peanut headed into one of the two bedrooms and returned

holding something. 'I found this hidden under the mattress. It's Cole's passport.'

'Brilliant work, pal,' said Eddie, taking it from him and slipping it into his jacket pocket. 'Now, where is the slippery wee turd?'

'He must be somewhere in Haghill. That's where all the action seems to be.'

'Maybe. Let's head back there and see if we can find him.'

* * *

Eddie called Jane on the drive back to Haghill to find out where they were. She told him they were at The Horseshoe Bar and they arrived to find Derek, Sharon and some of the customers helping clear up after the earlier aborted attack. Jane, Rose and Jennifer were sitting with The Bitches, a sheepish and shaken Jessica in the middle of them all.

'Derek, pal,' said Eddie. 'I hope there was no major damage?'

'Naw,' he replied. 'Brenda caused the worst of it throwing pint glasses. Hey, Peanut.' He grinned, shaking his hand. The two had become firm friends. 'It's good to have you back, pal.'

'I would say it's good to be back but I've arrived to all this shite.'

'Aye, it is bad timing. Still, it seems to have gone quiet now. Either that or we're in the eye of the storm.'

'Don't be so gloomy,' said Brenda, the big, blousy middle-aged woman who'd had her eye on Derek for a few years. 'The enemy's retreated after having their arses kicked.'

'Has anyone seen Cole Alexander?' Eddie asked the room.

Everyone shook their heads.

'Where is the little bastard?' he huffed.

'So he wasn't at home?' said Jessica.

'If he was do you think I'd be asking everyone if they've seen him, you fucking arsehole,' Eddie roared back at her.

Jessica pursed her lips and hung her head to avoid his rage. She might have been clever and wily but she was also an abject coward.

'Why don't me and Harry look around the scheme for him?' said Dean.

'You two are no' wandering about on your own after everything that's happened. It's too dangerous.'

'Then how do you suggest we find him?' he replied in frustration.

'We make him come to us. We've got his maw after all.'

Jessica chuckled but there was no humour in the sound. 'If you think that would work then you're a fool. He doesn't care about me. He doesn't care about anyone except himself.'

'And whose fault is that?' retorted Jane. 'You got him sent to prison, you turned him into what he is. Cole was the only one of your sons with any real heart and you destroyed it. Now look what's happened – you're all alone in enemy territory with no one to come to your rescue because no one gives a shite about you.'

Jessica seemed suddenly struck with the truth of her words and hung her head again.

'So that plan's out,' said Eddie. 'Oh Christ, why didn't I think of it sooner?' he exclaimed. 'You can still call him, Jessica, tell him your people have got hold of Dean. That'll make him come running.'

'He's not stupid enough to fall for that.'

'It's worth a try. Call him and if you warn him then Jane will go to town on your face with her knife.'

Jane handed Jessica back her phone, which she'd taken from her earlier.

'None of your fucking tricks,' Jane told her. 'And put it on speakerphone.'

Jessica nodded and dialled. Despair filled her when it just rang out. Cole finally picked up on the last ring before it went to voicemail.

'Yes?' he said coolly.

'My men have got Dean Savage.'

'Where?'

'At his flat.'

'That's strange because I'm there with them right now and he's no' here.'

Jessica's eyes filled with panic and she glanced at Eddie. 'Did I say Dean?' she said, attempting to sound casual. 'I meant Harry. I'm always getting them mixed up.'

'You get nothing mixed up. I take it I'm on speakerphone?'

Jessica looked to Eddie again, not knowing what to do.

'Aye, ya are,' he sighed.

'Good. Now here's what's going to happen. You, your sons and Jane are going to come to me nice and quietly and unarmed without any of The Bitches. Even though Rose has caused some havoc tonight I'll still leave her out of it. She's got the chance to change her ways and not follow in the footsteps of her older sisters.'

'Go fuck yourself, you arsehole,' yelled Rose.

'Be quiet,' Jane told her.

'Why the hell would we come to you?' Eddie asked Cole.

'So we can get this sorted out once and for all. And, judging by what my maw said, you want to talk to me, so let's parley.'

'We are not coming to you. I wouldnae trust you as far as I could throw you.'

'And I'm not coming to you, so it looks like it's a stalemate. I suppose I'll just have to take it up with Carly.'

'Carly?' said Eddie, voice going tense with nerves.

'Aye. I've still got a soft spot for her. I might see if she wants to pick up where we left off.'

'You'll leave her alone, you twat,' yelled Dean.

'Ooh,' taunted Cole. 'It looks like someone's still carrying a torch for her even though she's back with Jack.'

'You're bluffing. You don't know where she is.'

'Don't I?' Cole said before hanging up.

'Call him back,' Eddie told Jessica.

She tried but it went straight to voicemail.

'He's probably turned his phone off,' said Jane.

'We have to get to Carly,' exclaimed Dean.

'He was bluffing,' replied Eddie. 'He doesnae know where she is.'

'How can you be so sure?'

'Don't you see what he's doing? He wants us to go to her so we can lead him there. He hasn't been trying to get into Jack's good books, he's been working against him, using his name to set up this gunrunning ring. Carly's safe, I promise.'

'But...'

'I'm right, son. Trust me.'

Dean looked to Harry, who nodded.

'Okay, fine. God, I'm tense.'

'You need a pint,' said Eddie.

'Sharon,' called Derek. 'Get Dean a pint.'

'I'll have one too,' said Harry.

'Aye and me,' replied Eddie.

More drinks orders were placed. While everyone waited for their drink, Dean excused himself and headed into the bathroom. Once he was in there, he checked the stalls to make sure they were empty before taking out his phone.

'Carly,' he breathed when she answered. 'Are you okay?'

'Aye, I'm fine. Why, what's going on?'

'We've had some trouble but it's over now.'

'Is anyone hurt?'

'No, we're all fine. I think you could be in danger though. Cole hinted that he knows where you are. Is Jack with you?'

'No, I'm alone.'

'I'll come straight over. Where are you?'

'I promised I wouldnae tell anyone.'

'Carly, this is me,' he said tenderly. 'You know you can trust me. I won't tell anyone else, I swear. I just don't want you there alone if Cole does turn up. Jack wouldnae want you to be in danger. I'm sure he'd rather you break your word and keep yourself safe than stick to it and put yourself in danger.'

'Aye, you're right but you can't tell anyone else.'

'I promise I won't.'

'I'm on the caravan park at Plant Street.'

'On my way,' he said before hanging up.

Lifting the window, he slid out into the backyard and pulled it closed before running off into the night.

25

'Dean's been a long time in the cludgie,' said Harry as he sipped his pint. 'I'll go and check on him.' He returned, looking troubled. 'He's no' there.'

'What?' said Eddie. 'But he must be. He hasnae come out.'

'It's empty.'

'Why would he leave?'

'He was worried about Carly,' said Jane. 'I bet he's gone to her.'

'But he doesnae know where she is.'

'He probably called her and convinced her to tell him; they are still really close.'

'Oh hell, oh no,' he breathed.

Jane was rather alarmed by how pale her uncle had gone. 'Why, what's wrong with that? If Cole does know where she is then Dean will keep her safe.'

'I need to talk to you in private. You too, Harry.'

Jane was puzzled by how grimly the two men looked at each other. She rose and followed them into a quiet corner, out of earshot.

'I didn't want Carly and Dean getting together, you know that,' opened Eddie. 'And it wasnae just because they're cousins.'

Jane felt slightly sick as she felt to be on the cusp of some terrible revelation.

'Dean has the tendency to get a little obsessed,' he continued. 'With women.'

'Really? He doesn't seem the type.'

'It's only happened once before.'

'Maisie Summers,' said Harry.

'Aye,' replied Eddie. 'Women usually get on his nerves after a short time, for one reason or another but Maisie was different. They dated and she broke up with him.'

'Don't tell me he stalked her?' said Jane.

'No, nothing like that but he did batter her new boyfriend, put him in hospital. Me and Harry stopped the boyfriend from going to the polis by threatening his wee brother. Aye, shite, I know,' he added when Jane frowned. 'But we were only trying to protect Dean. You'd have done the same for one of your sisters.'

Jane's expression softened and she nodded.

'Dean changed. Before he was a bit lighter, no' so serious but after that incident there was a darkness inside him that wasnae there before.'

Jane looked to Harry. 'You said at one point that you think we shouldn't have interfered in Dean and Carly's relationship. Why would you say that if you thought he could be obsessed?'

'Because I didnae think it could happen again and I'm still no' convinced it has,' he added with a hard look his father's way.

'You've always said Dean was in a different league to you, violence wise. Is this what you meant?'

Harry nodded seriously.

'I know it doesnae sound that bad, beating up your ex's new boyfriend,' said Eddie. 'But you didn't see the change in Dean. I saw he looked at Carly the same way he looked at Maisie and knew he'd developed another obsession. Then he got with Destiny and I thought it was okay, he'd got over it.'

'Maybe he has and he just genuinely wants to protect Carly?' said Jane.

'I would think that if I didn't suspect he was the intruder at the flat banging on the windows.'

'What? But he can't be. He was with us when the intruder went to the house the first time.'

'He got an accomplice to do that in order to make himself look innocent. He knew I'd suspect him. It worked too. I immediately thought he couldnae be responsible.'

'But he's been helping us track the intruder and we saw them go into the Stewart brothers' garage on the CCTV footage.'

'Aye but Dean was the one who overheard the conversation between Jessica and the others at the garage. He was the one who listened in on the conversation at The Wheatsheaf too. He's the one who's given us most of our information, which he's constantly said points to Jack.'

'What are you saying?'

'I don't know yet.'

'Yes you do, you're just afraid to say it.'

'Because I'm not 100 per cent certain.'

'There is one way to find out.' Jane turned to call, 'Jessica, over here.'

Now the situation had calmed down, the arrogance had returned to the Alexander matriarch's eyes. She rose to her feet with stately dignity and swanned over to them.

'Yes?' she sniffed.

'What were you discussing with Alfie and the others the last time you met in the office at the Stewart brother's garage?'

'You mean the night there was a loud crash, which was no doubt your family spying?'

'Aye.'

'Well, if you must know, we were discussing Ross and Dominic's move to Bishopbriggs. We were wondering whether to recruit them or not. I was all for it but Alfie vetoed it because he and Ross do not get along.'

'Did you mention Berettas at all?'

'Berettas?' she frowned. 'No. We've never dealt in Berettas. They're too big and heavy. No one wants to carry around something that size. Only Glocks as they're lighter and simple to use. That's all according to Alfie anyway, I know nothing about them.'

'That confirms it,' Jane told Harry and Eddie.

'Confirms what?' said Jessica.

'Never you mind. Sit back down.'

With an indignant tilt of the head, Jessica strode back over to her seat.

'Dean was the one who told us they were discussing Berettas. He's been making things up this whole time to make it look like Jack's running the gun ring. He's been feeding us false information to make us turn against him so Carly will dump him.'

'I don't know,' said Harry. 'It all sounds a bit weak.'

'It explains why we haven't been able to get to the bottom of all this and that's thanks to Dean continually throwing us off the scent.'

'No, I cannae believe it. There's a big difference between beating up your girlfriend's new boyfriend and this. Anyway, he told me he's really happy with Destiny.'

'I looked into Destiny when I started getting worried,' said Eddie. 'She's been in France for the past three weeks on a photo shoot, she's got some big modelling job on. So where's he been when he said he's been seeing her?'

'I cannae believe he'd betray us like this.'

'It's no' his fault, it's his obsessive personality.'

'I'm calling Carly and warning her,' said Jane, getting on her phone. 'She's not picking up,' she said, face creasing.

'Oh Christ,' said Eddie. 'And we don't know where she is.'

'I do – in a caravan on Plant Street. It's no' far.'

'Then let's get over there,' exclaimed Eddie. 'Peanut, you're with us.'

'I really think you're jumping to conclusions here,' said Harry reasonably.

Jane ignored her cousin and hurried over to Rose and Jennifer. 'We've got to go somewhere. You two are in charge. Stay here, keep an eye on Jessica and look out for any trouble.'

'Why, where are you going?' said Rose, getting to her feet.

'I can't explain just yet. I need you to trust me, please.'

Rose swallowed down her fear, recognising something serious was happening. 'I do.'

Jane gave her hand a gentle squeeze. 'Thank you, honey.'

Rose watched her older sister leave with her uncle, cousin and Peanut.

'I wonder what's going on?' she said.

Jennifer wrapped an arm around her. 'Whatever it is, they'll sort it. Don't worry.'

'Worry? I'm terrified for them,' Rose rasped.

Carly was looking out for Dean and sighed with relief when she saw his car pull up outside the caravan. She unlocked the front door and opened it.

'I'm glad you're here,' she said when he got out of the car.

'Jack's no' come back and I can't get hold of him. I'm really worried.'

Dean stepped inside the caravan, closed the door and gently took her by the shoulders. 'You need to listen to me very carefully – we've found out that he's definitely in charge of this gun ring.'

'No, he swore he isn't.'

'He lied to you. He's only stuck you here to isolate you and keep you away from your family.'

'You're wrong, I know he wasn't lying.'

'He lied to you before, so why not now?'

'Because he's changed.'

'Men like Jack never change. It's all been a trick to keep you to himself. He sent men to kill us. Thank Christ we managed to fight them off with the help of The Bitches and Peanut.'

'Peanut's back?'

'Aye, just in time too. Jack cannae stand the thought of you loving anyone else, no' even your own sisters. He wants us all gone.'

'Jack would never hurt me like that, he knows what my family means to me.'

'He's a selfish bastard who only cares about himself. Now we have to leave before he gets here. I'll take you somewhere safe. Grab your stuff quickly so we can go.'

Carly didn't like the look in Dean's eyes. There was something wild in his gaze that she'd never seen before and it unnerved her. 'This doesn't make sense.'

'It's true, believe me, now we have to go. If he comes back, we're fucked. Grab your coat and shoes.'

'Where's the rest of the family?' she said, her suspicion growing.

'They're making sure Blair and his men and the biker gang

leave the scheme. They sent me to bring you home before Jack gets back.'

'Okay,' said Carly while slowly backing away from him. She stuffed her feet into her trainers. 'My jacket's in the bedroom. I'll go and get it.'

She raced into the bedroom and turned the lock, which was flimsy and wouldn't do a thing to keep out Dean but it made her feel slightly more secure. Her phone was in her jeans pocket so she took it out and dialled Jack's number but he didn't pick up.

'Where are you?' she whispered. He should have been back by now. What the hell was going on?

She was about to call Jane when there was a knock at the door. 'Carly, we have to go,' called Dean.

'I'm coming, I'm just packing my stuff,' she called back, already opening the window.

'There's no time.'

'Just one minute and I'll be with you.'

Pushing open the window, she looked left and right before sliding out, the space just wide enough for her to fit through. She landed in a crouch and gently pushed the window closed behind her. No one else seemed to be about, so she tiptoed past the caravan, hoping Dean wouldn't hear the crunch of her trainers on the gravel. She couldn't believe she was running from this man who she'd loved and trusted, the man she'd gone to after almost being raped by Rod Tallan but her instinct was screaming at her to flee. If she was wrong, then she could apologise later and beg his forgiveness but for now she had to get away.

Just as she dialled Jane's number, a hand shot out and grabbed her arm, the phone falling from her hand. It took her a moment to realise who the figure was in the darkness, which was only broken by the weak glare of the streetlights from the main road.

'Cole,' she gasped. 'What are you doing here?'

'You need to come with us,' he said in that dead monotone.

'Us? You mean you and Dean?'

He just nodded.

Realisation struck all at once. 'You two have been working together, haven't you?'

'Explanations later. Now it's time to leave.'

'And go where?'

'You'll see.'

'What the hell is this?'

'No time,' he said, his grip on her wrist tightening.

'Cole, you're hurting me,' she said.

His eyes narrowed and she saw the glint of a blade in his free hand.

'She's here,' he called.

'You wee rat,' hissed Carly when Dean emerged from the side of the caravan.

'Did you climb through the window?' Dean asked her curiously.

'Aye, I did.'

'Why would you do that? We're just taking you home.'

Cole rolled his eyes. 'Oh, give it up. She knows something's wrong.'

Carly pointed at Dean with her free hand. 'Traitor. What I can't work out is why you two would work together... Oh my God, you set up the gunrunning ring and you've been using Jack's name.'

'You're right,' said Cole. 'It's amazing how many people just accepted he was behind it.'

'So Jack knows nothing about it?'

Cole shook his head.

'I knew it,' she exclaimed. 'Everyone was trying to tell me he was guilty but I knew he wasn't. So why did you come to my flat telling me you wanted me back?'

'To make you think I'd changed.'

'Changed? You're worse than ever. You were the intruder at my flat, weren't you?'

'I was the first time. Dean did it the second time. He suggested your family look at the local CCTV footage so they'd link the intruder to the Stewarts' garage, enabling him to put the blame on Jack for everything and make them think he was trying to take you away from them,' he said, smiling at his own cleverness. 'It was all about you for Dean, but for me it was the money and taking Jack's position from him, which should have been mine by rights.'

'Jesus, you're smug. Get off me,' she added, trying to shake off his hand and failing.

'It's okay, you can let her go,' Dean told Cole.

'Are you sure?' he replied. 'You know what she can do.'

'I do but she'll behave, won't you Carly?'

'Why start now?' she retorted.

'We just want to take you somewhere safe,' he said gently.

'Where? Back home?'

'No. It's a place only me and Cole know about.'

'Why the hell would I go with you?'

'To get you away from Jack.'

'I don't want to get away from Jack, I love him.'

'He's not right for you,' said Dean ardently. 'You should be with me, no' him.'

'What are you talking about? We agreed to just be friends, you're with Destiny.'

'We had a one-night stand but that was it. You're the woman I want, no one else.'

'Are you saying you made up your relationship with her?'

'It was a useful cover story for when I needed to sneak away to meet Cole. It also meant it was easier for me to get rid of Jack.'

Carly's blood ran cold. Was that why Jack hadn't come back? 'What did you do to him, Dean?' she rasped, throat tight with anger and fear.

'Just ensured he's kept busy so I can get you away. He won't be able to find you either. Now let's go.'

Carly punched Cole in the wrist, forcing him to release her. 'I'm going nowhere with either of you. I'm going to find Jack.'

When she attempted to walk around them both, they barred her way.

'You're coming with us,' said Cole.

'What's it to you?' she retorted.

'It's what Dean wants and he's my business partner. We're gonnae take over from Jack.'

'That won't work, you idiots. No one will swallow that. You're better off giving it up now. How the bloody hell did you two become partners?'

'We realised the same person was standing in both our ways.'

'Jack?'

'Aye. It just made good business sense.'

'It's the stupidest thing I've ever heard. Now I'm leaving and you two will let me.'

As she spoke, she scanned the ground, hoping to spot her phone but it was too dark.

'We belong together, Carly,' said Dean, grabbing her hand.

'The fuck you do,' growled a voice.

Dean was knocked sideways by someone slamming into him.

'Jack,' breathed Carly. 'Look out, he's got a knife,' she cried when Cole lunged at her boyfriend.

Jack grabbed his arm, twisted it and punched him in the face, knocking him off his feet.

'Get the knife, babe,' he told Carly.

'I can't see it,' she cried. 'He's dropped it and it's too dark.'

He took her hand. 'Let's get out of here.'

Dean was already getting back to his feet so they ran over to Jack's car which was parked at the top of the road while Dean chased after them roaring Carly's name.

'Dean and Cole have been plotting against you,' Carly told Jack as they ran holding hands.

'Aye, I've just worked it out, with Elijah and David's help. I knew Cole was involved but I wasn't 100 per cent certain about Dean. Now I know for sure.'

Carly glanced over her shoulder and her eyes widened. 'Jack.'

He stopped and turned to face Dean, who slammed into him and the two went tumbling to the ground.

When she ran to help her boyfriend, arms wrapped around her from behind and began dragging her towards Dean's car.

Carly stomped on Cole's foot and she threw back her head. She didn't connect with his face but it did force him to release her.

'If you come with us,' he told her. 'We'll let Jack go.'

'Bollocks. He's standing in your way.' She glanced over at Jack and Dean, who were frantically fighting. Jack was tough, a good streetfighter but he wasn't trained in martial arts like Dean was and she gasped when Dean's fist snapped his head back.

'Jack,' she cried, rushing over to help but Cole once again grabbed her.

'I'm getting fucking sick of you,' she said before punching him in the face.

To her surprise, Cole shook off the blow faster than she'd anticipated and he tried to hit her back. She moved but he still caught her on the shoulder, knocking her off balance. Taking advantage of this, his hand fisted in her hair and he pulled her backwards. Carly cried out in pain, her nails ineffectually scraping at his hand.

'Carly,' she heard Jack yell.

As she had her back to him, she couldn't see him but she could hear the sounds of a violent fight. He needed help against Dean, so it was vital she take down Cole as soon as possible.

Carly scrambled in her jacket pocket for her baton, the only weapon she had on her. She attempted to smash it into his knee but failed, although she did catch him on the calf, making him cry out in pain and Carly found herself released. She turned as she got up, swiping at him with the baton again, forcing him to keep his distance. It was hard for her to believe that she'd once loved Cole. Now she hated him. He was the enemy and he was in her way. It was as simple as that. All that mattered was getting to Jack.

She and Cole circled each other, her anxious gaze continually slipping to her boyfriend. With a cry, Dean threw Jack and he hit the front door of another caravan, smashing it open and vanishing inside. Dean ran in after him and the sounds of a struggle continued.

Carly ran at Cole, drawing back the baton. He tried to punch her but she dodged at the last moment and tried to smack him in the arm with the baton. He snatched his hand away in time and she struck air. With a cry of rage, she hurled herself at him and they crashed backwards together into a wheelie bin, upending it. A winded Carly scrambled to her feet, hoping to get upright before Cole but he managed it first. When he tried to kick her in the ribs, she rolled. He missed but she crashed into a group of empty gas bottles stacked by the fence, knocking them into each other. She rolled one towards Cole, forcing him to jump over it, giving her time to get up. She picked up a smaller bottle and swung it towards him like a bowling ball. Cole raised his hands to ward it off and he staggered backwards so Carly took the opportunity to run to Jack. Hearing pursuing footsteps, she glanced over her shoulder and saw Cole running after her, this time clutching a second knife that he must have been carrying, face alight with anger. He was a very fast runner and rapidly gaining on her. Knowing she wouldn't reach Jack in time, she veered towards the nearest caravan, charging at the door without slowing and it snapped open beneath her weight. She turned and kicked the door shut in Cole's face. He fell backwards onto his bottom, blood trickling from his nose. She leapt back outside and ran past him, jumping when he tried to grab her legs. Carly raced towards the caravan in which Jack and Dean were fighting, the whole thing violently rocking from side to side. She was elated when Dean was hurled through the door, landing heavily on his back. Jack jumped out after him, blood running from a cut to his forehead. Carly snatched up a garden ornament of a small dog as a weapon and ran up to Dean, raising it over her head to bring down on him. Spotting her, he rolled and she missed. Turning, she saw Cole pelting towards them, holding the knife.

Jack grabbed her hand and pulled her into the caravan before slamming the door shut and putting his weight against it, attempting to hold it shut when Dean began throwing himself at it. Carly helped him, pushing down on the door as hard as she could.

'Carly, come out,' roared Dean. 'You belong to me, no' him.'

'I don't belong to anyone,' she yelled back. 'And I don't want you. Why don't you get it?'

'He's fucking crazy,' exclaimed Jack.

'You're not wrong. Why did I never realise it before? I need to call Uncle Eddie but I lost my phone.'

'Mine's in my left jacket pocket,' he said, sweat popping out on his face as he put everything he had into keeping the two men out.

Before Carly could grab his phone, the door erupted open and they were both thrown backwards.

'Carly, go,' yelled Jack, leaping to his feet when Dean and Cole burst in.

'I'm no' leaving you,' she cried back.

Their assailants gave them no time to recover and launched themselves at them. Dean went for Jack, the two men tumbling across the dining table while Cole ran at Carly still wielding the knife. She grabbed a vase sitting on the windowsill and smashed it into his face. He cried out with pain, blood pouring from various lacerations and he dropped to his knees. Carly delivered a kick to his chest that put him on his back. Snatching up one of the broken shards of the vase, she turned to help Jack just as he threw Dean through the window, the shattering of glass deafening in the confines of the caravan. Carly never thought she'd see the day she was happy to witness Dean being thrown through a window but she was elated by the sight.

Jack pulled her into his arms. 'Are you okay?' he panted, exhausted from the fight.

'I am but you're bleeding,' she said, the blood that had trickled from the cut to his forehead staining his face and neck.

'It's fine. Let's go while they're still down.'

Taking her hand, they ran for the door, which was hanging off its hinges. Jack came to a sudden halt, jaw going slack, a groan sounding in the back of his throat.

'What's wrong?' said Carly, who was standing behind him, waiting to go through the door.

He released her hand, his arm falling limply by his side. As he was taller than she was, Carly couldn't see what was going on. It was only when he slumped to his knees that she saw Dean standing in the doorway, the knife he held buried up to the hilt in Jack's stomach.

'No,' she screamed.

With a grunt, Dean dragged the blade sideways, opening up a large, ragged wound through which Jack's insides protruded. His body went into shock and began to violently tremble. As Dean yanked out the weapon, he dropped to his knees before toppling backwards.

'Oh God, no, please,' she cried, throwing herself down by Jack's side, letting the shard of vase drop to the floor. She pressed her hands to the wound in an attempt to close it, blood pouring through her fingers.

'Call an ambulance,' she screamed at Dean as he entered the caravan.

'It's pointless,' he replied coolly, his dishevelled appearance at odds with the ice in his voice. 'He'll bleed out before help ever gets here.'

'Stay with me, babe, please,' Carly told Jack, her voice cracking. Spotting a tea towel in the kitchen, she leapt up to grab it and rushed back to his side, pressing it against the wound but the crisp white linen was instantly stained with blood.

All the colour had drained from Jack's face. Even his dark eyes looked paler as they rolled open to look at her.

'I love you,' he murmured.

'I love you too,' she wept. 'Hang on, please.'

The blood continued to bubble up through the wound, pooling around him. She knelt in its sticky warmth and knew there was nothing she could do to stop it.

With the last of his strength, he took her hand and cradled it to his cheek. His eyes locked on her before slowly sliding shut. There was one long, gentle exhale and his hand went limp in her own.

'Jack?' she breathed.

There was a moment of absolute silence, which was broken by

her piercing wail. Carly buried her face in Jack's neck, wrapped her arms around him and sobbed.

'You don't need him any more,' said Dean. 'You've got me now.'

Fury the likes of which she'd never felt before took hold of Carly. After placing a kiss on Jack's unresponsive lips, she covertly picked up the broken vase shard and slowly rose to her feet, her hands and clothes stained with blood. She glared at Dean with bloodshot, hate-filled eyes.

He extended his hand to her. 'It's time to go.'

26

Carly nodded and took Dean's hand but as she stepped towards him, she sliced downwards with the shard, piercing his right hand. With an agonised cry, he dropped the knife. Carly dropped the shard and snatched up the knife before immediately turning, raising the blade in a wide arc and slashing Cole, who had only just got to his feet, across the face with it. He stumbled backwards, hands once again going to his already damaged face and he toppled over the dining table. Carly tried to slash at Dean but he moved. She kicked him hard in the chest and he fell backwards out of the caravan, landing on his back. Carly leapt out after him clutching the knife, teeth bared.

'I'm going to fucking kill you,' she screamed.

Dean scrambled backwards on his hands as she frantically began attempting to slash him. There was no control or thought to her actions. All she knew was that she wanted to hurt this man she'd once professed to love, to do to him what he'd done to Jack. Determined to see him bleed and for his insides to poke through his belly, she went at him with wild, uncontrolled fury. Dean blocked and dodged her blows.

'Jesus fucking Christ, stop her,' cried a voice.

Carly ignored the voice. She didn't care about it or anyone else. Vengeance was the only thing that mattered and she would have it.

Arms wrapped around her, pinning her own arms to her sides and the knife was torn from her grasp.

'Oh my God, she's covered in blood,' cried a female voice, one much beloved but Carly had gone way beyond rationality and reason, the burning thirst for revenge still holding her firmly in its grip.

'I'm going to kill him,' she screamed as Dean got to his feet. 'I'm going to fucking kill him.'

Jane was suddenly standing before her. She slapped Carly hard, bringing her back to her senses and stopping Carly's frantic struggle to free herself.

'What's going on?'

'He killed Jack,' said Carly before bursting into floods of tears.

A shocked Harry released her and she staggered into her older sister's waiting arms.

Peanut peered into the caravan. 'Oh, Jesus,' he sighed. 'Eddie, you'd better take a look.'

Eddie looked inside to see Jack's body sprawled on the floor, saturated with blood. 'Christ,' he muttered. He rounded on his younger son. 'You did this?'

Dean nodded. 'Serves him right. It's only what he did to someone else.'

Carly tried to charge at him again and Harry and Jane between them had to fight to hold her.

'Someone went out the window,' said Peanut, stepping around Jack's body and peering outside.

'Carly, was someone else in there?' Jane asked her.

Her sister didn't reply as she still fought to get at Dean.

Jane shoved her back against the side of the caravan with Harry's help and pinned her there. 'I understand you're upset but we need to know who else was in there?' she yelled.

Jane's authoritative tone got through to Carly and she finally went still. 'It was Cole. I slashed the shit out of his face.'

'Good for you.'

'He was working with Dean. They set up the gunrunning ring and put the blame on Jack.' Just the mention of Jack caused Carly to go limp and the tears to roll down her face. 'He's gone, Jane. He's gone,' she wept before collapsing forward onto her sister.

'I need to get her out of here,' Jane told her uncle.

Carly's head snapped up. 'Not until I've killed that fucker,' she snarled, pointing at Dean.

'That isnae happening,' replied Eddie as he and Peanut stepped out of the caravan.

'He's no' getting away with it.'

'Take her back to Haghill, Jane.'

'No, I'm not going,' cried Carly. 'I want justice.'

'Toni McVay will have to be told and she'll decide what's gonnae happen.'

'You won't serve up your own son to her. You'll blame someone else for Jack's death when he should suffer.' She rounded on Dean. 'I hope she scoops out your eyes for this, you fucking cunt.'

'Carly, please, you know we belong together,' he said, taking a few steps towards her.

Harry put himself between them and pressed a hand to his chest. 'You're going nowhere near her again. Do you fucking hear me?'

Dean looked past him to Carly. 'It was always meant to be us. It's right, we both know it.'

'Oh, Jesus, why can't you just stop?' Harry yelled at his brother.

'Get her out of here, Jane,' said Eddie.

'You're no' taking her from me,' roared Dean.

He shoved Harry out of his way and ran at her. Peanut leapt out of the caravan to meet him, grabbed Dean by the throat and threw him to the ground onto his back, using all of his considerable strength to keep him pinned there. Eddie punched his son hard in the face, stunning him and he went limp.

'Wait,' said Carly as Jane attempted to lead her over to the car. 'I have to say goodbye to Jack.' She knew there would be no funeral for him, no mourners or flowers. His death would be covered up by Toni McVay, so this would be the last chance she got.

Jane nodded and took her hand. Together they entered the caravan, Jane wincing at the sight of the awful wound to his stomach.

Carly knelt beside Jack and placed a gentle kiss on his lips before pressing her forehead to his.

'I'll dream about that life we planned together every night,' she whispered. 'And maybe if I dream it enough, it'll come true and this will all just be a nightmare.'

A tear spilled down Jane's cheek as she watched her sister and she hastily brushed it away.

After kissing his lips again and running her fingers through his hair, Carly got to her feet and stared down at him limply. Her face creased and tears slid down her cheeks. Jane wrapped her arms around her and hustled her outside.

'Peanut will drive you home,' Eddie told the sisters, recognising that Carly was in no fit state to drive and that Jane didn't know how. 'Don't tell anyone what's happened, no' even Rose. You say nothing to anyone until I get back, okay?'

Jane and Peanut nodded while it appeared Carly hadn't even heard.

'When you've dropped them off, come back for us,' Eddie told Peanut.

Eddie watched the three of them head to his car. Only once they'd gone did he turn back to Dean.

'Wake up,' he said, shaking him by the shoulders.

Dean came round and slowly sat up.

'I have to tell Toni McVay. She's the only one who can clear up this mess but she will want to kill you for this. You have to leave no' just Glasgow but Scotland. Head to Aunty May on the Isle of Wight.'

'But Carly…'

'Wake the fuck up. She never wants to see you again and if she does, she will try to kill you. What the hell were you thinking?'

'I did it all for her. I would be the one running things and I could give her more than Jack ever could.'

'This is fucking insane,' cried an appalled Harry. 'All the time you made out you were happy with Destiny when she wasnae even in the fucking country. I always knew you had a dark side but I didnae realise you were evil.'

'I'm no' evil, I did it for love.'

'You did it for obsession. You tricked us all,' he said, voice cracking with emotion.

Eddie gripped Dean firmly by the shoulders. 'You have to go otherwise you're deid and there will be nothing I can do to stop it. Despite what you've done, you're still my son and I love you but you have to leave right now. I can give you one hour's head start, that's time enough for you to go home and grab what you need. I take it armed men aren't really waiting at your flat?'

'Naw. Those men were working for me. I was worried you might be onto me and I wanted to put you off the scent.'

'I thought so. Go now, there isn't much time.'

'Toni will know you sent him away,' Harry told his father. 'And she'll come for us all.'

'No she won't, although I will have to tell her the truth. I'm banking on her no' bothering to hunt down Jack's killer. She'll be anxious to restore the equilibrium as soon as possible.'

'But she's known for taking assaults on people who work for her as personal attacks on herself.'

'This wasn't really about business, it was obsession, it's different. I think we can get away with it but you have to go now, Dean, and you can never come back. If you do Toni will kill you and I won't stop her.'

'But Carly...'

'Get her out of your fucking heid,' spat his father. 'You've lost her forever and unless you want to lose your life too then you'll leave.'

Dean sighed with resignation and nodded.

* * *

Peanut saw the sisters safely inside the flat before leaving. Jane had called The Bitches on the way and ordered them to go to their street and keep an eye out. She also called Jennifer and told her to keep Rose at the pub on the pretext of watching over Jessica Alexander.

Jane led her sister into the house. Carly was in the grip of shock, her body trembling and gaze catatonic as she no doubt relived Jack's death. Jane helped her remove her bloodied clothes and made her get into the shower. Carly stood limply under the spray, continuing to stare straight ahead as her sister scrubbed the blood from her body and stuffed her clothes, jacket and trainers into a bin bag ready to be disposed of. Jane briefly left her sister in the shower to change her own clothes, which had blood transferred onto them from Carly's. She put her jeans, jacket and T-shirt into the bag with Carly's clothes then helped her sister out of the shower, wrapped her in a towel and led her into her bedroom. Carly still stared straight ahead unseeing but at least the warmth of the shower had stopped the horrible shaking.

Jane helped her into her pyjamas and tried to tuck her into bed but Carly refused, speaking for the first time since they'd left the caravan park.

'I can't sleep yet,' she whispered. 'I'll just close my eyes and see him die over and over again.'

Jane's vision momentarily blurred with tears before she blinked them away. 'Okay. How about a brew instead?'

Carly nodded and groped for her sister's hand like a child. Jane led her into the kitchen and sat her on the couch. She then fetched Carly's duvet from her bed and tucked it in around her. The hot shower had done nothing to warm her up. Once that was done, Jane put the kettle on and prepared the mugs. Carly stared at the kitchen counter with tears rolling down her face.

'That was the first place we had sex,' she rasped.

'What was?' said Jane.

'The counter where you're standing. We had sex over it.'

'Oh,' said Jane, unsure what to say.

'It was wonderful.' Carly smiled sadly. 'I didn't know what to expect from him back then but he was sweet and tender. I thought he'd leave straight after but he stayed with me all night. It was so romantic. It was then I realised there was more to him than everyone thought. No' enough people saw who he really was, deep inside, I mean. They just hated him.'

'Plenty of people liked him too,' said Jane.

'Not his own family,' replied Carly bitterly. 'They were too busy being jealous of what he'd achieved, too stupid to realise they were only spiting themselves. Elijah wasn't a traitor in the end. Jack told me he and David helped him work out that Cole was the one behind it.'

Carly lapsed into silence again, staring straight ahead. Jane thought it best to remain quiet. Her sister was incredibly fragile, anything could make her shatter completely and it was her job to protect her.

The kettle boiled and Jane poured out the tea. She sat beside her sister on the couch and they sipped their drinks in silence. Jane's mind frantically ticked over the night's events. There were still pieces missing that only Carly could give her but she wouldn't press her until she was ready to talk. She couldn't believe Dean had been behind all this because he had some sort of weird obsession with Carly; that he'd killed a man who was not only Carly's boyfriend but a prominent member of the gangland community. What the hell would the fallout mean for her family? Would Toni kill Dean for what he'd done? Her own feelings for her cousin were jumbled. On the one hand, she wanted him punished but she didn't want him to get hurt. She still loved the good friend he'd been to her. Eddie, Dean and Harry coming to Haghill had seemed such a blessing after she and her sisters had struggled for so long with their father's illness. They'd all been so close and now it was ruined. It was her uncle she was the most worried about. Jane knew he'd send Dean away before Toni could get her hands on him but what would that mean for Eddie himself? It was such a horrible mess and she had no idea how it would turn out for any of them.

Eddie and Harry arrived over two hours later, both looking tired and devastated. Jane opened her mouth to speak but her uncle shook his head and she soon saw why – Toni McVay strode in followed by her second-in-command, Caesar. They had both clearly come straight from some posh event. Caesar was in a very smart suit with black tie. Toni was dolled up to the nines, diamonds around her neck and hanging from her ears. Her black gown was floor-length and strapless and showed off her generous bosom to the full. Jane ran an appreciative gaze over her, thinking how beautiful she was. Toni spotted that look and would have normally revelled in it but she was too pissed off to bother. Her black eyes were filled with fury and Jane experienced a moment of extreme anxiety as she feared she would take all that anger out on her family. Therefore, she was puzzled when all Toni's anger faded as her gaze settled on Carly, who still stared straight ahead, seemingly having failed to even notice their arrival.

Toni knelt before Carly and gently took her hands in her own.

'Carly?' she said gently.

She didn't respond.

Toni looked questioningly at Jane. 'Has she spoken at all?'

'Just a few words about Jack but that was a while ago now,' she replied.

Toni sighed heavily but it seemed with sadness, which surprised Jane. She had thought the Queen of Glasgow completely lacked empathy but it appeared not.

'Carly,' repeated Toni more forcefully.

Carly's gaze finally settled on Toni but she didn't speak or react.

'Did Jack tell you anything about what was going on?'

Jane was afraid this would be too much for her sister, that she needed time to recover before speaking but Carly nodded in response.

'What did he tell you?' said Toni quietly and patiently.

'That...' Her voice cracked and a tear spilled down her cheek. She took a deep breath and cleared her throat before continuing. 'Dean and Cole were working together. They were using his name to deal the guns. Elijah and David helped him work it out, he didnae say how. I thought Elijah was in on it but I was wrong.

That was all Jack had time to tell me before they attacked us.' Some of Carly's characteristic fire returned to her eyes. 'Have you killed Dean?'

'No. I've not been able to get hold of him, not yet anyway.'

'I want him dead,' Carly hissed.

Toni patted her hands. 'I understand that, believe me.'

'I want to be there when you take his eyes,' said Carly, her own eyes wide and unblinking.

Jane noticed Eddie and Harry wince and look down at the floor.

'The desire for revenge is good,' Toni told Carly. 'It will get you back on your feet. This has knocked you sideways but you're young and strong and you will recover.'

'I want to help find him.'

'Not necessary. I've got my own people who can do that. Just leave everything to me and your uncle, okay? We'll sort everything out.'

'Where will you put Jack?' said Carly, starting to tremble. 'I want to be able to visit him. Please put him somewhere nice, I cannae bear the thought of him being put in an incinerator and then thrown away.'

'He'll be buried in a graveyard, he can even have a proper funeral. The authorities need to know that he's dead. He's still on parole and if he goes missing then a police hunt will start for him. That I can't have.'

'Won't a murder investigation cause the same trouble?'

'No because I can control that. His body will be moved to an area where a lot of the local polis work for me. He'll be found by a passerby, who will be in my pay. I have someone waiting to confess to his murder, an old friend dying of cancer who wants a hefty payday for the family he'll leave behind. Jack's death will be immediately closed by the police with the minimum of investigation and he can have a proper burial.'

'Thank you,' Carly croaked, giving Toni's hands a gentle squeeze.

Toni wasn't used to people being genuinely grateful to her. She usually only got gratitude that was filled with fear but there was absolutely no fear in Carly Savage's eyes when she looked back at her, which only increased Toni's respect for her.

'You're welcome,' Toni told her. 'Now you need to look after yourself, to rest and grieve. Do you want to make the funeral arrangements?'

'Aye. His own family don't care enough about him to do it. Have you found Cole?'

'Nope but we're looking.'

'I fucked up his face. I hit him with a vase and then cut him with a knife. He'll need medical treatment.'

'I appreciate the tip.' Toni patted Carly's hand before elegantly rising to her feet. 'Jane, why don't you tuck your sister up in bed then come straight back?'

'Okay. Come on, honey,' she gently told her sister. 'Harry, can you bring the duvet?'

This time, Carly allowed herself to be led into her bedroom without protest and Jane tucked her sister in before returning to the kitchen with her cousin.

'This has hit her hard, hasn't it?' Toni asked Jane.

'Absolutely. I've never seen her like this before, no' even when we lost Maw and she was just a wean then.'

'I wanted her out of the way because she won't like hearing me say that I'm not going to pursue Dean. This was all down to his obsession with Carly. It's not business.'

'Even though he was involved in the gunrunning ring?'

'Aye. I've already dismantled that. I've got hold of Alfie and Hairy Bill. They will pay for the crime. Cole will too once I find him. Dean however I'm willing to leave alone for the sake of your family although God help him if I see his face round here. I hate a power vacuum, they always cause trouble and I need you lot to help prevent any fallout. David and Elijah will now run things between them. They make a good team and I want your family backing them up. I need you to hold Haghill as well as the surrounding districts. Your influence has extended beyond this scheme. Jack's death means you've all taken a step up the ladder. Elijah and David are the bosses around here now and you three are their lieutenants.'

'Really?' said Jane in disbelief. 'But after everything that's happened...'

'Jack was the boss, so all that lands on his shoulders, no' yours.' Toni's tone was no-nonsense, her gaze hard. The tough gangland boss was back.

Toni turned to Harry and took his chin roughly between her thumb and forefinger before aggressively pulling his face towards her so she could look into his eyes.

'I hope for your sake that you're no' a loon like your brother?' she demanded.

'Me? No,' he said nervously.

'Good because I'm letting Dean off out of respect for your family but I won't tolerate it a second time.'

'I'm nothing like him,' Harry said determinedly.

Toni's expression turned even colder. 'You're fortunate I'm classing this as family business, otherwise the repercussions for yourselves would have been much worse. Now get it together because I do not want to be dragged out of the opera again to deal with your family's shite. Do you hear me?' she yelled.

Eddie, Harry and Jane nodded.

'Good.' Toni treated them all to the full force of her black-eyed glare. 'Now, I need to go and speak to my contacts in the polis and call in quite a few favours. And look after that poor wee lassie,' she added, pointing in the direction of Carly's bedroom. 'No polis should come along pestering you but tell her the cover story, just in case. I don't know how much she took in earlier.'

'I'll make sure she understands,' said Jane.

'Good. Caesar, we're leaving,' said Toni grandly. She paused to look back at the Savage family. 'And if I were you, I'd keep my heids down and ensure things go flawlessly on this scheme from now on because you do not want to piss me off again. And make sure Dean never comes back to Glasgow, Eddie, because if he so much as sets foot in the area I will know and I will kill him, no questions asked.'

She glared at them all before leaving, Caesar giving them a warning look as he followed her out.

'Bloody hell, we were lucky there,' breathed Harry when they'd gone.

'Aye we were,' said Eddie. 'At least we can relax and let her clear up all the mess. As we speak, her people are destroying evidence and setting fire to the two caravans.'

'What if the polis do come sniffing round here?'

'Trust me, they won't. It means we can concentrate on moving forward and helping Carly recover.'

'I don't know how long that will take,' said Jane. 'She's absolutely devastated.'

'Like Toni said, she's strong and tough.'

'This isn't like watching our parents die of natural causes. She saw him being brutally murdered. He died in her arms. That's going to take some getting over and I don't know how to even start helping her. And what about you, Uncle Eddie? You've pretty much lost a son.'

'At least I know he's still alive and as long as he stays away from the city he'll be safe. Right now, that feels like a gift when only a couple of hours ago I thought he might be tortured and killed. Anyway, son or not, I'm fucking furious with him. He not only betrayed Carly and all of us, he sided with the enemy. I don't even want to look at him.'

'Is that how you feel, Harry?'

Harry nodded, gaze turbulent. 'I cannae believe what he did, it's mental. We're better off without him.'

Despite their words, Jane could see the pain in their eyes. This would haunt them all for years to come.

27

Carly found herself staring down into another grave, which was even more painful after only recently burying her father. Contrary to what she'd initially thought, Jack was given a wonderful funeral, paid for not only by her family but David and Elijah too. They'd managed to get him a spot in the graveyard close to Carly's parents and even though they hadn't known each other in life, it gave her a little comfort knowing they were so close. None of the Alexander family had bothered to turn up. Cole was still in the wind, having managed to evade the people Toni McVay had set on his tail. Jessica had moved to Bishopbriggs to be with her other two sons, none of whom were interested in saying goodbye to their cousin, who they'd hated and envied in equal measure. This left Carly as undisputed chief mourner. She was the one everyone paid their respects to after the coffin had been lowered into the ground but she barely heard them. All she wanted was for everyone to leave so she could be alone with Jack. Absently she shook hands and murmured thanks for the condolences. Peanut, The Bitches, Derek and the regulars from The Horseshoe Bar had all shown up, as had Elijah and his enormous brother Davey. Both appeared to be genuinely cut up about Jack's death. David himself gently took Carly's hand and told her to call him anytime if she needed anything. She found his presence a comfort and was grateful for the support and loyalty he'd shown Jack.

Her sisters remained firmly by her side throughout the entire ordeal but Carly envied them because at the end of the service they could walk away with their partners, still happy and secure in their relationships while all she had left of the love of her life was a hole in the ground.

'The car's waiting to take us to the wake,' said Jane gently when all the mourners had left.

'Just give me a minute.'

Jane nodded and she and Rose left to join Eddie and Harry waiting at the black limousine.

Carly turned to the grave and stared down at the coffin. Jack's death had caused a brief stir of interest in the city and all the stupid comments online and in the media about him getting what he deserved had stung Carly to the core. What the fuck did those idiots know? They'd never even met him. No one had questioned the official story. He'd died as a result of a mugging gone wrong, which to many people had been karma at its finest. Nothing had been questioned and the culprit was sitting in prison, waiting to be sentenced after pleading guilty. Toni McVay's cover-up had worked like a dream and Carly hadn't been questioned by a single police officer. But that had done nothing to ease the torment inside her. In fact, the pain only seemed to steadily increase each day and she couldn't escape his murder, her mind continually replaying it over and over again.

She stared down into the grave, wanting to talk to him but she was too conscious of her family watching from the car, no doubt whispering to each other about how concerned they were for her mental health. But how could she move forward when her future had been stolen from her by someone she'd once trusted with her life? The pain of Jack's loss was exacerbated by the pain of betrayal. She couldn't help but be tormented by the thought that she had been the one to condemn Jack to death. If she hadn't reconciled with him he'd still be alive now. His love for her had killed him. In fact, her love seemed to be toxic for every man it touched. Cole had turned into an evil, twisted creature, Dean had lost his mind and Jack was dead. She was a jinx, a Jonah and she shouldn't go near a man ever again. Not that she wanted anyone else. Jack was gone and she knew she could never love like that again.

The years rolled out before her, long and lonely when all she wanted to do was fall into the grave with Jack and be done with it all.

A warm arm wrapped around her shoulders and she looked up into the face of Derek, her second dad.

'Come on, hen,' he told her. 'Let's go and see him off in style.'

Carly wanted to be alone at the wake at The Horseshoe Bar, as she had been at her father's but her family wouldn't leave her alone, her sisters sitting either side of her, Eddie, Harry, Peanut and Derek ensuring they stayed close too. She wanted to sit and think of Jack but she couldn't get the breathing space to do so. Instead, people talked, bringing her mind back to the awful present when she ached to lose herself in the past. She didn't have many mementos of her relationship with Jack. The first time they'd been together their relationship had been a secret and they'd only recently reconciled. Her phone wasn't filled with photos from days out or holidays together. All she had were the photos she'd taken of him in Edinburgh, raising his wine glass in a toast to her in the restaurant where they'd eaten and another of him in bed, half asleep with a grin on his face. They hadn't had time to make memories together. She'd taken it for granted that they would and it had all been taken from them in a single moment by a psychopath she'd thought a friend.

Fresh pain bubbled up inside her chest and she knocked back her glass of wine, downing the contents in a couple of gulps, hoping to keep that horrible emotion at bay until she got home and could grieve in private. It felt like everyone was watching her and talking about her behind their hands, perhaps even blaming her for what had happened to him.

Suddenly she couldn't breathe and she slammed the glass down on the table.

'Carly,' said Jane. 'Are you okay?'

'I need to get out of here,' she choked before getting to her feet and rushing into the toilet. Fortunately, it was empty and she grasped onto the sink, attempting to catch her breath, heart hammering and head spinning.

Jane and Rose charged in after her. They spoke but it sounded to Carly like they were under water. Her legs gave way and she found herself on the floor. Rose left and quickly returned with Mary McCulloch.

'It's okay, sweetheart, you're just having a panic attack,' said the old woman kindly. 'It'll soon pass.'

'I feel like I'm dying,' Carly gasped.

'It feels that way but you're not. Focus on slowing your breathing. Take long, deep breaths.'

Carly obeyed and the terrible feeling soon passed, leaving her crumpled on the floor of the toilet, exhausted.

'We should get you home,' Jane told Carly. 'It's been a difficult day.'

Carly nodded and between them, Jane and Rose helped her to

her feet and she swayed slightly until her head cleared. All her strength had gone and her sisters had to support her as they left the bathroom.

'What's happened?' asked an anxious Eddie, who was waiting outside the door with Harry and Peanut.

'She had a wee panic attack,' said Mary.

'I can drive you home,' said Peanut. 'I've no' had anything to drink yet.'

'Yes please,' replied Carly.

'I've got you,' he said, wrapping a strong arm around her and helping her to the door. When people rose to speak to her, he brushed them away with a wave of the hand.

'Thank you,' croaked Carly, so grateful to him.

'Nae bother, hen,' he said, kissing the top of her head.

Peanut dropped the sisters off at home, by which time Carly was feeling a little stronger. She felt better just for being away from everyone. She changed into her pyjamas and climbed into bed, turning down her sisters' offer to watch a film together. Carly curled into the pillow Jack had used when he'd stayed over and finally she could let go of her grief, sobbing into the pillow until she fell into oblivion.

* * *

'Where are you going?' Jane asked Rose once Carly was settled in bed.

'I just need to nip out,' she replied, pulling on her jacket.

'Now?'

'I promised I'd let Tamara know how we got on.'

'Well, okay,' said Jane, thinking the support of her best friend could only be a good thing. 'But don't be too long. Carly needs us more than ever.'

'I'll be back as quickly as I can.'

Rose left the flat before her sister could object further. The moment she turned the corner at the bottom of the road, she called Tamara. 'Is he still there?'

'Aye,' replied her friend. 'He's been in there three hours, so he should be leaving soon.'

'On my way,' she said determinedly before hanging up.

Rose caught the bus into Bridgeton, and met with Tamara, who was waiting across the road from a red brick end-of-terrace house.

'Are you sure about this?' she asked Rose.

'Aye, I am. The bastard needs to suffer.'

'How's Carly?'

'A mess. I've never seen her like this before. I don't know if she'll ever get over it,' she said sadly.

'I don't blame her. I mean, Jack was murdered right in front of her. It's enough to fuck up anyone.'

The door to the house opened and Rose's eyes filled with malevolence when Mason emerged. His brother Alfie was in a coma in hospital with all his limbs broken but Mason had escaped justice, mainly because he was useless and thick. Toni McVay had seen it as beneath her to punish someone so weak but Rose didn't agree. She'd decided he not only needed to suffer but she also wanted to make sure that he could never hurt her family again.

'Going somewhere?' she said as he moved to unlock his car.

Mason frowned as she crossed the road towards him. 'Rose? What are you doing here?'

'I think it's wrong that you get off scot-free. You were as much a part of what happened as your brother.'

He smiled patronisingly. 'What do you know about it? You're just a wean.'

'I know more than you think.'

'Go home, little girl. You've no' got your sisters to back you up now.' Mason was a coward who only felt tough when confronting someone he considered to be weaker than himself. He thrust his face into hers. 'You don't want me to get nasty.'

'Nasty?' she laughed. Rose's expression hardened. 'I'll show you fucking nasty.'

Mason's body jerked, face contorted with pain before he dropped down behind his car. Rose pocketed the stun gun and looked around to make sure no one was watching before crouching beside him. After slapping some tape over his mouth, she grabbed his crotch and twisted harder than she'd ever twisted before, until blood began to stain his jeans, his screams muffled by the tape.

When she was satisfied enough punishment had been inflicted on him, she tore off the tape, shoved it into her pocket and got to her feet, glaring down at him curled up in agony on the pavement before casually strolling back over the road to her friend.

'Sorted?' said Tamara.

'Aye, sorted,' she replied. 'Let's head back to Haghill.'

The two girls walked to the bus stop together, both unable to stop smiling about what they'd just done. Rose felt that a little more justice had been served.

* * *

Carly was woken by a knock at her bedroom door.

'Are you awake?' called Jane.

Carly pushed herself up to a sitting position, pushing her hair back off her face. 'Aye. What time is it?'

'Five o'clock. You've been asleep for three hours. I didn't want to wake you but there's someone here to see you.'

'I don't want to see anyone.'

'It's Jack's solicitor. He's got something for you.'

She frowned. 'Solicitor?'

'Shall I tell him to come back another time?'

'No, I'll see him.'

Carly climbed out of bed, pulled on her dressing gown and slippers and followed Jane into the kitchen where Rose already sat, having returned an hour ago. The solicitor was a short, round man with sparse grey hair. His suit was expensive but strained across his corpulent belly.

'Carly Savage?' he said, rising to his feet.

'Aye,' she replied.

'The name's Steven Mortimer from Mortimer and Granger solicitors. May I offer you my sincere condolences.'

'Thanks,' she replied, confused. 'What's this about?'

'I'm here on behalf of my client, Jack Alexander. He came to me a month ago to arrange his will.'

'Will?' She frowned, taking a seat at the table.

'Yes. It's a very simple and clear will. Everything he had he left to you.' He produced a sheet of paper from his briefcase and read out the formalities.

'A month ago,' she murmured. 'But we weren't even together then. We broke up and only reconciled shortly before his death.'

'He did explain to me that you were his ex-girlfriend but he still wanted everything to go to you, which amounts to his car and the contents of his flat. He then came back to see me just three days ago. The terms of the will were to remain the same but he had something he wished to entrust to me to give to you.'

From his briefcase he plucked an A4 jiffy bag and held it out to her. Carly took the envelope from him and stared at it in confusion.

'Naturally I don't know the contents,' continued Mr Mortimer. 'They're for your eyes only. I'm just the delivery boy, so to speak,' he added with a kind smile. 'Now, if you could sign this to say you've taken receipt of it, I can be on my way. I don't want to intrude on your grief a moment longer than I have to.'

Still puzzled, Carly signed the piece of paper he gave her and handed it back. He then again delivered his condolences before leaving.

'Aren't you going to open it?' Rose asked Carly when she continued to stare at the envelope.

'I suppose I should.'

The envelope contained four things – a letter, a key, a small rectangular card and a diamond ring.

Carly opened the letter and tears welled in her eyes. 'It's Jack's writing.'

Carly,

This situation is dangerous and I've no idea how things are going to turn out. If they go as I hope, then soon I will be putting the ring in this envelope on your finger and walking you down the aisle. If I lose this particular battle, then please keep it as a gift from me. I hope you'll look at it from time to time and remember how much you were loved.

There was more to the letter, but it fluttered from her hand before she could finish it and she stared at the ring she held. He'd told her he wanted to marry her but this had shown how sincere he'd been. The ring was beautiful with a glittering diamond and when she slid it onto her ring finger, it fitted perfectly.

'Do you want me to finish reading it?' Jane asked her, picking up the letter.

Carly just nodded, still staring at the ring.

'Also enclosed with this letter is a key,' read Jane. 'It opens a safety deposit box at the address at the bottom of the page that contains all my money. There's also an access card that you'll need to gain entry to the facility. I've named you as a specified person on the account, so you'll be given full access to the box. The money's for our future together but if the worst happens, I want you to take it and do whatever you want with it, just as long as it makes you happy. That's all I've ever wanted, for you to be happy.'

'Oh God,' breathed Rose, eyes filling with tears.

'I don't intend to let anything take me from you, babe,' Jane continued reading. 'But if I fail, know that you were so loved and that you were the only good thing in my life. Thank you for being the only person in the world to see something good in me. Always yours, Jack.'

Jane and Rose anxiously watched Carly, wondering what sort of reaction she'd have to the letter but she just continued to stare at the ring.

'We should go to that safety deposit box,' said Rose.

'Not now,' replied Jane.

'Why not?' She took the letter from her sister's hand and looked up the address on her phone. 'It's open till six. That gives us plenty of time.'

'Carly's no' up to doing that yet. It can wait.'

'It was Jack's last gift to her. She should go.'

'Leave it, Rose.'

'She's right,' Carly told Jane. 'We should go. It was obviously important to him. Can you call a taxi while I get dressed?'

Twenty minutes later the sisters left Haghill and the taxi dropped them off outside a smart-looking premises opposite a church in the city centre. Carly wondered if she'd be denied entry but the access card did all the work for her. When she informed the staff that Jack had died, she was told she would still be permitted access to the box as she was named on the account but they would require a copy of the death certificate when it came through.

Rose and Jane were asked to sit in a waiting room while Carly was led deeper into the building where she was taken into a private room so she could open the box. She gasped when she saw all the money inside. However, that wasn't what grabbed her attention the most. Sitting on top of the money was a small, gold heart necklace with the initials J and C entwined together in elegant script. Something from him she could keep forever. She kissed the heart and fastened it around her neck.

Carly counted the money and was astonished to find it totalled 90,000 pounds. That money should have gone towards financing their new life together. Instead, it would continue to sit here until she could decide how she would move on. Right now, she couldn't think beyond getting through the day. Jack had wanted her to use this money to make her happy but how could she ever feel happiness again without him? There was no future any more, just the effort of dragging herself through each day, waiting for the moment when she would inevitably stumble and fall. The question was, would she have the energy or will to get back up again or would she lie down and die and join the man she loved?

ABOUT THE AUTHOR

Heather Atkinson is the author of over fifty books - predominantly in the crime fiction genre. Although Lancashire born and bred she now lives with her family, including twin teenage daughters, on the beautiful west coast of Scotland.

Sign up to Heather Atkinson's mailing list here for news, competitions and updates on future books.

Visit Heather's website: thebooksofheatheratkinson.com

Follow Heather on social media:

instagram.com/heathercrimeauthor

facebook.com/booksofheatheratkinson

ALSO BY HEATHER ATKINSON

Wicked Girls

The Savage Sisters Series

Savage Sisters

A Savage Feud

A Savage Betrayal

A Savage Inheritance

The Gallowburn Series

Blood Brothers

Bad Blood

Blood Ties

Blood Pact

The Alardyce Series

The Missing Girls of Alardyce House

The Cursed Heir

His Fatal Legacy

Evil at Alardyce House

PEAKY READERS

GANG LOYALTIES. DARK SECRETS. BLOODY REVENGE.

A READER COMMUNITY FOR
GANGLAND CRIME THRILLER FANS!

DISCOVER PAGE-TURNING NOVELS
FROM YOUR FAVOURITE AUTHORS
AND MEET NEW FRIENDS.

JOIN OUR BOOK CLUB FACEBOOK GROUP

BIT.LY/PEAKYREADERSFB

SIGN UP TO OUR NEWSLETTER

BIT.LY/PEAKYREADERSNEWS

Printed in Great Britain
by Amazon

48403456R00205